PROPHECY

Keeper of the Sphere
Book Three

D M Youngblood

Cover and interior artwork designed by Farah Evers Designs
www.faraheversdesigns.com

Editing by Jen Whitten Consulting
www.jenwhitten.net

This book is a work of fiction. Names, characters, places, and incidents either are products of the author's imagination or are used fictitiously. Any resemblance to actual persons, living or dead, events, or locales is entirely coincidental.

D M Youngblood
Visit my website at www.dmyoungblood.com

Printed in the United States of America

First Printing: October 2022
Wyked Words Press

ISBN 978-1-7325331-5-8

For Finn, furever in my heart.

PROLOGUE

S AMUEL A. JACKSON, the President of the United States, nods to his cabinet members as he enters the room for his weekly briefing. He's early; only about half the attendees are here.

He's almost always early. It's just a habit he formed long ago.

He pours a cup of coffee at the sideboard, adds a single packet of sugar and one container of non-dairy creamer, then settles into his seat. A file folder, stamped with a high-level classification status, awaits at each seat around the conference table.

While he waits for the briefing to begin, his mind drifts—as it tends to do often now.

He's a young-looking fifty-eight year old man, and is currently half-way through his second presidential term. Before that, he'd been a US Senator for a dozen years, so he's been in Washington for almost half his adult life.

Although he feels he's done some great things for the American people and significantly contributed to world peace, he's actually looking forward to the end of his term.

Simply put, he's tired.

The constant battles with the opposing political party, the convoluted process of finding and fixing many of the lingering issues of his predecessors, and the near-constant climate disasters as the planet heats up—well, it just seems as if he's playing whack-a-mole.

Some days, he thinks he'll finally whack the last mole and be able to move on to other important things.

But on other days, he feels he's losing the game.

By the end of his first term, his thick black hair had turned completely silver. Now, his face is far more wrinkled than it was only a year ago.

His two kids are off at college, and his wife—although always a classic and gracious First Lady in public—barely speaks to him anymore. When did he start losing her? He isn't sure.

Then again, maybe that's just the lie he tells himself. He's fairly certain he knows *exactly* when he started losing her.

The doors close with a solid *thunk*, and it shakes him from his melancholy. While he'd been distracted by his thoughts, the room had filled.

He clears his throat. "Good morning, everyone."

"Good morning, sir." Ben Thompson, the Attorney General, speaks. "If I may, I'd like to go first today."

Jackson smiles indulgently. "Sure, Ben."

"Thank you, sir." Thompson nods once, then continues without further hesitation. "We have a problem." He flips open the folder in front of him and waits as everyone else follows suit.

Skimming over the first page, Jackson frowns in confusion. "What exactly am I looking at here?"

Thompson clears his throat. "We've been keeping you fairly up to date on the killings of oil and gas executives, but now it's escalated."

Jackson barely remembers most of his briefings these days; they all sound the same. "Refresh my memory. Didn't those killings start some time last year?"

"Yes, sir. They started last August. The first victim was identified as Roderick Hartsfield the Third..."

Hartsfield? Jackson stops listening.

He's pretty sure he'd remember hearing *that* name in a briefing last August.

For just a moment, Jackson flashes back to six months into his first term.

In the Oval Office, Hartsfield sneers and throws an envelope on the president's desk. "These photos will be all over the tabloids by morning if you don't veto that fucking tax legislation."

2

Jackson flips through the photos with disbelief and a sinking heart. Now he knows what really happened that night he'd gotten drunk and passed out at a charity gig, when he'd woken with his pants off and a young girl's cold naked body next to him. Naturally, he'd panicked.

Then Hartsfield had shown up, confident and sympathetic. "I'll take care of everything," he'd said. "No one will ever know."

But it'd all been a set up. Someone had obviously slipped a drug into his drink and staged... this. Whatever this was.

He's reasonably certain he didn't do... these disgusting things... with that poor child. His eyes are closed in most of the photos, and he seems passed out and posed rather than caught in the act.

But photographic evidence, even faked, is hard to defend against. He knows no one would believe him.

Jackson raises his head and glares at Hartsfield, whose lips are curled in a nasty smile around his unlit cigar. "You won't get away with this."

"Won't I?" Hartsfield raises a brow, then leans forward with his fists on the Resolute Desk. "Think you can take me on, Mr. Goody Two-Shoes? I dare you to fucking try it."

Jackson slips the stack of photos back into the envelope for shredding later. "Congress will know something's wrong if I veto that bill. The Senators—"

Hartsfield barks out a laugh, then snarls, "—will do nothing. I own half the Senate, too, you fucking moron."

"—will override my veto," Jackson lamely finishes.

"No, they won't." Hartsfield slowly shakes his head. "You just veto it. That's your job here."

Jackson has to look away so he can think for a moment.

Although he's sure he never did what those pictures show, he can't prove it. And if they were released to the public, it wouldn't only end his political career.

It would end his marriage.

His daughters would never forgive him. Hell, they're older than that girl, they know about sexual predators, and they would be completely disgusted with him.

He knows he doesn't have a choice.

His shoulders slump. "Fine. You win. I'll veto the bill."

Hartsfield grins. "Good boy." He taps the envelope with one thick finger. "Just a reminder: these are copies. The digital files are ready to be sent to every newspaper in the country the minute you don't follow through."

That was only the first of many times he was told to either sign or veto certain legislation. He'd had to get quite creative on the excuses.

But now, he's free. Free of Hartsfield's blackmail.

He takes a deep breath, but it hitches in his chest as he thinks about the pictures.

What happened to the digital photos? Where are they now, and who has them?

Shit. This might not be over, after all.

"Sir?" Thompson prompts.

"Sorry," Jackson says, but doesn't give an explanation for his inattention. "Could you repeat that last?"

"To date, there have been forty-eight victims."

Holy shit.

He dimly remembers hearing about twenty or so. "So the killings have escalated, and you're just now telling me about it?"

Thompson's face reddens. "We, uh, had to finish the preliminary investigation and analysis."

"Correct me if I'm wrong," Jackson says, "but weren't they all beheaded?"

"Yes, sir. Well, except for the last one."

"What happened to the last one?"

"He was strangled on national live TV."

Finally. Some good news. "So we have someone in custody."

"No, sir." Thompson hesitates before continuing. He knows how this will sound, but he doesn't have much choice. "It, ah, wasn't done... ah, it... well, you see, it wasn't actually done by a visible person at the television studio. We believe someone used... magick."

Uncomfortable titters from almost everyone in the room.

"Ben, I want some of whatever it is you've been smoking," says Susan Jones, the Secretary of Transportation. She smirks and glances around to gauge the reaction to her snark.

Thompson's face turns dark red. "There's simply no other explanation. The medical examiner was quite clear that Marinelli—the victim—died of strangulation when his windpipe was crushed. Yet every witness said the same thing: at the time of the incident, no one even touched him. He was actually in the middle of a sentence when he died." He pauses before the next part. "And, it happened on camera. There was no one anywhere near him except for the news anchor, six feet away."

Silence in the room now, as everyone ponders that information.

Magick. It's a subject Jackson doesn't know much about, except what he's seen in movies. But he's pretty sure that's not the kind of magick they're talking about here.

Or is it?

What else but supernatural power could crush someone's windpipe from an unknown distance in front of witnesses and on live television?

Jackson isn't sure what he believes, but he's seen some mind-blowing shit since he became president and given access to highly classified intelligence on abnormal phenomena from the past several decades.

He notices Thompson watching, obviously expecting him to say something. So he takes a deep breath and says, "We all know there are still many things in this world that can't be properly explained by current science. At this point, I suppose it's entirely possible someone out there has the ability to... to manipulate energy in such a way as to kill someone from a remote location."

Jones snorts. "So you believe in magick now, Sam? What's next? Witches and vampires?" She laughs, but no one laughs with her.

There's just an uncomfortable silence.

Jackson narrows his eyes at her and wonders why she's so adversarial all of a sudden. "*Magick's just science that we don't understand yet,*" he says quietly. "So said Arthur C. Clarke, a brilliant futurist, inventor, and writer."

Jones blinks at him, then her face reddens as she looks away.

Now Jackson nods to Thompson. "What more can you tell me about these killings? Start from the beginning."

Thompson turns to Thomas Joseph Franks, the Assistant Attorney General. "TJ, would you mind taking the lead on that?"

Franks clears his throat and begins. "As Ben mentioned, last August, Roderick Hartsfield the Third was the first victim. At the scene, first responders reported the presence of two other bodies, but when investigators arrived there was only Hartsfield. The walls of his office were covered in scorch marks, but the sprinklers hadn't been deployed, and there was no evidence of a fire. A thorough search yielded no evidence— not a single trace of DNA that didn't belong to the victim. Then we got reports of the company's facilities being destroyed, and about fifty or so casualties. That's when we knew it wasn't a random attack." He pauses to take a breath.

"A couple of weeks later, there was a second beheading. Rhonda Sitwell was at a retreat with her top management team, but she was the only one beheaded. The rest were shot in the back of the head, point-blank, one bullet each. Very professional. Again, all the company's facilities were completely destroyed, again with several casualties.

"The killings continued over the next several weeks, sporadic at first but then with increasing speed and regularity. In a relatively short period of time we had a total of forty-eight beheadings, and roughly a hundred facilities destroyed. Mostly oil refineries and plastics manufacturers. Of course, the Bureau was immediately brought in on the investigation, but with no physical evidence, they didn't have much to go on. Then, in late October, the beheadings stopped as suddenly as they'd started, with none since."

"FBI come up with anything?" Jackson asks.

Franks shakes his head. "Nothing conclusive. Nothing we can use."

Jackson frowns. If even the FBI didn't have anything on this, it wasn't good. Maybe one of the dozens of agencies in the Intelligence Community knew something about this. It just didn't make sense otherwise. "What about the rest of the IC?"

But Franks shakes his head. "Nope. Not a damn thing. It's become a huge mystery."

Phil Roberts, the Secretary of State, speaks up. "Maybe it's some new radical Islamic jihadi group. Aren't they always splintering off?"

"Doubtful." Franks shakes his head again. "They would've claimed responsibility by now. Besides, Islamic State groups are not known to care

6

about environmental issues." He turns to Jackson again. "There are a few other details you should know. First, someone—or some*thing*—knocked out all the communications and security technology just before each attack." He holds up a hand to stop anyone from commenting, even though no one even thinks about doing so. "No, it wasn't something as simple as a jamming device or some cut wires. Whatever it was left absolutely no trace." He glances at Thompson. "Maybe like a magick spell."

Amazingly, this time, no one snickers. Not even Jones, who's keeping her eyes downcast.

Franks continues. "As I mentioned earlier, in each case the scenes were extraordinarily clean. I mean, yes, there was a lot of blood, but it only belonged to the victims, so it appears they didn't fight back. Also, there were no fingerprints, no DNA, nothing. Not even a single hair or flake of skin that didn't belong to the victims. Lastly, there wasn't a single witness in any of the cases. The closest we came was Hartsfield's secretary. She told investigators she'd heard some odd noises in her boss's office, opened the door, and got a glimpse of a group of soldiers in tactical gear before the office door was closed in her face. She was able to dial 911 from her cellphone, until it stopped working. Right before her follow-up interview, she disappeared, and hasn't been seen or heard from since.

"In Sitwell's case, ballistics analysis tried to trace the bullets used on the management team, but hit a dead end." Franks suddenly stops talking, as if realizing he's been babbling.

Jackson flips through the contents of the folder in front of him, skims over some of the more technical details of the situation, and frowns again. "So what you're telling me is: someone has killed a lot of very important people and destroyed valuable resources, and there's not a damn thing we can do about it."

"Well, not exactly," Thompson says. "The Bureau put their best profilers on the case, and came up with the one thing all the victims have in common. They're all the heads of companies that are responsible—or, I should say, have been held legally liable—for damaging the environment."

Jackson looks up from the folder and focuses intently on Thompson. "And?"

"And, using that criteria, we've compiled a list of about forty additional potential victims. The list is in the folder."

Jackson nods. "That's excellent. But you said the killings have stopped."

Thompson and Franks share a meaningful glance, then Thompson says, "The Bureau believes they'll start up again."

Jackson taps the folder. "So the names on this list—they're all in protective custody?"

Thompson grimaces. "Not exactly, sir. Roughly half of them are not here in the States, so they're out of our jurisdiction. For the rest, we're working with the Bureau to come up with a plan. Something along the lines of surveillance to capture and analyze any anomalies that could be useful to determine who's really behind these killings. Maybe there's some type of energy field disturbance, for example, or an unusual energy signature that we can record before it dissipates. At a bare minimum, we'll increase security presence for each of the potential victims."

"Fine." Jackson sighs. "Keep me posted."

"Yes, sir. Will do."

Jackson turns to Maria Medina, his Secretary of Commerce. "How's our production economy and Wall Street doing with losing all these facilities?"

"It's the oddest thing, sir. After the initial hits, the Dow and NASDAQ bounced back very quickly, and they've been stable since October. Of course, there have been supply chain issues off and on, but nothing that our reserves or trade agreements can't handle."

That, at least, was good news.

"If I may, Mr. President," interjects Bianca Haddad, the Administrator of the Environmental Protection Agency. Jackson gestures for her to continue, and with one long finger, she taps the open file in front of her. "Many of the remaining corporations on this list have Superfund sites. Most have been dodging our efforts to contain their contamination of our waterways for years."

"And?"

"Well... they're not necessarily nice people, sir."

She doesn't have to tell him that. Hartsfield had been a total asshole. He can only imagine how bad some of the others are.

But he decides to push a point. "So that makes it okay for them to literally lose their heads?"

Haddad blushes charmingly and pushes her heavy glasses up on her nose, but they slide down again almost immediately. "No, sir, that's not what I meant. I was just wondering if the people who're doing this basically think of themselves as the good guys. Heroes, saving the planet." She turns her intelligent gaze on Thompson. "Maybe the Bureau could add that to their profile."

Thompson blinks at her for a moment and wonders how in the world the Bureau had missed that important detail. "Interesting observation, Bianca. I'll pass it on."

"Keep me posted," Jackson repeats, and closes the folder. "Now, what's next on the agenda?"

"Sir, we have another problem," says General Joseph Carmine, the Secretary of Defense. His bushy gray eyebrows completely shade his light blue eyes from the overhead lighting, making them appear much darker. "Hostilities are quickly ramping up in South Asia, and it looks like it may escalate to a nuclear confrontation."

Shit. Jackson's heart sinks. He sure as hell doesn't need a fucking nuclear war right now, on top of everything else.

"But they've had a solid peace agreement in place for decades." Roberts, the Secretary of State, frowns. "I just met with them only a few months ago, and they were getting along fine."

Carmine nods. "It's been very sudden, this turn of events. We're watching it closely—as is the UN—but it may require an intervention."

Now, Jackson's head hurts. He sighs and rubs his forehead. "Keep me posted."

CHAPTER ONE

AFTER MY VISIT with Maggie at Ard na Mara, I'd ported directly to my suite at The Hacienda, since I wasn't quite ready to talk to anyone just yet.

And I had a few things to do.

First, I rummaged through my jewelry box until I found a thin leather necklace cord with a strong clasp. From my pocket, I took the blue glass bead I'd found on the beach at Ard na Mara and threaded the cord through the bead's hole. When I slipped the necklace on, the bead felt warm against my skin. Now, it'd always remind me of my time with her in the Sanctuary, but even more than that, maybe it'd help me to remember how her words had made me feel: confident, calm, and determined to do my job well.

Next, I tucked the magickal flask in the top drawer of my nightstand. Not only had that special mead helped to calm me and clear my mind, but that flask had stayed full even after both Maggie and I'd had quite a lot of it to drink. I didn't know if or when I'd ever need that mead again, but at least it was in a safe and accessible place.

With those tasks done, I freshened up in the bathroom, brushing out my wind-blown hair, redoing my ponytail, and washing my face. As I patted it dry, I frowned at the long, raised scars on my cheek. Had the wind at Ard na Mara made them so much redder than usual? I glanced at the matching scars on my upper arm—both caused by Mike's claws when we fought after the battle with Cromm last year—but they were pale and normal.

Wait. That battle with Cromm had only happened three months ago, in November. It only *seemed* like it'd been a lot longer.

Most of the time, I didn't even remember about the scars until I caught sight of them, like now. Somewhere along the line, I'd also stopped being self-conscious of the scars Cromm had left on my belly and thigh, where he'd taken slices of my flesh.

These were all battle scars. My *survivor* scars. In a way, I was proud of them now.

My eyes were still a bit puffy from all the crying I'd done before Maggie had found and comforted me, but a bit of magickal glamour took care of that.

I'd just finished hanging up the towel when the knock on my door came. "Dee? You okay in there?"

Kevin. And Arddhu was probably with him. It'd only taken them about five minutes to sense my presence.

"Be right out," I called.

I expected the worst: lots of yelling at me for acting irresponsibly, for taking out a target on national live television and running away afterward. So I took a moment to close my eyes, take a deep breath, and ground myself. I knew I had to stay calm during this discussion and not let my emotions free rein.

I opened the door and stared at my Consorts.

Uncharacteristically, Kevin looked like shit. His clothing was rumpled, his hair mussed as if he'd been constantly running his hands through it, and his dark green eyes didn't have their usual sparkle.

Arddhu just looked tired. Actually, way beyond tired: *exhausted*. His shoulders slumped, his normally lustrous long brown hair now hung limp and lifeless, and his warm brown eyes seemed haunted.

Immediately, I felt guilty for what I'd put them through.

"Let's sit in the living room." I'd started past them, but Kevin quickly pulled me into a hug.

"Thank the gods," he murmured into my hair. "I—*we* were so worried about you."

His arms felt good around me, but after a moment, I gently pulled away from him and turned to Arddhu. As soon as I put my arms around him, he crushed me against him without a word.

After another moment, I took each of them by the hand and headed to the living room. It was late morning, and the room was bright with natural light from the beautiful sunny day.

I sat between them on the couch, Arddhu on my left and Kevin on my right.

"Before we start, I want to apologize." I turned to Kevin first. "I'm sorry I had such a bad attitude and that I treated you like shit." Next I turned to Arddhu. "And I'm so, so sorry I was gone so long and made both of you worry about me."

"Where were you?" Kevin asked.

"Ard na Mara. I... I had a long talk with Maggie."

Arddhu frowned. "But my locator spells could not find you there."

Interesting; the Sanctuary blocked locator spells? "I was in the Sanctuary."

He shook his head. "What is that?"

I briefly explained what and where the cave was, not really surprised he hadn't known of it. He and Maggie hadn't been as close.

"Who built such a place?" Arddhu asked.

"Not a clue. I didn't even know it was there until we—" I gestured toward Kevin "—discovered it last Lammas."

Maggie, of course, had known about it. But as far as I could tell, after a quick search through the memories of prior Keepers, none of the other Irish Keepers had known of it. It was just another oddity in the collection of weirdness I'd seen in the past eighteen months or so.

"Well," Kevin sighed. "I'm glad you're home. When Arddhu's locator spells didn't work, we... we thought you might've been taken off-world."

Again.

I'd heard it even though neither had said it.

Shit.

No wonder they both looked so stressed.

"I'm so sorry I worried you both so much," I repeated. "I needed—" Ugh. How could I explain to them the real reason I'd left? Feelings of inadequacy, worries about hurting those I loved... maybe I didn't need to. "I just needed some time away," I finally said.

Arddhu's voice was low. "Kevin told me what you did with the target."

Of course he did.

I sighed. "I fucked up. I realize that, now." To Kevin, I said, "I didn't understand at first, what you were trying to tell me. But after I cleared my head, I knew what I'd done wrong: not thinking an action through. Then, on top of that, I completely discounted your opinion.

"I won't do anything like that ever again. I promise. I promise I will always take time to think about consequences before action." Now I took their hands in mine. "And that I will always value your—*both* of your—opinions. That is my most solemn promise to you both."

"You're not the only one to blame." Kevin picked at a loose thread on his shorts with his free hand and didn't look at me. "I admit I might have overreacted. Just a bit. So I'm sorry for that."

I almost laughed. That was so typical of him, to completely understate his reaction. He hadn't *overreacted just a bit*. He'd actually accused me of being no different than Ida, a tyrant. But I also heard what he hadn't said in his apology, and knew he was sorry for what he'd said.

I lifted his hand and kissed it.

"I accept your apology," Arddhu said, and I kissed his hand, too.

After a quiet moment, I asked, "Has there been any fallout from the media?"

"Surprisingly, nothing we can't handle," Kevin replied. "After you left, I called a quick meeting with Arddhu, Anthony, and the Morrigan, and let them know what happened. Anthony's been monitoring the situation closely, and he said although there's the typical conspiracy theory shit going around, nothing is too serious. He did mention it'll probably attract the wrong kind of attention, though."

"Like the FBI." I sighed and nodded. "They're probably the ones most interested."

"Close attention from law enforcement authorities may put further missions at risk," Arddhu pointed out.

"Probably." Suddenly restless, I released their hands, stood, and paced. "But let's say, for argument's sake, the Feds figure out some of the targets left on our list and install surveillance to try and catch us. Our anti-technology spells should block their spy tech, right? And if they put additional security around any of the targets, we could figure something else out. Like, borrow the Cloak of Concealment from the Túatha, or maybe some other spells to keep us under the FBI's radar." I stopped pacing and faced them. "But we don't have that many targets left. We can't stop now, we're too close to being done. And if we're extra careful, maybe we'll get lucky."

Arddhu sat quietly thinking it through, but Kevin was skeptical. "Just getting lucky isn't enough. What happens if they catch us?"

"That's easy. We just port away."

"Maybe not. What if they use some kind of technology that can stop us from porting?"

"Seriously? You really think they have magick to counter ours?" I snorted. "Not a chance."

Kevin met and held my eyes. "What if they have a deity working with them? Like Ares or Athena?"

I considered it for a moment, but no, that was impossible.

Wasn't it?

"You really think that's a possibility?"

"Hell, I don't know." He ran a hand through his hair, thought for a moment, then shook his head. "No, probably not. At this point, I'm just throwing shit against the wall to see what'll stick."

Frowning, Arddhu pointed at the wall behind me. "I do not see any feces on the wall."

Kevin sighed and began to explain the phrase, but Arddhu held up a hand and chuckled softly.

"No, Kevin. There is no need to explain, I understood the reference. I was what you call *kidding*."

This had to be a first; I didn't remember Arddhu ever joking before.

Kevin had raised his brows. "That's... wow. Okay, then."

To Kevin, I said, "Look, I get it. You're just trying to think of every possibility. But I can't let something that might not even happen stop me from completing the missions."

Arddhu nodded. "I agree with you. Earth needs healing, and to do that, we must remove those who are destroying her." He turned to Kevin. "We must resume the missions. I cannot see any other way."

For just a moment, I felt victorious.

Then, I remembered that resuming the missions would put others at risk. What if there was another Malsumis out there, helping the targets, and just waiting for us to show up? Or, even worse, what if there were more than one Malsumis?

How many Jasons would have to die so Earth could be healed?

It was one thing to risk my own life, but hadn't I promised myself last year that no one else would die if I could help it? I'd never forgive myself if something happened to Arddhu, Kevin, or the Morrigan because of my actions or decisions.

There *had* to be another way.

Wait. What if...

Mind racing, I sat in one of the chairs.

"Maybe there's a better option," I began. "What if I took out the rest of the targets remotely? Something like what I did with the last one, Marinelli, except not on national live TV this time. I could just, I don't know, give each of them a stroke or something. And I could also destroy the facilities remotely, too, so we wouldn't need the asset destruction teams either. It would minimize almost all risk."

I wasn't surprised that Kevin was the first to comment.

"That'd mean humans would know magick was used."

I shrugged. "Yeah, but so what? I mean, they'll eventually find out about me anyway."

Kevin's eyes were sharp on mine. "Dee—"

"I find no fault with your proposal," Arddhu interrupted. "It is, by far, the most sensible idea I have heard so far."

"And what happens when everyone finds out she's the one who did all the killings?" Kevin snapped at Arddhu. "Do you remember the witch trials? 'Cause I sure do. It wasn't pretty. And this could be so much worse." Then he realized he'd almost been shouting, and took a deep breath to calm down.

"But how would it be worse?" I asked. "I'm the Goddess of Earth, and so much more than just a witch. Humans can't hurt me. And if anyone threatens any of you, I can just eliminate them."

Kevin stared at me. "More killing."

I lifted an eyebrow. "You have a problem with killing now?"

"Of course not," he shot back. Then he sighed and ran a hand through his hair. "Dammit, Dee, humans have laws for a *reason.*"

"But deity is above human law," I pointed out. "Normally, we work within its constraints, yes, but in these extraordinary circumstances, I don't think we're really expected to."

"Long, long ago," Arddhu said, "humans feared us. And respected us." He looked at Kevin, then me. "Perhaps the time has come for them to fear and respect us once again."

Arddhu was right.

Mythology was filled with stories of humans fearing and respecting the ancient gods. Although I was the newest addition to this whole deity thing, it shouldn't make any difference. Deity was deity.

And I knew without even asking that the Morrigan would agree. As would all the other gods and goddesses.

Especially the Túatha, who'd ruled Ireland as great and terrible gods for millennia.

"Thing is," Kevin began, "in this modern era, we shouldn't have humans fear us too much. Fear can breed contempt, which can then turn to violence. Respect should be enough."

"But Arddhu has a point," I argued. "I mean, if we're going to make this planet healthy again, we have to take control. The humans won't like it, but they'll get used to it. They'll have to."

Kevin stared at me with wide eyes. "Now you're talking about *taking over?* As in, ruling the whole world?"

That actually wasn't a bad idea, but I shook my head. "Of course not. I'm not a dictator. But maybe the human leaders should know they're not the most powerful beings on this planet anymore. Maybe they should know they were never anything more... than what the gods allowed them to be."

Kevin studied me for a moment. "What *happened* to you at Ard na Mara?"

"Like I said: I had a long talk with Maggie. And I came to understand a few things, one of which is *I am the boss*, and I'd better damn well start acting like it."

Kevin blinked at me, but didn't say anything.

Arddhu's smile was wide. "This pleases me. I have long wanted you to embrace your divinity, and now it appears you have." His smile faded as he continued. "As for your idea of using your power to remove the targets and destroy the facilities remotely, I believe that is the most logical approach at this time. However, in all fairness, I strongly suggest it should be properly presented and discussed at a Council meeting."

I nodded. "Yep, I planned on that. I want everyone's feedback—and a thorough risk assessment—before I make a final decision."

"That is wise." Arddhu nodded again, and stood. "Now, I must rest. We will have more to discuss later."

He left for his room, which the Morrigan had given back to him after all the allies and their retinues had returned to their own worlds a couple of weeks ago. She'd taken over one of the other bedrooms, and Kevin had moved his stuff back into his old room at the end of the hall. My two consorts usually took turns staying overnight in my bed, but I had it to myself at least a couple of nights every week. I could stretch out and be as restless as I wanted, since I still didn't need to sleep as much as I did back when I was fully human.

"*Deirdre, You must be careful.*" Anu's voice in my head was soft. "*Do not succumb to the lure of power for its own sake. You must stay true to who You have always been.*"

Ah, yes. What was that old saying? Power corrupts, but absolute power corrupts absolutely, or something like that.

"*I won't, Anu. I don't ever want to be like Ida. I'll be careful.*"

Anu sent a warm flush through me, which felt a bit like an internal hug. "*That is good. Much love.*"

"*Much love, Anu.*"

While I'd been preoccupied, Kevin had become lost in his own thoughts. He probably didn't even know Arddhu had left the room.

"Why does it bother you so much?" I asked. "Me wanting to use magick to remove the targets, I mean."

"I'm just worried." He met my gaze. "You don't spend as much time online as I do. Especially on social media. Humans lose their damn minds over anyone who's different. Look how they treat brown people, for example. Or immigrants. Or gay people. When they find out about you—

and that the Old Gods are real—they're going to go crazy. Think pitchforks and torches, except updated to modern technology, like guns and pipe bombs. As much as you don't want to, you might end up having to move to Ida's world just to be safe from them."

I knew at least some of what he'd said was true. I'd seen it first-hand. In the little time I'd spent on the internet in my lifetime, I'd seen how ugly it could get. Nasty people were even called trolls, although Pete and Petunia would probably take offense at that.

Then again, I'd seen Pete in his battle mode, and it'd scared the shit out of me. Maybe they wouldn't be so offended, after all.

But to Kevin's point, I'd noticed how increasingly, online hostility was spilling over into the offline world, too. Hate crimes were at an all-time high, and mass shootings were a daily occurrence here in the States, where the ultimate answer to any problem seemed to be found in the unlimited number of weapons any one person could own. No matter what the problem, *more guns* was the answer for too many people these days.

Even minor disagreements commonly devolved into online death threats, escalated into offline stalking, or even progressed to actual murder.

But I couldn't let the possibility of violence stop me from the missions. I had to heal Earth, no matter what. That was my primary goal right now.

"I get what you're saying. I really do. But don't forget: I have an excellent security team and strong wards in place. And I'm not easy to kill."

Kevin sighed. "It's not just that, though, is it? Ares, Athena, and Kali are still out there, too. As soon as you get identified publicly, they'll probably stir up as much shit as they can, just to make everything worse. You'll be a target."

I nodded. "Ares, especially, since he really hates humans. I wouldn't be at all surprised if he tried to start a war somewhere." A shiver of unease crept up my spine; was that a premonition? Or just paranoia?

At that moment, Brianna entered the kitchen. "Dee, let me fix something for you."

Lately, I hadn't been eating as much or as often as I had back when I was fully human, but now my stomach growled loudly. Once again, her timing was impeccable. She had strong magick, knowing when I needed to eat and what I had a hankering for.

I smiled at her. "I'd love a bite to eat."

"Cool." She grinned and began pulling ingredients from the pantry and fridge. "I'll have it ready in just a few minutes."

Now, my thoughts turned to Arddhu and his health. He'd been getting so much more tired lately.

I glanced at Kevin; maybe he knew what was going on.

So I got up and moved beside him on the sofa, then spoke softly so my words wouldn't carry to Arddhu's ears. "Hey, is Arddhu okay? I've been worried about him."

"He will be." Kevin sighed and kept his voice as low as mine. "He wore himself out last night. He must've done at least ten locator spells to try and find you. I know he's been more tired lately, but those spells just left him completely drained."

Shit. Now I felt even worse about my actions.

"I want to do something," I said. "But I don't know what. Remember that ring he enchanted for me? His energy powered it. After I became the Goddess I stopped wearing it, thinking it'd help him feel better, but it doesn't seem to have made any difference."

"If you're talking about who I think you're talking about," the Morrigan softly said as she approached, "I can probably shine some light on the subject." She sat in the chair I'd vacated and crossed her long legs.

She'd finally adopted a more modern American style of black jeans and a red and black tee shirt, instead of her usual all-black outfit of knee-length coat, tunic, and leggings. Her long hair, blue-black and shiny as a raven's wing, was in a single braid that lay over her shoulder and reached her waist. In a nod to her new home here in the Arizona desert, she wore black flip flops adorned with shiny red sequins.

I smiled at her. "Please do."

"You haven't known him long enough to remember what he used to be like. He's been slowing down and gradually deteriorating over the past few centuries, ever since Ida forbid him from doing his annual Wild Hunt. He's maybe only a century or two from fading away completely."

What? Arddhu fading away... no way. I couldn't let that happen.

"I'd wondered why he stopped," Kevin murmured, then his voice turned harsh. "Gods, what a fucking *bitch* she was."

The Morrigan nodded at Kevin, her dark eyes flashing. "Class A."

The Wild Hunt... I vaguely remembered some bits of stuff I'd read over the years. There was something about the legend of Herne the Hunter in Britain, but I didn't know how any of it related to Arddhu.

"Could you please explain to me exactly what the Wild Hunt is?" I asked the Morrigan.

"Of course." She leaned back in her chair and got more comfortable. "Every year at Samhain, he assumed his Cernunnos aspect, gathered his prized stallion and fine pack of wolfhounds, and led a Hunt during the wee hours. Any humans foolish enough to be out and about instead of snuggled safe inside their homes were caught up and forced to ride with him for the duration of the Hunt, which sometimes lasted up to a week. At the end of the Hunt, those humans ceased to exist." She held up a finger. "But he is not to be confused with Wotan of the Norse people, who holds his own Wild Hunt galloping across the midwinter night sky. Or Herne of Britain, who leads a spectral Hunt confined to Windsor Forest."

"What did he—Cernunnos—hunt?"

The Morrigan smiled wistfully. "The finest stag in the world."

I blinked in confusion. "But isn't he the Lord and Protector of the Forest, and all its creatures?"

"Sure." She shrugged. "But that's during the rest of the year. This one time, the stag is honored to be brought down by Cernunnos himself. In turn, Cernunnos honors the stag's sacrifice with a blessing on his spirit."

"And the Hunt was a source of energy for Arddhu, rejuvenating him," Kevin added.

"So if I understand you correctly," I said, "the Hunt was—*is*—a vital part of him, something that helps makes him the Great One." The Morrigan nodded. "So why did Ida make him stop? Why did she care? It doesn't make sense."

"I'm not sure," the Morrigan said. "I never asked him. I just know he stopped, and it was because she commanded him to."

Kevin spoke. "I think I might know. I remember once, he told me something about her being jealous of him. I'd only seen the Hunt one time before he stopped doing it, and he was impressive. *Magnificent.* Imagine him, naked but for a loincloth, his antlers fully extended, and his tattoos glowing with power. He was the epitome of male strength and divine authority. I remember standing there, watching him pass by, and wanting desperately to join him. But he never asked." He shook his head. "Anyway, my theory is: she *despised* that annual reminder of just how powerful he was—in many ways, much more powerful than she was. She wanted him weak, so she could control him." Now his eyes grew distant. "Just like she wanted to control and punish all men."

What the fuck.

I thought back to when I'd first met Ida, during my transition to becoming the Keeper. I'd thought she was good, and kind, and supremely divine. The love I'd felt from her had been comforting and sweet. Hell, I'd even cried when she'd shed a single tear.

My teeth ground together as I realized how she'd manipulated me, manipulated my feelings, to make sure I'd do what she wanted.

What a fool I'd been.

I shook my head in disgust. "He should've just told her to go fuck herself."

"He couldn't." The Morrigan shook her head sadly. "He truly loved her, you know. He did almost anything she asked, up until about six months ago. I suppose that's when he realized it was hopeless, and when he finally gave up on her."

Six months ago... that was when he'd starting growing closer to me and spending more time here on Earth. Before Samhain, at the end of last October, he'd told Kevin and I that he wasn't Ida's Consort anymore, that she'd changed. Then after the Samhain ritual, he and Kevin had started giving me a much-needed massage that'd ended up with all three of us in bed together.

That'd been a helluva night, and it'd led to me choosing both of them for my official Consorts.

But poor Arddhu. My heart hurt for him, but at the same time I was furious. If she hadn't already been banished to another realm, I'd do it now in payback for how she'd treated Arddhu.

I took a deep breath and slowly released it. At least now I knew what was wrong with him, and had an idea of how to fix it.

"Thanks, guys," I said. "I think I know what I need to do."

The Morrigan's dark eyes glittered with something I couldn't quite identify. "Are you going to ask him to lead the Wild Hunt again?"

Just then, Brianna called from the kitchen. "Dee, lunch is ready."

"Not exactly." I grinned at The Morrigan and stood. "I won't be *asking*. I'll be *telling*." Then my stomach growled. "Right after lunch."

With two quick knocks on Arddhu's door, I announced myself. "It's Dee. May I come in?"

"Of course," was his muffled reply.

Closing the door softly behind me, I glanced around. I hadn't been in this room since he'd taken it over from Mike, but it seemed like he hadn't changed anything. It was filled with just the basics—bed, nightstand, dresser, desk, and chair—and every surface was completely devoid of personal effects.

Arddhu sat up in bed, his back against the headboard, waiting expectantly with a weak smile. The covers were pooled around his waist, leaving his chest bare. His shoulder-length brown hair was bed-mussed and wild, but it suited him and increased his attractiveness.

I glanced at the tattoos on his chest and shoulder, noticed something not quite right, and took a closer look.

The sharp lines of the leaves and vines weren't as well defined, and not as dark as they used to be. More evidence of him fading away.

How had I not noticed it until now?

I sat on the edge of the bed and forced a smile. "How're you feeling?"

"A little better. But I will require a longer period of rest to fully recover."

"I understand." I took his hand in mine. "And we'll make sure you're undisturbed for as long as you need. But I wanted to talk to you about something important, to give you as much time as possible to prepare."

He frowned with concern.

"Oh, it's nothing bad," I quickly assured him. "I just... well, I want you to resume the Wild Hunt."

His eyes widened and he leaned forward. A single beam of light from the window now lit up his face, making him seem to almost glow with excitement. "Truly?" His voice was hushed.

"Yes. Absolutely."

He squeezed my hand, then released it as he moved closer. Gently, he took my face in both hands. "You have no idea how much this means to me." He gazed at me with pure adoration.

One side of my mouth quirked. "Oh, I think I have some idea. I just had a little talk with the Morrigan."

He drew me close and pressed his lips against mine, softly at first before becoming insistent and speeding up my heart rate. After a moment, he broke the kiss to rest his forehead against mine. "You are my Lady, my Goddess, my Love," he murmured. "I pledge myself to You forever."

At his words, something inside me shifted and opened, almost as if he'd spoken some kind of spell that unlocked a hidden source of power. It felt like some of my life essence drained away. Not enough to weaken me, but definitely enough that it'd been noticeable.

He gasped, flinched, and pulled away, leaving his hands resting on my shoulders. His gaze was sharp on mine. "What did you do?"

Oh no. Had I hurt him somehow?

"Do?" I frowned. "Nothing. I—what's wrong? What happened?"

His eyes unfocused briefly as he sought the words to describe what'd happened. "Just now, a flood of energy flowed into me. I feel... younger. More alive. Rejuvenated." He focused on me again, and cocked his head. "I am no longer weary or require rest."

Oh, thank the gods, I hadn't hurt him. But I had no idea what had actually happened, or how. Without knowing either of those, how could I hope to repeat it for anyone else who'd need it? With a little luck, it would just happen, like it had this time.

"Well, whatever it was, I'm glad you feel better."

He rose up onto his knees and gently—but firmly—pushed me onto my back. His dark eyes burned with desire. "Now I will show you just how *much* better I feel."

Oh, how I adored him.

CHAPTER TWO

AFTER A NIGHT of glorious lovemaking, first with Arddhu then with Kevin, I rose early and headed to the training room for my morning tai chi session.

Normally, Kevin joined me. Sometimes the Morrigan, too. But for some reason, Arddhu never did, and I'd never thought to ask why.

As I slowly moved through the forms with my sword held in both hands, I thought back to last year, when The Hacienda had been crammed full of allies and their attendants. Many of them had joined in my morning sessions, watching me closely and duplicating the movements.

Had any of them continued practicing? Or had it only been something to kill time during their stay on planet Earth?

I'd left the training room door open, and that was probably the only reason I heard the squawk from the handheld radio base in the kitchen. "Base, this is Gate, come in."

Porting to the kitchen with my sword in hand, I picked up the unit and thumbed the talk button. "Go ahead."

"We have a group of... uh... visitors. They wish to speak with you personally." That was Randy; he and Joe were the security team on duty at the entry gate this morning. "They say they're an official diplomatic delegation," he added, almost as an afterthought.

Visitors? Odd. We never had visitors.

Curious, I sent out a probe using my witchy-sense. What came back was: *nonhuman. Earthy. Friendly*, mostly. *Respectful*, definitely. Clearly, the visitors didn't seem to be a threat.

Diplomatic delegation. Hmm. Probably to meet with me as the Goddess, not the Keeper, based on the sense of formal respect my witchy-sense had detected.

Hosting these types of delegations was probably one of my new responsibilities.

I thumbed the talk button. "Entry is permitted. Send them in."

"Will do. Out."

Quickly, I modified the wards to allow access to the property. It was hard to believe I'd set those wards in place almost two years ago, when I'd first moved in, and they still worked effortlessly. Anyone who didn't have access hit an invisible barrier and couldn't go any further than the front gate.

I sent the sword to my pocket universe and freshened my appearance with magick, tidying my ponytail and lifting the inner shield for a soft glow to reinforce my divinity. But I didn't change my leggings and tee shirt. If the visitors expected to see me look like Ida, with flowing gown and billowing hair, they'd be disappointed.

When I opened the front door, it was to a motley group.

Four beautiful, statuesque women, dressed in many-hued diaphanous gowns, stood together. Their hairstyles were elaborate: intricate braids and impeccable updos put the simple braided crown I'd worn at Samhain to shame. Honestly, they all looked like they'd just stepped out of a sumptuous painting of Classical Greek nymphs.

Surrounding the women were smaller, less human-looking creatures in odd clothing. Some had features that seemed to be carved from stone: all sharp angles and flat planes. Their clothing was mottled gray, brown, and black—like a bizarre type of camouflage.

Others had faces and bodies with indistinct features, more or less simply vague blobs of matter that resembled smoke or vapor. Still others flowed and rippled like water as they stood there, their blue and green clothing undulating as if they were underwater.

Several other creatures, varying in size from a dragonfly to not much bigger than a hummingbird, were interspersed throughout the group. Some glowed and others shimmered, but all hovered in the air on tiny wings that were only a blur.

"Hello," I greeted them. "I'm Dee Connor, the Keeper of the Sphere and Goddess of Earth. How can I help you?"

In response, the tall women knelt and the entire group bowed their heads.

The woman closest to me raised her head and spoke with a voice like wind through the trees in high summer, musical and light.

"We humbly ask audience of Thee, Great Goddess." She held her hands raised beseechingly. Her skin was so pale and flawless, it rivaled the finest porcelain. Her sky-blue eyes were enormous, and her lips were naturally pink. Her golden hair, braided atop her head in a complicated crown, was decorated with sprigs of pretty flowers and greenery. Her sleeveless gown consisted of several sheer layers in shades of green, from palest jade to darkest forest. A golden belt wrapped her slim waist in a style I'd only seen in historical dramas.

I clasped her hands in mine and gently—but firmly—raised her to her feet. "Please, there's no need for formal ceremony. You can just call me Dee." I turned and indicated the open front door. "Welcome to my home."

The other three women stood, but no one in the group moved to go inside.

"Our apologies, my Lady, but we cannot," one of tiny hovering creatures said in her high, piping voice. "There is too much iron present."

Was that the one about the same size as a carpenter bee? I wasn't exactly sure which one had spoken. But it didn't really matter.

"I sincerely apologize." I closed the front door. "Let's go around back to the garden, where we'll more comfortable."

As I led the group on the paver pathway around to the backyard, I searched my brain for information. Wasn't it the fairy folk who couldn't tolerate iron? Was that who these creatures were? Fairy folk?

I sat cross-legged on the patch of soft grass near the back patio, surrounded by flowering oleander and bougainvillea in white, pink, and red, and invited the group to join me.

The taller women gracefully knelt in a semicircle, and the smaller creatures settled in front of them. The tiny winged beings landed on the shoulders of the women, since they'd probably get lost in the thick grass.

"May I offer refreshment?" I asked. "Lemonade? Biscuits?" Too late, I realized I didn't have any drinking vessels small enough for the littlest critters that wouldn't risk them drowning.

The woman who'd spoken earlier replied. "That is most kind of You, but it is not necessary. Please do not trouble Yourself." She smiled. "I am Daphne, a Dryad of the Laurel Tree."

The rest of the group introduced themselves. Two of the other taller women were also dryads—one of oak, the other of ash—and the last was an oread of a mountain I'd never heard of. The smaller creatures were nature sprites of Water, Earth, and Air, and the tiny winged beings were, indeed, fairies.

"We wished to meet You and thank You, Great Goddess," Daphne said, as apparently the group's spokesperson. "We are thankful for Your healing of Earth, which has awakened us from our long sleep. Please accept our gratitude and devotion."

The entire group bowed their heads at the same time, as if rehearsed.

I don't know what I'd expected, but it hadn't been *this*. This was more like worship than a diplomatic delegation, and it made me uncomfortable.

"I'm honored to meet you all," I said. "But please, just call me Dee. Are there many more of you?"

Daphne lifted her head, and the others followed suit. "Oh, yes. Many, many more. Which brings me to the other purpose of our visit: to respectfully ask when You will awaken the rest of our kin."

Ah, so that was the real reason they'd come.

"Well, I'm not really sure. I'm trying to heal Earth as fast as I can, but... it's complicated. There are others who are trying to stop me." The faces around me—those I could actually see, anyway—clearly showed disappointment. To give some encouragement, I added, "I can say this: I will continue to heal Earth until all the waters run pure and clear, the air is fresh and clean, and the soil is free from toxins. I just don't know how long that will take." Then, I had an idea. "Daphne, I'd like you to join my Council. As an ambassador, you'd represent your kin. Not only would you be one of the first to know what's happening, you'd also be part of the decision-making process."

Her eyes widened. "I would be most honored to serve on Your Council, my Lady."

"But what about us?" one of the fairies asked. "Who will represent us?"

"And us, too?" asked the Water sprite, in a voice that bubbled like a stream over rocks. Her pale aquamarine dress softly billowed in the still air.

"Daphne has different concerns than some of us," the Air sprite explained, his voice as soft as a whisper of wind yet somehow understandable.

I'd just opened my mouth to reply when a scuffle on the patio caught my attention.

"… I'm telling you, She must do something about this *now*." Angus Og was usually calm and level-headed, but his face was bright red with fury as he yelled at Kevin. Despite the size difference between them, Kevin seemed to be physically restraining the bigger man fairly easily with just one hand clasped on Angus's arm and the other on his shoulder.

Sam, who'd been on security patrol near the house this morning, stood calmly nearby. His face was also flushed, but I wasn't sure if it was from exerting himself, embarrassment, or anger.

Angus looked over at me expectantly, and I cleared my throat. "Gentlemen, I'm in the middle of a diplomatic meeting. Can't this wait?"

"Absolutely not," Angus snapped.

I clenched my jaw on the rebuke that came to mind; I understood he was angry, so just this once, I let the disrespect stand and stayed calm.

Angus pointed at Sam. "One of your damn bodyguards—"

"Security personnel," Kevin corrected mildly.

"*Fine,*" Angus growled and rolled his eyes. "One of your *security personnel* just insulted me. I want his head. *Now.*"

"Once again, I meant no disrespect," Sam said to Angus. To me, he said, "I thought it was proper."

Angus Og rounded on him and thundered, "*I am not a fairy.* I have a wife and almost a dozen children. That I know of."

Oh.

Oh no. Why would Sam have used an offensive term to one of the most respected members of the Túatha?

Angus turned and pointed a chubby finger at the delegation. "*That* is a fairy," Angus roared.

The tiny creature on Daphne's shoulder shot into the air with indignation, and began squeaking in an unfamiliar language.

Oh.

Sam stared at the little fairy, who fell silent but continued to tremble in anger, then he cleared his throat. "I truly apologize."

Obviously, some diplomacy was required here. As well as a lesson in American cultural references.

"Angus," I began, with a calm and steady voice, "here in America, most people don't know there's a difference between the Túatha—who are also called the Fae and Faery—and fairies. It doesn't help that there isn't a big linguistic difference between *Faery* and *fairy*, either. And to make matters worse, some here even believe the Túatha are elves." His eyes widened in horror, but I continued. "Our movies and television shows confuse everything, as you'll see for yourself when you watch some of them. Thanks to you, those of us here right now know better, so thank you for clearing up the difference. But there will be lots of others who won't, and you'll be out there among them soon. And demanding their heads for a perceived insult simply isn't the answer. So I really must insist that you *not* lose your temper when something like this happens again. Instead, I want you to try to calmly educate them, as I've done just now." I paused and put a little iron in my next words: "Consider it a polite request from me."

Angus seemed to understand what I hadn't said: knock it the fuck off. He hung his head for a moment, then quietly said, "Er... I see. Yes, my Lady."

"Good. Now, if that's all, gentlemen..."

Kevin took his cue and released Angus but kept a hand on his shoulder to steer him back into the house, and Sam followed closely behind. "What d'you say we all have a drink," Kevin said.

Just before the panel in the window-wall closed, I heard Angus say, "Do you have any fermented goat's milk? I really *love*—"

I sighed and shook my head, then turned and addressed the delegation. "Please accept my most heartfelt apologies for the rude interruption. Where were we?"

The tiny fairy had seemed to calm down; she'd returned to Daphne's shoulder. "He was very rude," she squeaked.

I nodded. "Yes, he was."

But Daphne's enormous eyes were still fixed on where Angus had stood. "The Túatha have truly returned?" Her voice was barely above a whisper.

"Yes. Since Yule."

"Why?" Now she turned those unsettling eyes on me, but whether she was frightened or just shocked, I wasn't sure. "How?"

"Well, we needed their help to defeat the—er, Ida, so we freed them from their banishment. And that's when the power of the Goddess came to me."

Daphne swallowed visibly, then nodded. "Oh. I see." After a moment, she seemed to compose herself. "Will they be returning to Eire, then?"

"Probably."

She turned to one of the other dryads, and it seemed as if they communicated silently. The other dryad nodded, then Daphne turned to me once again. "Please forgive me, my Lady. We try to stay out of their way, so we'll need to let our sisters in Eire know of their return."

Was this another situation like with the trolls? "Out of their way? Have they hurt you? Any of you?" I'd quickly glanced at the rest of the group to include them.

"Not recently, no," the Air sprite said.

I frowned, but before I could ask, Daphne replied.

"A long time ago, they slaughtered all the troll-kind in Eire, and then attacked a small group of sprites. After that, we all hid from the Túatha."

Shit. "Well, not all the trolls are gone. There's a mated pair near Ard na Mara."

Once again, Daphne's eyes widened, but this time with joy. "Truly? That is wonderful news. The troll-kind has always been friends to sprites, fairies, and dryads."

I made a mental note to talk to the Dagda about leaving all the other creatures alone. "So, to get back to what we were talking about, after I became the Goddess is when I started healing the Earth."

"Yes, of course," Daphne nodded. "We believe Ida ceased caring for Earth some time ago, which allowed mankind free rein to destroy the forests, mountains, and lakes." She paused, and continued in a soft voice. "That is what caused us to slip into hibernation. But some of us simply ceased to exist instead: those who could not leave their locales at the time of destruction."

"Did they suffer?" I wasn't sure I really wanted to know the answer to that, but I had to ask. I needed to know the truth so I could fix it and make sure it never happened again.

She blinked away the tears shimmering in her eyes. "Yes, many of the hamadryads did. As their trees were struck by the cruel biting axes, they died slowly, painfully, and horribly."

I winced at the torture they'd suffered. "I'm so sorry. I promise you, I will do everything in my power to make sure that never happens again." I wasn't exactly sure how I'd do that, not yet. I wasn't so naïve to think we could stop the lumber industry from cutting down any more trees, but maybe I could make sure there were protected groves for the dryads and hamadryads.

She bowed her head again. "We are grateful for Your compassion and consideration."

After a beat of respectful silence, I gently steered the conversation to less emotional ground. "Now... as to your concerns regarding my Council: I don't have room for everyone, but I can accept three representatives. Since I've already invited Daphne and she's accepted, the rest of the dryads and oreads must agree to her as their representative.

"I'd like the nature sprites to nominate someone to represent them, and the fairies to do the same. To give you all time to meet your kin groups and decide on your representatives, we can meet again in a few days."

I'd barely taken a breath when one of the fairies replied, "That won't be necessary, my Lady. We choose Alanna." He nodded to the fairy on Daphne's shoulder.

Alanna hovered closer to me, fluttered her wings, and bowed deeply. "I am honored to serve on Your Council, my Lady."

Next, the Water sprite spoke. "My Lady, we choose Ferris to represent us."

Ferris was a Mountain sprite, his features sharp and angular, as if carved of rock. He nodded to the other sprites. "Thank you all," he said in his gravelly voice. "I will be fair and honest in my representation of you and the others who have not yet awakened." He turned toward me and bowed his head. "I, too, am honored to serve on Your Council, my Lady."

Lastly, one of the other dryads spoke. "We appreciate Daphne's willingness to serve on the Lady's Council. She is quite competent and resourceful. We will abide by her representation."

Daphne seemed overwhelmed at the words, actually blinking away tears. "Thank you, my sisters. I will do my best to deserve your confidence in me."

With that settled, I addressed the group. "Thank you. *All* of you. I appreciate your coming here to let me know how important my mission to heal the Earth really is. I'll make sure your concerns are heard, and I'll do everything I can to protect your environment."

To my three newest Council members, I added, "The next Council meeting will be in a few days."

Wait.

How would we contact them with the details? Somehow I didn't think any of them had email accounts or phones.

"Um, how can we communicate with you? For the actual date and time of the meetings, I mean."

Daphne blinked in surprise. "Why, just send the message through Gaia, my Lady."

Through Gaia? The Earth itself?

"I'm sort of new at this," I admitted. "I'm not sure what you mean."

"Oh. I see." She smiled. "I apologize. Simply place Your hand like so," she pressed her palm against the ground in front of her. "Then, speak our names and the message. We will hear."

Oh. That was fascinating. I'd had no idea I could do that. Who else could I talk to that way?

"Thank you. As soon as I find out when the meeting will be, I'll send word. And I will personally make sure there won't be any iron at the meeting location."

"Thank You, my Lady," Alanna said, and fluttered her wings again. Maybe she did that flutter to express emotion?

Ferris simply grunted, which sounded a lot like two huge rocks grinding together.

Daphne smiled again. "We look forward to it, my Lady."

After escorting the group to the front of the house, we said our farewells and they headed toward the gate, back the way they'd come.

I went inside and sat at the kitchen island, my head full of the last hour or so: my first meeting with some of the incredible legendary creatures of the planet. What wonders would I see next?

Actually, I thought I'd handled it all pretty well. Had I finally reached the point where not much surprised me anymore? In the almost two years since Mike had knocked on my door, I'd met trolls, deities—good, bad, and nasty—the Túatha, and now dryads, nature sprites, and fairies. I'd seen magick, battles, had half my arm cut off—and then had it restored when I became the Goddess.

Then, my thoughts turned to Mike.

I'd finally stopped grinding my teeth with anger every time I thought of him, but it still hurt that he'd betrayed me. Betrayed all of us, really. Once in a while, I missed him, the old Mike, who'd been close to a friend. Sometimes, I expected him to walk through the door from the garage.

I shook my head and forced my thoughts elsewhere.

The incident with Angus still bothered me, but I wasn't sure if I needed to mention it to the Dagda. It'd just been a simple mistake. Angus didn't need discipline or punishment, just more education on the way things were here in this time period. Here in America, and on Earth in general.

A lot had changed in the past three thousand years, while they'd been banished.

And from Angus's reaction, he'd probably need another lesson soon, this time on elves.

"I heard the dryads paid you a visit." The Morrigan entered the kitchen, interrupting my thoughts. "That's fantastic."

Word had gotten around quick. Maybe security had told her?

"Well, it was only a few who represented all who've awakened because of my healing sessions. Apparently the rest are still in hibernation. But the delegation wasn't just dryads. There were also nature sprites and fairies, too. I've added one of each... um, type? Kind? Species? To the Council."

She raised a brow. "I'm impressed. Nature sprites are notoriously antisocial and fiercely independent. It should've taken several visits—and more than a few expensive gifts—to convince them to agree to something like that."

I blinked at her. "Really? They didn't seem like that at all."

She just stared at me.

"I was wondering, what are the dryads called in Ireland? I mean, that was the Greeks' name for them, right?"

She shrugged. "We never had any special name for them. But you have to know, the Greeks went overboard. They named *everything*. For example, a dryad is categorized by the type of tree she's associated with, and also by location. So, for example, a dryad for a mountain laurel is named differently than a meadow laurel, and also for the specific mountain or meadow location." At my look of surprise, she continued. "I'm totally serious. It's beyond crazy how meticulous the Greeks were. But back to your question; in Ireland, we just called them tree spirits."

"What about the nature sprites and fairies?"

"Nature sprites were always just nature sprites. Fairies were fairies, although we did distinguish between light, dark, and neutral." Her dark eyes flashed. "But don't *ever* call a Túatha a fairy. It's a grave insult, one usually punishable by death."

"Yeah." I snorted. "Already went through that earlier with Sam and Angus Og."

Her eyes widened. "Oh no. Poor Sam is dead?"

"No. Angus brought his grievance to me—as he should have—and I turned it into a learning opportunity. For *both* of them."

"Wow." Now she eyed me with admiration. "I'm even more impressed."

I laughed it off. "The real problem is with human popular culture, which confuses the Fae with fairies and elves."

She grimaced. "Yes, I know. I saw part of a movie the other night that was deeply disturbing. Some of the characters were clearly Túatha, but someone had put ridiculous pointy ears on them and called them *elves*. Elves were never that powerful, only the Túatha." She shook her head in disgust. "Then Kevin explained the movie was based on books written early in the twentieth century, in a genre called *fantasy*, which meant everything was all made up. But if the humans have seen that movie—and others like it—and think it's all real, it won't help the Túatha when they start living among them."

I sat there, speechless.

Once in a while, I was rudely reminded that the Morrigan, for all her somewhat modern outlook, was an ancient being who was still learning about our culture.

This was one of those moments.

It'd probably be a good idea to not get into a long discussion on pop culture right now.

Instead, I said, "Well, with a little luck, from now on Angus will take my suggestion and explain the differences between the Túatha and other beings, instead of wanting someone's head over it."

She nodded. "Should the opportunity arise, I too will explain the differences, purely in the interests of coexisting in peace with humans."

"Thank you for that."

Hopefully, every little bit would help. The last thing we needed was some kind of war between the Túatha and humans—or any other category of unusual creature, for that matter.

And I'd do whatever I could to prevent another Túatha slaughter of any creatures.

I stood. "I need to go take a look at the VIP tent, try and remove all the furniture from it. Maybe order some plastic stuff as replacements. I promised the fairies an iron-free meeting location for the next Council meeting."

"That's very thoughtful of you. But what is the frame of the structure itself made of? Or the foundation? Would either of those have any iron, by chance?"

"Shit." I was an idiot. Of course, the tent's frame was probably steel, and if I remembered my high-school chemistry class correctly, steel was made by adding carbon—and a few other things—to iron. "You're right. Maybe it'd be better to just make a meeting space outside. After all, the weather's perfect for it right now."

She nodded. "It's very nice this time of year."

Right now, in mid-February, the highs were only in the low eighties, which was pretty close to perfect. The Morrigan had hated the triple digit heat and higher humidity of the monsoon last September, when she'd taught me battle magick out on the property. She'd complained quite loudly, in fact.

"With a little luck," I said, "it'll stay like this for another couple of months."

She cocked one brow. "That's entirely up to you, you know."

Ah, yes. How could I have forgotten?

Once upon a time, Mike had told me I manipulated the weather at Ard na Mara, turning its typical cool cloudiness into warm sunshine. At the time, I hadn't consciously known I'd done it, or even how I'd done it.

Now, as the Goddess, I could do so much more than just keep clouds away or warm up the air. No, I could cause terrible storms, too, if I so desired.

But something like maintaining pleasant weather for the duration of Council meetings was relatively benign.

"Thanks for reminding me." I smiled at the Morrigan, then raised a brow. "By the way, you never told me what position you'd like on the Council."

Her reply was quick. "I wish to advise you on political affairs."

"Done. You are now my Chief Political Advisor."

She blinked at me as if she'd expected me to argue, then bent her head for a moment. "Thank you. I am honored to serve on your Council."

"Well, I feel pretty honored myself, to have the Goddess of Battlefield Death as my Chief Political Advisor."

Then the prayers grew loud in my mind, and although someday soon I hoped to answer them while I did other stuff, for now it was still too new.

I had to concentrate fully during the process and keep distractions to a minimum.

"I'm sorry," I said. "The prayers are piling up. I'll talk to you later."

As I walked away to find a quiet spot, I felt her gaze on my back, assessing me.

Hopefully, with approval.

Some time later, I left my suite, feeling a bit drained from the prayer session. They'd been increasing over the past few weeks, but this time there'd been so many for healing and protection from storms, it'd almost been overwhelming.

Now, on my way outside, I ran into Anthony and Brianna in the kitchen, putting away groceries. I updated him on the diplomatic delegation, the problem with the VIP tent, and that I was going to create an outdoor meeting space instead.

"That makes sense," he nodded. "The meeting is next week, by the way. I'll let the attendees know they have to leave all iron at home."

After getting the exact date and time, I smiled and thanked him, then opened the panel in the window-wall and stepped out into the warm sunshine.

Remembering Daphne's instructions on communicating with her and the other ambassadors, I crouched in the grass and placed my hand flat. Next, I willed my message down into the ground. "*Daphne, Ferris, and Alanna, this is Dee. The Council meeting is next Thursday at nine in the morning. Come to the same place as last time, my home.*"

Almost immediately, I heard each of them reply in my mind.

Neat system, I had to admit.

Now, it was time to create the meeting space. As I walked toward the open land beyond the VIP tent, I reviewed the requirements.

There should be enough room for a full Council meeting, with green grass, some trees, maybe some flowers. All native, of course. Nothing that was high maintenance or needed a lot of water to survive. For the table and chairs, I could use some type of natural material like wood, but not put together with nails. Maybe magick would do the trick.

Wait. Wood probably wasn't a good idea, since Daphne was a dryad. Somehow it didn't seem right.

What if I used stone? Would that offend Ferris, the mountain sprite?

So many new things to worry about.

But first things first: I needed a location.

I studied the landscape for an area suitable for a meeting space. It had to be large enough to accommodate up to twenty attendees, and the ground had to be level. Ideally, it shouldn't have much vegetation, because I didn't want to remove any wildlife habitat. Most of the open land on my property consisted of plain dirt, but patches of desert scrub and wild mesquite trees were just about everywhere.

Ah, there: just beyond the dry wash and its yellow border of blooming creosote was a nice level patch that looked promising. Eager for a closer look, I started to hop over the wash, but then I realized it wouldn't be that easy for others. Especially since the steep banks were covered in loose gravel. Besides, later in the year, the wash would run with muddy, fast-moving water from the monsoon rainstorms, which would make it nearly impossible to safely cross.

Before I went any further, I created a sturdy little bridge over the wash with nearby rocks, desert soil, and my magick. I also included short walls along each side for additional safety.

Smiling at my ingenuity, I crossed my new bridge and closely inspected my chosen location.

It seemed perfect for my needs. It was nice and level, and didn't have many rocks at all. And there weren't any trees, bushes, or scrub to displace. As an added bonus, I didn't see a single hole in the ground, which would've been a good indication of a rattlesnake den or some other critter's home. I could hardly believe my luck.

I took a deep breath, stood in the center of the area, and turned slowly while I mentally mapped out the design of every feature I wanted to include—plus some ways I could make the space truly special.

After I was satisfied and had the design fixed in mind, I began thinking the objects into existence.

Starting with the dirt, I covered it in a circle of soft, thick grass that would never need mowing or fertilizer. Next, I created several mature mesquite trees around the grass edge, so their wide lacy canopies provided just the right amount of sun-dappled shade. In between the trees, I added a short hedge of colorful native flowering plants but left one space open for the entrance to the area. There, I added two swelling mounds of bush morning glory in full bloom, and laid a wide pathway of smooth pebbles all the way from the grass to the little bridge.

I paused to study my creation: a lush green space in the middle of a brown, dusty desert, filled with native plants that would flourish in the hot, dry climate with no additional help from me. I really liked how the space seemed naturally enclosed yet open and inviting, and it reminded me a little bit of the ring of oak trees in Garrett's office.

Now, for the final touches: furniture. Again, I used my magick to form and harden the shapes using just the desert soil. Not exactly stone, so it shouldn't offend Ferris, and it wasn't anything made of modern steel, so it wouldn't bother Alanna.

A vast round table, matching chairs, and a sideboard for refreshments now filled the green space. I'd even remembered special chairs for Alanna and Ferris so they could sit high enough at the table to see—and be seen by—everyone.

An unexpected wave of dizziness forced me to abruptly sit in one of the new chairs.

From the position of the sun, I'd been at it for over an hour, although it hadn't seemed like it. Maybe I'd used too much energy at once? Maybe creating from scratch was an enormous power drain? If so, I'd need to remember for next time, and take it a little bit slower.

I drew energy from Earth to replenish what I'd used, and it didn't take long for me to recover.

The dappled shade prevented the sun from being too hot, but the air itself was quickly warming. I'd definitely need a climate control system for any Council meetings held in summer.

But for now, I was done.

With a final glance of satisfaction, I turned and headed back to the house.

Kevin was in the kitchen, on a break from teaching his computer class in the VIP tent.

"How's it going?" Unfortunately, I'd asked just as he'd stuffed half a bagel into his mouth, so I had to wait while he chewed and swallowed with an apologetic look on his face.

"Great," he finally said. "I think this'll probably be the final session with this last group of Túatha. They're just about ready to be on their own." He paused, studied the other half of the bagel for a moment, then continued. "You know, the Morrigan's done a fantastic job teaching them how to look more human. Some have even started wearing contact lenses, although Dagda absolutely refuses. He says he'll just use magick to modify his appearance if and when he needs to. Honestly, I can't fault him for that. Even though contacts have gotten better over the years, they're still a pain in the ass."

That was the first I'd heard of the Morrigan showing them how to look more human. I hadn't checked in on any of the classes, and it'd been weeks since I'd met with the Dagda. What else had I missed?

"How are they handling social media?"

"They have a really hard time recognizing sarcasm, but other than that, they're picking up the lingo easily. Even abbreviations and slang. And since some want to tie their social media accounts to websites, I'm planning some breakout sessions to cover that."

"Websites? What kind of websites?" Oh gods, I hoped none were planning on doing anything illegal.

"Mostly storefronts and blogs, that sort of thing. One has a cooking show, so he wants to be able to sell cookbooks and gadgets. Another wants to sell scarves and shawls made from that shimmery iridescent fabric the Túatha are famous for—or will be someday, probably. Some even have brick-and-mortar businesses planned, like restaurants, art galleries, and day spas, so Anthony's helping them with the legalities of setting those up."

Cooking shows? Clothing? Restaurants? Fucking *day spas*?

I was stunned.

While I was glad the Túatha were finding their entrepreneurial spirit, I wasn't sure it was such a great idea to have them out among the humans so soon. Were humans ready to coexist with Túatha? For that matter, were the Túatha ready to coexist with humans?

At our last meeting, the Dagda had promised that none of his people would use their magick, but it was probably just a matter of time before one of them slipped up.

Or there was an incident like the one between Angus Og and Sam.

Or something even worse.

Unsurprisingly, Kevin picked up on my unease. Somehow, he always managed to read my mood or what I was thinking.

"Don't worry, Dee. They're not going to do anything against the rules. No magick lessons, no spells, no apothecaries, no Fae weapons. Only legit human-like businesses, like bookstores and restaurants. Oh, and handcrafted things like cloth, musical instruments, and artwork."

I was still a bit skeptical, but at the same time I was curious and couldn't wait to see what the Túatha created. "Well, I'll definitely check out their shops. They've got some really unique ideas."

He'd just opened his mouth to respond when Arddhu and the Morrigan entered the kitchen.

"I understand we will be meeting outdoors for the Council meeting," Arddhu said.

I nodded. "It's to accommodate the wishes of Alanna, our new fairy ambassador. No iron allowed within fifty feet or so."

"I see. Well, I am at your disposal should you require assistance in finding or creating such a suitable space."

"Too late, already done." I grinned. "I finished it just a little bit ago, and I think everyone will love it."

He blinked at me for a moment, and his smile had a hint of sadness. "Your progress continues to impress me, and I am proud of all you have accomplished."

"But something's bothering you."

He shrugged, which was probably the first time I'd ever seen him do that. A lot of Kevin was rubbing off on him, it seemed. "I must admit it stings a little that you no longer need me."

"Whoa, whoa, whoa. I never said I don't need you. I will *always* need you. Just not for the easy stuff that I can do myself."

The Morrigan snorted. "Creating a meeting space in this inhospitable hellscape is *easy*?"

Inhospitable hellscape?

I blinked at her. "I thought you loved it here."

She snorted again. "I *like* it here. I love *Ireland*." After a pause, she added, "But I must admit there is much beauty here that I haven't seen anywhere else."

Arddhu rested a hand on my arm. "I look forward to seeing what you have created."

"Me too," Kevin said, mouth full of bagel.

"And me," the Morrigan said.

And with their words, an unexpected butterfly fluttered around in my stomach. The meeting space was my first big created-from-scratch project, and the fact that these ancient deities would be judging it made me surprisingly nervous.

I could only hope they'd like it as much as I did.

CHAPTER THREE

T HE COUNCIL MEMBERS were due to arrive in only ten minutes. But before then, I wanted my closest and dearest advisors—my *family*—to have an advanced look at the meeting space I'd created. So Arddhu, Kevin, the Morrigan, and I headed out to the site a bit early.

The grove of mesquite trees I'd created were tall enough to be seen as soon as we rounded the VIP tent: a spot of vibrant green among the surrounding brown and gray.

"Whoa," Kevin breathed. "That's a little oasis out there."

I smiled. "No palm trees for this oasis, though. I used mesquite trees and Bermuda grass for green, bougainvillea and California poppies for color."

"Even from here, it's really pretty," the Morrigan said.

As we crossed the little bridge, I explained how I'd created it to be especially useful later in the year, when the monsoon storms flooded the wash and made it hard to cross for meetings.

"Well done," Arddhu said.

I followed them on the path into the meeting space, and although it was comfortable now, I started the climate control system to keep the temperature fixed for the duration of the meeting, even if it lasted into the afternoon.

My family milled around the area, closely inspecting my work. I watched their reactions, wanting them to love what I'd created. In a way, it was as if this space was my final exam for being admitted into a secret organization of immortals.

"How did you make this table?" Kevin asked, skimming his hand over the smooth surface. "Did you teleport stone from a quarry somewhere?"

I shook my head. "No, I formed it with desert soil and magick. Same as the chairs, and the sideboard."

One brow rose. "I never would've guessed it hadn't been hewn from stone."

"And the plants, grass, and trees?" The Morrigan turned from the bougainvillea toward me. "How did you make those?"

"I just *thought* them into existence."

She stared at me. "So, the furniture you transformed, but you created the living things from nothing."

I nodded slowly. Was that a big deal?

Arddhu sat in one of the chairs. "I must admit: this is not what I had expected. It is much more complex. Not what I would describe as you did, as *easy stuff.*"

"Well, it did seem easy. Besides, isn't that one of the powers of the Goddess? To create?"

Arddhu replied, "Yes. As is the power to destroy."

"That's why this was easy for you," the Morrigan added. "There's no way you could've done most of this last year."

"Right," I agreed. "As the Keeper, I couldn't create something from nothing. I could only transform existing matter." Such as the raincloud I'd made from the moisture in the Ard na Mara air, which then rained down onto Mike's head.

Good times.

The Morrigan touched my arm to get my attention. "You've done a skillful job here. It's a well-designed space that's both functional and beautiful."

Did that mean I'd passed the final? Was I really and truly deity now?

I grinned at her just as Brianna and Anthony appeared, followed by a few helpers sent from the firm. Most of them carried platters of food to the sideboard, while others wrangled hand-carts loaded with beer, wine, and booze.

Oh shit. I'd forgotten to make a bar.

As the guys with the hand-carts glanced around, I quickly used more desert soil and magick to form a beverage station near the sideboard.

"Sorry," I called to them. "There it is."

They smiled and nodded, and began unloading the carts with swift efficiency.

Now Arddhu was beside me. "The Túatha are here."

The four of us lined up to greet the attendees, but not like the formal receiving line of last year's alliance meeting. These Council meetings would be more informal, just the way I wanted.

First were the Dagda and Manannan, followed by Lugh and Ogma. Unlike the last time we all met, when we'd worked on stripping Ida of her power and banishing her, this time they all wore twenty-first century clothing. Now I saw first-hand what Kevin had told me about the Morrigan working on modernizing the Túatha's appearance to better fit among humans.

Even so, seeing the Dagda and Manannan in jeans and polo shirts with their long silver hair and kaleidoscope eyes was a bit jarring. Lugh and Ogma made the casual look work much better, since they'd transformed their eyes with magick or contact lenses.

"Welcome," I greeted with a smile. "The meeting will begin shortly. In the meantime, please help yourselves to refreshments."

Reshep arrived next. The last time I'd seen him, only a few weeks ago, he'd been ashen and exhausted, with dark circles under his eyes. Now, he seemed well-rested and rejuvenated. Color had returned to his complexion, and his dark eyes sparkled. He smiled warmly at me. "It is good to see You again, Lady." Then his gaze shifted to the Morrigan beside me, and his smile broadened. "And you as well, Morrigan." She joined him as he moved away, their heads close in a private conversation.

Then Randy was next, dressed in khaki pants and a polo shirt. I'd never seen him in anything other than jeans or tactical gear, so either he thought this would be a more formal meeting, or he wanted to make a good impression.

"Ma'am," he greeted me.

"Welcome to our first Council meeting. You're not on duty here, so please feel free to speak your mind and help yourself to the refreshments."

He nodded, but didn't head to the bar, just moved off to the side. Maybe he thought he was still security, despite this being more of an administrative function.

From past experience, I knew most of the attendees would wait until after the meeting to eat any food, but as I'd expected, they'd already been to the bar and were imbibing freely.

But, glancing around, I realized everyone wasn't here. We were missing three attendees.

I turned to Arddhu. "Our newest ambassadors confirmed they'd be here, but I don't see them. I hope nothing's happened."

His attention was elsewhere as he responded, "I believe this may be them."

I followed his gaze. Coming around the side of the house, Nat and Sam escorted a tall woman with flowing gown, and a short stocky creature, unmistakably Daphne and Ferris. I only saw Alanna hitching a ride on Daphne's shoulder because of my enhanced vision.

Randy spoke. "Looks like they used the front gate instead of the portal, like everyone else."

Shit. I'd completely forgotten to tell them about the portal.

Then again, could they even use it? Well, I'd ask them later.

As they drew closer, I smiled warmly. "Be welcome."

Daphne had slowed, eyes huge with wonder as she took in the little grove. "Oh, my Lady, this is truly quite beautiful."

High praise, coming from a dryad. "Thank you. I'd hoped you'd like it." To Alanna, I said, "This entire area is an iron-free zone. I keep my promises."

She bent her tiny head in reverence. "Thank You, Lady."

"My Lady, it seems You thought of everything." Ferris had noticed the special chairs I'd made for him and Alanna, and pointed them out to her before turning to me. "You keeping Your promises is priceless to us. For far too long, we were treated as less. Beneath all others in status. And more promises have been broken than were ever kept." His tone seemed more sad than angry.

"I'll see what I can do about fixing that," I said. "But in the meantime, please help yourself to the refreshments. The meeting will begin shortly."

The trio moved off, eyes wide in wonder, and the Morrigan and Reshep immediately engaged them in conversation.

Arddhu, Kevin, and I stood together for a moment, giving the rest of the group time to mingle for a bit.

"This is all very well done," Arddhu said. "In particular, the special seating. It seems you truly did think of everything."

I snorted. "Not quite. I totally forgot about including a bar for drinks, and only remembered when the guys showed up."

"But not many would've remembered to make special seats," Kevin pointed out.

I shrugged. "It just seemed like the right thing to do." I glanced around, and judged it was time to call the meeting to order. "Everyone, please take a seat, and we'll begin the meeting."

Alanna fluttered down into her seat, Ferris easily stepped up into his beside her, and Daphne gracefully sat in the seat on Alanna's other side. Ferris actually smiled, which softened his chiseled-rock features.

Of course, Kevin sat on my right, with Anthony and Randy next. Arddhu sat on my left, with the Morrigan and Reshep next to him.

After a brief hesitation, the Dagda sat beside Reshep, and the rest of the Túatha took the remaining open seats.

I noticed Reshep was visibly uncomfortable with the Dagda beside him, his posture stiff and body turned slightly away from the Dagda. I remembered after we'd freed the Túatha last year, he'd mentioned he didn't want them on his world. I'd never asked him why, and now, with this palpable tension between them, I'd need to find out.

Right after this meeting.

Unfortunately, the three new ambassadors also seemed uneasy with the Túatha, but I knew why: they still hated the Túatha for the troll slaughter and other nasty things they'd done. Daphne was only frowning, and Alanna looked everywhere but at the Túatha in front of her, but Ferris's bright smile of a moment ago had been replaced by a thunderous scowl.

I took a deep breath and began.

"Thank you, everyone, and welcome to our first official Council meeting. As you all know by now, we were successful in our plan to free the Túatha de Danann." I nodded to the Dagda and made brief eye contact with the other three. "Last year, some of you performed a crucial role in our plan to strip Ida's power and banish her, and for that I am most grateful. Just to reiterate once again for those who weren't present at the time, Anu decided on her own to gift the power of the Goddess to me, and I've accepted the solemn responsibility that comes with the power. I'm well on my way to a full transformation to divinity." I made contact with each of the attendees in turn as I spoke.

"But I'm not Ida, and I won't be that sort of Goddess. So, no bowing to me. No formality here. And please, stop using *my Lady.* Each and every one of you can just call me Dee." I paused to take a breath.

"Of our original group of twelve allies, only four remain. After some discussion and serious consideration, I've restructured that alliance into this Council. For the benefit of our newest members"—I indicated Alanna, Ferris, and Daphne—"I will now introduce each member and their assigned office."

I started on my left. "Arddhu is Chief Information Advisor; as one of the oldest among the world's deities, he has a wealth of knowledge and an extensive library to look up anything we need to know. The Morrigan is Chief Political Advisor, and will help keep me from getting us into a war. Reshep is Chief of Military Operations, in case we *do* get into a war." Now I turned to my right. "Kevin is Chief Technology Advisor; go to him to learn how to use modern conveniences such as the internet or computers. Anthony is Chief Administrator; he knows almost as much as I do about anything we'll be discussing in these meetings. Randy is Chief of Security; his team keeps us safe from intruders or threats.

"For the rest of you, our newest members are Daphne, the Dryad Ambassador; Alanna, the Fairy Ambassador; and Ferris, the Nature Sprite Ambassador."

My throat was parched by now, so I stopped to take a long drink of water. So far, no one had even tried to interrupt.

"Next, I'd like to announce my nominations for the remaining vacant positions. I'd like the Dagda and Manannan to serve as Joint Chiefs of Magick; you'd both be responsible for advising me on any matters related to the use of magick, defensive or otherwise. Lugh, as Chief Diplomatic

Advisor, you'd be responsible for diplomacy, which includes representing me on any delegations to other realms or pantheons. And, Ogma, as Chief Public Relations Advisor, you'd manage my social media presence, requests for interviews, and that sort of thing. Now, none of you have to decide immediately—"

"I accept," the Dagda interrupted, followed by the other three.

Wow. That was quick. Somehow I'd expected a bit more discussion.

"Thank you." I nodded. "Let me know if any of you have any questions about your responsibilities, or what's expected of you."

I took another drink of water and steeled myself for the firestorm of reaction I expected regarding the next topic.

"Now, I'd like to talk about something that's very important to me. The Goddess usually searches for a Consort, if she doesn't already have one, at some point in her... um... tenure. In my case, it's a bit more complicated, as I've already been in such a relationship for some time, but with two gentlemen. I realize this is a break with tradition, but I love them both deeply, and it just didn't seem fair to choose between them. So, I've decided to appoint *two* Consorts: Arddhu and Kevin."

But no one seemed at all surprised, not even the new ambassadors. I certainly hadn't expected the ancient deities, normally so traditional, to be so liberal.

"Any questions or concerns?"

Everyone shook their heads. So far, this was going almost too easily.

"Okay," I continued. "I'll turn to the next agenda item. Dagda, do you think you and your people are sufficiently up to date on the events that occurred on Earth while you were... um... away?"

He nodded. "Yes, we are now familiar with the three thousand years of what is now history." Then he frowned as he glanced around the table. "But I must say, I am appalled with the current state of affairs. Earth is vastly overpopulated with arrogant and selfish humans, who negatively impact the planet on a daily basis. Their constant aggression and deep hatred of each another has created an environment in which peaceful caretakers of the planet cannot exist, let alone thrive. So many wars. So much death. It's an abomination." He shook his head in disgust. "In addition, the pollution and widespread destruction of the once-abundant natural resources has resulted in the extinction of many species of flora and fauna."

From the corner of my eye, I saw Daphne nod enthusiastically, and I was hopeful they'd be able to use their common ground to work together without issues.

Then the Dagda turned his disconcerting gaze on me. "As the Goddess, You have started to correct this, for which we are truly grateful. But we— the Túatha—would like to expedite this effort in any way we can. To that end, please advise us what we can do to help."

I hesitated for a moment before I replied. After all, what could he and his people do to help? For all I knew, they'd only hinder my efforts.

"I'm not really sure what you or your people can do, specifically."

"For one thing, our magick could help clean the environment so Your work to heal the planet is not wasted. For another, we could help humans relearn basic respect for Earth, her flora and fauna, and perhaps even each other, with educational outreach."

I wasn't surprised he'd had suggestions ready. He'd obviously given this some thought.

"I'm definitely interested in hearing more," I said. "Let's have a break-out session after this meeting to discuss it in more detail."

He nodded in agreement, and I took another sip of water before continuing.

"For the benefit of our new members as well as those who aren't aware of recent developments, here's a recap: last year, we compiled a list of ninety humans who are destroying the planet with their polluting industries. Our mission objective was to eliminate the humans as well as their facilities, which would ensure they couldn't easily resume operations and continue polluting the water or air. We successfully eliminated about fifty targets from that list and their facilities. But late last year, we paused the mission to deal with some other issues that'd come up.

"Now, I think we're ready to resume the mission. But because it's inherently risky—we took a few casualties last year—I wanted to explore alternatives. In fact, I have an idea I'd like to present., but first I should mention something that gave me the idea.

"A few weeks ago, I removed a target and his assets. But I did it by myself, without a team, using magick right from here. Arizona, I mean. Although it was successful, I made one major error: I did it publicly, in front of a fairly large number of witnesses." I faltered for a moment after Reshep's startled gasp, but doggedly continued. "So, here's my idea: I'd like to eliminate the rest of the targets and their facilities the same way: remotely, using magick. Doing it this way would reduce the risk of anyone on our teams getting injured or captured, and it'd also be the quickest way to stop the constant damage to Earth." I glanced around the table. "So, what does everyone think?"

Reshep spoke first. "You said you removed the target publicly. How and where, exactly?"

"He was in an interview on national live television. I... I crushed his windpipe while he was speaking."

He blinked at me. "And so you propose to crush the windpipes of the remaining targets, all at once?"

"No. I was thinking something more like natural causes. Heart attacks or strokes, for example."

"And then you would destroy their facilities all at once, using magick?"

"Yes."

"Does human law enforcement know it was you?"

"No." If they did, they would've visited by now.

Reshep shook his head. "Although it is a reasonable idea, something about it bothers me."

"Thank you," Kevin interjected. "I'm glad I'm not the only one that doesn't like this idea."

Anthony cleared his throat. "I'd like to take a moment to talk about the consequences of destroying the facilities of almost fifty corporations last year." At my nod, he continued. "Those facilities were primarily used in the global production of heating oil for homes and gasoline for vehicles, and their loss caused quite a bit of global economic chaos. Because of the heating oil shortage, thousands of people froze to death in their homes over the winter. Here in the US, gasoline shortages have been mostly averted due to periodic releases from the reserves. But other countries have instituted rationing for their dwindling gasoline supplies, which has affected the global supply chain for everything from food to clothing to new vehicles. And it was a very bleak holiday season for many of the world's children, as store shelves were empty of popular toys."

He paused to take a breath, which seemed loud in the stunned silence.

"Most of the remaining mines and refineries on the list of targets have boosted their production to make up for the reduction in supply, but that's causing a corresponding spike in pollution. In conclusion, I strongly recommend another option than destroying those remaining facilities. To do otherwise risks bringing the entire global economy to a screeching halt."

Oh gods.

In the extended silence, Kevin's muttered "*fuck*" seemed incredibly loud.

I'd had no idea. All this time, I'd had no idea.

And yet, hadn't there been a lot more prayers over the winter? Prayers for money, for food, for warm clothing, for holiday toys. Why hadn't I put the pieces together and realized what had happened?

Now, I knew why I hadn't been making much headway on healing the planet. The damage had actually increased, making up for the decrease in production from those destroyed facilities.

The mission—Ida's entire *plan*—had been seriously flawed from the beginning, and I hadn't even realized it until now.

I felt like an idiot.

Arddhu's voice was subdued. "Perhaps the remaining facilities could be converted somehow? Could their ability to harm the planet be removed without impacting their basic functions?"

Anthony shook his head. "I doubt it. It'd be incredibly expensive to try such a conversion, and not even the firm has that much money."

Struggling to overcome my shock, I forced myself to concentrate on the problem at hand. "Could they be converted magickally?"

Kevin answered. "I'm not even sure that's possible. I mean, technically anything is possible with magick, but think about it. Let's take an oil refinery as an example. It probably uses a very complicated—and specific—industrial chemical process to transform crude oil into petroleum for vehicles. So you'd have to study how that process works in detail, then come up with some other way to do it." He quirked a wry smile. "No offense, love, but you're not an industrial chemical engineer. It'd probably take you years of trial and error."

Shit. He wasn't wrong. If anything, he was understating it. It'd take me *decades*, since I completely sucked at anything related to science.

"Not to mention all the highly qualified employees at those facilities," Anthony said. "Whatever you came up with, they'd all have to be retrained. It would take significant effort." He paused for a moment, as if debating whether or not to continue. "There was another unintended consequence I didn't mention earlier. All those employees of last year's destroyed facilities? The ones who weren't on site at the time, I mean. Well, none of them had jobs to go back to. Here in the US, unemployment soared, as well as participation in social safety net programs like food stamps. Then winter hit, with the heating oil shortages and global trade issues, and... well... it's been a helluva mess for the past several weeks."

Honestly, at this point I felt like curling up and crying. I'd never intended to cause so much harm. I'd thought I was making things better. Not worse.

"Is there anything we can do to help them?" I asked him. "Send some money, care packages, that sort of thing? Anonymously, of course."

He pursed his lips in thought for a moment, then nodded. "I think I can find a way to do that."

"Great." I took a breath before continuing. "So, maybe we should wait before removing any more of the targets. There's a lot we still need to discuss, and more than a few decisions to make."

"That would be wise," Arddhu said.

"We can help," the Dagda insisted. "We've spent quite some time learning the current technology, but truly, it is crude and clumsy. Our magick could transform how humans live on this planet. Not only would it be non-polluting, but it could also—as I mentioned earlier—help the humans to live more in harmony with Earth. We could start today. Why shouldn't we?"

The Morrigan turned toward him. "Do you really want to expose yourselves to humans like that?"

"Why not?" Lugh shrugged. "People in Eire have known of us for centuries. Why not go global?"

"Right," I agreed. "I've heard for months now how humans no longer believe in the gods. But if we do this—and do it right—they'll *believe* again. And maybe that'll stop any gods from fading away."

"I won't deny there are quite a few who are gone," the Morrigan said. "Let's face it: the little bit of power we get from being mentioned in humans' movies and television shows is just that: a trickle. It's barely enough to sustain us. But what you're suggesting would put all of us at risk of far too much exposure."

"Exactly," Kevin said. "It could end up being a Pandora's Jar. I mean, sure, it could go absolutely perfect and be a really good thing to have humans worshipping all the gods again. But it could also go horribly wrong and be a disaster. After all, humans haven't exactly been kind to the gods. Just look at history."

"I think there's a lot more evidence for the gods being unkind to humans," I countered. "Even so, I think it'd be worth taking our chances. And besides, if we can pull this off, humans will be happy again. With clean air and water, people won't get so sick anymore. The planet will cool down. Weather will stabilize, with fewer deadly hurricanes, tornadoes, floods, or earthquakes. It'll be a paradise, like it was a long time ago. I could even send a wave of healing over the entire planet, and cure everyone who has cancer or whatever. Everyone would be happy."

Kevin stared at me like I'd lost my mind. "Have you already forgotten that humans are never happy for very long? It's just not in their nature."

Shit. He had a damn good point.

"And you're forgetting something else," the Morrigan said. "All that divine intervention will only cause even more unintended consequences. You might end up making things worse with widespread healing like that. Besides, if you make things too easy, they'll never learn the lessons they're supposed to, to make them better humans."

"What about answering prayers?" I asked. "Isn't that divine intervention?"

She shrugged. "Not if you don't give them what they ask for directly. Usually, I either connect them to other humans who can provide what they need, or I ignore them."

I couldn't believe what I'd just heard. She just *ignored prayers?*

"Wait. So if someone desperately asks you for healing, you just ignore them?"

She laughed, but not unkindly. "No one's ever asked the Goddess of Battlefield Death for healing. Victory on the battlefield, yes. Revenge against enemies, also yes. Not healing."

"But you answered those others, right?"

"Of course. Not recently, though. Back in the old days. Not now."

"Why not now?"

"Too many unintended consequences with divine intervention. I learned my lesson."

I glanced at the other deities. "Have the rest of you stopped answering prayers, too?"

The Túatha looked away, refusing to meet my gaze. But they were forgiven; they'd been banished for the past three thousand years.

Reshep simply nodded, but didn't explain or comment.

"I'm exempt." Kevin sighed. "I'm not really a god, anyway."

Arddhu replied. "Yes, for the most part. As the Morrigan stated, the risk of unintended consequences is too high in these modern times."

I shook my head. "And yet you were all so pleased when I told you I was receiving prayers and answering them."

The Morrigan shrugged again. "You're a newbie. We thought it'd be better for you to learn these things on your own."

I stared at her, unable to form a proper reply. I didn't know if I should feel betrayed or just plain pissed.

Then I thought about the poor humans. No fucking wonder they'd become so cynical about the gods. Their prayers probably hadn't been answered for centuries.

"You know, this sucks," I said. "You guys are supposed to *advise* me, but I don't remember anyone mentioning any of this. When we came up with the plan for removing the targets, nobody brought up unintended consequences. And when I got the power of the Goddess, nobody said anything about divine intervention being bad."

"Well, for one thing," the Morrigan jabbed a finger at me, "you were only the Keeper when we worked on that plan. For another, we weren't advisors, we were allies. And yes, we *are* advising you. Right here, right now."

Both of us had gotten a bit testy.

Before it could escalate further, Arddhu rested a hand on my arm.

"You are correct, Deirdre. On those two occasions you mentioned, we did not counsel anything different. As far as unintended consequences go, we bear just as much responsibility as you. And as for divine intervention, it is commendable that you consistently answer prayers." He made brief eye contact with the Morrigan and Reshep, as if to convey something unspoken.

"If that's settled," Lugh said, "I'd like to go back to something else you said—something about if we're successful, the humans will be happy." I sighed and nodded for him to continue. "What about the aggressive humans? The ones who're never content with the land within their borders, and who always want to take it from their neighbors? And the ones who kill for entertainment? Do you plan on making *them* happy, too?"

"Of course not," I scoffed. "But, honestly, I just threw an idea out there for discussion."

The Morrigan leaned forward and rested her arms on the table. "Earlier, you mentioned you'd like to return the planet to the paradise it used to be." She shook her head. "Some of us were there, ages ago. We can tell you: it was *never* a paradise. There's always been war, hunger, death, disease, and greed, not to mention murder, theft, and mayhem." Her expression softened. "Sorry, but there's no such thing as utopia. It's just a fantasy."

Now, I realized how idiotic I'd sounded. Paradise, indeed. "I do know that," I insisted. "I guess I just want to make it better than it is now."

She smiled warmly. "And you will. *We* will, all of us. We'll help. It'll be better." She held my gaze. "Just not perfect."

"I know it won't be perfect." I quirked a grin. "I'd never want to put you out of a job. There'll probably always be battles. And wars. I just hope for fewer innocent casualties."

She grinned in reply, and our testiness was forgotten.

"To return to the agenda topic," Reshep said, "I propose this: we move forward with eliminating the remaining targets. I believe removing them in a single magickal action would send a strong message to the world that the time of unbridled corruption and pollution is over. However, we cannot have chaos on a global scale, so I think the facilities should be left to function for the time being. Until such time as we can figure out how to convert them in some way."

That seemed like a good compromise.

"Okay," I nodded. "Let's vote on that. All in favor of me taking out the targets magickally and remotely, but leaving the facilities untouched for now, say *aye*."

Reshep, the Morrigan, Arddhu, and the Túatha immediately agreed.

Daphne murmured with Ferris and Alanna for a moment, then said, "We have no opinion on this. We trust You to do whatever is necessary."

Randy shrugged and pointed to the ambassadors. "I'm with them. I don't really have an opinion on this."

Kevin was the sole holdout. "I'm sorry, I have to vote no. I've got a bad feeling about this. But since I'm outnumbered, can you at least promise me that you won't take out any of them publicly?"

I met and held his gaze. "I promise you: I absolutely will not do it publicly." I addressed the rest of the Council. "Okay, so we officially have a change in the mission plan. I truly appreciate everyone's honesty and patience."

"Oh," Anthony interjected. "I just had an idea. On the facilities and repurposing them, I'll talk to the firm. I'm sure they have some resources that could be useful to us."

Damn. How could I have forgotten about the firm? It had deep pockets and global tentacles, so of course it'd be able to help.

Probably.

"That's a great idea," I said. "Thanks." Then I glanced at the agenda. "Okay. Next agenda item: we need to visit some of the other pantheons.

First, to personally give my condolences for the losses of Tyr, Marisha-Ten, and Nayenezgani. Also, we need to let them know what's been going on. I don't know how many worked with Ida, or even if they knew her, but some might be concerned I'm no different than she was. Or, maybe they've heard about what happened with Ares, Athena, and Kali, and they think I'm planning on taking over."

"Or," Kevin added, "maybe those three have already won some other pantheons over to their side. We could be looking at another war between the gods."

Another war between the gods? I hoped not. Humanity would never survive it. Maybe not even the planet.

Our side. Their side.

I hated thinking of it like that, choosing sides. But that's really what it came down to, wasn't it? Those three could be out there saying absolute shit about me.

"Okay, that's another reason to visit other pantheons," I said. "We should pursue diplomatic alliances with as many pantheons as we can, just in case it does come down to those three against us."

Lugh spoke. "As Chief Ambassador, I'll get started right away on planning the diplomatic missions. If I may, I'd like to suggest a visit to the Norse pantheon first. I think they'd be the friendliest."

"That sounds great." I nodded. "Anyone have any additional business?"

Ogma spoke. "As your Chief Public Relations Advisor, I'd like to begin creating your public persona. I'll schedule some media interviews and a few other in-person appearances, of course well-presented, so we can get ahead of any damaging information that may start floating around."

"Just let me know what you need from me." His famed reputation for eloquence of the written word made him the perfect choice to help me craft my image. Although the mere thought of public appearances made me nervous, I knew I'd be in good hands with him.

"We still haven't discussed the elephant in the room," Kevin said. "What are we going to do about Ares, Athena, and Kali?"

"Has anyone heard anything?" I glanced around the table. "Do we even know where they are?"

Arddhu shook his head. "I have heard nothing."

"It's almost as if they've disappeared." Reshep frowned. "However, I have heard of a sudden escalation in hostilities between two long-standing enemies in South Asia. Both countries have nuclear weapons technology. It is possible that Ares could be behind this. After all, he craves the brutality and horrors of war more than anything else."

Shit. The absolute last thing we needed right now was a nuclear war.

"I'll see what I can find out," Anthony said. "The firm might have some resources in that area, as well."

"Keep me updated." I nodded. "If Ares is whispering in the ears of two armies, I'll need to stop him."

"No," Kevin corrected. "*We'll* need to stop him." His gaze locked with mine, but one side of his mouth quirked. "You don't have to go running off to do everything yourself, you know."

"You're right." I flashed a quick grin. "Of course." To everyone else, I said, "Does anyone have anything else they want to discuss before we adjourn?"

"Yes." The Morrigan leaned forward. "There's one thing that's been sort of bothering me about removing the remaining targets remotely with magick. We all agree it's the sensible thing to do." She glanced around at the others before resting her gaze on me. "And we all know that you're quite capable of doing it quickly and easily. But just because we *can* do something doesn't mean we *should*. It's one thing to go into battle with our swords raised, meeting our opponents face-to-face. It's another thing to kill someone silently with magick, while he sleeps comfortably in his bed with his wife snuggled at his side and his innocent children tucked in their rooms next door. It's not honorable, according to the timeless rules of battle engagement."

Ouch.

She'd just called me out as dishonorable, and it stung more than a little. I stared at her, trying to think of something to say that wouldn't be taken as an insult.

But it was Arddhu who spoke next. "That is true: it is not an honorable battlefield death, according to the old ways. Ida was a product of those old days, for she also preferred the battlefield. She did not use the internet, social media, or modern technology.

"However, times have changed. And, although the battles of last year were exhilarating for so many of us old ones, it is no longer necessary, or appropriate." He indicated me with a graceful wave of his hand. "Deirdre is truly a Goddess of the Modern Era, as she clearly demonstrated when she removed the last target on live national television with magick, a method which is firmly rooted in today." He smiled at the Morrigan, with just a hint of sadness. "The old ways are over, my friend. It is time for the new ways. And I believe there is just as much honor on Deirdre's battlefield as there was on our own."

I swallowed, hard. I hadn't expected him to advocate for modern methods like that. As far as I knew, he still didn't even have electricity in his realm.

"You make your argument well, old friend." The Morrigan's expression softened. "And yes, you have convinced me." Her dark gaze shifted to meet mine. "Life is full of hard choices. We get some of them wrong, despite our best intentions." She shrugged and smiled wryly. "We're gods, but we're not perfect. However, I would be remiss if I didn't mention that you've done remarkably well in such a short period of time, adjusting to your new godhood. Most humans would be drunk on the power you now wield, but you have shown restraint, and learned valuable lessons from your mistakes."

Wow. These two were going to make me cry in a minute. I'd never dreamed of having such strong support from two ancient deities.

"Thank you both. Your words mean everything to me." To the rest of the group, I said, "If no one else has anything to add, the meeting is adjourned. Please enjoy the refreshments."

As everyone swarmed the sideboard and began feasting, I glanced at the food but immediately lost interest. I just wasn't hungry. That was one of the weirdest things about this transformation to deity: sometimes, I was still ravenous after eating a big meal, other times I couldn't force myself to eat a single bite, and sometimes there was every variation in between. My appetite was in chaos these days.

No one even noticed when I slipped away.

CHAPTER FOUR

I LEFT THE meeting space and walked out onto my property in the warm afternoon sunshine. It was still only February, but the rest of the year stretched out before me as unbelievably busy.

Ostara, the Spring Equinox, was only a few weeks away. Finn's Cove would hold a feast but no ritual, and it was just another event I'd been forced to miss last year because of Cromm.

I'd missed so many things because of that asshole: Yule, Imbolc, Ostara, and Beltaine. And I'd still only have half of my right arm, too, if the power of the Goddess hadn't unexpectedly restored it. I'd truly expected to need my prosthetic hand for the rest of my life, and it still amazed me that I didn't.

Beltaine, on the first of May, was one of the most important rituals in the Wheel of the Year for Finn's Cove. From Maggie's memories, it'd include a sacred bonfire, festival, and feast, but its main purpose was to promote fertility for the land, livestock, and people.

According to tradition, there'd be a lot of couples sneaking off to fuck, too.

Sometimes, the Sacred Rite was performed with the avatars of the God and Goddess. They joined together, sometimes in private but most of the time in public, to symbolize the union of Earth and Sky, May Queen and King, or Goddess and Consort.

It'd be my first Beltaine as Lady of the Cove and the Goddess. I wasn't sure if I'd be expected to participate in the Sacred Rite, or even how that'd work with two Consorts. But there was still plenty of time to figure that out.

Then there was the rest of the Wheel of the Year: Midsummer, Lammas, Mabon, Samhain, and Yule.

A neat line of stones in the desert soil stopped me from walking any further, and I looked up in surprise. I hadn't realized I'd walked so far.

I'd reached the old portal, the one I'd used to travel to and from Ard na Mara, back before I received the power of the Goddess and could teleport anywhere I wanted.

For just a moment, I thought about those days with wistful fondness. Things had been simpler then, even as I'd thought they were infinitely more complicated than when I'd just been an accountant. Back then, as the Keeper, I'd only been responsible for protecting the Sphere. Of course, after Ida gave me the mission to eliminate the threats to Earth, it got more complicated. Nothing like things were now, though.

Responsible for the entire planet? Who would've ever expected such a thing?

But really, I wouldn't trade these days for those, not for anything. Having the power of the Goddess meant I could do incredible, wonderful things. Fantastic things for the greater good of the entire world.

"Dee?" Kevin's footsteps crunched behind me. "Everything okay?"

"Yeah." I turned and smiled. "I was just thinking."

He wrapped his arms around me and lightly rested his chin atop my head. "After everyone started eating, I didn't see you. I got worried."

I snuggled against his chest, so warm and strong. "So you tracked me down."

His low chuckle rumbled in my ear. "Locator spells, for the win."

"What if I didn't want to be found?" I teased.

His arms tightened around me briefly, then released me. "I didn't stop to think maybe you didn't want to be disturbed. I'll leave you be." He turned to go.

Shit. "Wait. I was just teasing," I explained. "If there's ever a time I want to be alone and undisturbed, I'll definitely let you know."

He nodded. "Okay. Sounds good." He gazed off in the distance for a moment. "I thought you and the Morrigan were going to get into it, for a minute back there." Now he met my eyes. "You know we care about you and only want the best for you."

"Yeah, I know. And as much as I value the opinion of the Túatha, Reshep, and the others on the Council, it's you, Arddhu, and the Morrigan who are my closest advisors. Hell, you're more than that. You're my *family*. I trust each of you completely." I stepped close and pulled him to me. "I won't ever do anything to jeopardize that. Promise."

Resting his forehead against mine, he sighed. "It's hard sometimes. I mean, I never want to put any limits on you, but I worry. I don't trust humans at all. Given half the chance, they wouldn't hesitate to hurt you."

"Hey, I'm still one of those humans you say you don't trust," I teased. "Well, sort of. I guess I still *think* of myself as just another human, more or less, even though I'm not. Not anymore."

One brow quirked up. "I've got news for you: even when you were the Keeper, you were never *just another human*." He cocked his head thoughtfully. "Now that I think about it, I think I loved you from the first time I met you. I just didn't know it yet."

I frowned. The first time we'd met, he'd been an arrogant asshole intent on scaring the shit out of me. He sure hadn't acted like he'd even *liked* me, let alone *loved* me. But just as I was about to call bullshit, my witchy-sense told me his words were *truth*.

Huh.

So instead, I continued to tease him. "Is that so? And why in the world would you have loved me back then?" I fully expected him to answer something about my boobs or ass.

"You were fearless. I mean, I used every trick I could think of to intimidate you, but you never once backed down. That one time, for example. There you were, stark naked, head held high and fire in your eyes, and you never yielded an inch. You were so *fierce*."

I blinked up at him. He hadn't taken the bait like I'd thought he would; he'd stayed completely serious.

That time he mentioned... I'd only been naked because he'd shown up at a vulnerable moment: after I'd showered and before I'd had a chance to get dressed. Interestingly, he hadn't sensed how scared shitless I'd been. I must've been better at acting than I'd thought.

"And then," he continued, "that time in the shower? When you actually used your magick against me?" He shook his head. "I think that's when I really fell for you. Head over heels, in fact."

Ah, yes, I remembered. He'd barged in on my shower—another vulnerable moment—and pestered me until I'd basically lost my patience and pushed him away with the power of the Keeper.

I smirked. "You know, back then I just thought you were an arrogant asshole."

He still didn't smile. "I *was* an arrogant asshole. For centuries, in fact. I prided myself on how much of an arrogant asshole I was."

"So, what changed you?"

He hesitated. "Honestly?"

"Of course."

"You," he said. "After Cromm took you, I knew it was my own damn fault it'd happened. If I hadn't taken you off Earth to begin with, you would've been safe from him. When I thought I'd never see you again..." He shook his head. "That's when I realized how fucked up I was. All those things I promised you, after we got you safe to Arddhu's world? That I'd never hurt you and that I'd protect you? That wasn't just bullshit, you know."

Even if my witchy-sense hadn't just told me he'd spoken the truth, I would've known it. He'd been nothing but loyal and dependable ever since my rescue from Cromm's world.

"I know it wasn't bullshit." I held his gaze. "But if you hadn't changed, we wouldn't be here right now."

His arms tightened around me. "Oh gods, I know. *Believe me*, I know." He sighed. "But I still worry. You deserve better. So every day, I try my damnedest to be worthy of you. Of your love."

I swallowed the lump that'd formed in my throat.

Shit.

Truly, I'd known he loved me, but this... this was way more than he'd ever said to me, and way more than I ever thought I'd hear.

In this moment, I didn't think I could love him any more.

I pulled his head down and kissed him hard, then spoke against his mouth. "You *are* worthy. Don't you *ever* fucking think you're not."

Just then, Arddhu's voice in my head startled me. "*Deirdre? Where are you?*"

"*I went for a walk. Kevin's with me; he came to find me.*"

"*We are meeting with the Dagda in the VIP tent now for the break-out session you requested.*"

"*On our way.*"

Kevin's questioning look let me know he'd sensed I was communicating through a mental link. "Arddhu's waiting for us. We need to get back." I pulled away from him and took his hand in mine. "I want some mead before he drinks it all," I added as I tugged him toward the tent.

He grinned. "We could just port there, you know."

"I know. But I like holding your hand and walking with you. It's romantic." I caught myself grinning like a silly lovesick girl.

"Oh?" His lips curved into a sly smile, the one that always sent a shiver—the *really good* kind—up my spine and made my heart speed up. "Is that all you like doing with me?"

"Mmm." My voice was husky. "Later, I'll show you *exactly* what I like doing with you."

"Can't wait." The tone of his voice and the look he gave me... well, he'd just made it almost impossible for me to concentrate on the next meeting.

We didn't talk on our way back, just held hands while we walked. When we entered the VIP tent, Arddhu, the Morrigan, the Dagda, and Reshep waited in the lounge area.

"Sorry," I said as I poured myself a glass of mead. "I just needed to stretch my legs for a bit." I sat in the unoccupied chair next to Arddhu.

The Dagda smiled. "It did seem to be quite a long meeting. Hopefully this one will be much shorter." He leaned forward. "As you know, my people have been learning the use of computers, the internet, and other new technologies in preparation for launching online businesses as well as brick-and-mortar establishments such as restaurants. What I propose is this: we—the Túatha—also resume our traditional roles as caretakers of Earth, and do it quite visibly, using websites, streaming entertainment, and public outreach. For example, education of young and old on what it means to care for the planet and its environment. In the course of these efforts, we would also work with the oil and gas industry as well as other corporations that currently violate clean air and water standards. Perhaps we could even interest them in converting their facilities to solar, wind, or water as their sources of power, replacing the use of coal, oil, natural gas, or nuclear energy." He glanced around. "That is what I propose."

Holy shit. That was a lot. That was *huge*. A total game-changer for Earth.

While I blinked at him and tried to find the words to express how much I loved his idea, the Morrigan spoke.

"But, just as I mentioned earlier, that would expose you and your people to humans. I'm not sure that's a good idea."

The Dagda shrugged. "As Lugh also pointed out earlier, Eire has known of the existence of the Túatha for centuries. We are comfortable revealing ourselves to humans."

I found my voice. "Just as long as you don't harm anyone. We don't need human law enforcement agencies on our backs."

"Of course." He nodded. "I also remember quite well the promise you extracted from me last year. We will not harm any humans. We will simply educate them, and restore their respect for their world."

"Not just humans," I said. "Other creatures, too. Like trolls, sprites, dryads, and fairies."

He raised a brow, but nodded. "Of course."

"As for your idea, I like it." I glanced around. "What about everyone else?"

"I still have some reservations," the Morrigan said. "But I say let's give it a shot."

Arddhu also agreed. "I am very interested to see how the humans respond."

"As am I," Reshep said.

Kevin shook his head. "I'm still worried about any of us putting ourselves out there like that. It's a risk."

The Dagda cocked his head to one side. "Does the lion concern himself with a dung beetle? I am not worried."

Well. That was one way to look at it, I supposed. Not sure I'd ever heard it put that way before, though.

"You can go forward with your idea," I said. "Make sure you keep in touch with Anthony. The firm has extensive resources that we can leverage to help with most of this."

"Of course," he said again, and leaned back in his seat with a satisfied smile.

"May we spend a few moments on the plan for removing the targets?" Reshep asked. "I'd like to ask a few more questions."

"Sure." I refilled our mead glasses.

"How do you think the humans will react to approximately forty of their captains of industry suddenly dropping dead of apparent natural causes at the same time?"

"Well, they'd probably figure out there was something—or someone— to blame, and freak out a little. But even if we spaced it out a bit, like a few every day for a week or so, it'd still be suspicious. No matter what we do or how we do it, people will still see the connection."

Arddhu nodded. "That would be true even if we continued removing the targets as we did last year."

Good point.

"You know," Kevin said, "it's always bothered me that all those killings—the missions—didn't make the prime time news. It's almost as if someone kept it all quiet. Normally, wouldn't multiple beheaded prominent businessmen cause a panic? Or at least be a news story for a week or so?"

"Now that you mention it," I said, "you're right. It should have. Too bad Anthony isn't here. Maybe the firm had something to do with covering it all up."

"If they did," the Dagda said, with raised brows, "then this firm is very powerful, indeed. It might be a good idea to work with them a bit more closely."

"But back to your question," Kevin said to Reshep. "Social media would go absolutely nuts. It's already full of conspiracy theorists, but they'd just use this latest thing to promote even crazier shit. And the gun nuts would buy lots more guns and ammunition, thinking that the world was ending. There'd probably be a surge in violence."

"Not only that," the Morrigan added, "it'd draw attention from law enforcement agencies. Everyone from government goons to local sheriffs would get involved. It'd probably be just a matter of time before you'd get a not-so-friendly visit."

Ugh. What a mess. "But really, what choice do we have?"

Reshep nodded. "I don't see that we do have a choice. But, unlike with other actions, we can try to anticipate all the consequences this time, and maybe even avoid some of the worst of them."

"How?" Arddhu asked. "How could we avoid any of the consequences?"

"What if we got ahead of the story?" I mused aloud.

"What do you mean?"

"What if I had a press conference immediately after I took out the targets? I could explain what I'd done and why. Ogma could help me craft the statement so it'd have the maximum effect. And maybe we could have additional press conferences in the weeks after. I could talk about how I'm healing Earth and how it benefits everyone. Or maybe we could hire a small camera crew to follow me around and do a mini documentary."

Then again, I really didn't like that last idea.

Arddhu shook his head. "I do not like any of those ideas."

"Me neither," Kevin said. "How about, instead of press conferences, you film a video? We could do it ourselves right here and upload it to the social media sites you'll be setting up with Ogma."

"I like it." I hadn't really liked the idea of getting up in front of a bunch of reporters, but thought it'd be effective.

"Perhaps You should also consider meeting with the leaders of the world," the Dagda said. "Speak to them directly about what You're doing. Especially after the targets are removed—it could be a good opportunity to convince them to be better stewards of the planet."

"Absolutely not," Arddhu objected. "I have no love for the human world leaders, especially the Americans. They are selfish and greedy, and would see Deirdre as a threat to their own power." He shook his head. "They would wish to harm her."

"Or try to use her power," Kevin quietly added. He turned to the Dagda. "It's not a bad idea, but you've been gone too long. You underestimate the humans. They're much worse than they were in the old days. Even though they seemed more brutal back then because they had less sophisticated weapons, they've become more self-centered and unhinged from reality."

The Dagda sighed. "I see your point. We watched some of the documentaries of the most recent fifty years or so. Humans have become a terrible scourge on the planet."

Oh for fuck's sake. I needed to get this back on track immediately.

I cleared my throat. "Can we get back to discussing the consequences of me doing a clean sweep of the targets?"

"I like that." Reshep smiled at me. "With your permission, we will call this Operation Clean Sweep."

More than a few chuckles sounded among us, and some of the tension had drained, too.

The Morrigan spoke. "As your Chief Political Advisor, I see no reason to not do all the targets at once. It's just like removing a bandage from a wound; you don't peel it off slowly and prolong the pain. No, you tear it off quickly so the pain is only momentary." She shrugged. "The consequences will be the same regardless of whether it is done fast or slow."

"When, though?" Kevin asked. "I mean, should it be before or after the diplomatic missions?"

I frowned. "Why would that matter?"

"Well, what if Ares, Athena, and Kali have been meeting with the other pantheons? If so, why wouldn't we want to talk to those pantheons as soon as possible, to try and counteract anything they're trying to do?"

"In that case," the Dagda said, "diplomatic relations would seem to be the immediate priority."

"Yes," Arddhu said. "It makes sense to visit the pantheons first."

"Forging diplomatic ties with other uncertain deities is a strong political strategy," the Morrigan agreed. "I highly recommend it."

Reshep nodded. "Those visits would also be the perfect opportunity to explain your long-term plan for removing the targets and healing Earth. It is better for them to hear it from you, than from others who have incentive to lie. And trusting the other deities with the truth shows good faith."

"Okay," I said. "It's settled then. We'll delay Operation Clean Sweep until after the diplomatic missions. Dagda, can you have Lugh come back here in the morning? We need to get started on those visits as soon as possible."

The Dagda nodded, and after we adjourned, he left the VIP tent.

Arddhu refilled all our glasses with the last of the mead.

"I believe we resolved many issues today," Arddhu said.

Not all of them, though. I turned to Reshep. "Can I ask you something?" I didn't wait for him to reply. "Last year, when we freed the Túatha, you said you didn't want them on your world. And I sense some lingering animosity between you and them. So before we go much further, I'd like to know why."

He hesitated for only a moment. "They have powerful magick. Last year, I did not want them using it in my realm. My people could have been hurt."

My witchy-sense told me he spoke the truth, but I couldn't shake the feeling that he wasn't telling me the whole story.

He held my gaze unblinkingly as the silence stretched out.

"That's it?" I finally asked. "Anything else you want to tell me?"

He slowly shook his head. "That is all."

So be it.

"I've extracted a promise from Dagda that neither he, nor any of his people, will use their magick to hurt anyone. So far, he's held to that promise." Now I glanced around at the others. "If any of you hear otherwise, please let me know immediately."

Murmurs of assent.

"Thank you all for your wise counsel," I added as I set my glass on the table and stood. "Now, if you'll excuse me, I require some private time."

I ported directly to my suite and collapsed on the bed. For some reason, I was exhausted.

Probably nothing a bit of sleep couldn't fix.

CHAPTER FIVE

ASHES AND SMOKE. Screams and panic.

Fire and soot rained from the sky.

Everywhere around me was devastation and death.

I threw a shield up to keep the fireballs from igniting more of the surrounding area—as well as myself—but winced as each one hit. It was as if the shield was an extension of my body.

Of course, the shield didn't do a damn thing for the superheated air; every breath I took was agony, searing my throat and lungs.

Where was my family? Were they dead? Or were they somewhere safe from this hell?

Wracked with a coughing fit, I almost dropped the shield. My energy was fading fast, and I didn't know how much more I could hold it.

"Deirdre, you must wake."

Anu's voice was like soothing cool water in my fevered brain.

Wait. I was dreaming? This wasn't real?

"Wake, Deirdre. Wake now."

At her insistence, I opened my eyes even as I gasped for breath, heart pounding in my chest like I'd just run for miles.

I was in my bed. The sun streamed through my patio window, and birds sang in the backyard.

Everything was normal, completely normal.

It'd all been a dream.

Well, more like a nightmare.

I took a deep breath and calmed, then sent gratitude to Anu.

"Thank you, Anu. That was horrible."

"Yes, it was. Much love, Deirdre."

For a moment, I was still disoriented. When I'd curled up for a nap, it'd been late afternoon. But by the angle of the sun, it was now early morning. Which meant I'd slept through the entire evening as well as the night.

Huh. I must've been more tired than I'd thought.

Shaking off the nightmare, I took a quick shower, then dressed and left my suite.

Arddhu and Kevin were at the kitchen island while Brianna made breakfast.

"Good morn," Arddhu smiled. "I trust you are well rested?"

"I can't believe I slept so long." I sat next to him just as Brianna placed three plates on the granite. Each was piled with fluffy scrambled eggs, crispy bacon, and savory hash browns.

"We figured you needed it," Kevin said. "So we didn't wake you."

Too busy eating to respond, I just nodded. For the first time in what seemed like weeks, I was absolutely starving.

As we ate, Brianna paused in cleaning up to stare off into the distance. Suddenly, she began cooking more food. After a moment, she got two more plates from the cabinet.

I didn't have to wait long to find out who they were for: the Morrigan and Reshep entered the kitchen from the direction of the hallway to her bedroom. The Morrigan's grin was lazy and sensuous, like that of a satisfied cat, while Reshep's eyes sparkled as he brought her hand to his lips.

Oh. I hadn't realized they'd begun a relationship, but I was beyond happy for them.

"Good morning," she sang, and sat next to me just as Brianna placed the last two breakfast plates on the granite and resumed cleaning up.

"Morning," I replied. "To both of you."

Reshep met my gaze over the Morrigan's head, and nodded respectfully.

Fuck that serious shit. Grinning, I gave him a thumb's up, and his face split into an answering grin.

Between bites, the Morrigan asked, "What time are we meeting with Lugh?"

"As soon as we're all done eating," Kevin replied.

"You must've been really tired last night," she said to me. "You feeling better now?"

"Yeah," I nodded. "I don't think I woke up even once. I wonder if it's the transition to deity that's messing with me. I mean, sometimes I'm not sleepy for days, then something like last night happens. It's the same with eating; sometimes my stomach rolls over if I just look at food, then other times it's like I'm starving." I shook my head. "It's like I don't even know my own body anymore."

"Hmm." Arddhu studied me thoughtfully. "Yes, it is quite possible your transition is the cause of the disruption. Has there been anything else unusual? Changes in your powers, for example?"

I thought for a moment, then shook my head again. "Not really. Nothing I've noticed, anyway."

Kevin pushed his empty plate away. "Keep us posted if you start to see anything else. We've talked about this before, but since you're the first human to deity transition we've all had the privilege to witness first-hand, it's also a great learning experience for us."

"Sure." I, too, pushed away my empty plate. "Brianna, you've outdone yourself again. This breakfast was perfect."

She turned from the sink to grin at me. "You'll give me a big head if you keep that up."

A few moments later, it was time to head to the VIP tent. While the rest of us scooted our stools under the counter, the Morrigan and Reshep shared a deep kiss.

"I'll catch up with you later," she murmured to him, and he nodded.

On the way to the tent, none of us spoke. Lost in our own thoughts, maybe.

Lugh waited for us in the lounge area, since this was an informal meeting. After greetings, he got right to it.

"Dagda has already briefed me on your discussion with him yesterday. After giving it some thought, I still think the first official visit should be to Asgard. It would serve three purposes: to convey your condolences for Tyr, participate in the funeral games, and request a formal alliance. The latter, of course, is in case Ares, Athena, and Kali have been seeking alliances of their own."

"Wait." I frowned. "Funeral games?" I only had a vague idea of what those were, and I sure hadn't expected to participate in any.

"It's customary for many cultures to have their best warriors as well as honored guests participate in feats of strength and skill to honor a fallen warrior or royal personage. In this case, you and anyone you take with you would be the honored guests."

"So I guess it'll be just the five of us going."

He leaned forward slightly. "I should also mention it's possible that Tyr's surviving family members will challenge you to a contest, or ask for payment, to settle the blood-price."

Blood-price? "But I didn't kill him. Ida did."

He nodded. "True, but his family might still hold you responsible, since it happened when he was your ally." He spread his hands. "Look, I'm not saying it's a certainty, just a possibility. I'd be remiss if I didn't mention it, so you'll be prepared if it does happen."

"Okay. Got it."

"So, the delegation will consist of: yourself as the Goddess of Earth; Arddhu and Kevin as Consorts and Advisors; the Morrigan as Chief Political Advisor; and myself, as Chief Ambassador. That should be sufficient to show respect and honor." Then his brows furrowed. "Um, I'm assuming Tyr's body has been preserved in some way since his death?"

"No." I shared a quick glance with the Morrigan and Arddhu. "It was... he was..." I struggled to find the appropriate words to describe how Tyr had been torn into unrecognizable pieces.

"He was dismembered," Arddhu supplied. "Ida murdered him in his own home, on Asgard. Under the circumstances, we thought the most respectful thing we could do was to leave his remains for his loved ones to take care of."

"I... see," Lugh said, still frowning. "That both complicates and simplifies things. Complicates because usually there's a ceremony for handing over the body. And simplifies because I'm assuming he's already been given proper burial, so those rites won't be part of this visit."

Arddhu nodded. "We do have some of his jewelry and other personal items. Just a few things that were left behind when he stayed here last year."

"Excellent." Lugh seemed a bit relieved. "That'll do for the official hand-over part of the ceremony. I'll have a nice wooden box made, for presenting those items."

Now Kevin leaned forward. "What happens if that's not good enough? What if, somehow, they're offended?"

"Slim chance, but in that case, I'll accept full responsibility. That will leave the rest of you free from consequences."

"I don't like the sound of that," I said.

He smiled reassuringly. "Trust me, it sounds worse than it really is. Normally, it's just a formal challenge to a skills contest in the funeral games. And I assure you, I can more than take care of myself in that regard."

If it'd been anyone else who'd said it, it would've seemed arrogant. But from him, it was just confident.

"When do we leave?" the Morrigan asked.

"I'll need only a few days to arrange everything," Lugh replied thoughtfully.

"How long will we have to stay?" I asked.

"I'd assume anywhere between three to five days. Three is customary for a simple diplomatic visit, but five is typical when funerary games and rites are included. However, it's been several months since Tyr's death, so the official games and rites have probably already taken place. I'd expect this to be a three-day visit, with a simplified version of the games."

Three days in Asgard. I wasn't sure if I should be excited or apprehensive.

"What's the dress code?" the Morrigan asked.

"I strongly recommend your best ceremonial armor."

"Oh, good." She grinned. "I've been wanting to dust off the old outfit."

"Um." I glanced at the others. "I don't have any ceremonial armor."

"Except for you." Lugh shook his head. "The Goddess must be gowned."

"And don't forget to glow," the Morrigan added, teasingly.

Every time we went anywhere, she reminded me to glow. As if I'd forget. Well, I did forget back when I'd first become the Goddess.

Now, she probably just said it to fuck with me.

"So, this is just a dog and pony show," I groused.

"I am not a pony," Arddhu objected. "Nor am I a dog."

It would've been funny in other circumstances.

But before any of us could explain the phrase to Arddhu, Lugh continued, with a shake of his head.

"I'm sorry, but you *are* the Great Goddess. Goddess of Earth. You must look the part."

At our first alliance meeting last year, Athena had worn gorgeous ceremonial armor, all shiny gold and brilliant white. She'd looked every inch a Goddess.

I decided to argue.

"So Athena and other goddesses can wear ceremonial armor, but I have to wear a stupid flimsy gown?"

Lugh frowned. "That's different. You're not just any goddess, and this is a formal diplomatic mission. It's traditional."

"It's protocol," Arddhu agreed.

"It's customary," the Morrigan added.

It was bullshit, that's what it was.

My mind had started working on some really impressive designs that would fit all the necessary requirements.

Defiant, I raised my chin. "I've heard tradition is simply a guide and not a rule. I've also heard that traditions need updating now and then. In that vein, I've decided to change this particular one." I grinned. "But don't worry. I promise, no one will mistake me for anyone *but* the Goddess." At Lugh's doubtful expression, I added, "Trust me."

While Lugh worked on making the logistical arrangements for our visit to Asgard, I worked on my ceremonial armor.

Most of the time was spent designing it, which included several hours on the internet doing research for the necessary details. It helped to know the armor would never be used in actual battle, just to impress other deities.

The actual fabrication phase was as quick and easy as when I'd made the green space for the Council meeting. I only had to think it into existence.

On the day of our departure, I met the others at the portal.

Kevin was the first to see me approach. He'd been in the middle of a sentence when his jaw dropped, which made the others turn to look.

Four pairs of eyes stared at me in total silence, and I barely kept from smirking in smug satisfaction.

My golden breastplate, molded to fit my body and curved to a point at my waist, was embossed with Celtic knotwork and spirals. I'd made it low enough to show a bit of cleavage but not be too revealing. A matching pauldron on each shoulder joined to a gold gorget of open knotwork that encircled my neck.

A short battle kilt, constructed of white leather strips, fell to mid-thigh. I'd designed it to tease with flashes of bare skin when I moved, but wore fitted briefs for modesty.

Celtic spirals decorated the gold bracer on my right arm from wrist to elbow. On my left, a much shorter one curled around my bracelet, to show it off rather than cover it up. Matching greaves wrapped my legs from knee to ankle, with white leather low-heeled boots beneath.

As a final touch, I wore a simple circlet of gold. I'd left my dark brown hair unbound, but magickally boosted its length and volume so its wavy fullness fell to my lower back, like a dark cape. My makeup was much more dramatic than usual, with dark eyeliner, mascara, blush, and lip color magickally applied.

For the first time, I'd chosen to hide my facial scars.

And yes, I'd remembered to glow.

I knew I looked divine.

Arddhu, bless his heart, was completely speechless as he stared at me. He'd chosen a dressier version of his dark green leather armor with soft black trousers, and looked quite regal and handsome. In one hand, he held the ornate wooden box of Tyr's personal effects.

"Wow, Dee." Kevin finally found his voice. Sort of. "Just... wow." He wore what he called his feasting outfit, and it was also my favorite. Green leather armor embossed in gold Celtic knotwork covered his torso, with soft trousers in darker green. His dark hair fell past his shoulders in soft waves, except for the warrior braids at each temple. He truly was the epitome of a gorgeous Irish demi-god in his prime, and my heart swelled.

"Well done." The Morrigan grinned from ear to ear. "*Very* well done. I'm proud of you." She'd chosen a fancier and less practical version of her battle armor: tight-fitting breastplate and leggings in black leather with blood-red accents, and a blood-red cape.

Lugh, in his ornate silver and white Fae armor, had eyed me from head to toe with a wry grin. "I sincerely apologize. You were absolutely right. No one will mistake you for anyone but the Goddess." He shook his head. "And I will never doubt you again."

"I'll hold you to that," I quipped. Poor Arddhu still hadn't said a word, nor had he taken his eyes off me. "Are you okay?"

"I... you..." he stammered.

"C'mon, snap out of it," I teased. "Focus."

"Forgive me." He shook his head. "You truly look divine, and I find I am quite distracted."

It was pretty cool to get such a compliment from one of the most ancient deities alive.

"Thanks." I grinned. "Shall we go?"

He opened the portal to Asgard, and we stepped through.

We arrived on the Bifröst, the shimmering road also known as the Rainbow Bridge. Its constantly shifting iridescence of every color and hue was almost mesmerizing, and I couldn't take my eyes off it. The surface felt as hard as glass or concrete, but it was so much more beautiful than those mundane materials. This sparkled as if made of the most exquisite rainbow moonstone, and it went on for as far as the eye could see, in either direction.

A soft sound caught my attention.

Not far from where we stood, a bright white guardhouse with a shiny gold roof stood beside the road. A tall, imposing man, covered from head to toe in gold armor, had stepped out of the guardhouse. He walked toward us with a lethal-looking golden spear in one hand. Only his pale face was visible, with a bushy red-gold beard and mustache.

Lugh immediately stepped forward to meet him.

"Greetings, Heimdallr, Keeper of the Bifröst, Watchman of the Gods. I am Lugh of the Túatha de Danann of Midgard. Accompanying me is a diplomatic delegation consisting of four other deities of Midgard. We are here to formally express our condolences on the death of Tyr."

The golden man, Heimdallr, studied each of us carefully for a moment. His eyes on me were piercing; it was if he burrowed into my soul and weighed its merit. When they moved on, I tried not to sigh with relief.

Finally, he nodded and stepped aside. "I bid you welcome to Asgard, Midgardians." His deep voice had a surprisingly pleasant musical quality. He turned, using his spear to indicate the shining city that rose into the sky beyond a wide meadow. "You may enter."

Lugh thanked him, and we proceeded past the guardhouse. Strangely, our footsteps were muffled, as if the Bifröst swallowed them.

On our left, far from the road, a thick forest of tall trees hid the horizon, from which I heard birdsong. On our right, the tall grass and flowers of the meadow danced and rustled in the light breeze. The air itself tasted sweet, as if honeyed.

As we walked, Lugh broke the silence. "I already know this is your first time here, Deirdre. But what about the rest of you?"

"Once," the Morrigan said, "a very long time ago."

"Unfortunately," Arddhu said, "I have had no reason to visit until now."

"Ditto." Kevin swiveled his head, taking everything in with unmistakable awe.

"What about you?" I asked Lugh.

"I've only had a couple of brief visits," he replied.

Using my enhanced vision, I studied the legendary realm ahead of us.

Built on a hill, the city was surrounded by a massive wall, impossibly high and probably just as impossibly thick, with huge gates located at widely spaced intervals. The main entrance seemed to be directly ahead of us, and stood open invitingly. Beyond, I glimpsed a clean, well-maintained road of gleaming white paving stones.

Hundreds of buildings of all shapes and sizes clung precariously to the hillside. I'd somehow expected to see a drab city of wooden houses, like something out of a historical drama, but that's not at all what awaited us. Some of the buildings were bright white with shiny gold roofs, while others were pale or neutral shades topped with copper or bronze. A few were brightly colored, splashy blue or red or green. One extremely large building reminded me of a temple or palace: its walls were golden, with grand white columns in front and a red tile roof.

But these were nothing compared to the massive and ornate building at the top of the hill, which left absolutely no doubt it was the seat of power in Asgard.

Brilliantly white with tall, stately columns and a shimmering roof that rivaled the Rainbow Bridge itself, the building dominated the city below and seemed to touch the sky.

I could only imagine the opulence inside.

Lugh's voice interrupted my thoughts. "By the way, this is the famous Plain of Iðavöllr. It's where the Æsir hold important gatherings."

Wildflowers of every hue waved gently in the breeze and danced with the silvery-green tall grass, while bees buzzed and butterflies fluttered.

"It's also where Ragnarök, the battle to end the gods, takes place," Kevin added, then shrugged. "According to Norse mythology, anyway."

I stared at the peaceful plain and tried to imagine it someday full of blood, death, and destruction, but I failed. It was just too pretty. Maybe Ragnarök was, indeed, just myth and not the future.

We could hope.

"Seems like something Ares would instigate," the Morrigan quietly said.

Shit. That was the last thing we needed.

"All the more reason to cement this alliance with the Æsir," Arddhu pointed out.

"Yeah," I agreed.

By now, we'd gotten close enough to the main gate that the two nearby guards had come to attention. They watched us approach with open curiosity, not caution or suspicion, as I would've expected.

"Welcome to Asgard," said the one on the right. "The All-Father awaits you in the Great Hall."

Huh. Either Heimdallr had sent a message from the guardhouse, or Asgardians had telepathy.

"Where's the Great Hall?" I asked.

"I know the way," Lugh said, at the same time the Morrigan said, "Just up the road a bit."

"You will be escorted," the second guard said. "They're waiting just inside."

True to his word, as soon as we passed through the wide gates, another pair of guards stepped up, nodded respectfully, then turned crisply to lead us through the city. Along the way, people paused their errands to watch us pass. They seemed curious and friendly, quickly resuming whatever they'd been doing as soon as we passed.

The main street was wide and well-kept, and although the connecting side streets were narrow, they too were clean and in good repair. Almost every intersection seemed to have some type of fountain or public water source. Some were large and ornate, like those seen in modern romance movies; others were small and simple, little more than a water spout over a stone bowl. At each, the water was crystal clear and filled with rainbows as it sparkled in the sun and cascaded into lower basins. The sound of so much water flowing was almost musical.

The street rose in a steady incline up the hill, and even though I was in decent physical condition, I was really glad I'd made sure to make my boots with sensible heels. This was a lot of walking.

We passed shops and markets, temples and shrines, modest homes and palaces, taverns and restaurants. People were everywhere, stopping to watch us before resuming their business. It all seemed so normal, but no one could ever mistake this place for a typical city of Earth. Everything had an otherworldly feel or look to it. Nothing resembled anything Earthlike, from the graceful, flowing dresses and tunics of every color, to the décor of the buildings, and the complete lack of visible modern technology.

No streetlights, telephone or utility cables, or satellite dishes here.

No vehicles of any kind, either; it seemed Asgardians walked everywhere. Once or twice I thought I heard the rumble of cart wheels, but never actually saw any carts or wagons. At other times, I thought I heard hoofbeats. Maybe only foot traffic was allowed on this main avenue, to keep it clean for visitors and pedestrians.

Trees and flowering shrubs dotted the edges of the street, and lined many of the cross streets. They added a sweet perfume to the air.

But for such a large active city, it was almost unnaturally quiet. No shouting or loud noises, just the subdued murmurs of the people as we passed.

If I had to guess, Asgard probably hadn't changed in centuries.

The bright, shining palace at the top of the hill loomed above it all, and it still seemed a long way off.

But as it turned out, the palace wasn't where we were headed, because our escorts abruptly turned right onto a wide, paved entranceway leading to a massive stone-and-timber building.

"Your destination, the Great Hall," one of the guards said. Then both of them turned and left us.

I studied the hulking building before us. It rose two stories and spread to what seemed an entire Earth city block. High up on the wall facing us, just under the roofline, were several square openings without any glass. They allowed air and light to enter, but the rest of the walls were solid, without any windows. Was that for privacy, or security?

Two additional guards stood at the huge entrance doors, which seemed to be solid wood slabs, each ornately carved with a beautiful tree framed in knotwork. The guards opened the doors, which swung smoothly and noiselessly.

Lugh took the lead, guiding us into the dark interior. He spoke quietly to yet another guard, who then announced us with a voice that rang out in the cavernous Hall.

"Lugh of the Túatha de Danann of Midgard, leading a diplomatic delegation to express sympathy on our loss of Tyr."

As Lugh led us down the aisleway toward the far end of the Hall, I glanced around. Lining the walls on each side were enough long tables and benches to seat hundreds of people. Various banners, tapestries, and shields with unique insignia covered the walls, all the way up to those high square windows.

Just to one side of the aisle, a large rectangular hearth was built into the floor, with courses of brick raising it to maybe two feet high. The flames were low, and didn't give off much light or heat, but they didn't need to. It was a warm day, after all, and plenty of light came from the upper windows and the torches in the wall sconces.

We drew closer to the two thrones and the Æsir who sat in them, and I'd be lying if I said I wasn't nervous. After all, these were the Norse Gods and Goddesses of myth and legend. They were insanely famous, the subjects of countless novels, comic books, and movies.

The butterflies in my stomach were crazed, as if they were fluttering about on the Plain of Iðavöllr in frenzied, nectar-sucking joy.

In the large curved throne on the left of the dais sat Odin, the All-Father.

His single blue eye rested icily on each of us in turn, and he seemed devoid of any emotion except for a ghost of a smile of recognition for the Morrigan. Me, he studied with casual interest, but when that wintry eye fell on Kevin, it narrowed with obvious suspicion before moving on. His other eye was covered with a simple leather patch, and I remembered reading something about how he'd sacrificed his eye for knowledge long ago. His face was deeply seamed with age, his pure white hair long enough to brush his shoulders, and his white beard was braided and adorned with silver and gold beads that glimmered in the light. His knobby fingers gripped the arms of his throne firmly.

For being the King of the Æsir and such a legendary deity, I would've expected him to dress royally, but he wore a simple tunic and trousers in drab colors.

A raven perched on each of his shoulders, their heads cocking this way and that as they stared at us. Two enormous gray wolves sat perfectly still at his feet, alert and watching us intently with their yellow eyes.

I shivered under those cold gazes.

A woman sat on a smaller throne beside Odin, and I assumed she was his wife, Frigg. Her beautiful silver hair shone in the light, bound in intricate braids that fell to her waist. Her face was unlined, somehow retaining the smoothness of youth despite her age, and her dark blue eyes watched us with curiosity. Unlike Odin's chilly regard, hers held warmth and friendliness as she smiled at each of us. Also in contrast to her husband, she had dressed with regal elegance, in a pretty blue overdress trimmed in gold braid with a light blue chemise beneath. She fairly dripped with expensive jewels, as earrings, necklaces, bracelets, and rings flashed in the light.

Behind the thrones, I sensed there were others in the shadows, but whoever they were would have to wait. We'd stopped at the foot of the dais and now fanned out in a line, ready for presentation to the King and Queen of Asgard.

Lugh stepped forward, dropped to one knee, and bowed his head.

"Greetings, Odin, All-Father, Lord of the Æsir, Ancient One, Raven God, and Friend of Midgard. I am Lugh, son of the Dagda, and the Shining One of the Túatha de Danann of Midgard." He rose and introduced each of us, beginning with Arddhu at the far end—which, I quickly realized, would put me last.

"My companions from Midgard are Arddhu, also known as Cernunnos, the Lord of the Forest and Consort to the Goddess; the Morrigan, Goddess of Battlefield Death and Chooser of the Slain; Kevin, also Consort to the Goddess," now he gently tugged me forward, "and Deirdre Connor, Keeper of the Sphere and Great Goddess of Midgard."

Immediately, the butterflies in my stomach stopped, and my nervousness disappeared.

Unlike the others, I didn't bow or take a knee. Right or wrong, I saw Odin and Frigg as equals. So I simply nodded respectfully while maintaining eye contact with him. That's the only reason I caught the flicker of surprise in his eye before he blinked and it was gone.

A few heartbeats later, his gravelly voice echoed in the hall.

"I have heard rumors of a new Goddess of Midgard. And now, here you are. I bid you and your companions welcome to Asgard, but tell me: why are you here?"

I noted the lack of reverence in his tone and decided to reciprocate. And I didn't know if Lugh had planned to reply or not, but since Odin had asked me, I thought it only fair that I was the one to answer.

"First of all," I began, "thank you for agreeing to this audience. We are here to offer our sympathies and condolences on the loss of Tyr, a great warrior of Asgard. As you know, he aided our efforts to eliminate the threats to Earth—er, *Midgard*—in preparation for my healing the planet." I paused, but he remained silent. "Tyr was a good man and a strong ally. He is sorely missed," I finished.

After a moment, Odin turned his head and nodded to someone in the shadows off to our left. A woman approached with soft footsteps, her pretty features composed and serene. Although her dark hair was generously streaked with silver, her face was unlined, making it difficult to pinpoint her age. She wore a simple brown overdress with a pale yellow long-sleeved chemise. She stopped in front of me, bowed her head briefly, then met my gaze unflinchingly. "I am Keki, the widow of Tyr. I am grateful for your words of comfort."

Tyr had been so loud and boisterous, it was hard to believe such a quiet woman had been his wife. Then again, who knew what he might've been like in the privacy of his own home.

Arddhu had passed the box of Tyr's personal items down the line, and now I presented it to Keki. "On his last visit to Midgard, he left a few items behind."

She stared at the box for a moment before taking it from me almost reluctantly, then met my eyes again. "Thank you. Blessings on you all." She glanced at Odin, then turned and quietly left the hall.

Now, the woman beside Odin stood. "I am Frigg, Queen of Asgard and wife of Odin, All-Father. Please accept our hospitality and join us for refreshments." She indicated the nearest table, which had been filled with trays of food and pitchers of drink sometime in the past few minutes.

"Of course," I smiled. "Thank you."

The others who'd been standing in the shadows now came forward to join us at the table. Although we didn't plan it, somehow all of us visitors ended up on one side of the table, with the Asgardians on the other. Odin sat opposite me, his single eye fixed on me even while the platters of food were passed. That shrewd gaze measured, analyzed, and judged me.

It made me uncomfortable, but I hoped I hid it well enough.

The others hadn't identified themselves or been introduced. I smiled at the huge red-haired, bearded fellow on Odin's right. "You all have me at a disadvantage, it seems. You know who I am, but I do not know all of you."

His smile was kind, and crinkled the corners of his eyes. "Forgive my poor manners. I am Thor, son of Odin, and Protector of Mankind."

"Very pleased to meet you, Thor." I took a passing tray and spooned what looked like mashed potatoes onto my wooden plate.

The young woman beside him, with a beautiful mane of long, thick hair the color of summer wheat, introduced herself as Sif, Thor's wife. Her blue eyes sparkled in the firelight, and she also smiled kindly.

A platter of roasted light-colored meat was next, and I placed two small pieces on my plate before passing it on. It looked and smelled like chicken, but I couldn't be sure since I didn't even know if they had chicken on this world. For all I knew, it was some weird Asgardian creature.

"I am Iðunn," said the pretty young woman on Frigg's left. Her light brown hair was elaborately braided around her head. "And this is my husband, Bragi." The man beside her was handsome, charming, and attentive as he carefully filled her goblet from a pitcher while flashing us a quick friendly grin.

Beside me, Kevin had already started digging in to his food. Tentatively, I tried the meat, and sure enough, it tasted like chicken. But what I'd thought were mashed potatoes were sweeter, almost as if honey had been added. Or maybe it was some other kind of vegetable. The crusty bread, though, made me think of what Garrett served at his pub: hearty, full of whole grains, and delicious.

As I ate, I sensed rather than saw someone lurking behind the columns of the Hall. It was distracting, and I hadn't realized anyone else had noticed until Odin spoke.

"Loki, if you wish to join us, then do so. Stop prowling about in the gloom."

A moment later, a tall, lean figure emerged from behind a nearby column. Clean-shaven among these heavily bearded gods, Loki glided forward and sat at the far end of the table next to Sif—who immediately shifted closer to Thor—and studied me with open curiosity.

His eyes were startlingly blue, even bluer than Odin's, and his face was all lines and angles. Strong jaw. Fine, noble nose. Wide, thin lips. Longish auburn hair with copper highlights that glimmered in the torchlight.

So. This was the infamous Loki, Trickster God of Mischief, the subject of many novels, blockbuster action movies, and probably countless women's fantasies.

He was handsome, yes. And there was something about him that was intriguing.

Sif had passed the meat platter to him, but he shook head. "No, thank you," he murmured while accepting a drink from the servant. His long fingers wrapped gracefully around the mug as he lifted it to his lips and drank deeply, without taking his eyes from mine.

An elbow bumped into my side, and I turned toward Kevin, who nodded at Odin. Apparently, I'd been asked a question.

Oops. Only then had I realized I'd been staring at Loki. Or rather, we'd been staring at each other.

"I'm sorry?"

"I asked if you will require another Asgardian warrior to join your alliance now that Tyr is no longer available?"

Ouch. What a fucking cold way to put it. Unless he was deliberately baiting me... I decided to reply politely, and not take the bait.

"No. Tyr assisted us in our battle preparations last year, along with many other deities of warfare. But that battle has since been fought and won, and that old alliance is now my Council of Advisors."

Seemingly satisfied, he nodded and took a bite of food.

"But what of the next battle? Won't you need another Asgardian warrior for that?" Thor asked, a bit enthusiastic.

"Not really. The enemies of Earth—um, Midgard—will be removed by magick instead of with battles. By me."

"What about after?" Sif asked. "After these enemies of Midgard are removed, what then?"

"I've been healing the planet from its environmental damage, so after I eliminate the enemies, I'll just continue to clean the air, soil, and water. After I'm done, Midgard will be like it used to be, with healthy thick forests and abundant wildlife."

"Just so the humans can destroy it all over again." The sarcastic voice came from the end of the table.

Loki.

I didn't really want to discuss our plans in detail at this point, so I just shrugged. "I won't let that happen."

"Good luck with that. You may as well be Sisyphus, rolling a boulder uphill for eternity." He laughed. "Humans are notoriously chaotic and selfish, rude and slovenly. As long as they're around, you won't be able to stop them."

Okay, now he was definitely getting annoying.

"Like I said: I'm going to fix it."

Loki smirked, one brow cocked. "And like *I* said: good luck with that."

"That is enough, Loki," Odin growled. "Do not antagonize our honored guests."

"Yes, All-Father." He dropped his gaze and picked at the knot in his wooden mug with a thumbnail.

But his words made me defensive. To Odin, I said, "I know it's a big job. But I have to try."

Odin studied me for a moment, then nodded. "Sometimes it is all we can do."

Frigg smiled warmly at me. "It will be wonderful to see Midgard made beautiful once again, as it was for many centuries. It has only become intolerable for the last century or so." She shuddered. "The trash and pollution are quite horrific to those of us who remember what it was like before."

Arddhu spoke. "Much of that deterioration can be blamed on Ida, the previous Goddess. She had removed herself from the affairs of the planet and ignored her responsibilities." He turned to me and smiled. "Deirdre, however, has already shown herself to be the antithesis of Ida."

"How so?" Odin asked.

"For one, as she has already mentioned, she has formed a Council of Advisors, something Ida would never have done. For another, she has immersed herself in her duties."

The Morrigan added, "And she's been answering human prayers again."

"Is that so?" Now Odin's gaze was sharp on me. "That is... interesting."

It felt odd to be talked about in the third person while I was sitting right there. I swallowed a sip of ale then asked, "Do you—all of you—answer prayers too?"

Odin nodded. "Of course. I have many thousands of followers now. Not as many as in the old days, true, but the numbers are finally rising for the first time in centuries." His gaze dropped to his plate. "Unfortunately, the Vanir were not as lucky."

At my frown, Thor explained. "He means Freyr and Freyja. They were forgotten and faded away. Fairly recently, in fact," he added, softly.

"Oh, no." I set my mug on the table. "I'm so sorry. Are there any others who are in danger of fading away? Maybe I can help."

"And just how would you do that?" Loki scoffed. "It's so typical of a newly-made deity, thinking you know more than us ancient ones." He gestured rudely to the servant to refill his mug.

I blinked at him. What the *fuck* was his problem? It was as if he wanted to pick a fight for some reason.

Well, I wouldn't let him.

I kept my voice calm and spoke directly to Odin. "I was thinking maybe I could help boost worship for anyone who's in need of it. Ogma of the Túatha is my Chief Public Relations Advisor, and we plan to craft a social media presence."

Odin nodded. "That is interesting. We have some marketing and promotional specialists here, as well. They've helped increase our reach on Midgard. Perhaps, if I mention your plans to them, they can work with Ogma for a similar campaign."

Who would've ever thought I'd sit here with Norse gods and talk about social media and marketing?

The absurdity was off-the-charts ridiculous.

"I'm sure he'd be honored to assist in any way," I said.

"Are you kidding?" Lugh grinned. "He'd *jump* at the chance to work with the Æsir."

"There you go." I smiled at Odin. "Sounds like a plan."

"Are you ready for the games?" Thor asked.

Although we'd discussed this days ago with Lugh, I asked, "What sort of games?"

Thor's eyes lit up. "Feats of strength and skill, such as wrestling, archery, and axe throwing. Sometimes we even have a bit of gaming as well, since we have tafl and chess boards aplenty. And there are dice, of course." It was obvious he enjoyed the games, and probably had been looking forward to them ever since Lugh arranged this visit.

"How long will they last?" I asked.

"We do not wish to keep you from your duties overlong," Odin replied. "Three days will suffice. Five chambers have already been reserved for your use."

Thor beamed. "The games will begin in the morning. Everyone will participate. We even have events for the children."

As if on cue, Odin and Frigg stood. "Please eat, drink, and enjoy yourselves. We bid you a restful night."

Night? Already?

I glanced up at the windows, which were now dark and barely visible in the shadows. Around the hall, additional torches had been lit and I hadn't even noticed.

Maybe time passed differently on Asgard than it did on Earth.

With another glance around the hall, I realized there were no electric lights, just smoky torches and the hearth fire. Was Asgard another realm without any modern technology, like Arddhu's world? What was I supposed to pee in, a chamber pot or an outhouse? Then again, even Arddhu had a modern bathroom, so maybe Asgard wasn't completely primitive.

Iðunn and Bragi were the next to bid us goodnight. Thor and Sif spoke quietly for a few moments, then Sif also left. Thor moved closer to the Morrigan. "It has been too long, Morrigan," he said, smiling. "It is good to see you again."

Lugh turned to me and spoke softly. "I'll see to the chambers and make sure all is in order." I nodded, and watched him leave. As he passed the hearth, he stopped to speak with a servant, who turned and led him toward a darkened hallway.

When Loki stood, I thought he, too, was leaving, but he sat across from me instead.

"Please forgive my earlier rudeness. I truly meant no disrespect." He held his mug out for the servant to refill.

"Then why were you? So rude, I mean?"

"I was testing you."

Testing me? More like testing my patience.

"Why?"

"Because he's an asshole and likes doing that sort of thing," Thor said, without a trace of animosity.

Loki drank from his mug, then grimaced and motioned to a servant. "To Helheim with this ale. Bring the mead."

The servant left and quickly returned with several cups and a large jug. She poured for each of us and left the jug on the table, then retreated into the shadows.

Loki lifted his voice with his cup. "Raise your cups and remember our fallen friend, the brave warrior Tyr. May he drink the nectar of the gods, feast on only the finest portions, and fuck every shieldmaiden in Valhalla. At least twice."

"*Skål*," Thor said, and the rest of us echoed the toast and drank.

It seemed I wasn't going to get an answer to my question anytime soon.

Loki gestured to the servant, who again stepped forward and refilled our cups.

"This is one of Odin's finest meads," he continued. "The bees feast on the flowers of the Plain of Iðavöllr and make a sweet, rich honey. Ripe berries are then added, using an ancient recipe known only to a few."

It was a fine mead, almost as good as Garrett's. "It's very good," I said, and took another sip.

"Nice armor, by the way." His gaze dropped to my cleavage, traveled across my breastplate, skimmed over my bracers, and studied my bracelet with interest before returning to my face.

"Thanks." I kept my expression neutral.

"None of you have luggage with you. If you wish, I could help find comfortable clothing."

"That won't be necessary," I said. With only a thought, I changed my fancy armor to my favorite faded jeans and a light sweater, but left my face and hair as is.

Loki raised a brow. "Well done." He turned to the others. "Can all of you do that?"

Kevin quickly replied, "*I* can." With a wave of his hand, he changed into his jeans and classic Dark Side of the Moon tee shirt.

Loki grinned. "Excellent."

"Unfortunately, neither of us have that particular gift," Arddhu said, indicating the Morrigan and himself.

"Not sure about him," Kevin said, as Lugh reappeared and sat beside Thor.

"What about me?" Lugh asked while he poured a cup of mead for himself.

I clued him in. "Can you change your clothes using magick, like Kevin and I just did?"

"Sure." He closed his eyes, and his shiny armor transformed into what I'd first seen him wear: tunic and trousers in the shimmery iridescent cloth of the Túatha.

"Bravo." I laughed and finished my mead, and Loki immediately refilled my cup. I narrowed my eyes. "You trying to get me drunk?"

He lifted a brow. "Are you still so human that you get intoxicated so easily?"

Well, no. Since I'd become the Goddess, alcohol sort of evaporated in my system, not affecting me at all.

I shook my head but didn't reply.

"By the way, I also can change my appearance using magick." In mere seconds, he became an identical twin of Thor, even to the clothing.

But that wasn't exactly the same thing as just changing clothes.

Thor laughed boisterously. "Loki is a master shapeshifter."

Loki-as-Thor laughed just as boisterously, then winked at me. "So he says now. But there were times he was not so amused."

It was uncanny how he'd even duplicated Thor's voice perfectly.

Loki-as-Thor morphed into Loki-as-Sif. "Isn't that right?"

Again, he'd duplicated her voice exactly.

Now, Thor's laugh seemed a bit forced as he stood and stretched. "Well, my friends, it is time for me to retire. The games begin early. Good night." He turned and left the hall without another word to Loki.

Loki had already returned to his normal appearance. He smirked and drank from his cup.

Hmm. There was a story there, and from Thor's reaction, it wasn't an amusing one to anyone other than Loki.

Arddhu was next. "I, too, shall retire. Lugh, where are our chambers?"

Lugh stood and pointed. "At the end of that corridor. All five rooms are the same, but I'll come with you."

Arddhu held my gaze briefly before he turned and left with Lugh.

Just as I set my empty cup down, Loki refilled it.

Ugh. I didn't want any more.

"No more after this, please."

"Pity." His face fell in disappointment, but it was probably fake. "I miss new people visiting and staying up late, talking and drinking."

The Morrigan also stood. "Well, kids, as much as I'd like to stay up talking and drinking with you, I'm off too."

Shit. Now it was just me, Kevin, and Loki—if only for the next few minutes or however long it'd take me to finish this last cup of mead.

"I was wondering something," I said to Kevin. "How can it be night already? It feels like we just got here."

"Not to me," he said, stifling a yawn. "It feels like it's been days."

"That's Asgard's magick," Loki explained. "The older someone is, the more it affects them. And anyone who's not Æsir will especially feel it weighing on them."

Ah, so that's why it'd affected the others. "But I remember reading somewhere that you aren't Æsir. So why doesn't it bother you?"

He shrugged. "I've lived here for thousands of years. I've adapted."

"It's weird how I'm not tired," I mused. "Not like the others."

Loki cocked his head, studying me with narrowed eyes. "That is very interesting, indeed. It must be because you are so young." He shifted his gaze to Kevin. "You know, you and I are very much alike."

Kevin snorted. "I'm nothing like you."

Loki cocked a brow. "Are you quite sure about that? I've heard... stories. Maybe you're more like me than you realize."

Kevin shook his head emphatically. "That was a long time ago. That's not me now."

Loki smirked. "A leopard can't change its spots."

That phrase was familiar; where had I heard it before? I frowned, trying to remember. Oh wait—that's what Lugh had said about Kevin last year.

Shit. It seemed a lifetime ago.

Kevin shook his head again. "Bricriu is dead. And good riddance to him."

"I suppose time will tell." Loki returned his gaze to me. "What about you, Keeper of the Sphere? Or should I call you Great Goddess? Or Lady?"

"Dee. Just call me Dee." I frowned again. "What do you mean? What about me?"

"Dee," he repeated deliberately, as if tasting my name. "Do you believe Bricriu is dead? Do you truly trust the trickster beside you?"

"Kevin is my Consort." Irritated, I pushed my half-empty cup away. "Be respectful when you speak of him."

Both eyebrows rose. "*Two* Consorts? How progressive. But then again, since you are newly-made, I suppose it makes sense. After all, you are a modern Goddess, with modern ideas."

I couldn't tell if he'd just mocked me or not, but I'd had enough. I stood. "If you'll excuse us, it's time to say goodnight."

Kevin also stood.

"Of course," Loki replied. "I look forward to competing in the games. Have a pleasant evening."

It seemed to me the games had already started. Word games. Mind games.

We left him sitting alone at the long table, surrounded by the leavings of the feast, and I felt his gaze follow me until we reached the hallway to our rooms.

CHAPTER SIX

MY ROOM WAS small but cozy. I sat on the bed to test it, and it seemed quite comfortable, although it was only a bit bigger than a twin size. The sheets and blankets were soft, and the pillow was large and fluffy. They even smelled nice, with a hint of aromatic herbs.

The room had no windows, and of course, no electric lights. A small brazier in the corner kept the space dimly lit. Surprisingly, it didn't generate any smoke, but I didn't see a vent in the ceiling, so it probably used some unique Asgardian fuel. A small chest and mirror were against one wall, with a ceramic basin and jug of water for washing.

As I'd suspected, there wasn't a toilet; the large bowl tucked under the bed confirmed the Asgardian use of chamber pots.

Although I wasn't sleepy, I changed into a sleep shirt and shorts, and snuggled beneath the covers anyway, thinking maybe the warmth and coziness would lull me to dreamland.

Instead, the nightmare came—the same I'd been having over the past few weeks.

The planet was on fire.

But this time, I heard no screams from humans or animals among the ash falling like snow from the dark sky.

Coughing uncontrollably, I stumbled through thick clouds of smoke, searching. I blinked through the stinging tears, trying to see clearly. The smoke cleared for just a moment, and I saw what I was looking for.

Amazingly, I'd found a patch of unscorched earth. It even had soft, green grass. I fell to my knees and drew a ragged breath into my scorched lungs, then pressed my palms against the ground and sent healing deep below. Next, I stood and sent healing up into the air, hoping to clear it of the smoke.

Oh shit. I wobbled on weak and shaky legs, and realized I'd used too much energy. I'd better replenish from Anu's reserves before I collapsed and fell.

If I fell, I might not get back up again.

But there were no reserves to tap into, and Anu didn't answer my call.

I stared at my bare left wrist and fought off panic.

What the hell was going on? Where was Anu?

Oh gods. Where was the Sphere I was supposed to protect?

Just then, as I'd expected, my legs gave out.

I began falling to the patch of soft grass...

... and woke gasping for air, sitting up in bed, and covered in sweat.

Shit. Goddamn fucking *fuck.*

What the fucking hell.

It'd all seemed so *real.* I even thought I could smell a whiff of smoke.

"*Be calm, Deirdre,*" Anu soothed. "*All is well.*"

"*These nightmares,*" I sent to her. "*They're bad. And I think they're getting worse.*"

"*All is well,*" Anu repeated. "*You are safe.*"

I took a deep breath and released it, then realized there was no way I'd get any sleep now. I changed back into jeans and a shirt, and quietly left my room.

In the main chamber of the Great Hall, the only sound was the crackle of the fire in the hearth. Something about an open fire had always drawn me, and this time was no different. I sat on a bench near the hearth and stared at the flames.

"Lady." A soft voice greeted me from only a few feet away, and as she stepped forward into the firelight, I recognized her from earlier as one of the servants.

"Is there anything I can get for you?" she asked.

"Could I have some water, please?"

She nodded, left, and quicky returned with a pitcher and cup. After filling the cup, she handed it to me and left the pitcher on the bench beside me.

"Thank you," I said, but she'd already returned to wherever she'd come from.

Did she just stand in the shadows and wait for someone to request something? Or did she leave the room? I wasn't familiar with servants or their habits, or even if Asgardian servants were similar to Earth servants.

What the hell. I shook my head, annoyed with myself.

No, Asgardian servants were probably nothing like Earth servants.

The water was sweet and cool, with just a hint of apples. It was delicious, and I was thirstier than I'd thought; I drained the cup and poured another, then drained that one, too. Staring into the flames, I let my mind wander anywhere it wanted, as long as it wasn't about the nightmare.

Lugh wanted to plan other diplomatic missions as soon as we returned home, and I suspected the next two would be similar to this one. We had to convey our condolences on the loss of Marisha-Ten to the Japanese pantheon, and of Begtse to the Tibetan pantheon, and both of them would probably also observe the tradition of funeral games. He'd already reported there was no surviving Gallic pantheon for us to visit on the loss of Belatucadros.

How incredibly sad.

I couldn't imagine being the last remaining member of a pantheon of deities, and then dying.

An entire pantheon, wiped out.

Well. At least he'd died in battle, as a God of War should.

Somehow, it seemed much worse to fade away due to the loss of worshipers, like the Vanir that Odin had mentioned earlier. How many others, in all the pantheons of the world, were in danger of fading away? How many were already lost?

It was all so sad.

Then again, how many pantheons had deities like Cromm or Malsumis? Or even worse? Maybe the universe was better off without them.

And what about Ares, Athena, and Kali? Where were they, and what were they up to? I really needed to find out as soon as we got back, and do something about them.

My mind turned to Loki. Would we need him to get our alliance with Asgard? Was his opinion or judgment important to Odin?

For that matter, what about Thor? To get our alliance, would we have to court *all* the Asgardians, or just Odin?

"Penny for your thoughts."

The soft voice startled me, and my head jerked up.

As if my thoughts had conjured him, Loki sat on a bench nearby, close but not too close.

"My thoughts are not for sale," I replied. "At any price."

He said nothing as he watched me. The servant brought a cup to him and disappeared again.

"Is your room not to your liking?"

"The room is fine."

"I sense that you don't trust me. You've only just met me, yet you don't trust me." He cocked his head. "Why is that?"

"I've read some of the stories." I snorted. "Do you blame me?"

"Those are just that: stories. They're not truth."

"In my experience, stories usually have a kernel of truth to them."

"A kernel is about all the truth there is to any story about me. Maybe more like a seed than a kernel. In most of them, the only truth is the use of my name. In one or two, there are possibly some things I may have said at one time or another."

"So, just to be clear, you never dressed Thor up as a bride and yourself as his female attendant to recover his hammer?" It was one of the only legendary stories I remembered at the moment.

"Of course not." He laughed, but it seemed bitter. "Nor did I ever give birth to an eight-legged horse, or tie my testicles to a goat for laughs." He shook his head. "You humans have such vivid imaginations." His sharp gaze pierced mine. "Ah, but I misspoke. Technically, you are not exactly human, are you? You are deity. So, of course, you are excused from my sweeping generalization."

I shrugged. "I still think of myself as human. I've only been the Goddess for a couple of months, so it's all still new to me: the whole idea of immortality and the power of the Goddess, among other things."

Now why the hell had I said any of that? I hadn't intended to get into any meaningful discussions with Loki. Fuck.

"Yes, it must be an incredible adjustment to go from human to deity," he agreed. "I can't imagine what you're going through. My situation was quite different, as I was never anything other than who I am now."

"Wait. So you were just... born... or came into being... just like you are now? An adult, I mean, with all your magick and everything?"

Despite myself, I was fascinated. This wasn't something I'd ever talked about with other deities. Kevin had told me how he'd become immortal, but I'd never asked Arddhu or the Morrigan.

He nodded. "As far as I know, yes. I don't remember a *before*. I mean, a time before my existence began."

Of course, I had to ask. "How long ago was that?"

Now he frowned. "I'm not really sure. It seems like forever ago." He paused for a moment, thinking, then shrugged. "When you live a long enough life, the very meaning of time changes. Calendars and clocks, and the division of time into convenient increments, are relatively recent inventions. For most of my life, time was only marked by events."

For a moment, I wondered what it would be like to live without the standard concept of time. Then I wondered if I, too, would eventually lose track of time—or if it would be different for me since I was a child of the modern era. Hell, in a thousand years, there might not even be any time keepers at all. Or maybe, time would be reckoned completely different by then.

In that distant future, if someone asked me how old I was, would I be able to answer?

Nonsense questions. I shook my head and returned to the present.

"But if you had to guess, how old would you say you are?" I pressed.

"You are so very persistent." He laughed softly, then stared at the flames for a moment. "Based on my earliest memories, I would say somewhere between twenty-five to thirty thousand years."

My witchy-sense advised he told the truth.

Holy fucking shit.

The things he'd seen in all that time...

He noticed my reaction and smirked. "You asked."

"That's just..." I shook my head, unable to find the right words to express myself. "Holy shit."

He shrugged again. "That's why time—as you think of it—becomes meaningless after so long." He drank from his cup, then changed the subject. "By the way; I sincerely apologize for offending you earlier." He sighed and stared into the flames again. "Sometimes I just can't help being who I am."

"And who are you?"

As if transfixed by the dancing fire, he didn't take his eyes from it as he replied. "I am Loki. God of Mischief. Master of Magick. And Lord of Fire."

I was familiar with the God of Mischief title, but not the other two. I studied him openly as he stared unblinkingly at the fire, and the flames seemed to dance across his features as if alive. Slowly, he stretched his hand toward the hearth, and a long tongue of orange flame flowed over the hearth wall to within mere inches of his fingers, as if in response to his nearness.

As if like was drawn to like.

"God of Mischief," I echoed. "Do you consciously cause trouble, or does it happen just because you're there?"

He blinked, as if waking up from a trance, and dropped his hand to his thigh. The tongue of flame wavered for a moment, then returned to the confines of the hearth, becoming part of the fire once again. "Both. I freely admit that sometimes I like to poke the bear, as humans say. Just to see what will happen."

"Is that what happened earlier? You poked the bear, just to see what I'd do?"

"So many questions." His lips quirked. "You are like water on stone, never giving up until you wear your opponent down." Sadness touched his features. "Which reminds me of my ex-wife."

"Is that good or bad?"

"Both. I did love her. Once. Before it all turned to shit." The bitterness had returned.

"You didn't answer my question," I reminded him.

"Relentless." He laughed softly, and despite everything, I found myself smiling. "Yes. I wanted to see what you would do."

"And? Did I meet your expectations?"

"Actually, no." His gaze held mine as he became serious again. "I expected you to respond sharply. To be cruel. To tell me to go fuck myself."

Well, I *had* thought of doing that, but only briefly.

"That's not me. Not how I do things. Besides, this is a diplomatic visit. It wouldn't be very tactful of me to behave like that, would it?"

"It wouldn't be the first time a diplomatic visit turned into a good old-fashioned Loki bashing."

"So you—what? Go on the offense first, poking the bear to justify the attack when it comes? Did I get that right?"

His sharp gaze pinned me, almost uncomfortable in its intensity. "That is quite an astute observation, young Goddess. Are you, by any chance, reading me?"

"*Reading* you?" I frowned. "What does that mean?"

He shook his head and spoke as if to himself. "She's a Goddess, but doesn't even know what I'm talking about. How is this possible?" He shook his head again, then continued. "I'd assumed that when you received the power of the Goddess, you also received the knowledge of how to wield it."

I snorted. "Hell no. I've been learning as I go." He stared at me in disbelief, which made the heat rise in my cheeks. "Wait a minute," I said, "you mean to tell me, back when you were born... or whatever... you just *knew* how to use your magick, right from day one?"

"That which I was born with, yes. Not that which I have learned since."

Learned? I thought magick had to come from somewhere or someone else. Like when I'd become the Keeper and the Sphere—Anu—had gifted me with magick. Or when I'd received the power of the Goddess. Sure, the Morrigan had taught me battle magick last year, but that'd simply been learning how to use the magick I'd already had at the time, just as Mike did when I first became the Keeper.

"But doesn't magick have to come from somewhere?" I frowned. "Either inherited, or given by someone else?"

He shook his head. "It is much more common for practitioners to learn their craft than it is to have it bestowed on them, like a gift. Some may have natural-born talent, yes, but most do not, and they must devote many years of hard work to become proficient." He paused. "Even Odin had to learn his magick. It was never simply given to him."

"Who taught him?"

He raised one brow. "I did."

A moment ago, he'd said one of his titles was Master of Magick, so it made sense he'd been the teacher. I couldn't even imagine the amount of magickal knowledge he had. Mine could probably fit in a thimble.

A miniature thimble, at that. Really, really tiny.

But it didn't have to stay that way. What if I could learn magick from a genuine master?

I studied Loki for a moment, considering whether I should ask or not. He met my gaze unblinkingly.

"Would you teach me?" I blurted out.

One side of his mouth quirked. "I knew you were going to ask me that." He drank from his cup, then nodded once. "Yes. I will teach you. But only under three conditions. First, I will not teach you anything I taught Odin. Second, I will not teach you anything that you could use against me. And third, you are not to tell anyone that I'm teaching you, or what I teach you. Do you agree?"

All three seemed to be reasonable conditions. "Yes, I agree."

"Swear it." He spit on his palm and offered his hand.

Eww. We were really going to do that?

Ugh. Fine.

I followed suit, and we clasped hands, mingling our saliva.

"I swear," I said, trying not to think about how gross this was.

But he didn't let go of my hand, and instead gripped it tighter as his gaze sharpened on me. Heat flooded my body from the top of my head to the tips of my fingers and toes.

"What are you doing?" My voice was soft as a whisper.

He didn't reply, but as his eyes dropped to my abdomen, the heat flared there, almost uncomfortably so, before suddenly dissipating.

When he finally released my hand, it was completely dry instead of the sticky mess of saliva I'd expected it to be.

"I see congratulations are in order." His voice was soft.

I blinked at him. "For what?"

He raised a brow. "You are with child."

What? No. Impossible. I'd been taking my herbs regularly, and I knew with complete certainty I hadn't forgotten, not even once. There was absolutely no way I was pregnant.

"It is still early yet," he added. "Perhaps only a few weeks."

I could only stare at him with my mouth open, unable to form a single coherent word. Then, I had the craziest urge to laugh. It was so strong, I was afraid if I gave in, I wouldn't stop. So I bit down hard on the inside of my lip instead, and said nothing.

"I take it you weren't exactly planning this."

I shook my head, still unable to speak.

He winced. "I am truly sorry. I didn't mean to shock you." He moved next to me and put a comforting arm around my shoulders. I immediately felt his heat. He radiated it, like the small electric heater in the family room of my childhood home. The one I'd curled up in front of until my exposed skin had turned red.

"It's impossible," I said. "I've been so careful." He had to be playing a trick on me. He was the infamous Trickster, after all. He just *had* to be lying.

Anu's soft voice filled my mind. *"No, Deirdre. Loki is correct. You are indeed with child."*

I clenched my jaw as anger flared through me.

"And just when were you planning on telling me?" I shot back.

Unsurprisingly, she didn't respond.

"It'll be fine." Loki's voice was calm and reassuring. "You are young and healthy. And I have no doubt you will be an exceptional mother."

My mind was still reeling. Did I even *want* a kid? Honestly, I hadn't given it much thought. It was a lot easier to just keep taking my herbs and leaving it to think about for some other day.

Shit. My responsibilities were hard enough as it was. And there was so much stuff coming up, how the hell could I possibly handle being pregnant? Then afterward, dealing with a constantly eating, shitting, and crying infant?

And whose was it? Arddhu's or Kevin's? Loki said I was only a few weeks along, and they'd both shared my bed around that time frame, so either could be the father.

Oh. What if neither of them wanted a kid?

For just a moment, I imagined myself with a son or daughter, and my hands dropped to my belly protectively as I was flooded with unexpected fierceness.

Mine.

None of the rest of it mattered.

This little one was the result of the incredible devotion between me and the two men I loved most in the whole world. Even if neither of them wanted it, I did. Even if this was a spectacularly bad idea, I didn't care.

Mine.

I turned toward Loki with a warm smile. "Thank you for telling me."

He returned the smile, and it seemed genuine; the corners of his eyes crinkled with it. Then he cocked his head, as if listening to something only he could hear. "It is morning. Your companions are awake and will be here in a moment. We'll speak again soon about the magick lessons." He returned to the other bench just as doors opened and closed at the end of the hall and voices approached.

Huh? It was morning already? A quick glance up at the windows confirmed it.

The time here on Asgard was definitely passing oddly.

Arddhu, Kevin, the Morrigan, and Lugh entered the main room with low laughter. I watched Kevin's curious gaze flick to Loki then to me, but he didn't comment.

"Morning," I greeted them, and they responded in kind.

Loki drained his cup and stood. "The games will begin within the hour, so I suggest we break our fast." He indicated the tables against the wall, where at some point servants had brought out platters of food and pitchers of drink, completely unnoticed by me.

"Good, I'm starving," Lugh said as we headed toward the tables.

"Everything okay?" Kevin asked quietly.

"Sure." I smiled, hoping it was normal enough to set him at ease.

He was always so perceptive about my moods, but my current situation was one thing I wasn't ready to talk about. Not here, not now.

He seemed not to notice anything amiss, and I relaxed as I sat at the table with the others. Although I wasn't really hungry, it'd be rude if I didn't eat at least a little bit. Besides, it'd probably be a good idea to eat for the baby.

Oh gods.

The baby.

The shock of that simple phrase ran through me and I almost dropped the platter I held. Keeping my cool until it was time to break the news would be one of the hardest things I'd ever had to do.

But I couldn't think about it now. I had to focus on being sociable to our hosts. And then there were the games that would start shortly.

The Morrigan passed a platter of fresh fruit and creamy cheeses, and I was thankful for the lighter fare. Unsurprisingly, Kevin's plate was piled with quite a bit of everything.

"What more can you tell us about these games?" Arddhu politely asked Loki.

"Well, Thor loves showing off in the feats of strength, so unless you wish to be seriously injured, I'd stay away from those. There will be footraces, swordplay, and the rope pull. The axe throw is popular among most of the Asgardians who are not Æsir. Others, like myself, prefer the games of strategy, such as chess or tafl." He paused, then added in a quieter voice, "Tyr was the champion of the wrestling matches, so in remembrance of him, they will not be held today."

"I see." Arddhu seemed thoughtful. "It has been far too long since I enjoyed a challenging game of chess. I believe I will enter that competition."

"Your warning doesn't scare me," Lugh said to Loki. "I can heal myself if I'm injured. So, I'll give the feats of strength a go." He grinned. "Imagine the bragging rights I'd have if I bested Thor."

Oh, I could imagine, all right. We'd probably never hear the end of his boasting.

"The swordplay sounds interesting," the Morrigan said. "I think I'll give it a shot."

"What about you, Dee?" Lugh asked. "What'll you pick?"

"Well, I've never been a very fast runner, so the footraces are out. I'm not great with a sword, so no swordplay for me. I'm not good enough at chess for a tournament, and I don't know how to play tafl." I shrugged. "So I guess I could try the axe throw."

"It's easy," Loki said. "Even small children easily compete."

Was that supposed to make me feel better?

When I didn't comment, Loki turned to Kevin. "And what of you, Poison-Tongue? Which event will you participate in?"

Kevin's lip curled at the deliberate use of the insulting old moniker.

"Doesn't matter," he countered. "Whichever you choose, I'll easily beat you."

Loki laughed with delight. "I accept your challenge."

"Good morn, Midgardians," Odin's voice boomed as he entered the hall with Frigg and the other Æsir close behind. They took seats at the table and began passing platters. "I trust you all rested well."

"Very well, thank you," Arddhu responded. "Our accommodations are quite comfortable."

Bursts of small talk peppered the rest of breakfast, until Odin stood.

"Come, Midgardians. The games await."

CHAPTER SEVEN

A RDDHU, KEVIN, THE Morrigan, Lugh, and I followed Odin outside, along a side street, and through a gate in the massive wall. A huge crowd had already gathered, and as soon as Odin mounted three steps to a small platform, everyone hushed.

"My people," Odin addressed them. Turning to us and nodding, he said, "Honored guests." Next, he spoke to us all. "Welcome to the funeral games in honor of our beloved Tyr, a warrior well known for his bravery and skill in battle, as well as at feats of strength and on the wrestling ground."

"Hail, Tyr," the crowd respectfully replied.

Odin waited a beat before thundering, "*Let the games begin.*" His people roared their approval.

What a showman. His timing had been impeccable.

Odin stepped away from the platform to talk to a small group, and I glanced around me.

Near the city wall, sections had been created for multiple events: spear-throwing, swordplay, archery, and the axe throw. Queues of eager participants had already formed at most of them.

Further out in the field, a large group began a confusing event that seemed like a strange combination of hockey, baseball, and American football: some players held sticks while others ran back and forth frantically between two goals. As I watched, a player hit a ball with his stick and another player caught the ball, but was immediately tackled to the ground by at least ten other players.

It made absolutely no sense to me.

Off to my left, several long tables and benches were set up with multiple chess and tafl boards, and quite a few older gentlemen had already chosen their seats to begin games. Beyond them, children had their own section where they fought with wooden swords, played a scaled-down version of the strange ball game, and ran in short footraces. Even further beyond, the adult footraces had begun.

Scattered between these areas, several food tents and drink tables saw bustling activity. Almost everywhere I looked, people had a mug, cup, or plate in hand as they watched events.

Between the food, the fresh air, and the sweetness of the meadow grass trampled underfoot, the smells were amazing.

"Welcome to the games, my friends," Odin called to us. "Enjoy yourselves." Then he was off, headed toward the ball game with Frigg at his side.

"See you guys later," the Morrigan said, and went to the swordplay event, where Sif was already choosing an opponent. Likewise, Arddhu left for the board game area, with Iðunn and Bragi joining him. Lugh spotted Thor lifting a boulder in the designated area for feats of strength, and quickly left to challenge him.

Kevin frowned. "Where are the contests for magickal ability?"

"There aren't any." Loki studied Kevin with interest. "Why? Are you seiðmenn?"

I wasn't familiar with that term Loki had used, but before I could ask, Kevin replied.

"I know a fair bit of magick, yes."

Huh. It must mean a user of magick.

"I must confess I am intrigued." Loki smiled. "Let's have our own contest, shall we?"

"Yes." Kevin didn't hesitate. "Let's do that."

Shit. I didn't think this contest was such a good idea. Yes, Kevin knew powerful magick, but did he know that one of Loki's titles was Master of Magick?

This could end badly, and I wondered if I should try and stop it.

Loki glanced around. "We can use that empty space over there, where the wresting ground would normally be."

They headed toward the area, and I couldn't believe they were really going through with this.

"Um, guys," I said, following them. "I don't think this is such a good idea."

Loki met my gaze over his shoulder. "Don't worry. I promise to keep it friendly. Besides, I'd never harm a guest of Asgard."

Although his words seemed sincere, it was the twinkle in his eye that worried me.

Reluctantly, I joined them, if only to bear witness from the sidelines. They stepped over the barrier into the deserted space, spoke quietly out of my earshot for a moment, then nodded and shook hands.

Kevin drew close. "No interference. For any reason. Agreed?"

"But I don't know what the rules are," I protested.

"Doesn't matter. You don't need to know them. Do you agree to not interfere?"

I held his gaze. "Are you sure about this?"

"Absolutely." He didn't hesitate. "I'll be fine. Don't worry."

"Okay." I nodded. "Then I promise, I won't interfere."

He flashed me a quick grin then returned to Loki, who took a coin from his pocket and waited for Kevin to call it.

"Heads," Kevin said.

Loki tossed the coin and they both watched it land on the soft grass.

"Heads it is." Loki bent and retrieved the coin. "You first."

They stood facing each other, roughly ten feet apart. By now, others had realized something was about to happen and began to gather on the sidelines.

Kevin rapidly fired off several fireballs, but Loki quickly and easily created a shield against them. The red fireballs fizzled out as soon as they made contact with the transparent blue-green barrier.

"You call that magick?" Loki scoffed. "That was child's play."

"Just warming up," Kevin said.

Now it was Loki's turn. He held both hands out with palms facing the ground. His lips moved as he silently spoke his spell, and the earth under Kevin's feet heaved, making him stagger and lurch first one way then the other. The growing crowd of spectators murmured in response.

As the tension grew, my hands, up to now resting on a wooden post holding the rope fence enclosing the area, gripped the wood and squeezed.

While Kevin regained his balance, Loki uncoiled a magickal rope. Bright red and orange, it snaked through the air and curled around Kevin's torso, trapping his arms against his sides.

I opened my mouth to yell *unfair*, then remembered I'd promised not to interfere. In silence, I ground my teeth instead.

But Kevin broke through the magickal rope easily, and it vanished as it fell away.

"That was lame," Kevin sneered.

Loki snorted. "As you said, just warming up."

Now it was Kevin's turn again. He conjured a monstrous shadowy beast that had a dog's body and tail, the wings of an eagle, and the full mane of a lion. Snarling and dripping foamy saliva from its massive jaws, it leapt toward Loki's throat, and the crowd gasped.

Loki simply waved a hand, and the creature disappeared in a puff of black smoke.

"So you like to play with animals," Loki said. His hands moved gracefully in the air, and seconds later a gigantic bird appeared. It reminded me of ancient pterodactyls I'd seen in artistic renderings, with a wingspan of several feet. As the monster hovered, I felt the air move around me, as if it were actually alive. The watching crowd—which had grown even bigger in the last few minutes—let out a breathless moan. The creature's long, serrated beak repeatedly snapped shut in anticipation of closing on Kevin's head. It emitted a piercing shriek that made me wince, and flew at Kevin surprisingly fast for its ungainly size. I clenched my jaw even harder to keep from crying out, and dimly recognized my teeth had started to ache.

But Kevin, not bothered in the least by this deadly monster, simply waved a hand. It halted in midair with a strangled croak, then fell to the ground and lay motionless before disappearing into smoke.

"That's the best you've got?" Kevin jeered. "I have to say, I'm not impressed."

Actually, neither was I. This wasn't at all what I thought it'd be. These were just harmless phantoms, and Kevin was holding his own just fine. I forced myself to relax, unclenching my jaw and my grip on the wooden post.

Kevin's turn again, but instead of summoning some new fantastical beast, he called his sword from his pocket universe. Loki summoned his own sword, and its long blade shimmered with engraved runes that glowed faintly green.

My heart jumped into my throat at this newest development. I'd thought it wouldn't be an actual fight, with actual weapons.

They flew at each other, whirling in a blur of motion and moving way too fast for me to see anything of consequence. The two long blades flashed in the sun, and golden sparks appeared every time they made contact. Again, the ever-expanding crowd released a low moan, and I grimaced, wondering who'd end up with the most injuries.

After what seemed like an hour but was probably only a few minutes, they abruptly broke apart, and studied each other while catching their breath. I examined each of them closely, but could only stare in disbelief.

Neither was injured. Not a cut or a scratch on either of them. Not even a single rip or tear in their clothes.

Then, Kevin's blade flickered, as if it were just a projection.

What the hell? They weren't using real swords?

They'd certainly *looked* real, even reflected the sun like real metal. And they'd clanged loudly every time they'd made contact with each other.

Well, shit. This was definitely some next-level magick, and I was almost embarrassed that I'd thought differently.

Almost.

Now, as if on some unseen signal, both swords disappeared and were replaced with daggers—one in each hand. Two daggers each? This was getting ridiculous.

But this time, I knew the daggers weren't real, so I wasn't concerned.

Again, they whirled and slashed, and it was impossible for me to see what was really going on, and I narrowed my eyes.

Maybe that was the whole point. Part of the show, so-to-speak.

Once again, they broke apart to catch their breath. The daggers disappeared, but this time nothing replaced them. The contestants circled each other warily for a moment, then Loki abruptly turned to the crowd.

"Good people of Asgard," he began, voice conversational yet boosted for all to easily hear. "Poison-Tongue has acquitted himself well in both magick and blade. I ask you, then, how shall we determine the winner of this contest?"

The crowd immediately chanted, "*fight, fight, fight.*"

Fight? Wasn't that just what we'd all watched? It didn't make any sense.

Then the person next to me took up the chant, and I heard it more clearly: it was *flyte*, not *fight*.

I searched my brain for the scraps of mythology I'd read, then finally remembered something useful. According to legend, Loki attended a feast and grossly insulted all the other gods and goddesses. Afterward, he was hunted down and imprisoned, in the prelude to Ragnarök.

A flyte was a contest of insults, and the Asgardians wanted such a contest between Loki and Kevin.

I relaxed again. That wasn't so bad. After all, in the old days, Bricriu was well known for his wit and sarcasm. He could certainly hold his own against Loki.

As the crowd chanted louder, Loki grinned and accepted a mug from one of the bystanders, then drained it and gestured for quiet. "Flyte it is, good people of Asgard."

Kevin had also taken an offered mug from someone and drained it. Both mugs were immediately refilled, and Loki began the flyte.

"Poison-Tongue, you look like a bitch cowering under the cruel hand of her master. Are you so afraid to match wits with me?"

Kevin laughed. "Why should I be, Trickster? After all, you're just a flea on the hind end of a mangy old mutt."

A few chuckles broke out among the bystanders, but for the most part, people had quietly settled in so they wouldn't miss a word.

"Hah," Loki snorted. "Not very original. Then again, neither are you. Speaking of hind ends, I hear you like it up the ass. So be a good little boy and bend over for me."

"That's lame." Kevin rolled his eyes. "I expected a battle of wits, but I see you've come unarmed, old man."

"Going for the tiresome lines already?" Loki faked a yawn. "This flyte will be over quickly."

"I accept your surrender." Kevin grinned.

"Nice try, Poison-Tongue. It's not that easy to defeat me." He faked another yawn. "You are boring me to tears. I'd heard you had a sharp wit, but it was clearly a lie. You are a witless oaf of an imbecile."

"My wits are fine. You're nothing but an addle-brained goat fucker."

Loki laughed. "Better a goat fucker than born from a goat's arse."

Back and forth the insults flew, using repulsive names or degrading sexual slurs. Their mugs were kept full at all times; they only needed to hold their mugs out for someone to gladly fill them.

Meanwhile, the crowd had swelled, and now all four sides of the contest arena were full, several rows deep. I even spotted Odin among the people, watching closely.

"Is your ass jealous of all that shit coming out of your mouth?" Kevin said.

The crowd *oohed* at that one, and Loki rolled his eyes. "Oh, like we've never heard *that* one before. Can't you for once come up with something original?"

On and on it went, raunchy and dirty, and even sort of funny in its absurdity. The Asgardians loved it all, sometimes howling with laughter while at other times wincing in discomfort. More than once, Loki and Kevin had to shout to be heard.

Then, the insults came faster. And nastier.

"You fuck yourself with dog entrails," Loki sneered.

"You bathe in sheep urine," Kevin countered.

"You feast on goat shit soaked in women's moon-blood."

"You gobble goat's balls marinated in pig semen."

Eww. This latest round was absolutely *disgusting*. And what was with all the goat references?

Then, something changed again.

Loki's eyes glittered as he took a couple of steps closer to Kevin and growled, "I will shove my cock down your throat until you choke on it."

"Not before I gouge out your eyes and fill the sockets with goat shit," Kevin snarled.

What the *fuck?*

I'd never seen Kevin so feral, so absolutely brutal.

This so-called contest had devolved into something cruel and appalling. Even the crowd had stopped laughing.

I'd lifted the rope without realizing it, intending to step into the arena; a firm hand on my arm stopped me.

Odin shook his head. "Leave them be."

"But this is nasty. And disgusting. It's not funny anymore."

"It rarely is." He'd already turned his attention back to the flyte and resumed watching dispassionately.

"I will slit you from throat to ass, remove your intestines, and stuff them into your big mouth," Loki spat.

"I'll slice off your cock and balls, roast them, and shove them up your ass," Kevin countered.

Back and forth it went, threats of dismemberment mixed with vulgar sexual perversions.

Then, Kevin shocked me to my core with his next words.

"I will slaughter your loved ones, cook them in a feast, and laugh when you eat every bite."

I could only stare at him. Had those horrifying words actually come from the same lips that kissed me so sweetly?

Something flickered in Loki's eyes, and his lips twisted into a mocking grin. "Ah, but you see, Poison-Tongue, your barb is toothless. Unlike you, I have no loved ones." He'd spoken so softly, I'd almost missed it.

Kevin frowned, as if he hadn't understood. Loki's sly gaze slid to me for a moment.

Oh no.

Don't you fucking dare, I screamed at him silently.

Loki stepped close to Kevin, until they were only inches apart. With cold venom dripping from every word, he said, "Last night, while you slept so peacefully, I fucked your Consort in every hole she has. She screamed my name with her pleasure, over and over, until this morning."

At the same time that someone in the crowd gasped, Kevin's fist shot out and connected with Loki's face with a sickening crunch. Blood instantly gushed from his nose, and Loki raised both hands to cover it protectively.

"*Forfeit*," he bellowed, stumbling away from Kevin. "He has forfeited the match."

Kevin's jaw clenched, then he closed his eyes, sighed, and shook his head. He approached Loki and they talked quietly. A moment later, Loki's hands dropped and Kevin held his hand over the injury, healing it. A bystander offered a wet cloth, and Loki used it to clean the blood from his face.

Loki studied Kevin for a moment. "You know you lost, don't you?"

"Yeah." Kevin shrugged, then grinned. "It was worth it." He offered his hand, and Loki took it.

Then, unbelievably, they embraced and began laughing, as if they were best friends who'd just shared a hilarious joke.

What the *fuck* was going on here?

CHAPTER EIGHT

FTER THE GAMES ended for the day, the Great Hall was packed for the traditional feast. It was loud, rambunctious, and completely insane.

Wine, ale, and mead were being consumed in massive quantities, with quite a bit ending up on the floor as servants carrying heavily-laden trays were jostled and bumped into. Several dogs roamed the Hall and left the puddles of alcohol alone in favor of the food morsels that rained down onto the floor. A few brief fights broke out between some of the dogs, but for the most part there were plenty of scraps for all of them to share in the feast.

With such a massive amount of people crammed into the Hall, the strong body odor of humanity mixed with the food odors and the woodsmoke from the hearth, and made it hard to breathe. The small upper windows didn't seem to do much to air out the place, and it didn't take long for the room to become uncomfortably hot and cloying.

A group of burly Asgardian warriors slapped Kevin on the back and congratulated him for his impressive performance at the flyte, and I barely stopped myself from rolling my eyes.

I didn't think it was all that impressive. It'd seemed more like something a couple of teenaged boys would do, especially with all the references to shit, piss, and sex. And what was with all the references to goats?

But then again, what did I know?

As I picked at my food and tried my best to ignore the chaos around me, I felt more than saw Loki's gaze on me, but I pretended not to notice.

I was still pissed at him for provoking Kevin with such a terrible lie. I didn't even blame Kevin for punching him. In fact, I felt like punching him right now, too.

The group of warriors continued on, and in their wake, a wave of nasty funk hit me and made my stomach roll over.

I had to get the hell out of there before I vomited right where I sat.

Dodging Asgardians, harried servers, and snarling dogs on the way, I politely nodded at the guards and slipped through one of the open side doors.

Ah. Fresh air. And blessedly cool, too.

I took a deep breath of it and looked around.

The cobbled square was well lit with multiple torches, giving me a glimpse of a small garden tucked between the Hall and another building.

Perfect.

It was a delightful little space. A few trees rustled in the slight breeze and a simple fountain gurgled happily. It was wonderfully peaceful. A small brazier nearby provided subdued lighting that didn't interfere with my night vision. In the night sky above, millions of stars twinkled.

But I didn't recognize a single constellation, reminding me I wasn't on Earth.

I sat on the bench near the fountain and breathed deeply. For the first time all day, I relaxed, and my stomach settled.

It'd been a stressful first day on Asgard.

After the flyte, Thor had politely reminded me about participating in the axe throwing event I'd completely forgotten mentioning at breakfast. But I hadn't wanted to be the only one of our delegation to not take part in the games, so I'd reluctantly—but bravely—gone with him to the designated area.

The weapon had been razor-sharp, with a long, thick handle, and I'd quickly realized this event could be deadly if I fucked it up.

He'd spent a few minutes explaining the two commonly-used methods of throwing. Since I was a first-timer, he'd recommended I use the two-handed method. He'd showed me how to grasp the handle—but not too tightly—and how to stand properly, with my body facing the bullseye target set up some distance away. Lastly, he'd walked me through a couple of practice swings, then pronounced me ready for my first throw.

Unfortunately, I'd fucked it up.

Thankfully, no one had gotten hurt.

Somehow, I'd accidentally released the axe too early, and it'd spun end-over-end toward the crowd of bystanders. I'd stood frozen in horror as people jumped out of the way—one older man had actually tripped and fallen in his haste to move—and the axe had landed harmlessly on the grass. After a few stunned seconds, everyone had laughed and shouted good-natured taunts at me.

I'd never been so fucking embarrassed in my entire life.

Thor had assured me it happened often, and pleaded with me to give it another try, but I'd refused.

Then, a child—who couldn't have been older than four or five—stepped up for his very first axe throw, and it'd gone perfectly. He'd even hit the target, although not in the center.

Which hadn't made me feel any better.

Unfortunately, the feast had started right after the games ended for the day, so I never had a chance to talk to Odin about becoming allies. I could only hope tomorrow would be a better day, and we'd have our meeting with him sooner rather than later.

"Penny for your thoughts." Loki sat beside me on the bench, leaving a respectable distance between us.

I sighed but didn't reply. *Of course* I couldn't have more than five minutes of peace and quiet.

Besides, I was still pissed at him.

"I noticed you didn't eat, so I thought you might not feel well. I can help."

So that was his excuse for watching me, he'd been concerned?

"Why are you here? Why do you keep pestering me?" Immediately, I felt bad; that'd come out harsher than I'd intended.

"*Pestering* you?" He laughed softly. "Lady, believe me: if I were pestering you, you'd damn well know it."

There'd been a note of sharpness in his voice, and I opened my mouth to snap back at him. But something in his shadowed expression stopped me, and we just sort of studied each other for a moment.

He sighed and held out his hand, offering a small vial. "A gift. A potion for pregnancy sickness, nothing more."

I hesitated; he was the most famous Trickster in history. Could I trust him? But my witchy-sense told me he was truthful. Although I could make my own potion, I recognized the peace offering and accepted it, slipping the vial into a pocket. "Thanks."

He nodded once, then turned toward the fountain. "I also wanted to apologize for the flyte. I shouldn't have poked the bear, but I just couldn't resist."

"True to your nature once again, huh?"

He shrugged. "That's always been my failing. I can't help who I am."

"Bullshit," I snapped. Then I softened my tone. "Look, if Bricriu could become Kevin, you could change, too. Become a better man. One who doesn't end up destroying Asgard."

"Ah, you speak of Ragnarök. It's just a myth, you know. It's not real, and it's certainly not the future."

"Are you sure about that? What if it *is* the future? And what if you could stop it from happening by changing your nature now? Even if Ragnarök never happens, you'd be a better man. It'd be a win-win."

"I've seen the future. The world doesn't end with me commanding a ship made out of fingernails." He'd said it sarcastically, and now he shook his head in disgust.

Despite myself, I was intrigued. Divination was one aspect of magick I hadn't worked with yet.

"Okay, I'll bite. How *does* it end?"

"I've seen many endings. It could be any one of them." He shrugged. "Or none of them."

A whiff of smoke made me think of my recurring nightmare for a moment. "Do any of them show the world destroyed in ash and smoke? Fireballs raining from the sky?"

From the corner of my eye, I saw Loki turn his head to stare at me.

"One or two," he replied softly. "You've seen it too, then?"

"Not really. I've never done divination." I met his gaze. "It's a recurring nightmare I've been having lately."

"It is always the same?"

"Mostly. Only tiny differences each time. But the same basic theme. As I said, ash and smoke. Fireballs from the sky. Death and destruction."

He sighed, frowning. "Divining the future is not precise. Any seemingly insignificant thing can change the outcome from one minute to the next."

"Sounds complicated."

"Sometimes, it can be. Of course, it all depends on the method, the diviner, the question asked, and a myriad of other variables."

I sighed, looked up at the night sky again, and changed the subject. "It's beautiful here."

"We have an almost identical environment to certain areas of Midgard. Our stars, of course, are different. And our moon has a different cycle." After a brief pause, he continued. "I miss Midgard. Over the centuries, I've spent quite some time there, but not lately."

"Why not?"

"Too many wars for my taste."

"Asgard doesn't have conflict?"

He smirked. "I wouldn't say that. But we haven't had any full-on battles in centuries."

Huh. Must be nice. Seems like some combination of the nations of Earth were constantly fighting.

"Ready to start learning magick?" he asked.

I blinked at him. "Here? Now?"

He snorted. "No, not here. We'll go where it's safe to practice magick and not be observed or interrupted."

"But my people will wonder where I am."

"It will be as if only moments have passed." He cocked his head. "Have you never manipulated time?"

"I know others who can, but I've never done it myself, no." It'd honestly never occurred to me that it was something I could learn to do.

"I promise, they won't even know you're gone." He stood. "Shall we go?"

He guided me through the empty yet well-lit streets of Asgard. Apparently, everyone was either tucked away in their homes or at the feast in the Great Hall.

The main part of the city, with its closed shops and other businesses, gave way to what I thought of as the suburbs: small homesteads with modest roundhouses and pens for sheep and goats. Further out were estates of rolling fields, with large rectangular buildings set quite a distance from the road.

"Out here are the halls of the Æsir," Loki said. "Most of them, anyway."

Many were huge and reminded me of the Viking longhouses I'd seen in movies. One or two were flashy Greek revival mansions with marble-columned porches, set atop low hills.

Loki stopped at a large house set closer to the road, lit with magick balls of light instead of torches.

"Here we are." He held the heavy wooden door open for me.

I stepped through into a spacious cobbled courtyard. A colonnaded walkway lined three sides, and potted trees were tucked beside benches and chairs. Through glass windows and doors of iron scrollwork, I glimpsed the rooms beyond, all of which opened onto the courtyard.

At the far end, an iron bench, flowering trees, and plants were nestled around a fountain that gurgled pleasantly. A small, shallow pool in the center of the courtyard reflected the night sky.

"The Seer's Mirror," he said, indicating the pool. "We'll come back to it later. First, what do you know of battle magick?"

"Not much. The Morrigan showed me some basic stuff last year, but it was nothing like what I saw earlier, in your contest with Kevin."

He nodded thoughtfully. "And what of your command of the elements?"

"You mean using water, air, fire? That sort of thing?"

"Yes."

"I, uh, actually haven't done any of that. Wait—does manipulating the weather count? I have a bit of experience with that."

He sighed. "This might take longer than I thought."

"So?" I frowned. "You said you'd manipulate time."

He held my gaze. "The longer I stretch it out, the greater risk of unintended consequences. For example, our time bubble could affect your unborn child in some way, although I don't believe it will be harmful. However, you should know this is my first time teaching a pregnant student." He studied me. "If you do not wish to continue with lessons because of this, I understand."

Oh, hell no, as long as it wasn't harmful to the baby. Besides, I'd really been looking forward to learning from a master of magick. "No, please, let's continue."

"As you wish. Then, we'll start at the beginning, with the basics. Pay close attention, so we can cover as much as possible in the shortest amount of time without the need to repeat lessons unnecessarily."

And with that, we began.

"Please, I just need a short break," I said.

Ugh. It'd sounded like I'd begged.

Then again, maybe I had.

Loki was a harsh taskmaster. We'd been at it for what seemed like hours with no break, and just now he'd said battle magick was next.

He opened his mouth to argue, but something he saw in my face made him relent.

"Fine. Only a short break." He waved a hand, and a platter appeared on the small table near the bench, followed by a pitcher and cups. The condensation dripping down the side of the pitcher made me realize how thirsty I was.

We sat and enjoyed a light snack of savory cheese, salty olives, and light but tasty bread, washing it all down with more of that delicious apple-flavored water I'd had at the Great Hall earlier in the day.

My head was almost spinning from all I'd learned already.

We'd covered the basics of magick first: manipulation of energy and time. Next was conjuring objects and creatures like those I'd seen him and Kevin do earlier. He'd also shown me how to maintain my energy without having to draw from a source, which would be useful in any non-Earth environment, like Asgard.

I'd learned how to communicate with the elements and use their power to protect with shields or destroy with weapons. And I'd learned how to create duplicates of myself to bewilder an enemy.

Or just to have a bit of fun.

After a moment, Loki broke the companionable silence. "You are a quick learner, and are doing very well so far."

"Thanks." I wouldn't let it go to my head, though I did feel a warm sense of satisfaction from his encouragement.

A moment later, we'd finished our break and went back at it, this time with battle magick unlike anything the Morrigan had shown me.

In addition to learning some of the moves I'd seen him perform during the contest with Kevin, he also showed me why they'd appeared to move too fast to see: he'd put up a specific magickal shield. Such a shield was usually used to confuse an opponent, but he'd used it earlier to hide both his and Kevin's movements from the onlookers, since neither of them had really wanted to hurt the other.

And now, I could do it, too, although I hoped I wouldn't need it.

Next, I learned how to conjure weapons that could either pass through a body harmlessly, or be real enough to maim and kill.

Once again, I'd just learned some of the secrets from his magick battle with Kevin earlier, but I'd never be able to admit it to anyone else.

"Enough battle magick," Loki said. "It is time to return to the Seer's Mirror."

I followed him to the pool in the center of the courtyard.

"As I mentioned earlier," he began, "divining the future can be useful in many situations. Using it to guide your decision-making is one of the most important. Employing a pool of still water is, of course, only one method of divination. There are many others. For right now, it will do. Simply concentrate on whatever it is you wish to see, then gaze into the pool. Don't let the reflection distract you; it is better to allow your vision to unfocus slightly. I will be nearby if you need assistance."

I nodded and knelt on the wide stone border of the pool. Somehow, the light breeze didn't disturb the absolute stillness of the dark water, which reflected the stars as if in a mirror.

What did I want to see?

Should I find out where Ares, Athena, and Kali were, and what they were up to? Or, maybe something a bit more personal: what would my future child be like?

As tempting as either of those were, though, I knew what I really wanted to ask.

What would happen after I removed the targets and healed the planet?

Concentrating on that question, I stared into the depths of the pool with my eyes unfocused, as Loki had advised.

After a moment, images appeared in quick flashes, like a video montage of photos, flipping from one to the next.

Flames rose from villages and cities, farmers' fields and old-growth forests, and the smoke was so thick it blotted out the sun, turning the sky to a dark orange-brown and the world to a hellscape.

The Earth was on fire.

Blackened bodies—human and animal—were strewn everywhere. But not all of them had been burned beyond recognition. No, some looked almost as if they'd simply curled up to sleep, which meant they'd probably died of smoke inhalation. Mothers with children in their arms. Couples hugging each other tight. Entire families lay next to each other.

A small girl, completely untouched by the raging fires, looked peaceful, half-covered by a fleece blanket. Her beloved doll, also remarkably untouched, lay in her arms.

Massive office buildings had been reduced to monstrous skeletons of rebar and cinder block. What had been neat rows of houses were now piles of rubble. The burnt husks of delivery trucks, cars, and SUVs blocked roads, bridges, and tunnels.

The suffering had been unimaginable, and my stomach rolled.

I closed my eyes and fought to keep the bile from rising further. It had to be my imagination, but I swore my mouth tasted of smoke and ash. I concentrated on taking deep breaths and slowly exhaling.

"Are you all right?" Loki, now beside me.

"No." My voice rasped, as if I'd inhaled smoke. "It was horrible. Fire. Smoke. Death." I shuddered and opened my eyes, but the scenes had been etched on my brain and I couldn't unsee the horror. "Earth was like something out of a nightmare." *My* nightmare, in fact. I'd definitely noticed the similarities. "It was like the recurring nightmare I mentioned earlier."

He helped me rise, then guided me to the nearby bench and offered a flask. "It's just mead."

Would it take the ashy taste from my mouth? I took a quick swallow, then another, and handed it back. "Thanks."

He capped it and set it next to me. "I know this will be difficult, but we must discuss your vision. First, exactly what did you ask to see?"

"What would happen after I finished removing the targets and healing Earth."

"Now, describe the vision, from beginning to end."

It only took a moment for me to tell him what I'd seen.

"Yes, that is very disturbing," he agreed. "I understand your reaction now. But you were never shown exactly what happened? What had caused that future?"

I shook my head.

"Okay." He took a deep breath and let it out. "Remember earlier, when I said there are many possible futures? That nothing is ever written in stone until it has actually happened?" He waited for my nod before continuing. "What this means is, the future you just saw can be prevented from happening."

"That's what I was hoping you'd say."

"However, sometimes it's impossible to know the exact cause—and appropriate solution—until it's almost too late. So, unfortunately, you may be unable to completely stop it."

Shit. "Well, that's depressing."

"The thing is... with this vision, I strongly believe there are other forces at work against you. Probably to prevent your stated mission of removing the enemies of Midgard and healing the planet."

I blinked at him, wondering if he was specifically referring to Ares, Athena, and Kali, or if there were others out there I didn't know about. "What would you recommend?"

"If I were you..." He pursed his lips for a moment, thinking. "I would assume the event—whatever it is—happens soon after you heal the planet. So, long before then, create another world. Create a healthy, pristine version of Midgard and fill it with all its plants and animals. A refuge, if you will."

"A contingency plan, in other words." His idea made a lot of sense, and I liked it. A lot.

"Yes." He nodded. "Just in case."

I had more questions.

"Is there any way I can go back into the vision, maybe find out more details about that future? Like, exactly what causes it?"

"No, I'm sorry. It doesn't work that way. Usually we only see flashes and snapshots, not the whole picture. It's up to us to interpret what we see, and find meaning where there may be none apparent."

That reminded me of what Maggie had told me last year: from beyond the veil, she could only see snippets of events, like scattered pieces of a jigsaw puzzle. And sometimes, it was almost impossible to put them all together in the right order.

It all made sense. But I felt like I still had so much to learn.

I let the silence draw out as I took in my surroundings to clear my head of that awful vision.

Through the iron scrollwork on the doors and windows, I glimpsed beautiful furniture, stately sculpture, colorful frescoes, and lots of gleaming marble and gold. It looked like he'd filled the place with museum replicas.

"Your home is very beautiful. And so different from the other places we passed on our way here. It's like something out of ancient Rome."

"Thank you." He glanced around with unmistakable pride. "I've always admired the era of Classical Greece. So I modeled my home on the elite villas of the period, making it as authentic as I could without sacrificing most modern conveniences." He hesitated, then asked, "Would you like to see inside?"

"I'd love to."

From the casual comments he made as he guided me through his home, I corrected my earlier assumption.

This artwork, these sculptures, weren't simply reproductions of museum pieces. They were real antiquities from the height of Greece's cultural beauty, and could only have been brought here from then and there. It reminded me once again that I was in the presence of an ancient deity.

Seen up close, the frescoes were amazingly detailed. Scenes of mythology, nature, and fantastic beasts, beautifully rendered in full color on plastered walls.

Each room of the house opened to the courtyard for fresh breezes, and I had to admit I loved the architectural style of it—but it wasn't at all practical in a climate like Arizona's summer, where we relied on air conditioning for more than half the year.

I pointed at the ornate double doors at the end of the colonnade. "What's in there?"

"My private quarters." He raised a brow. "But you don't need to see that." He continued walking past, and I quickly followed.

He was absolutely right. I didn't need to see that.

Next, he opened a similar set of double doors. "This is the bath. I modeled it on the Roman Imperial period."

It was an enormous room, artfully separated into three chambers with moveable panels and potted palms. Each chamber had its own small pool, beautifully tiled with mosaics of dolphins, fish, and other marine life. The skylights in the plastered ceiling would make it bright and cheerful in daytime.

"The first is a caldarium or hot water bath," he explained. "Next, the tepidarium, with warm water. The last is the frigidarium, although I rarely use it. I don't personally care for cold water. I only installed it for authenticity and for guests."

The white marble floor was highly polished and laid with gorgeous rugs. Colorful frescoes of more playful marine life adorned the walls. A few scattered couches and tables were piled with neatly folded towels and robes.

"It's gorgeous."

The next room we entered was also beautiful. But intriguing.

Couches lined the three walls, with small tables placed near each. The walls were a deep, rich red, and ornate oil lamps hung on long chains in the corners. The entire floor was covered in a smooth pebble mosaic of a frolicking pair of goats.

It wasn't quite a living room, but what was it?

"For this room's design," he explained, "I chose the andron from the Greek Classical Period. It was typically the men's dining room, used mostly for drinking and dinner parties. If any women attended—which was rare except for entertainment purposes—they sat in chairs while men reclined." He glanced around with pride. "But I don't use it for that. Just for snacks and such during parties. I have a normal dining room, with a long table and chairs, for dining."

The details were amazing. I almost felt as if I'd stepped back in time to tour an ancient palace.

Then we entered the kitchen, and I was jarringly returned to modernity.

Sleek black stainless steel appliances, gleaming black marble countertops, and stylish lighting completed what seemed to be a professional chef's workspace.

"Whoa," I breathed.

He shrugged. "I wanted something I could actually cook in, without smoking up the place."

"Wait. So you *do* have electricity in Asgard. Why didn't I see any lights in the Great Hall? There are only torches and braziers."

"*They* don't have it. *I* do." He grinned. "Well, it's not really electricity as you know it on Midgard. This is all powered by magick."

"Magick." I stared at him. "That's... fascinating."

Seeing my obvious interest, he explained how he'd created a reservoir of magickal energy, sort of like a massive battery, that served as the power source for the appliances and any other technology he wanted. The appliances still plugged into the wall like they did on Earth, but the power to the plugs was delivered from his reservoir of magick, instead of electrical lines or a power plant.

It made me think of his suggestion earlier, of creating a refuge, a sort of duplicate of Earth. Maybe if I did do that, I could power it with a reservoir of magick, like he'd done here.

It was worth thinking about some more.

I wandered the kitchen and took a closer look at the appliances: a huge French-door refrigerator and freezer with black glass doors; a wall of ovens that included a bread oven, microwave, and convection oven; a five-burner smooth glass cooktop; and a high-performance range hood. He even had the latest in technology: a two-drawer dishwasher beside the enormous stainless steel sink.

"So you actually cook, then?"

He nodded. "It's quite enjoyable. Some specialty ingredients are difficult to get, of course, but we have a concierge group that makes weekly shopping trips to Midgard and other worlds. They can get me pretty much anything I need."

I shook my head. This was all absolutely unbelievable, and I'd never for a minute thought there was anything like this place in the whole world.

"I'm impressed." And I really was, it wasn't an overstatement and I wasn't just trying to be nice.

"Thank you." He seemed pleased with my reaction. "And I know I'll be equally impressed with what you do."

"Well, I hope so." My vision and nightmare came back to me, and I sighed. "Unless I fuck it all up and somehow make a terrible mistake." My stomach ached just thinking of it.

"We all make terrible mistakes. You honestly think Odin hasn't done horrible things?" He didn't wait for me to reply, just continued on, with a bit of added venom. "Believe me, the myths don't tell the half of it. If humans knew the truth about him, they wouldn't worship him at all. They'd call him a monster and relegate him to the dustbin of history."

I blinked at him. Well. That'd been quite the rant.

I shook my head. "But if I'm the one who ends up destroying the world..." I couldn't even finish the sentence.

"For what it's worth, I don't think it's you. And I don't think the world will be destroyed. Damaged, yes. But not destroyed." He hesitated before continuing. "Look, I've also seen the future in the Seer's Mirror. I've seen you alive and happy, many millennia from now. You... and your daughter."

My daughter?

For just a moment, I forgot everything else. That Earth's destruction was only one of many possible futures—he'd said so, earlier—and instead, my brain locked onto those two words.

A daughter. I had a baby girl inside me.

The tension that'd built up in me melted, and in its place was a strange mixture of joy, apprehension, and longing.

"Thank you," I said. "I needed to hear that."

"You are quite welcome." He offered his arm. "Now, we must return to the Hall."

Rather, we returned to the small garden. He closed his eyes for a moment, and when he opened them, he met my gaze. "Time is now released to flow naturally."

"Thank you again," I said, softly. "For everything."

"You are quite welcome. It's been a pleasure, Lady."

As I watched him disappear into the darkness, I remembered the vial he'd given me. I sniffed the contents; the potion smelled minty. One cautious sip told me it didn't taste bad at all, so I took a bigger sip and returned the vial to my pocket. A moment later I slipped back into the Hall.

It was even more of a madhouse than before I'd left, with shouting, singing, laughing, jostling, and spilled food and drink. As I made my way through the tables and dodged the harried servers, I skidded on a couple of puddles of ale—or worse—but somehow managed not to fall.

Quite a bit of good-natured slap-and-tickle was going on between the servers and those being served, even between the women. Oddly enough, none of the servers seemed to mind; they simply laughed along with everyone else, as if it were just a big game.

How I made it to my seat without being groped, I'll never know.

As I sat, Kevin finished his conversation then turned to me. "Everything okay?"

He'd almost had to shout to be heard, so I leaned close and spoke directly in his ear.

"Yeah. It was too stuffy in here, I just needed some fresh air." A servant immediately filled the cup in front of me, and as I took a long drink, my gaze fell on the heaping platters of food. Suddenly, I was ravenous. "Could you pass that platter of meat, please?"

Kevin didn't say a word, just watched me eat with a bemused expression. He knew as well as I did that I rarely ate this much at one sitting, but I couldn't worry about it right now.

Loki's pregnancy potion had worked wonders. No more upset stomach, and a healthy appetite to boot.

Of course, I'd love to tell Kevin—and Arddhu—that I was pregnant, but that was just the emotional, warm-and-fuzzy part of me. The fact-based, rational part knew I had to wait until I had the pregnancy confirmed with modern methods. How could I tell them I'd only just found out from Loki and Anu?

So, for now, I had to keep the news to myself, and remember to pick up a home pregnancy test as soon as I could.

After I cleaned my plate, I sat back with a contented sigh, then stifled a yawn and drank some ale. Thank goodness alcohol wouldn't affect the baby, like it would a human. If I'd had to stop drinking, everyone would know immediately something was wrong.

From a nearby table came a strong tenor voice, and the Hall quieted.

> There once was a god of war
> He was strong, aye, and brave, too.
> Honest and truthful, and more besides
> In battle he was fast, aye, and clever, too
> None could escape his wicked blade.
>
> In the furs, though, he took his time
> And oh the women were quite content
> Though not among each other.
> 'Tis said there are sons a-plenty
> Aye, all across the nine worlds.
>
> To him we drink our finest ale

We mark our blades with his runes
And bleed a goat on eve of battle
For him to give us great victory
Aye, to him we drink our finest ale.

As the song faded, all around us, Asgardians banged their mugs on the tables and chanted Tyr's name.

After a moment, I joined in, feeling the need to be part of this tribute. I hadn't known Tyr well, and we hadn't spoken much outside of the business of alliance meetings, but he'd been well-respected by all. And, he'd been murdered because of me. The least I could do was show him the traditional respect due to a fallen warrior.

Another group began a lively—and dirty—drinking song, banging their cups and mugs against their table and covering the scarred wood with spilled ale. Laughter and good-natured jeers accompanied the singers, and I couldn't help but laugh along with them.

I'd never experienced anything like this, and I was a bit surprised to realize I was enjoying myself.

"Hey-ho, the bard is here," someone shouted, somehow making himself easily heard over the noise. A space was immediately cleared in the center of the Hall, and someone placed a padded stool there.

A lone gentleman, silvered hair neatly bound at the nape, sat on the stool and removed a stringed instrument from its case. That seemed to be some type of signal, because the Hall hushed. After another moment, the bard began to play. The notes rang out pure and clear, enrapturing everyone within the Hall.

"Oh, I love harp music," I whispered to Kevin.

"It's actually a lyre," he whispered back. "See there, at the bottom, how the strings go over a bridge before going into the wood? A harp doesn't have that."

I blinked at him, yet again impressed by his knowledge.

After another moment, the bard's rich baritone accompanied the song, but I didn't recognize the language. Even so, based on the reactions of the listeners, it didn't seem to be particularly sad or mournful but neither was it a joyful ditty. Most likely, it was some myth or legend that the

Asgardians were familiar with. It was a beautiful song, and my skin broke out in goosebumps at certain notes.

After the song ended, the Hall broke out into applause and cheers, then Odin's voice boomed. "Bothi, I would ask you to please sing in Midgardian English, for the benefit of our honored guests."

"Of course, All-Father," Bothi replied, then nodded in our direction before beginning another song—this time, a sweet tale of enduring love between a man and his woman.

A moment later, Kevin put his arm around me, and I snuggled closer to him. Around the Hall, other couples did the same, with one or two stealing a quick kiss.

The bard continued singing songs—some quiet and poignant, others lively and humorous, still others legendary sagas—long into the night, not even stopping after Odin and Frigg rose from their seats and left the Hall. Finally, the last notes of the last song died out, and as he packed away his instrument, the Hall rang long and loud with cheers of appreciation. Bothi bowed in acknowledgment, then he, too, left the Hall.

If I'd expected the night to end at that point, I was mistaken. Soon enough, more ale was served, the leftover food was cleared away, and more impromptu singing broke out. At this rate, the party would go all night, maybe even until the morning.

But for once, I was ready to try and get some sleep.

"I'm going to bed," I told Kevin, stifling a yawn. "I'm exhausted."

"I'll come with you." He glanced around. "I've had enough."

Arddhu saw us get up to leave, and joined us, followed by the Morrigan and Lugh.

I'd just opened my door when Lugh asked, "Can we all talk for a few minutes? We haven't had much privacy since we got here, and I wanted to give a quick update."

"Sure," I said, and waved them into my room. After everyone was inside, I quickly set a sound shield around us and closed the door.

"Wow, yours is bigger than mine," Kevin said, looking around.

I just blinked at him. "You're kidding, right?" My *bathroom* in Scottsdale was bigger than this room.

Lugh chuckled. "All the guest rooms are small, by design. They don't want visitors staying any longer than they absolutely have to."

That made sense. But it seemed wrong, somehow. Not very hospitable.

"So, what's up?" I asked him, and stifled another yawn.

"So far, I've been unsuccessful at getting Odin to commit to meet with us so we can present our case for becoming allies." He sighed and shook his head. "I'll keep trying, though."

"We still have time," the Morrigan pointed out.

Yeah. One more day and night, in fact, although I was ready to leave now, honestly.

"What if we force a meeting with Odin in the morning, then leave for home?"

"Why?" Kevin's gaze on me was sharp. "What's wrong?"

"Nothing. It's just... well, after the fiasco of today's games, I'm just not looking forward to tomorrow."

"What fiasco?" the Morrigan asked. "Kevin's flyte was amazing. I did fantastic in the swordplay, and the rest of us did well, too. Tomorrow can only get better."

I huffed. "Not for me. Mine was a *disaster*." My cheeks heated just thinking about that awful axe throw.

Kevin laughed. "Oh come on, it wasn't that bad."

"I could've *killed* someone."

"But you didn't," Kevin said.

Lugh grinned. "I'd advise you to stay away from the sharp pointy objects, then. Maybe try one of the chess matches. Or the footrace."

Not likely. "I suck at all that stuff."

"Then perhaps you should remain on the sidelines," Arddhu said.

"Somehow," Kevin mused, "I don't think either Odin or Thor would allow her to just be a bystander."

"You are most likely correct," Arddhu agreed. He turned to Lugh. "Was there anything else?"

"No, that was it," Lugh said. "See you all in the morning." He left, closing the door behind him.

"Me, too," the Morrigan said. "Night-night, everyone."

Arddhu kissed my forehead. "Rest well, my Lady." Then he followed the others, leaving Kevin and I alone.

I sat on my bed. "I have to ask you something. After all those horrible things you and Loki said to each other, how in the world could you two laugh and act like nothing happened? You even *hugged*, for fuck's sake."

He shrugged. "Most of it was for show. I mean, sure, he's a pisser, but it was a flyte. Nothing in a flyte is really personal."

"But you... the killing loved ones thing... and all that other shit... how was that *not* personal?"

He laughed as he sat beside me. "Dee, that was the whole point. It's supposed to be like that. Thing is, you're not supposed to *take* it personally."

I raised a brow. "Seems to me you took it very personal when he lied about fucking me all night."

He winced, then studied his nails. "Yeah, I know. He got me on that one. I guess I didn't have as good control as I thought I did."

"Hey, you're not jealous, are you? There's nothing between Loki and me. Well, except professional courtesy. If that's what it's called, when two deities have a working relationship." I was babbling, I knew it, and I hated it. Somehow I felt guilty for something I had no reason to feel guilty over. It'd just been some magick lessons, for fuck's sake.

But they were lessons I couldn't tell anyone about, since I'd given my word. My spit-bound vow, in fact.

His gaze lifted to mine. "Oh, yeah, I know. I mean, no, I know there's nothing between you." He shrugged again. "Like I said, I just lost my control for a minute. It was like, he knew the right button to push, and he didn't just push it—he *slammed* it." He took my hands in his. "I know you love me. And Arddhu. And you know you're my world. And his."

The warmth in his eyes made my heart overflow with love. "Both of you are my world, too."

He rested his forehead against mine. "You know, years ago, if anyone had told me someday I'd enjoy sharing my woman with another man, I would've told them to go fuck themselves. But here we are. And Arddhu's become such a good friend, one I didn't even know I wanted. Or needed. It's like we've all become a family."

Which was nothing short of amazing, since they'd started out sort of hating each other.

Then again, Arddhu had started out hating *me*, too. Because I was American, and he didn't have a high opinion of Americans.

We'd all come a long way, I supposed.

"Hey, want to stay here tonight? With me?" I already knew what his answer would be, but I'd asked anyway.

He snorted. "Of course."

The bed was small, but just big enough for us to snuggle up under the covers and hold each other close. And for once, I had no problem falling asleep.

CHAPTER NINE

THE NEXT MORNING, Kevin and I quickly washed and dressed. I dropped the sound shield as we left my room. I'd actually had a wonderful night's sleep, without even a whiff of the nightmare.

The rest of our group was already at breakfast, but evidence of the feast lasting well after we'd all gone to bed surrounded us. Asgardians littered the floor or tables, snoring loudly and twitching in their sleep as if battling enemies in their dreams.

It made quite the weird backdrop to breakfast.

Odin, Frigg, and the other Æsir didn't show up until we'd finished eating. Servants quickly placed plates in front of them, refilled our cups with surprisingly good coffee, then disappeared back to wherever they'd come from. I'd never get used to having servants hovering or lurking in the shadows. It just wasn't for me.

Odin studied me as he ate. "Thor has offered to tutor you for the axe throw this morning, so that you may compete for the prize."

Oh, hell no.

I smiled politely at Thor. "Thank you, but actually, I was thinking of trying the tafl or senet matches instead."

Odin's blue eye fixed on me sternly. "Goddess of Midgard, I would prefer for you to compete in a more suitable contest, so I may evaluate your combative skills. To that end, I suggest either the axe throw or swordplay."

Shit. I couldn't believe he'd just called me out. I quickly considered my options, but I didn't see how I had any. If I said no, it'd probably doom efforts for an alliance. But if I said yes, not only could I seriously injure someone—or myself—but I might also make a complete fool of myself.

Thor spoke up. "All-Father, perhaps she does not wish to compete in those events."

Odin didn't respond to his son, but neither did he take his gaze from me. "I have heard you wield a sword well. Perhaps the swordplay arena will be to your liking instead of the axe throw."

He certainly was insistent. And persistent.

Lugh spoke. "All-Father, we wished to meet with you this morning to discuss some important matters."

But Odin stayed focused on me with that unblinking eye. "We shall meet after the games."

Shit. There was no way I was getting out of this.

Fine.

I inclined my head. "As you wish, Odin All-Father. Today, I will compete in the swordplay arena."

Finally satisfied, he nodded once and turned his attention to his plate. It wasn't until then that I realized I'd been tense the entire time, and forced myself to relax.

As I finished my coffee, I went over everything I'd learned about swordplay from Kurt, Mike, the Morrigan, Kevin, and Loki. And, of course, Siobhan, the warrior Keeper from long ago, whose memories I'd inherited.

But all too soon, it was time for the games.

Once again, Odin led us from the Hall. This time, however, he headed straight for the swordplay arena.

"You'll be fine." The Morrigan spoke quietly into my ear. "Just remember to pace yourself so you don't tire too quickly."

"Kick ass," Kevin said.

Arddhu smiled. "I have full confidence in your abilities."

Lugh just nodded encouragingly.

They all stayed behind the barrier as Odin and Thor escorted me to the table near the arena, where a selection of swords had been arranged.

"We shall choose the weapons for you and your opponent," Odin explained, "so neither of you have the unfair advantage of a familiar blade." Without waiting for a reply, they began examining the weapons.

"Who's my opponent?" I asked.

"I am." Sif stepped forward from the gathering crowd.

Shit. The legendary Sif was my opponent? This was getting worse by the minute.

While she openly evaluated me, I did the same.

She was several inches taller than me and her arms were longer, but we seemed roughly about the same muscle mass. According to mythology, she had quite the reputation as a warrior, so with her longer reach, that made two strikes against me.

With a critical eye, I studied her armor of boiled leather. It protected her from neck to knee, unlike my jeans and tee shirt. So I quickly reproduced her armor for myself, including the tall, sturdy boots.

"These are your weapons." Odin presented two identical swords to us.

I hefted mine experimentally. It was heavy—I'd have to use both hands to wield it—but the grip was a good fit for my small hands. It was also well balanced despite being well over a foot longer than Ire, my Celtic shortsword.

Sif and I spent a few minutes warming up and continuing to assess each other. She, too, used a two-handed grip, and her practice swings were graceful and steady.

Quite a crowd had already gathered around the arena, but so far they were quiet. So quiet, in fact, I clearly heard the noise of the strange ball game taking place far out in the field.

"What are the rules?" I asked.

"There is only one." Sif's smile was somewhat feral. "No killing blows."

"Two, actually," Odin corrected, his eye fixed firmly on me. "No magick."

Well, shit. There went the one thing that could've evened the playing field for me. Maybe, just maybe, the loss wouldn't be too embarrassing.

The crowd of onlookers buzzed with excitement, and my stomach jittered from nerves. I'd never had an audience before.

Except for my practice sessions when Mike had watched. But that was different.

As I scanned the crowd, my gaze fell on Loki. He nodded once, slowly, as if to say, *you can do this; remember what I showed you.*

Oh.

Of course. I thought back over what I'd learned last night, and instantly recognized several techniques I could use today.

Almost as if he'd known I'd be in the swordplay arena today.

I nodded to him in response, then joined Sif in the center of the roped-off arena. My nerves—and stomach—settled, and as I focused on Sif and the match before me, the crowd faded away.

If she'd noticed I'd copied her armor, she didn't mention it.

She thrust out her sword, pointed toward the ground. "Touch your sword to mine to begin," she softly said.

I complied, and the match began.

Sif was a powerful and agile warrior; each time I parried a strike, our swords clanged in the morning stillness and sent intense vibrations up my arms. Within minutes, my hands grew numb from those damn vibrations. After I blocked another strike, I spun away to give myself some time. Only a couple of seconds, so I could slip a shield over my hands to deflect the vibrations. Odin might technically consider it cheating, but I didn't. It simply leveled the playing field between Sif and I.

When I turned again to face her, I was ready to resume.

For the first time since the match had started, I went on the offensive, using some of what Loki had shown me last night. She blocked every blow, but I kept it up, steadily advancing and forcing her to retreat.

Next thing I knew, she lost her balance. Giving in to a sudden mean streak, I took advantage of the opportunity and shoved her just hard enough that she landed on her ass.

The crowd gasped, and she glared at me with fire in her eyes.

Shit. Why the hell had I done that?

I stepped closer to offer her a hand up, but she ignored it and quickly got to her feet. I shrugged and readied myself for the match to continue.

She wasted no time, coming at me with a ferocious grimace. Parry, parry, lunge, parry. Over and over and over. Despite the coolness of the morning, sweat dripped down my neck and back. Even with the energy boosting techniques Loki had shown me, my muscles were tiring.

Despite my best efforts, she clearly held every advantage over me. The most I could hope for was an honorable loss.

Sif feinted left, and I was too slow. Her blade sliced into my shoulder, and I hissed.

She smiled triumphantly, and it galled me. I launched a flurry of attacks, but somehow she blocked each one.

Fuck, this was frustrating.

Then, in the middle of a parry, I had a sudden opening. I took it without hesitation, and my blade took a chunk out of her upper arm. She grimaced but never even faltered in returning blows.

That marked a turning point in the match; from then on, we both landed more hits than we blocked, and it wasn't long until we were a sweaty, bloody mess.

Parry, parry, lunge, thrust, parry.

My arms ached, and I knew I was lagging. But Sif seemed to be tiring as well; she panted as much as I, and her movements were slower and losing accuracy.

Still we kept on, attacking and counterattacking, until we both began to stagger a bit after each blocked blow. At this point, neither of us could be considered winning, and yet I couldn't see either of us surrendering, either.

I'd lost all concept of time, too. I had no idea how long we'd been at this. All I knew was it felt like hours.

Parry, thrust, parry, lunge.

How in the hell could either of us be declared a winner of this damn thing?

Just when I thought it wouldn't end until both of us had collapsed to the ground, Odin's voice boomed.

"Enough. I declare this match a draw."

Oh, thank all the gods.

Sif and I lowered our swords and stood staring at each other, chests heaving as we caught our breath. The onlookers cheered, chanting Sif's name, then, to my surprise, mine as well.

Finally, she took a step toward me, offered her hand, and I clasped it.

"Well done, Lady. It's been quite some time since I've had such a well-matched female opponent."

"You are phenomenal," I replied. "It took everything I had just to keep up with you."

"Aye." She grinned. "Plus a little extra."

My heart sank. If she'd known I'd used magick, Odin probably knew, too. "Lady Sif, I sincerely apologize."

"For what? You made it a proper match of skill, not of strength alone, and one of the best in my recent memory." She shook her head. "Truly, you have nothing to apologize for."

Humbled by her generosity, I could only thank her.

She grinned again. "Let's go get cleaned up. There's a special place I'd like to show you."

Leaving our swords behind, we pushed through the crowd and headed away from the grounds.

Her special place turned out to be a small pool fed by a hot spring, tucked away in a dense thicket near her home.

She peeled off her armor and handed it to a waiting servant, who took it away for cleaning. She stood in her sweaty underclothing and raised a brow at me. "I noticed you changed your Midgardian clothing into a replica of my armor. Do you wish it to be cleaned?" She motioned to another servant, who stepped close and began to clean her wounds.

"There's no need. I created it with magick, so I'll just get rid of it with magick, too." I changed my armor into a long tee shirt. "Just like that."

"Convenient," she said, then grimaced as her servant cleaned her upper arm, where I'd taken a chunk of flesh.

I winced in sympathy, then got busy healing my own cuts and used magick to clean away the dried and crusted blood. When I looked at her, I caught her eyeing my smooth skin with a bit of envy.

"I can heal your wounds, if you'd like."

She grinned and waved away her servant. "Oh, I would definitely like."

Each cut only took a few seconds to heal, and as a final touch I used my magick to clear away the dried blood, too.

"You have my thanks," she nodded, inspecting my work. Then, as she headed toward the pool, she added over her shoulder, "This will feel wonderful after that long contest."

Shallow steps had been carved into the side of the pool, and rock ledges underneath the surface served as bench seating. The water was a bit cooler than my spa back in Scottsdale.

A servant arrived with two wooden mugs of mead. We clinked and drank, then set them aside and relaxed in companionable silence for a moment.

"This is nice," I said.

She raised a brow. "Just nice?"

I didn't want to seem ungrateful, but it wasn't as nice as my spa, with its jets. I smiled. "You should come visit me someday. I think you'd really enjoy the Earth version of this. It's called a spa or hot tub."

She frowned, suddenly wary. "Oh, I've heard of Midgardian hot tubs." She seemed as if she were ready to defend herself. "I must speak plain. I have no wish of being seduced."

I almost spit out the sip of mead I'd just taken. "Oh, no. That's not... um... they're not always used for seduction. Mostly, they're just for sitting in, like this."

She blinked at me, still wary. "So, to be clear: you didn't just invite me to have sex with you?"

"No, I most certainly did not." Shit. I hope I hadn't offended her by saying that. What if she thought I thought she wasn't attractive? But she relaxed and drank her mead, not offended in the least, and I breathed a sigh of relief. "I was just commenting that I have something similar to this. That's all."

"I see." She sighed. "Midgard is so complicated."

"It can be, yes. But then again, I find Asgard complicated."

She studied me. "I suppose it could be, especially to a first-time visitor." She drank some mead. "Where did you learn to fight?"

"I had an instructor. After that, the Morrigan and Kevin showed me a bit, too."

"From yesterday's flyte with Loki, I'd say Kevin seems a formidable opponent. As for the Morrigan, she participated in our games many years ago, so I am somewhat familiar with her techniques. But it is your instructor I am curious about. Was she a famed warrior?"

For just a moment, I thought back to the sessions I'd had with Kurt, who Mike had hired to teach me combat techniques and sword fighting.

Now, that all seemed so long ago.

"He was Swedish, I think. His first name was Kurt, but I never did find out his last name."

"Kurt?" Sif's eyes grew wide. "White hair? Ice blue eyes?"

"That's him." I'm sure I looked as surprised as she. "You know him?"

"Yes," she nodded. "Kurt Alfsson. His father was King Alf of Denmark, and his mother was the famed shieldmaiden Alfhild. He has visited Asgard many times over the centuries to train our youngest warriors." Her eyes held newfound respect for me, as did her voice. "You are fortunate indeed to have been trained by Kurt Alfsson."

"Wait—you said *over the centuries*."

She nodded again. "All-Father held him in such high regard, he requested an Apple of Immortality from Iðunn."

It'd obviously made Kurt immortal. Although this explained some of the mystery I'd sensed about him and which Mike had never explained, it also left me with more questions.

"Mistress." A servant approached. "The All-Father has requested you bring our guest to the Great Hall for the feast."

Sif nodded. "Tell him we are on our way." The servant nodded and left to deliver the message.

She stood and stepped out of the pool. I was right behind her.

"I must return to my hall to dress. Do you require a gown?"

"No, thank you." As Sif watched, I changed my soaking wet shirt to jeans and a lightweight sweater, instantly drying my skin at the same time.

She cocked a brow and gave me the once-over. "That is a handy bit of *seiðr* you have there. I wouldn't mind being able to change my clothing with just a thought."

I shrugged. "It's the power of the Goddess. I couldn't do it otherwise."

"A worthy power." She smiled. "I'll see you at the Hall, then?"

"Meet you there," I smiled in reply.

146

Retracing my steps to the Great Hall, I fell in with a large group of Asgardians also on their way to the feast. A few of them stared at me and whispered, but thankfully they left me alone.

Inside the Great Hall, I saw the rest of my companions were already seated at the table closest to the dais, where Odin and the royal family were. Dodging the servants who bustled through the room with platters heaped with food and clay pitchers of drink, I slid into the open seat between Kevin and the Morrigan.

"Where'd you go?" Kevin passed a platter. "I saw you and Sif take off, but I was starting to get worried."

"She took me for a soak in a hot spring near her place. It was a bit like my spa, except without the jets." I piled chunks of savory roasted meat on my plate before passing the platter to the Morrigan.

"Where did you learn some of those fancy moves?" She took the platter and glanced sharply at me. "I didn't teach them to you. And I've sparred with Kevin, so I know he doesn't know them either."

"Yeah, I was wondering about that, too," Kevin said.

Shit. I couldn't tell them the truth, I'd sworn to Loki I wouldn't. But as much as I didn't want to lie, I didn't have any choice.

I knew Kevin would be able to detect the lie, so I wrapped it in a bit of magick, something else I'd learned from Loki, and made my voice sound casual.

"I found some useful stuff in the Keepers' memories." Neither of them would know otherwise, since only the Morrigan had been acquainted with Siobhan.

I drank some of my ale so I wouldn't have to look at either of them, but I felt Kevin's heavy gaze for a moment before it passed, and knew my efforts at subterfuge had been successful.

"Well, you did quite well," the Morrigan said, passing the next platter. "Sif is one of the best warriors on Asgard. A drawn match is rare."

"I was just lucky." I shrugged. "I really thought I was going to end up on my ass."

The Morrigan leaned in close and spoke quietly. "You should not say such things, especially here, in the Great Hall, with so many others near. Putting yourself down does you no favors, especially with Asgardians. Just say *thank you* and accept the praise." She smiled, then, to soften her words. "I only say this as your advisor, to counsel you as best I can."

I immediately saw her point, but the Hall was noisy enough—with people talking, platters clattering, and dogs barking—that hopefully nobody else had heard.

"I understand." I nodded. "Thank you."

Glancing around, I saw Sif had entered the Hall and was now seated at a nearby table. She saw me, smiled, and lifted her mug. I reciprocated.

Then the room quieted, for Odin had stood.

"The games in honor of our beloved Tyr have ended. We recognize the accomplishments of all the participants, including our honored guests from Midgard." With those words, he gestured to us and nodded once. "Thor, please present the prizes to the winners of each event." As Odin returned to his seat, Thor moved to one side of the dais.

As he announced the winner of each event, shouts of congratulations and cheers of support rang through the Hall. Every winner received a prize from Thor: a finely-tooled leather belt for the runner; a beautifully decorated quiver for the archer; a rune-inscribed axe for the thrower.

On and on it went, until Thor paused and exchanged a brief glance with Odin. I would've missed it if I hadn't been watching, but I didn't have to wait long to find out what that look meant.

"And now, for five special awards. The first is to Arddhu of Midgard, for his exceptional skill at the chess board."

Arddhu was so surprised, he sat unmoving for a moment before rising to accept a finely crafted wooden case. Thor opened it to show a stunning carved chess set inside. Polite applause scattered through the Hall.

"For Lugh of the Túatha de Danann of Midgard, in recognition of his remarkable weight lifting ability—nearly as remarkable as my own—" there were more than a few chuckles at his words "—please accept this pendant."

As Lugh accepted the item, Thor explained its significance to him: it'd been made from a piece of the boulder Lugh had lifted in the contest. Apparently, it was traditional to let them drop to the ground after lifting, and sometimes they broke apart on contact. Thor had asked a master craftsman to take one of the smaller pieces from Lugh's boulder, set it into gold, and attach it to a heavy gold chain.

Lugh received a bit more applause, and even a few scattered cheers.

"For the Morrigan of Eire of Midgard, for her outstanding skill with a blade." The Morrigan received a dagger of fine dwarven steel, complete with a tooled-leather scabbard. Like Arddhu, the Morrigan received spotty applause.

"For his impressive wit and sarcasm employed in the flyting with Loki, I present this next award to Kevin of Midgard, formerly known as Bricriu of Eire." Kevin blinked with surprise, but stood and accepted his prize with grace, to loud applause and more than a few cheers.

Kevin's prize was a gorgeous piece of Celtic knotwork wrought in gold and jewels, but I didn't know what it was. A pendant, maybe? No, it didn't have a chain.

"What is it?" I whispered when he sat down again.

"It's a cloak pin. I haven't seen one like this in centuries. The workmanship is exquisite."

"Last but not least," Thor continued, "for her surprising skill with a sword against Sif, my exceptional warrior wife, and which resulted in a rare and extraordinary drawn match, this dagger is awarded to Deirdre Connor, Keeper of the Sphere and Great Goddess of Midgard."

In hindsight, I should've expected it, but honestly I'd thought a draw was only a small step above a loss.

I stood to a fair amount of applause, and met Sif's eyes. She smiled and nodded at me, and I continued to the dais.

"Well done, Lady," Thor murmured as he passed me the blade.

Unable to resist, I slid it out of its plain leather sheath and gasped. The blade itself was expertly knapped clear crystal, joined to a handle of polished obsidian. I lightly tested the edge against my thumb and even that was enough to slice through my skin. It was a wicked sharp blade, and beautiful as well.

"Thank you." I met Thor's gaze. "This is magnificent."

He smiled and nodded, and I returned to my seat in somewhat of a daze. My companions leaned closer to get a better look at my prize and murmur compliments.

Then Thor took his seat, and Odin stood once again.

"Good people of Asgard, new friends from Midgard, enjoy this feast as we honor Tyr, remember his deeds, and celebrate the games." He raised his cup. "*Skål.*"

The toast was returned with a roar that shook the dust from the rafters, and the feasting began in earnest.

I'd eaten half the meat on my plate and drank most of my ale when my gaze fell on Loki. He smiled and raised his cup, and I raised mine in reply.

"It was very nice of Odin to give us all prizes," the Morrigan said. "Even though we didn't win any of our contests."

"Maybe he wants to be allies as much as we do," I suggested.

She pursed her lips in thought. "It's possible, although I'm more inclined to think we need him much more than he needs us."

She had a point. Ares, Athena, and Kali were more of a threat to Earth than they were to Asgard, although if they destroyed Earth, Asgard would be destroyed, too, since they were connected.

I turned my attention to the rest of my food, and was just thinking about asking Kevin to pass the meat platter again when two things happened simultaneously: Odin rose and left the room, and Thor approached our table.

"The All-Father has granted your request for audience," he said. "Please, come with me."

CHAPTER TEN

W E FOLLOWED THOR down a corridor on the right side of the Hall and into a small chamber. A large table and carved wooden chairs filled most of the space, and Odin sat waiting at the head of it. Twin ravens sat on the posts above his shoulders, watching us closely with their shiny dark eyes.

We sat, and servants quickly poured goblets of mead for each of us. Leaving the pitcher on the table, they closed the heavy door behind them, cutting off the noise from the Hall.

"You said you wished to discuss important matters," Odin said to Arddhu. "I am now ready to hear your words."

Arddhu's eyes met mine, and I nodded. Let him open the discussion. I'd jump in when and where necessary.

"Respectfully, we formally request an alliance between our two peoples," Arddhu said. "Especially as it relates to defending Midgard against three deities who are actively working against the long-term survival of the planet."

"If you are referring to Ares, Athena, and Kali," Odin said, looking toward the door and nodding, "yes, we are well aware."

Loki had entered, and now he also sat at the table. The room was silent as he apparently waited for some cue from Odin before speaking. "We have had a visit from Ares, who has also requested an alliance." Loki met my gaze. "Of course, we heard his urgent plea but politely declined."

Odin spoke. "We declined, not for any reasons you may think, but simply because we have no wish to involve Asgard in any of Midgard's quarrels."

"But it's not just a quarrel," I said, and all heads swiveled toward me. "And it doesn't just involve Midgard. Asgard is also involved, since it's connected to Earth. If Ares successfully destroys Earth, Asgard will also be destroyed."

"There are many realms physically connected to Earth," Arddhu added. "All our fates are entwined. If Earth is destroyed, so too are all the connected realms. Countless billions of lives are at stake, All-Father."

Odin's single eye stared at each of us in turn for a moment, then fixed on me. "I am well aware that the worlds are connected. I am, after all, Protector of the Nine Realms. But what is this nonsense about Ares planning to destroy Midgard?"

Before any of us could reply, one of the ravens cawed, and it startled me so much, I flinched. Odin turned to the raven, and as the long moment of silence stretched, it seemed they were locked in conversation.

After another moment, he slumped in his chair and muttered, "Shit."

I bit my lip to keep from laughing inappropriately. He'd been so eloquent and formal until now, somehow his muttering of that single word seemed humorously incongruous.

"Father?" Thor asked, concerned. "What is it?"

"It is true." Odin shook his head. "The Olympians have created another world and will destroy Midgard before fleeing." He turned to me. "What are your plans to counter this? Before I agree to ally with you, I must know how you will deal with the Olympians."

The Olympians? What about Kali? My brain stuttered for a moment.

"Well?" Odin demanded.

Dammit. I didn't *have* a plan. Not yet. But I couldn't exactly say that.

"We're not exactly sure where they are, so I'll have to gather more information before deciding what to do with them."

"Some goddess you are." His lip curled in disgust. "They are on Olympus even as we speak. How do you not know this?"

Loki interrupted. "All-Father, she is but a young goddess, and has little experience dealing with situations such as this."

Odin sighed heavily. "Of course. I had forgotten." He shook his head again, but spoke a bit more kindly. "As I see it, you have few options. Banish them to another realm, or destroy them. Choose one."

"I was actually hoping I could just talk to them and convince them to leave Earth alone."

He snorted. "It is never wise to allow enemies the opportunity to destroy you. You must destroy them first."

"I understand that. And you're right, it probably won't be an option. But I want to try it first anyway, because the very last thing I want to do, as a new goddess, is destroy other deities unless I absolutely have no other choice." I smiled weakly. "I must try diplomacy first."

He studied me for a moment. "That is commendable, and appreciated by those of us who are other deities. However, in this case, diplomacy will most likely fail, and you will have little choice in the matter. And when these meddlesome Olympians are eliminated, the threat to Midgard and all the other realms is also eliminated."

"Of course," I agreed. "And believe me, if, as you say, diplomacy fails, I *will* eliminate them immediately."

Odin's brow rose. "You believe you have the power to do so? With no assistance from any others?"

I raised my chin a bit. "Of course I do. I have the power of the Goddess."

"And the power of the Sphere," Arddhu said.

"With some wild forest magick thrown in for good measure," Kevin added.

"All-Father," the Morrigan said quietly but firmly, "she has the power."

He studied me for a moment longer, then nodded. "Then you have your alliance, Lady. But do not fail. I do not wish to hasten Ragnarök."

Finally. He'd made me work for it, but at least I didn't have to play any more stupid games.

"Thank you, All-Father," I said.

He raised his cup. "Let us toast this new alliance between Asgard and Midgard."

We all raised our cups and drank, and with competing squawks, the ravens flapped their wings simultaneously, as if they, too, celebrated.

As I placed my cup on the table, Loki's voice spoke in my head. *"Well done, Lady. Now, for all our sakes, please don't fuck it up."* Shit. As if I needed any more pressure.

In unspoken agreement, we didn't return to the celebration in the Great Hall but simply made a beeline to my room.

Once again, I slipped a sound shield around us as soon as the door was closed.

"Well, we have our alliance," Lugh said. "So I consider this visit a resounding success."

"And we know where Ares, Athena, and Kali are," Kevin added.

"Actually, not Kali," I pointed out. "Odin specifically said, *the Olympians*. Kali is definitely not an Olympian."

"Oh fuck." His eyes widened. "You're absolutely right. How did I miss that?"

"You weren't the only one," the Morrigan said with disgust. "I guess I was too busy thinking about what Odin said about their big plan."

Arddhu shook his head. "It is worse than we had thought. We must confront Ares and Athena as soon as possible."

I sighed. It seemed those two troublemakers were my top priority now.

It was always something. Why couldn't I catch a damn break?

"We'll worry about that when we get back," I said. "Let's try to get some sleep."

That night, Arddhu stayed with me, and I slept peacefully in his arms through the night, as I had with Kevin the night before.

The nightmare didn't trouble me, and it was wonderful.

The next morning, we collected our things—including the precious gifts we'd been given—and after another hearty breakfast, we said our goodbyes to the Æsir and took our leave of the legendary Asgard.

At the guardhouse, Heimdallr wished us farewell, and at about the same spot where we'd arrived, Arddhu opened the portal.

We stepped through, and I took a deep breath of *home*.

It was mid-morning in Scottsdale, and at about ninety degrees it was already too warm for my jeans and light sweater. As we walked toward the house, I changed into shorts and a tee.

It never got old, being able to do that.

I glanced around, appreciating being home. It was another gorgeous day in early March, with a cloudless blue sky and a light breeze rustling the palm fronds. It was the sort of day that drew thousands of people from colder climates, and one of the main reasons Arizonans loved living here.

The Morrigan was the first to speak. "So now that we know where they are, why don't we take a little trip to Olympus?"

"I've been thinking about that," I said. "Maybe I should go myself. Keep it low-key. If we all went, they'd probably think we were starting a war."

She snorted. "They're the ones who are starting the war. Besides, I don't think you should go alone."

"I second that," Kevin said, and Arddhu wasn't far behind with his agreement.

"Why not?" I protested.

Any answers were delayed when Joe, on duty near the backyard, saw us approach. "All quiet while you were gone," he called.

"Good to hear," I replied with a smile.

"You four should go discuss your differences of opinion," Lugh said with a smirk. "As for me, I'm going home." He waved goodbye, then quickly turned back to the portal.

But I was exhausted. Despite the good night's sleep, I just wanted to relax and not think for a while.

"You know, I don't want to do this right now," I said to the others.

"The sooner we talk about it," the Morrigan said, "the sooner we can resolve it."

"Please, not right now," I repeated, opening a panel in the window wall and stepping inside. I ported the crystal dagger to my room and plopped down on the couch. "I'm tired and getting cranky. I just want some quiet time."

Especially after the zoo that'd been Asgard for the past three days. Between the feasting, the games, and the lessons with Loki, I was *so done*.

And that wasn't even taking my big news of the pregnancy into consideration.

"Well, you're not going to get it just yet," Randy said as he entered the room. "There's a delegation at the gate. This time it's Native American."

Native? What could they—oh. They were probably here about Jason. Or maybe Nayenezgani.

I modified the wards accordingly. "Okay, wards are open."

Randy radioed the front gate, and I sighed. So much for a bit of peace and quiet.

Before anyone could remind me about dressing appropriately for meeting an official delegation, I changed my shorts and tee into a pretty sundress and set my glow to a medium level.

"Hey," Kevin said, taking Arddhu by the arm. "You don't need either of us, so we'll be in the office, on the computer."

I nodded to them and asked the Morrigan, "Will you stay?"

"Of course."

We stood in the shade under the porte cochere, waiting for the delegation. A moment later, a long shiny black SUV arrived and parked in front of us.

Several gentlemen got out, dressed in a variety of clothing styles. One wore a suit with no tie and dark sunglasses, two others wore business casual. The last of the four wore a cowboy hat, ostrich leather boots, bolo tie with a button-down shirt, and a large, ornate rodeo-style buckle on the tooled leather belt around the waist of his jeans.

The gentleman in the dark suit and sunglasses took the lead. His crisp white shirt was unbuttoned at the neck, which showed off a carved turquoise bear amulet. His long dark hair was liberally streaked with silver and bound in two braids that lay over his shoulders, and his tanned face was deeply seamed. He removed his sunglasses and met my gaze with startling gray eyes.

"Greetings, Earth Goddess. I am Sani Cooper, President of the Southwestern Native American Inter-tribal Council. These are my associates." He turned and briefly introduced the other three, noting that all were elders of local tribes.

"Welcome to my home, gentlemen. This is my Chief Political Advisor, the Morrigan, who is also the Irish Goddess of Battlefield Death." That got a few impressed murmurs among the group. "Please come in and make yourselves comfortable while I round up some refreshments." I led them to the living room area, where I realized there wasn't enough seating and quickly created a couple of extra chairs. If anyone noticed my use of power, they didn't comment on it.

I turned toward the kitchen to gather refreshments, and blinked as Brianna was already there, putting the finishing touches on trays of tea and biscuits.

"Trust me," she murmured. Picking up one of the trays, she nodded at the second one in a wordless request.

"Always," I replied, and took the other tray.

I did trust her; it was part of her magick to know what food to serve when.

She served the tea and I followed with the biscuits.

Three of the visitors were on the sofa, and Sani had chosen one of the chairs. He smiled at us both, and the corners of his eyes crinkled into deep creases. "This is quite thoughtful. It has been a very hectic day for us."

Brianna returned his smile, placed her tray on the coffee table, and left us to our business.

I placed my tray beside hers and sat in the chair nearest Sani, since he seemed to be the one I'd be speaking with the most. The Morrigan took the last open seat.

"These are delicious," one of the other gentlemen said—I think his name was Joseph—after a bite of biscuit. "And the tea is paired perfectly." The others nodded and smiled in polite agreement.

Intrigued, I took a bite of biscuit and tasted a delightful burst of lemon, with a hint of something fragrant, almost flowery. Next, I sipped the tea. Citrusy and herbal, with a hint of honey sweetness, it was, indeed, perfect with the biscuit.

Once again, Brianna had outdone herself.

"To what do I owe the honor of your visit?" I asked Sani.

"We are here for several reasons," he replied. "First, we bring greetings from the Algonquin people of Quebec, and a gift from them in gratitude for Your destruction of Malsumis, the Evil God of Chaos and Tricks."

Malsumis? I blinked at him for a moment, confused. Oh wait—at that first mission, the one that had claimed his life, Jason had mentioned that Malsumis belonged to the Algonquin people. I'd completely forgotten until now, to be honest.

Sani carefully set his tea on the table beside him and produced a small box from his inside jacket pocket. Nestling the box in both hands in a somewhat formal gesture, he offered it to me. "This is their thank-gift."

Although I hadn't expected anything, I wasn't sure of the protocol here. I sure didn't want to offend by refusing. So I took the box, removed the lid, and found a simple stone pendant on a delicate silver chain.

Simple, but gorgeous.

The carved sphere of brilliant blue turquoise was naturally marbled with swirls of creamy white and splotches of dark green, making it look like a miniature Earth.

"This is stunning. Please tell them I'm pleased I was able to remove an enemy of my friends."

He smiled and nodded. "I will do so."

I set the box aside. "You mentioned your council is inter-tribal. Does it include the Navajo people, by chance?"

"Oh, yes." Sani nodded again. "I, myself, am of the Diné."

"Please accept my deepest condolences on the loss of Nayenezgani, Slayer of Alien Gods, and one of my allies. He was fierce and fought bravely in last year's war against Cromm Crúaich of Ireland. We wouldn't have been victorious without him, and we honor his memory and courage."

While I'd been speaking, Sani had bowed his head. I'd thought it'd been in respect, but when he looked up at me after I'd finished, tears shone in his eyes.

"I had not heard the Slayer was no more. He was beloved by many. My people will mourn deeply." He inclined his head. "Thank You for telling us."

He sipped some tea and nibbled on a biscuit, and I waited a moment before continuing.

"On a related topic, I'd like your help, if I may. We lost another warrior last year, but unfortunately I don't know his full name or tribal affiliation. I only know his first name was Jason, and he gave his life defending us against Malsumis. He fought bravely and should be honored by his people, but I don't know how to make that happen."

Belatedly, I realized I could've asked Anthony to get Jason's information from the firm, but it was too late now that I'd mentioned it to Sani.

He smiled warmly. "It seems You were his people, and You have already honored him. But if it will ease Your discomfort, we will include Jason in our upcoming ceremony for fallen warriors."

That would have to be enough. "Thank you."

Sani sipped his tea, then set the cup down. "As to the other reason for our visit, I fear I must now be blunt. You are Earth Goddess. Surely You are aware Earth is suffering. What are Your plans?"

I hesitated for a moment and glanced at the Morrigan; how much should I say?

She smoothly responded. "She has already started healing the planet. In fact, you should have been hearing Earthsong again."

Sani nodded. "Yes, one of our village Grandmothers has heard what you call the Earthsong, and has wept with joy. Unfortunately, not everyone is able to hear it, but we look forward to the day we can all listen to the Earth sing her song."

I smiled at him. "That should be within the next couple of months. I'm close to beginning the final healing phase. When that's done, the air and water will be pure and clean again. Forests will regrow. Plants and animals will thrive again."

"That is wonderful news," Sami said. "I will tell my people to watch and wait."

Unexpectedly, he placed his hand over mine on the armrest. A sudden flash of power jumped from me to him, and his eyes widened.

I'm sure I looked just as surprised.

Sani blinked at me in wonder, then squeezed my hand. "Earth Goddess, You have taken away the pain and swelling in my hands and knees. I am grateful to You yet again."

So I'd—what? Healed his arthritis? Without thinking or even knowing about it?

Huh. This was new.

I glanced again at the Morrigan, whose gaze met mine with as much surprise as I felt. To Sani, I said, "I'm glad I was able to help you. You have honored me with your visit."

Releasing my hand almost reluctantly, he flexed his fingers with a grin, and took a final sip of his tea. The others had already placed their empty cups and plates on the coffee table; they'd completely devoured all the biscuits and tea. He placed his cup with the others, then stood. "We will leave You in peace now. Thank You for Your hospitality, Earth Goddess."

Everyone else stood, me included.

"Please don't hesitate to contact me if I can help you and your people with anything." I escorted them to the front door.

Sani had been the only one who'd done any talking. Why had the others come along, anyway? Just to say they met me?

"Certainly," Sani replied.

"Be well," I said in farewell, and they piled into the SUV and drove off.

I closed the front door and leaned against it with a sigh.

"You did well," the Morrigan said. She nibbled at her biscuit, made a face, and put it back on her plate. "Healing him was a nice touch."

I shook my head. "I didn't even know I was doing it. It just happened."

"Ah. I wondered why you were so surprised." One eyebrow rose. "How interesting."

Before I could even begin to pick up the dishes, Brianna was back.

"I'll take care of this," she said, and smiled with satisfaction at the devastation on the trays.

"So what was the significance of the tea and biscuits?" I asked. "They really loved it all."

Brianna smiled again. "Oh, it wasn't official or anything like that. I just had a hunch they'd enjoy some bright, natural flavors like citrus and herbs." Her smile faded when she saw the half-nibbled biscuit that the Morrigan had left on her plate. She eyed the Morrigan for a moment, took the trays to the kitchen, then returned with a package of large chocolate chip cookies. She opened it and offered two to the Morrigan, whose eyes lit up as she snatched the cookies from Brianna's hand. A second later, she reached into the package for another two, hesitated, then grinned as she grabbed two more.

Holy shit. *Six cookies?* I'd had no idea the Morrigan loved chocolate so much, but now that I knew, it could be useful for future reference. Like, for a bribe or two.

Brianna gave the Morrigan an answering grin, then went back to the kitchen and began cleaning up.

Between bites of cookie, the Morrigan asked, "So which realm are we visiting next?"

"Hell if I know. I'd have to ask Lugh."

As she enjoyed her chocolate fix, I debated whether or not I should ask her opinion on my situation. I trusted her to keep it secret, and I trusted her judgment.

So I asked, "Hey, do you have a couple of minutes? I could use your opinion on something."

"Sure," she replied around a mouthful of cookie.

"Let's go for a walk." I didn't want to take a chance of being interrupted—or overheard—by the guys.

She shrugged, and we headed out past the patio.

Then I faltered. Where to start?

"I think I'm pregnant," I blurted.

"I'm not surprised." She'd finished chewing this time. "I figured you were."

"What?" I stopped in my tracks. "How?"

She shrugged again. "Intuition, maybe. Nothing you said or did." We continued walking. "Anyone else know?"

I couldn't lie to her. "Me. You. Loki."

"*Loki?*" She laughed. "How'd that wily old snake find out?"

"He sort of scanned me or something, then asked if I knew I was with child. Of course, I didn't. Then Anu confirmed it." I sighed. "Shit. I don't even know how far along I am. I don't really remember when my last period was."

She nodded. "A lot's been going on. It's easy to lose track sometimes." After a few more steps, she added, "So what do you want to do?"

"Well, first I want to take a home pregnancy test. Then I'll have to find a doctor. Oh, and I'll have to tell the guys. Then... well, actually, that's as far as I've gotten."

She stopped and turned toward me, eyes bright. "I know. Let's go on a field trip to the local drug store."

She seemed so excited, I had to laugh. Then I sobered. "It wouldn't be that much fun. We'd have to take security with us."

"So, bring Nat along. It'll be a girl's day out."

She made it all sound so simple.

Then again, maybe it was. Maybe I was just making it more complicated than I needed to.

"Okay. It's a date. Um, so-to-speak."

She opened her mouth and said something, but I didn't hear it. The sudden cacophony in my head was deafening, as if a thousand panicked voices cried out at the same time. No, wait... not exactly voices. I discerned humans yelling and wild animals screaming.

What the hell was going on?

With effort, I blocked the noise and took a breath. "Did you hear that?"

She frowned. "Hear what?"

Not knowing what I was looking for, my eyes darted from horizon to horizon as I tried to pinpoint the source of that infernal noise. Then I saw the haze of smoke rising far to the north, and pointed. "That."

It was probably a brushfire, which were fairly common here in Arizona. But it seemed way too close to the Phoenix metropolitan area, and somehow, it seemed different from others I'd seen in the past.

Then again, this time I could hear and feel the terror of hundreds of forest animals and humans in the fire's path.

"I have to go," I said.

"Wait." She reached out to me.

But I couldn't wait. Every moment delayed was just more destruction, so I ported directly to the site.

Surrounded by searing flames and thick smoke that made my eyes burn and sting, I stumbled through charred vegetation and quickly realized

I was too close to see anything useful. I needed to see the bigger picture. I needed a bird's-eye view.

I rose about a hundred feet into the air and surveyed the damage.

The flames had already burned a significant area of open brush as well as partial woodland. A small group of houses at the edge of the tree line were in the direct path of the fire. A little further down the road, a sleepy little town was also in danger.

Judging by the terrain, I figured I was somewhere in the Tonto National Forest between Scottsdale and Payson, near the Mogollon Rim. This was a popular area for Phoenix residents to have vacation homes and cabins, but there were also lots of small towns scattered along the forest roads.

Those towns would also be in immediate danger. Unless I did something, and did it now.

My first thought was to pull water from the closest lake—Roosevelt Lake to the southeast—and douse the fire with it. But the area was just too massive, and I wasn't sure how I could move that much water such a long distance.

Then I remembered my lessons with Loki.

Using the elemental magick he'd shown me, I reached out to Fire and asked it to stop.

Nothing happened, except the flames seemed to grow and leap even higher. I thought I heard gleeful laughter, but it could've been my imagination.

Shit.

I closed my eyes and tried again, this time adding the strength of a command to my request.

A moment later, I sensed rather than heard a long sigh. When I opened my eyes, the flames had winked out around me as far as I could see, leaving a smoky, charred mess behind. I thanked Fire for complying, but didn't get any response.

Next, I connected with Water and asked it to soak the ground just enough to keep the dormant Fire from reigniting.

Water didn't give me any shit, just complied immediately.

Still floating in midair, I surveyed my work and breathed a sigh of relief. Most of the trees and the entire group of houses had been saved. The small town down the road was safe.

I'd been in time to make a difference.

Then my eye caught the group of people beside the dirt road about a hundred yards away. Some looked like local residents from the small town down the road, but others were dressed in firefighting gear.

And every single one of them held their mobile phones up.

Recording me.

Shit.

I hadn't stopped to think about being seen. All I'd thought of was getting the fire out as soon as possible. In hindsight, I should've made myself invisible.

Too late now.

But I immediately ported back home, right where I'd left the Morrigan. Surprisingly, she was still there. Her nostrils flared at the odor of acrid smoke rolling off me. I glanced down at my pretty little sundress, now ruined with soot, and fought off a wave of dizziness.

"I take it you saved the day," she said drily.

"Yeah." Now I was even more exhausted, and had to tap into Anu's reservoir for a boost of energy to even stay on my feet. "But I was seen doing it. And I was recorded by mobile phone cameras. Quite a few, actually."

She sighed. "Well, it was bound to happen sooner or later. It's one of the reasons I wanted you to wait." She shrugged. "But that doesn't matter now. And you probably saved some lives, so there's that."

I desperately wanted to change my clothes, but first I wanted a shower—a real one, not a magickal one—to get the stink off me.

As we headed back to the house, I asked, "What do you think will happen?"

"Honestly, I have no idea. Kevin's the one to ask. He's got a better handle on the effects of social media than I do."

It probably all depended on the answers to two questions: how long until the videos were uploaded to the internet, and how many views would they get?

CHAPTER ELEVEN

A S IT TURNED out, it didn't take long at all for the videos to hit the internet and cause a viral response.

By the time I'd showered off the stink of smoke and dressed in clean clothes, the Morrigan had corralled Kevin, Arddhu, and Anthony. They waited at the kitchen island with concerned expressions, which made me nervous.

Wordlessly, Kevin placed his cellphone on the granite in front of me and touched the screen. A video began to play, and even with the audio of people talking excitedly and swearing prolifically, I could still hear the crackle and pop of the brush fire in the background.

Whoever posted the video, probably one of the local residents, had apparently been recording the fire's advance toward the small group of houses when I showed up. I watched myself suddenly appear on screen, rising above the smoke and flames, then hovering in the air. "*Do you see that?*" someone asked, while someone else simply said, "*what the fuck.*" The video shook a little as it zoomed in on me, probably from the person's excitement.

My heart dropped as the screen was filled with my clear and recognizable face. "*Holy shit,*" someone said, and the camera zoomed out again, just in time to capture the sudden extinguishing of the flames.

At the time, I hadn't realized my hands had reached out toward the fire, since I'd had my eyes closed while I'd worked my magick. But seeing it on the video made it fairly obvious to anyone watching that I'd put out the fire.

The audio was a mess of confusion, surprise, and even more profanity. The person recording said a few choice words himself, but he continued to keep the video centered on me while I finished up my elemental work. Then, he'd captured the moment I'd turned and seen the crowd, and even zoomed in on my face again. My expression of dismayed surprise was almost comical. Of course, that was when I'd ported home, captured on the video as my sudden disappearance. Immediately, the audio erupted in even more excited profanity. Finally, mercifully, the video ended.

"This is just one of the hundred or so videos uploaded in the past ten minutes." Kevin tapped the screen and closed the app. "So, you're pretty much famous now." He didn't look at me as he put his phone away, and I knew he was pissed at me for being so careless.

I tried to smile. "Um... oops?"

Arddhu shook his head, but didn't seem too upset. "It was inevitable. These devices are in such widespread use, I am actually more surprised it took this long."

That didn't make sense. "But this was the first time I've done anything like this."

"He means other deities," Anthony explained. "It was just a matter of time before someone somewhere got a video of some deity doing something impossible. It's just that the deity happens to be you."

Oh.

I smiled sheepishly. "Well, maybe we can make lemonade out of these lemons." At Arddhu's puzzled expression, I clarified. "Maybe we can turn this to our advantage."

"That's possible," Anthony said. "But it could also cause a lot more problems. These videos have already gone viral." He was turned toward me, so he kept talking and didn't see Arddhu's confused expression. "The way I see it, people will split into at least two factions: those who believe the videos are real and think you're some kind of angel sent by their god; and those who will never believe this really happened and that the videos are what's called deep-fakes."

Kevin had been fiddling with his phone again. Now, he said, "Well, there's at least one problem with your theory. Since there's more than one video, taken from more than one angle and uploaded by more than a single source, a deep-fake theory wouldn't gain any traction. But, to your point, I think most people will probably think it's some kind of movie-promo stunt. They'll say there were invisible wires holding Dee up, and a fake fire. Something like that."

"But the fire damage was real," I protested. "They were there. They were terrified of losing their homes."

Kevin shrugged. "Sometimes, people believe the most ridiculous shit instead of the truth."

This was madness.

"We should definitely discuss this further." Anthony gestured at Kevin's phone. "In the meantime, I'll continue to monitor social media for the fallout, and meet with Ogma to come up with some options. As you said, Dee, there's always a chance we can use this to our advantage."

"We should probably have a Council meeting next week," the Morrigan said. "I don't think we need to include everyone, though. Just the key members."

I knew what she meant; we didn't need to get the new ambassadors involved in this. Instead, we'd brief them at the next full Council meeting.

"That's a good idea," Anthony said. "If you all agree, I'll get it on the schedule and notify the appropriate members."

We all did agree, and Anthony left.

I studied Kevin, who continued to stare at his screen with a frown. He was probably watching the other videos, if I had to guess. He must've sensed me watching him; he looked up at me.

"I just have a bad feeling about all this," he said.

"She'll be fine," the Morrigan told him. To me, she asked, "Isn't it time to go see Nat?"

Oh. That.

"Why? Is something wrong?" Arddhu asked, frowning.

"Nope," she said. "just some girl stuff."

"Girl stuff?" He continued frowning.

"Probably something to do with their reproductive organs," Kevin said.

"Oh. I see." Arddhu held up a hand. "We will talk when you return."

We left the guys in the kitchen and headed toward the guest house.

"Works every time," the Morrigan said, and I had to laugh.

Randy answered my knock, and when I asked for Nat, he stepped aside. "Sure. Come on in. I'll let her know you're here." After doing so, he went to the kitchen, where he was prepping vegetables for some kind of dish.

A moment later, Nat entered the living room with a towel around her neck and sweat glistening on her face. She looked like she'd been working out. "What's up?"

"We need to go on an errand, and we'd like you to come along," I explained.

From the corner of my eye, I saw Randy glance up in surprise before immediately ducking his head down again.

"My shift starts in a couple of hours," Nat said with a frown.

"We'll be back way before then," the Morrigan assured her. "This is just a quick run to the store."

"Okay," Nat shrugged. "Let me change and I'll be right back."

Within a few minutes the three of us were on our way to the drug store a couple of miles away.

It'd been so long since I'd driven anywhere, I'd almost asked her to drive instead. Mike used to drive everywhere, but then I'd just ported where I'd needed to go.

But by the time I'd pulled into the parking lot, it felt good to be behind the wheel again.

I parked in a spot near the entrance and double-checked my glow to make sure it was completely off. I wanted absolutely no attention whatsoever. This was just a quick in and out.

Inside the store, we headed straight for the pharmacy area in the back, where I assumed the pregnancy tests were located. But on the way, the Morrigan got distracted by the hair care aisle and waved us to continue on without her.

Thankfully, my assumption was correct; the pregnancy tests weren't far from the pharmacy counter. For a moment, I just stared at such a wide selection.

"Shit," I mumbled. "Why are there so many?" I wished I'd done some internet research on which ones were the most accurate and reliable.

Nat pointed to a box on the shelf. "That's a good brand. And it has two tests, so you can retake it if something happens to the first." She smiled wryly. "One time, I accidentally dropped it in the toilet."

That was good to know.

"Thanks." She hadn't asked any questions, so I was also grateful for her professionalism.

On our way back to the checkout in front of the store, the Morrigan rejoined us. She'd found a hairbrush she liked.

"I'll get that for you," I told her.

The cashier was polite and friendly. I don't know why I expected anything different, but she didn't bat an eye at the pregnancy test.

Of course not. Why would she? Sometimes I was such an idiot.

I paid with my debit card and declined to apply for a loyalty card, and after a moment she handed me the bag and a receipt long enough to use as emergency toilet paper. I'd just taken them when all hell broke loose.

"That's her," someone said, way too loudly and excitedly. "I'm telling you, that's *her*."

Reluctantly, I turned toward the voice. Two women were at the entrance, actually standing on the pad that held the automatic doors open. One of the women pointed her finger at me.

"You're that woman on the fire videos," she said. "You an angel?"

The other woman scoffed. "Angels don't shop *here*, Karen."

"Maybe she's an alien, then," the first woman said, not taking her eyes off me.

What the fuck.

They blocked the exit, and unless I forced my way through them, I was trapped. Sure, I could probably just port us all home, but disappearing in front of everyone would probably make things even worse. Besides, I didn't want to leave my SUV in the parking lot.

In my moment of indecision, Nat took control. She barreled forward confidently, with a forceful "Excuse us, ladies." She never stopped, just kept on walking, and the women stumbled out of the way.

The Morrigan and I followed on Nat's heels. I'd almost made it through the door when someone grabbed my right arm.

It was the first woman, still loud and demanding. "Hey, you can't just leave," she said. Her friend was fumbling with her phone.

Shit. That's the *last* thing I needed.

I'd just opened my mouth to say something—not exactly sure what—when Nat grabbed my left arm. "Sorry ladies, gotta go," she said.

Unfortunately, the woman hadn't let go of me, and now I felt like a toy being fought over.

Without warning, Nat punched the woman in the face. She immediately screamed and released my arm. As we ran to the SUV, Nat said, "Keys." I gave them over, gladly. We piled in, and I noticed my hands shook a little. Adrenaline, I figured, as we backed out of the parking spot and waited for traffic to clear on the street.

Nothing like that had ever happened to me. Was this what I could expect from now on? Shit, I hoped not. The celebrity life just wasn't for me. Maybe I should lay low for a while. Maybe I should pick up a pair of those enormous sunglasses, the super-dark ones that celebrities used.

"Shit," Nat said, watching in the rearview mirror. "That other bitch came out and snapped your plate."

That *was* shit.

Traffic had finally cleared, and now she turned onto the street and headed home. For the whole ten minute drive, I kept turning in my seat, irrationally expecting to see the flashing lights of a police car in pursuit.

Of course, we made it home with no issues. The rush of adrenaline left me a bit shaky still, so I collapsed onto a stool at the kitchen island. The Morrigan and Nat joined me, and we sat in silence for a moment.

"Nice right hook," the Morrigan told Nat.

Nat and I shared a glance, and that's all it took. She burst out laughing, and then I couldn't hold it in, either. The Morrigan joined in, and for the next few minutes the three of us laughed so hard, we were almost hysterical.

Finally, taking a deep breath, I wiped the tears from my cheeks and dug around in the bag for the hairbrush. I ported the bag with the pregnancy test to my room.

"Happy birthday." I handed her the brush.

"Huh?" She frowned. "It's not my birthday."

That got me going again, which got Nat going again too. This time, the Morrigan didn't see the humor, and just shook her head.

"Sorry," I gasped. "It's just an expression."

"I see." She cocked a brow. "Well, I think I'll go read for a while."

After she left, I took another deep breath. My face and stomach hurt from all the laughing, but it felt good.

I couldn't actually remember the last time I'd laughed so hard.

"That was a fun errand," Nat said.

I shook my head. "I really didn't think something like that would happen. Otherwise, I never would've gone. I would've just ordered it online."

She smiled ruefully. "Well, you're a celebrity now. It'll probably only get worse."

Shit. She must've seen the videos from the brushfire. "I guess I should probably stay out of sight from now on."

She eyed me. "Or, you could just tell me what you need, and I'll get it for you. It's no big deal."

She had a point. "Thanks. I appreciate it."

She studied me for a moment. "So... what will you do if it's positive?"

"Find a doctor, I guess."

"The firm probably has someone you can see. The less questions the better, right?"

"That's what I was thinking, yeah."

She nodded. "I'll see what I can find out for you. So you don't have to talk to Anthony about... well, it."

I smiled at her. "You're a godsend, Nat. Seriously. Thank you."

She opened her mouth to say more, but just then the handheld radio base came to life with a call from the guardhouse: the Scottsdale police department was at the front gate, wanting to interview me.

Shit. That hadn't taken long.

I quickly modified the wards and thumbed the talk button. "Okay, send them in."

"I'll get Anthony," Nat said, and hailed him on her handheld. She took a moment to brief him on what happened.

It was smart of her to call him, since he was my legal representative in addition to being my assistant and Chief Administrator.

In the living room, I paced nervously. I'd never been in trouble before or talked to police, so I was too keyed up to sit.

Anthony showed up a heartbeat later.

"Nat, please stay and give witness testimony. Dee, just answer truthfully, and stay calm. You've got nothing to worry about."

That made me feel better. So while Nat and I sat, he went to the front door and greeted the two officers.

After the introductions, we learned the woman Nat punched had filed a formal complaint, and the officers were duty-bound to investigate. However, neither of the two women had mentioned their own actions and how they'd provoked a response. It only took Nat and I a few minutes to explain everything, and one of the officers mentioned the cashier had corroborated our story.

The officers sympathized, and asked if I wished to pursue assault charges. I didn't need to see Anthony's subtle head shake to know I should decline. To wrap up the investigation, the officers planned to review the store's security camera footage, and would contact us if they had any additional questions.

As Anthony showed the officers to the door, I slumped in my chair.

The entire visit had taken less than ten minutes, but the surge of adrenaline now left me drained.

"See? No problem," Anthony said.

I thanked him, and after he left, Nat stood.

"I'll get back to you on what we talked about earlier." She grinned. "Thanks for the adventure."

"Sure." I went to my suite to do the pregnancy test.

This was actually the first one I'd ever done; I'd always been responsible with birth control and had never had any pregnancy scares. I supposed that's why part of me didn't really believe I was pregnant, despite both Loki and Anu telling me so, and neither had any reason to lie.

The instructions were incredibly simple, and I didn't accidentally drop the damn thing in the toilet. But the test immediately and clearly showed a positive result, almost before I'd even finished peeing on it. I didn't even need to wait the expected five minutes.

Seeing those two bright pink lines on the little test window made it all real for me in a way it hadn't been until just this moment.

I stared at that little window for a moment, then started laughing and couldn't stop.

It would've made an interesting photo: me, sitting on the toilet, pants down around my ankles, a pregnancy test strip in one hand and the other on my belly as I laughed so hard my stomach muscles cramped and tears streamed down my cheeks.

It wasn't even that funny. Maybe it was just the stress and adrenaline peaks from the past couple of days. Or maybe it was hormones. I'd heard something about hormones causing laughing jags.

Shit. How could this have happened?

Well, I mean, I knew *how*, but I'd been so careful with my herbs. I was pretty sure I hadn't forgotten to take any. Maybe it had something to do with my transition to deity.

Oh shit. What if Arddhu's wild forest magick had negated my birth control? Kevin had told me Arddhu was a fertility god, so it would make sense if his power had blown through my defenses.

So-to-speak.

I got myself back together, sent both the used and unused tests to my pocket universe, and splashed some cold water on my face. Then, my legs shook so badly I had to sit on the toilet lid for a moment.

My mind was a jumble of all the challenges involved with having a baby and raising a child, healing Earth and being the Goddess, and dealing with the threat of war. Oh, and then there were Ares, Athena, and Kali.

It was all too much. Just too fucking much.

Breathe. One step at a time.

First, I'd see the doctor that Nat would find for me. In the meantime, I had more healing to do for Earth, prayers to answer, and a Council meeting to prepare for, all of which should keep me plenty busy so I wouldn't obsess too much over this.

I hoped so, anyway.

CHAPTER TWELVE

T HE COUNCIL MEETING was scheduled for the end of the third week of March, just a little over a week away. We'd had to push it out a week due to the Túatha having prior commitments they couldn't reschedule. Something about business licensing meetings with various city councils.

So, in the meantime, I continued the healing sessions for Earth and answering prayers. Anthony and Ogma continued to assess the social media reaction to the viral videos of me extinguishing the brush fire.

Just as Kevin had predicted, a lot of conspiracy theories were floating around. But there were also a surprising number of people who believed in me, which meant now I had even more prayers to answer.

Something else had happened, too, something I hadn't planned for, although in hindsight I probably should've expected it.

Only a couple of days after the videos were posted, an enterprising young journalist had somehow identified me by name, based on some old college photos I hadn't even known were out on the internet. Now, there were a number of tabloids trying to guess who—or what—I really was, and some of the stories were absolutely insane: the most far-fetched ones claimed I was a government experiment gone wrong, or some kind of genetic mutation, or an alien-human hybrid.

It'd be hilarious if it weren't so fucked up.

Ogma and Anthony had been busy with the social media accounts they'd set up for me, fielding requests from various media outlets, podcasters, radio talk show hosts, and journalists, all of whom wanted statements or interviews. So far they'd been turned down, but we knew we'd need to do something soon. We really needed to figure out how to handle all this attention, and use it to my advantage.

But it was also scary. How long until someone found The Hacienda, or even Ard na Mara? So far, the only things anyone knew about me as the Keeper Goddess was I lived in Arizona.

Anthony pointed out that Mike had used some kind of shell company set up by the firm when he'd purchased The Hacienda for me, so it should be almost impossible for anyone to find me. But even if they did, the wards would keep them from getting past the gates or perimeter fencing.

On the other hand, it wouldn't keep anyone from flying a helicopter or drone overhead and taking photos or otherwise invading my privacy. So, as a precaution, I added a special layer of wards to the entire property to hide us from view. Anyone flying a drone or other aircraft would only see empty desert.

Which would also work for satellites, probably.

Not a perfect solution, but it'd have to be good enough.

Another new development had started keeping me busier lately: the need to intervene in more frequent and extreme climate-related events. Just in the past week alone, I'd shifted a huge snowstorm from the East Coast out into the Atlantic; calmed a tsunami off Japan by working directly with Water; redirected a freak string of tornadoes in Oklahoma; and stopped catastrophic flooding in Afghanistan, again by working with Water.

But this time, before I'd even ported away to any of those places, I'd made myself invisible so nobody could film me.

Wielding the power of the Goddess was fucking *awesome*. And I was incredibly grateful to Loki for showing me how to work with the elements. It'd truly made all the difference in some of these near-disasters.

Another piece of good news was I hadn't had that nightmare since returning from Asgard. But I continued feel tired more often than I used to.

Nat had heard back from the firm with the name and number of a local OB/GYN, but I hadn't called for an appointment yet. I wasn't sure why; Nat had assured me—based on her discussion with the firm—the doctor had been advised of my divinity. Discretion was guaranteed, as was the accommodation of any special needs I might have.

Maybe I was putting it off because it'd make the pregnancy more real, somehow.

But I did take the second home pregnancy test. It seemed a waste not to. Of course, it was just as positive as the first had been, but this time I didn't have a paroxysm of laughter.

Immediately after, I sent the used test back to my pocket universe and sat on my bed, thinking. Would I be a good mother? How far along was I? Was it even a good idea to think about raising a child? How would Arddhu and Kevin take the news? Would they be happy?

My brain reeled with the deluge of questions, and I knew I'd gotten myself worked up and tense.

"Peace, Deirdre," Anu's voice in my head was soft, soothing. "All will be well. I promise."

How could she promise such a thing? There'd been that vision I'd seen during my visit to Asgard...

"There are many possible futures," Anu said. "No single one is certain."

Which was pretty much the same thing Loki had told me. I took a deep breath and released it. Anu sent a wave of comfort through me, and I relaxed even more.

"Thank you, Anu. Much love." And I meant it, too. I did love her.

"Much love, Deirdre."

Well, there was nothing else for it. I'd just have to continue taking it one step at a time and doing my best with everything.

One morning, I woke but didn't want to leave my nest of soft blankets. It wasn't like I wanted to avoid anyone or anything; I just felt lazy, for a change. I couldn't even remember the last time I'd just relaxed in bed, dozing in a state of peacefulness between awake and asleep, listening to the birds sing sweetly outside my patio door.

Unfortunately, my serenity was broken by a brisk knock on my door.

"Wakey-wakey, Dee," Kevin said. "Time to rise and shine."

Shit. He must need me for something, otherwise he probably wouldn't have disturbed me.

"Okay," I called. "I'll be right out."

After a quick shower, I dressed in jeans and a tee shirt, and left my suite.

Kevin waited at the kitchen island with Arddhu, the Morrigan, Anthony, and Brianna. As soon as he saw me approaching, he said something to the others I didn't catch. They turned to face me and began singing *Happy Birthday*.

It stopped me in my tracks.

Today was my birthday? Birthdays didn't mean as much to me now as they had when I was young; I even struggled to remember how old I was. Thirty-five? No—that was last year. I'd been on Arddhu's world after being rescued from Cromm, and completely forgotten about my birthday back then.

So now I was thirty-six, but since I was becoming immortal, getting ever closer to forty didn't quite mean as much as it used to.

Then I remembered Kevin had asked me months ago when my birthday was, and said he'd plan something special.

And he hadn't forgotten, despite all the craziness since then.

With a dopey grin on my face, I listened to them sing. Honestly, they did a pretty damn good job of harmonizing, and it made me wonder if they'd spent time rehearsing. It wouldn't surprise me if they had.

When they finished with a grand flourish, I applauded enthusiastically and gave each of them a birthday hug or kiss.

"Aw, thank you, guys. That was really sweet."

Now I saw the granite island had been set with six plates, and Brianna wasted no time dishing out a savory breakfast of fluffy eggs, crispy bacon, hash browns, and toast with creamy butter. The final touch was a carafe of fresh-brewed coffee.

My stomach growled loudly, and Brianna grinned. "I'm so glad you're hungry this morning."

"Me too," I replied.

We all sat and devoured the mini feast.

It was, of course, delicious.

Afterward, I sipped my coffee, reveling in the warm glow of contentment. "You are all awesome. Thank you for making my birthday special."

"Oh, we're not done yet." Kevin's eyes sparkled with mischief. "We have a few more things planned."

Arddhu presented a small gift-wrapped box that he'd pulled from his pocket. "Bright blessings on your annual day of birth."

The last time I'd had birthday gifts was before I'd gone away to college, when my parents had given me a gift certificate to the local bookstore. They were dead before my next birthday.

Now, I blinked away tears and unwrapped Arddhu's gift. It was a gorgeous bracelet made of the clearest, palest aquamarines I'd ever seen, set in scalloped gold links.

"It's absolutely beautiful." I loved how the stones sparkled in the morning light streaming through the window wall.

As he helped me with the clasp, he said, "It is the traditional jewel for those born in March."

I kissed him. "Thank you."

Then Kevin gave me his gift: a matching aquamarine necklace.

"Wow, this is amazing." I lifted my hair up as he fastened it around my neck, then I kissed him, too. "Thank you."

Next up was the Morrigan, with her gift of matching earrings.

"Holy shit." I eyed the three of them. "Nice, how you guys planned this. I feel like a queen." They grinned with obvious satisfaction as I put the earrings on, then I hugged the Morrigan and thanked her.

Anthony's gift was a larger box, which contained a fancy tablet with all the accessories to convert it to a laptop.

"It's the latest tech, has all the bells and whistles, and it's screaming fast," he said.

"Oh man, I'm so jealous," Kevin murmured as he stared at it. "I've wanted one of those for weeks, but they're sold out everywhere."

Anthony nodded. "I would've still been on the waiting list if the firm hadn't bought a thousand of them straight from the manufacturer."

"Holy shit. A... *thousand*?" Kevin stared at him with wide eyes.

Anthony nodded again. "I've got three more on the way, so one's yours if you want it."

"Dude. Yes. I mean, wow. Thank you."

"You are such a great guy," I told Anthony. Impulsively, I hugged him, and after only a slight hesitation he hugged me back. "Thank you."

Brianna seemed a bit shy as she handed me her gift, something thin and flat. "I didn't know what to get you. Anthony helped me."

Intrigued, I opened the box.

A photograph of Arddhu, Kevin, and the Morrigan, in a simple yet elegant bright silver frame.

My family.

Each of them smiled warmly at the camera—at *me*—and in some magickal way, I could actually *feel* the love in their gazes.

"Oh, this is perfect." I hugged Brianna. "Thank you."

"You have no idea how many times I had to retake that photo until it turned out that perfect," Anthony said with a wry grin.

"Hey, it wasn't my fault Kevin kept making me laugh," the Morrigan said.

Arddhu seemed thoughtful. "Perhaps we should not have had so much mead that day."

"Well, we had fun, didn't we?" Kevin countered. "Just like I said we would." To me, he added, "Remind me later to show you the outtakes."

"Don't you dare," the Morrigan warned. "Never in my life have I ever acted so silly." She turned to Anthony. "You told me you deleted those."

As they bickered good-naturedly, I grinned at them and tears stung my eyes. In this moment, the love I felt for this motley group of gods and mortals overflowed my heart.

Into a lull in the back and forth, I blurted, "I love you guys." I wiped my eyes and sniffled. "I don't think I've ever had a better birthday. Seriously."

Kevin tenderly brushed a stray strand of hair from my face. "I didn't forget what you told me about past birthdays. I wanted to try and make up for the ones we missed, and the ones that went forgotten before that."

"Oh, you've done that and more." I squeezed his hand.

Now he grinned. "We're not done yet."

"On that note," Anthony said, "we'll leave the rest of you to it." To me, he said, "Happy birthday again, Dee. We'll catch up with you later."

Brianna echoed his birthday greeting, then they both left the room.

"Ready?" Kevin asked the others, who nodded.

"What's going on?" I asked.

"You'll see." He smirked. "But first, close your eyes."

I trusted them, so I did as requested.

Someone took my hand. "Okay, now, just step forward," Kevin said.

When I felt the change in air pressure against my skin, I knew I'd just stepped through a portal. I heard waves crashing on a distant shore and seagulls squawking overhead.

"Okay, you can open them," Kevin said.

I did.

The sun was low on the horizon, shining directly into my eyes, and I had to squint for a moment. The deep blue sky was splashed with ribbons of pink, orange, and red.

The four of us stood on a narrow deserted cobblestone street that followed a high shoreline. Far below shimmered a body of water that was bluer than any I'd ever seen. A few colorful fishing boats made their way to the harbor, done for the day. Far from shore, some luxurious yachts anchored or cruised among a dozen small, rocky islands; the brilliant white of the ships was startling in all that gorgeous blue. The air smelled slightly fishy and salty, with a heavy dose of perfume from the profusion of flowers everywhere.

"Where are we?" I asked.

"Santorini, Greece," Kevin said. "The village of Oía, to be precise." He turned toward me. "You once said you'd always wanted to visit. And we're just in time to watch the famous Santorini sunset."

I stared at him, speechless. How did I deserve this man?

He grinned, then nodded behind us. "It's off-season, so we've got the place mostly to ourselves right now. Except for the locals, of course."

I turned toward where he'd indicated. Hotels and resorts, white-washed and hugging each other as they clung to the slope of the low mountain rising above them, seemed deserted. Everywhere I looked, the bright colors from hundreds of flowering shrubs and plants—red, purple, yellow—contrasted sharply against all that white.

It was absolutely, stunningly, gorgeous.

Then the light-show began, and I had no more words.

The four of us stood silently watching the sun dip below the horizon in a sensational play of brilliant color above the Aegean.

The Morrigan seemed wistful. "It was a lot bigger in the old days, before the eruption. And it's too touristy now."

"When was that?" Sadly, I didn't remember much of world history from my high-school days.

She pursed her lips for a moment, thinking. "I think it was almost four thousand years ago or so now. I'm not really sure. We didn't reckon time the same way back then." She shrugged. "The Santorini name is fairly recent, only around nine hundred years old. Before that, it was called Thera. And before that, it was called Kallístē, which is Greek for the *most beautiful*."

"I remember hearing about the eruption," Arddhu said. "But I did not pay close attention. After all, it was a world away."

"It was way before my time," Kevin said. "I'm a youngster compared to you two."

She shrugged. "I wouldn't have known much about it either, if it hadn't been for a traveler from the region. He said his name was Dion, and oh, we had such a grand time together." She seemed lost in some memory, then shook her head. "Did you know, some of the early Greeks actually thought Eire was Hyperborea? They thought Apollon, their God of Light, stayed the winter every year." She snorted. "Such nonsense. If he had, I would've known about it."

I'd never heard of a connection between Greece and Ireland before, and I was fascinated.

"Others thought Hyperborea was Britain, Scandinavia, or even Gaul," Arddhu said. "There were many theories and opinions over the centuries, but later, when the globe had been explored to the fullest, no one had ever found such a place."

"If I remember right," Kevin said, "it was supposedly a warm place surrounded by a freezing northern climate. But just like Shangri-La, it was only make-believe."

The sky had darkened enough for stars to appear, and I shivered in the chilly air. I'd dressed for Arizona, which was much warmer this time of year, so I simply magicked a sweater over my tee shirt.

Kevin took my arm. "Hey, let's go check out some of the stores before they close."

So the four of us strolled the mostly-empty streets, occasionally ducking into a small shop to admire the beautiful artwork or jewelry. We stayed away from the typical tourist stores with their windows full of cheap reproductions of famous Greek statues.

At first, the shopkeepers were surprised to see non-locals in their shops, and seemed happy to see us—until they realized we were just browsing. At one, the older couple behind the counter didn't hide their scowls as we left without buying anything, and I felt bad. Before going into the next shop, I pulled a wad of money from my pocket universe and stuffed it into my pocket.

The next store was a ceramics workshop, and I was pleasantly surprised to see a small hand-lettered sign that the shop accepted US currency. So I chose a beautifully decorated shallow drinking bowl, identified as a kylix on the little card accompanying it, and smiled as it was carefully packed in bubble wrap and boxed. Sure, it was sort of expensive, but the artist's grateful smile was well worth it.

After we left, I made sure no one was looking then sent the package to my pocket universe.

A couple of hours later, we returned to the cliffside and found a short wall to sit on. All the hotels had turned on their lights, and now the hillside was lit in a soft glow, like fairy lights.

It was breathtakingly beautiful. I gazed out at the dozens of tiny islands, some with pinpricks of lights and others completely dark, and tried to imagine what it'd be like to live here.

"Ready to go?" Kevin asked.

"I could stay here forever." I sighed. "I'm not ready to go home yet."

"Oh, we're not going home just yet. And I think you'll like our next stop just as much as this. Maybe even more."

Once again, he asked me to close my eyes while Arddhu opened a portal. This time the air was balmy, and the sun was much warmer. I heard waves on a beach and wondered if it was Ard na Mara.

"Okay, you can look now."

A pristine white sand beach stretched for miles to either side of me. And beyond that was the clearest aquamarine water I'd ever seen.

Nope, this wasn't Ard na Mara.

The sun was high overhead in a cloudless blue sky; it'd been nighttime just a moment ago.

"Now where are we?"

"A small, uninhabited island in the Bahamas," Kevin replied.

Near a clump of tall palm trees and other lush vegetation, he called in a large duffel bag from his pocket universe and spread an enormous blanket on the warm sand. He handed a swimsuit to the Morrigan—a black and red one-piece, of course—and she ducked behind some dense bushes to change. He waved a hand and changed his clothing to tropical print swim trunks, but Arddhu simply stripped down to his bare skin.

"Well? Change into your suit." Kevin eyed me. "And don't forget to take off your jewelry."

I didn't need to be told twice. I magicked my clothes into a swimsuit and sent the aquamarine jewels to my pocket universe.

The four of us waded into the warm water. It was so clear, I could see tiny creatures scurrying along the bottom, away from my feet. I'd never experienced anything like this before.

It was spectacular.

For what seemed like hours, we swam, splashed, and played like children. Even Arddhu played. I'd never seen him like this, and it warmed my soul. Finally, skin pruning, I begged leave and headed back to the blanket, where a warm breeze rustled the fronds of the palm trees overhead. Sitting cross-legged, I watched the three of them continue to dunk each other, laugh, and play. My face hurt from the constant grin plastered there.

All the planning that had gone into this... I shook my head. How could I ever truly thank them for how special they'd made this day for me? Tears stung my eyes yet again.

I was so full of love right now for these three immortals.

My family.

After they came back to the blanket, Kevin pulled a low folding table from the duffle and set it up. How the hell had that fit in there? It was probably some next-level magick.

Next, he set out a small feast on the table: crusty bread, an assortment of cheeses, fresh fruit, and ripe olives. Lastly, he added a bottle of chilled white wine and four glasses, and poured one for each of us.

"You thought of everything," I said.

Kevin grinned but didn't reply.

The Morrigan raised her glass. "To our birthday girl." The others joined in the toast, and we all sipped.

Then I made my own toast. "To the best family I could ever ask for." The Morrigan stared at me in surprise, and I added, "What? That's what you are. All of you. You're my family."

"That's fine." She'd recovered her composure already, and now raised her chin. "But don't you fucking *dare* think of me as your mother."

Her eyes flashed in warning, and I almost spit out my wine.

"Of course not. I was thinking more like..." I almost said *aunt*, but she probably wouldn't like that, either. It was never a good idea to ruffle the feathers of the Goddess of Battlefield Death, even if she wasn't in her raven form. "A sister," I finished.

She apparently didn't mind that; she quirked a little smile, nodded once, and settled.

We nibbled on our feast and drank our wine as the warm breeze dried us off, then curled up next to each other and snoozed contentedly while the sun sank toward the horizon. It was nice being so close to the ones I loved, and the phrase *puppy pile* came to mind, making me grin.

Finally, Kevin roused us and said it was time to pack up and go home.

I was torn; part of me didn't want this day to end. It'd been so nice, not thinking about anything other than my family and being with them.

I almost felt guilty, like I'd just played hooky from all my responsibilities.

But nothing lasted forever, and we needed to go home.

While the Morrigan changed out of her suit and Arddhu dressed, Kevin and I changed our clothes with magick. I retrieved my birthday jewelry from my pocket universe and put everything on, then he and I shook the sand out of the blanket and folded it. He packed everything back into the duffel and sent it to his pocket universe.

Arddhu opened the portal, and everyone but Kevin and I stepped through. Before I followed, I turned for one last look at this little private paradise, to fix it in my memory.

"Maybe we'll come back," Kevin said. "Just the two of us." Then he took my hand and we stepped through the portal.

Back home in the living room, I pulled him close.

"Thank you for a perfect day," I said, expecting a kiss.

But he shook his head. "Nope, not done yet." He glanced at his watch. "It's time. Let's head out to the tent."

Tent? The *VIP tent*?

Oh no. What had he done?

Or, more accurately, what *more* had he done?

The three of them didn't say a word on the way there, but from their little grins it was obvious they were enjoying the surprise. At the entrance, Kevin held the door open and gestured for me to enter.

It was dark inside; even with my enhanced vision I didn't see anything at first. But as soon as I stepped over the threshold, everything happened at once: the lights came on, I saw the crowd waiting, and the shouted "*surprise*" was almost deafening.

It was obvious some of them were already quite drunk.

"It's about time you showed up." Randy's voice boomed. "We're already shitfaced."

I couldn't help but laugh. He'd always been boisterous and loud, but this was the first time I'd ever seen him so... unfettered.

Glancing around in amazement, I saw Reshep with a large group of Túatha, Garrett among them. There were the Asgardians, including Odin and Frigg, Thor and Sif. Even Loki. And over there: Anthony and the rest of the security team—Nat, Joe, Steve, and Sam—which made me wonder who was on security duty if they were all here. And there was Brianna, nibbling at the selections on the food tables; she must have the night off. The firm must've sent staff to take care of the food and drink, and probably the security, too.

Nat handed me a cup, and led a toast to "the birthday girl."

Everyone drank, then it was somewhat chaotic as each guest came forward to offer individual greetings.

"Happy birthday, Lady." Reshep was his usual semi-formal self, although his eyes brightened noticeably when the Morrigan drew close to his side. "I am honored to attend this celebration of Your birth."

"Thank you. I'm glad you're here." He and the Morrigan moved off, heads close as they spoke.

Odin and Frigg were dignified and stately as they simply offered their best wishes. Thor and Sif were as warm and friendly as they'd been on Asgard.

"Nice feasting hall you have here," Thor said, glancing around.

"Thanks." I'd noticed someone—probably Anthony—had removed the large table and chairs, and added a lot more casual seating.

As they moved off, Loki offered a box to me with a polite birthday greeting. As soon as I opened it, a dozen white birds burst out, startling me into dropping the box. The birds fluttered wildly over my head for a moment before they vanished in a puff of white smoke. Smirking, Loki made the box disappear with a wave of his hand.

"Neat trick," I said. And it was. Even if it did spook me a bit.

Next, I spent some time with Garrett and the Túatha, enjoying updates on their business ventures.

As I made my way through the crowd to Kevin, I noticed a DJ setting up in the far corner.

Kevin grinned at me. "Oh, yes: there *will* be dancing."

Holy shit. He'd even remembered I'd told him once how much I'd missed dancing. When was that, months ago? Had to be.

Impulsively, I pulled his head down for a deep kiss. The surrounding guests cheered loudly.

"You are absolutely incredible," I said. "I love you."

He raised a brow. "We'll see if you still feel that way after I beat your ass at both karaoke *and* the dance off."

Hours later, sitting on the floor against the wall near the bathrooms, I still couldn't wipe the grin from my face.

What a day.

It'd been epic. So many incredible moments.

I'd been given awesome gifts, seen a Santorini sunset, swam in warm Caribbean waters, and had a picnic on the beach.

And then this party... well. There'd been the usual, expected things, like dancing with Arddhu and then Kevin, then others. So many others. There'd even been group girl dancing. First with just Nat and Brianna, then the Morrigan and Sif had joined in.

But then, I'd never expected Frigg to join in, too, and was even more surprised to discover she knew how to dance to popular Midgardian music. Pretty damn well, too.

There were so many other things I'd never expected to see.

Reshep and Arddhu, both normally so reserved, in a heated free-for-all dance contest to old disco music. Loki had even conjured a mirror ball and suspended it above the dance floor. Even more surprising? Arddhu's winning moves, copying those made famous in a popular movie of the disco era. I'd laughed so hard, tears had rolled down my face.

Or when the Morrigan took down the Dagda in a Broadway show tunes karaoke battle.

Or the tap dance contest between Garrett and Loki. Somehow, I hadn't expected Loki to win.

Or Odin versus Kevin in a death metal karaoke match, and Odin easily winning.

Or Nat and Sif in a rap battle that ended in a draw. And a lot of laughter.

Kevin had even talked me into singing karaoke duets with him, and Arddhu had showed me how to dance gracefully to ballroom music of the Big Band Era.

And there'd been a *lot* of slow dancing. Arddhu and me, Kevin and me, the Morrigan and Reshep, Odin and Frigg, Thor and Sif. And some other pair-ups as well, both among the Túatha and between them and my security team. Even Nat and Anthony had paired up for one song.

Fuck.

It'd been a helluva party.

Now, beyond exhausted, I glanced around at the aftermath.

The last of the guests either slouched with drooping eyelids in chairs or snored loudly on the sofas or floor.

Unlike almost everyone else, Loki was sprawled in a comfy chair in the lounge area, wide awake and studying the glass of alcohol in his hand with a level of concentration that was disturbingly intense.

Garrett caught my eye from across the room, smiled and waved, then left.

Odin and Frigg had left some time ago, but now Thor and Sif waved farewell and left.

The Dagda nodded once to me, then roused and gathered the snoozing Túatha. Some of them stumbled a bit as they followed him out the door.

Nat and the rest of the security team were huddled on the floor around a coffee table playing some dice game that involved dollar bills and lots of drinking. Randy, eyelids drooping, looked ready to keel over, but Nat seemed wide awake. Based on the pile of money in front of her, she also seemed to be winning.

Reshep was passed out on one of the couches, with the Morrigan snuggled close, an arm draped casually across his midsection.

Arddhu sat in a chair nearby, deep in thought. He looked tired, but was still awake. What was he thinking so seriously about?

Kevin and Anthony stood near the bar, talking quietly and nodding occasionally.

The staff had already cleared the food tables, and after a quick word with Anthony, they quietly left.

The DJ had finished packing up his gear. On his way to the exit, pulling his wheeled case behind him, he smiled at me as he passed by. "Goodnight, birthday girl. Are you even old enough to drink?" He didn't wait for a reply, just kept on going, right out the door.

Ha ha. Mister funny guy.

I closed my eyes for a moment.

Thirty-six. Officially closer to forty than thirty. But I was immortal now. Or, near enough. How much longer would I mark the passing of each year? And when would birthdays become meaningless completely? At a hundred? Two hundred? A thousand?

"Penny for your thoughts."

I blinked up at Loki, who stood nearby. The glass he'd been studying so intently was gone now.

"I was just thinking about birthdays."

He shrugged. "After a while, they become meaningless to us immortals."

"That's just what I was thinking."

"Enjoy them while you're still young, Lady." He smiled. "For now, I bid you good night and final birthday blessings." He turned and sauntered out the door.

A moment later, Anthony stopped to speak to the security team, then left, while Kevin came my way.

"How're you doing, birthday girl?" he asked.

He'd caught me in a yawn. "Exhausted. But very, very happy."

He offered his hand. "Time to call it a day?"

I nodded, and took it. As we passed the couch, I glanced at Reshep and the Morrigan, both deep asleep, and quietly turned off the nearby lamp.

Arddhu joined us as we reached the door. "It was a celebration for the ages." He nodded at Kevin. "Well done, my friend."

All three of us crawled into my bed, fully dressed, with me tucked between my two loves.

"Thank you for an awesome birthday." I kissed each of them. "I love you both so much."

We snuggled in to each other and sleep took us quickly.

CHAPTER THIRTEEN

WE COULD'VE USED the VIP tent for the Council meeting since Alana wasn't attending, but I'd wanted to have it in the green space I'd created. After all, it was a beautiful morning, only in the mid-eighties and sunny.

As usual, Brianna had set up the sideboard with enough food for a small army, and the bar was fully stocked. After everyone was seated, I convened the meeting.

"Thank you all for coming." I read from my notes. "The agenda for today is: we'll update everyone on how the diplomatic mission to Asgard went; decide when to remove the remaining targets; discuss the progress made since our last meeting regarding the Túatha's efforts to educate humans on becoming better stewards of Earth; discuss available assistance from the firm for the facilities belonging to the remaining targets; and discuss social media engagement." To Lugh, I said, "Would you please give everyone a brief summary of our visit to Asgard?"

It only took a few minutes, since the only thing relevant to this Council was that we'd secured an alliance with Asgard, and there was only one question.

"When and where will our next diplomatic visit be?" the Morrigan asked.

Lugh frowned. "I'm not really sure. Technically, we should pay our respects for the loss of Marisha-Ten, but they're not responding to my inquiries."

Anthony cleared his throat. "Let me see what I can do to help. Maybe they're being overly cautious due to the escalation of hostilities in South Asia."

Oh yeah. That. I looked to Reshep. "Do we have more anything on that?"

He shook his head. "Not really, no. Nothing concrete."

"Has anyone heard anything about Ares, Athena, and Kali?" the Dagda asked.

"Odin told us Ares and Athena are on Olympus," I said. "But he never mentioned Kali, so we have no idea where she is or why she's not with them. As for Olympus, maybe I should go there and see if I can talk some sense into those two."

"Olympus is a very big place." The Morrigan raised a brow. "You know where they are, then?"

"Well, not exactly, no."

"Then I suggest we find out exactly *where* on Olympus they are staying, before you go."

"I think that's a great idea," Anthony said. "I'll ask the firm to send a team to scout Olympus for an exact location."

Spies. He was talking about sending spies. And it really was a good idea. Why the hell hadn't we thought of it sooner?

"Thanks. Keep us posted, please." I glanced at my notes and skipped down a couple of agenda items. "Dagda, would you please give us an update on how it's going working with the humans?"

"Of course." He sat a little straighter. "For the past several weeks, we've held local and online workshops on Earth stewardship, and they've been fairly successful. Each workshop has been filled to capacity, and most of the attendees have been young people, which is very encouraging. We've also been using our magick at night, in less populous areas, to help clean the environment." He nodded at me. "You should find your Earth healing sessions a bit more effective because of it. Our magick is sort of a boost for yours."

"That's great news." I smiled. "I can definitely use all the help I can get."

He returned my smile, then became serious once again. "As far as repurposing the facilities that currently belong to the remaining targets," he glanced at Anthony before continuing, "that effort is not bearing fruit as quickly. There is much work to do, and it is not as easy since it involves advanced science and technology."

Anthony nodded. "The firm is having difficulty working through some of the more complicated calculations and theories. But, teaming up with the Túatha has produced some great ideas that hopefully will be ready for testing soon."

Not as good news, but it could be worse.

"Sounds promising. Keep me posted." Again, I glanced at my notes. "As you all recall, at our last meeting we agreed to proceed with removing the remaining targets magickally, in what we dubbed Operation Clean Sweep. Now, we need to decide when to do it."

"Remind me: how many targets are left?" the Dagda asked.

"There are forty-two remaining from the original list," Reshep replied.

"Then, I think it should be done as soon as possible," the Dagda said.

Everyone but Kevin nodded in agreement.

"Well, today's Friday. I'd like to allow the targets one last weekend with their families. But I'll be in Finn's Cove for the spring equinox festival early next week, so the soonest I'm available is midweek. Will that work?"

Again, nods around the table.

Except for Kevin.

"Okay. So that's settled, then." I glanced at the agenda.

"I have a suggestion," Ogma said. "I think we should do a video explaining why Operation Clean Sweep is necessary. We could release it right after you do it, and we can use the momentum from the viral brushfire videos to reinforce the advantages of the Operation."

Arddhu frowned. "I do not think it wise to brag about removing the targets with magick."

"It's not bragging," I argued.

"Actually," the Morrigan interrupted. "I think a brag video is a brilliant idea." She turned to Arddhu. "Remember, things are different for Dee than they were for any of us. There is value in using this technology

192

to... to..." she glanced at Anthony and Kevin, not sure of the phrase she was looking for.

"Control the narrative," Anthony offered. "Get out in front of an issue and sway popular opinion in the direction you want."

"Yes, exactly." She smiled at him in thanks. "Politicians do this all the time. And quite well, I might add. Just look at how often the worst humans have been elected to high offices, especially here in America. They could've murdered someone and the voters wouldn't have cared. So the way I see it, right now Dee is more or less a politician."

"Oh hell no," I said. "I am *not* a politician. I'm just someone trying to undo centuries of damage to the planet we're all stuck living on for the foreseeable future."

The Morrigan shrugged. "It's all how you look at it. And even without the label of a politician, you are a leader right now. All I'm saying is, use the tools that other leaders have successfully used. In this case, a video."

"You know, I still have serious concerns." Kevin glanced around the table. "Some of you weren't around during the witch trials. The Túatha were banished, and Dee wasn't born yet." He paused, as if searching for the words he wanted to say. "It was *horrible*. It started out with one or two places going through some tough times—drought, famine, plague—and needing something or someone to blame. It ended with thousands of innocent people tortured and murdered in the most brutal ways imaginable. All because of mob mentality."

He took a breath and turned to me. "Right now, sure, they're sort of enamored with you even though they don't really know who or what you are. Not for sure. Some think you're an angel, for example, while others think you're an extraterrestrial. But the minute you do something they don't like, they'll turn on you. It's called mob mentality. It even happened before the witch trials, in a little place called Rome."

"I remember Rome," Arddhu nodded. "The mob completely controlled the city at times, usually when they did not get their way. At times, the people rioted after chariot races when their favorite team did not win."

"We've had something like that happen here in America, too," I pointed out. "People rioted when their sports team won a championship."

"I've read accounts of the witch trials," the Dagda shook his head. "Much happened while we were away. Very disturbing, indeed."

"Look." I sighed. "I know you've all been gods and goddesses for a lot longer than I have. And that's actually why you're all here right now: I need your experience and wisdom to help guide me. But the Morrigan was right: I'm the only one of us who's from this time, this age of man. I know humans better than you think I do, since I've been one my whole life. I'm pretty sure I can win over public opinion. And I think there'll be a side benefit when I do: they'll accept the existence of other gods and goddesses a lot easier. And we'll be able to do some great things together. As a team."

In the thoughtful silence, the Dagda was the first to speak. "Until now, my people have been advised to—lay low, I believe you humans say—and not draw too much attention to our otherness. We have taken great pains to do so, altering our appearance and adopting human customs as much as possible.

"It has been incredibly difficult to continue to hide our true natures while showing the humans how to become better stewards of the Earth. We miss living openly as the Túatha, using our magick freely. And we especially miss being worshipped.

He fixed his unnatural eyes on me. "So, if you do this video, and the humans react favorably, it could help us cement our own place in this strange new world we find ourselves. Without reservation, I vote yes on Operation Clean Sweep, the video afterward, all of it."

"As do I," Manannan said.

"And I," Ogma said.

"Well," the Morrigan said, "if we're taking a vote, then I'm a yes."

"I, too, agree," Reshep said.

Arddhu nodded. "I also vote yes."

"I'm a yes." Anthony said.

Kevin seemed miserable. "I'm sorry, but I have to vote no. I know I'm outnumbered, but for the record, I have a very bad feeling about this."

"I know." I touched Kevin's hand and spoke gently. "I do understand. And I respect your opinion. But yes, you've been outvoted." To everyone else, I said, "Thank you all for your confidence in me."

I turned to Ogma. "Can we work on the script for the video over the next couple of days?"

He nodded. "I can have a draft ready in about an hour." He waved a hand toward Anthony. "He's got the good camera. Could we record it this weekend?"

"Sure." I glanced at the agenda. "Now, can you give us an update on social media engagement?"

He nodded again. "All the posted brushfire videos have gone viral, which means they've been watched, shared, and liked at a very high rate. In turn, this has driven a fifty percent increase in traffic to your website and each of your social media accounts. So far, the overall reaction has been overwhelmingly positive, and I think that'll continue with the video after Operation Clean Sweep, too."

"Thank you," I smiled at him. "That's it for the agenda, then. We'll plan to meet again in a couple of weeks to discuss the public reaction to the video, and next steps. Any other business to discuss?" Head shakes all around. "Then, again, thank you all. This meeting is now adjourned."

While everyone else headed for the food, Kevin slumped in his seat, picking absently at a nail and staring off into the distance.

I hated seeing him like this. I probably couldn't change his mind, but somehow I had to ease his fears.

I had to try. Later, after everyone left.

It was another gorgeous evening, a bit on the cool side but clear enough for millions of stars to twinkle in the blue velvet sky. Crickets chirped in the desert beyond my backyard oasis, and the low landscape lights beautifully lit the palm trees around the spa.

Earlier, I'd left an old-fashioned note—with little hearts I'd drawn in red ink—in Kevin's room for him to meet me here. Now, I relaxed in the bubbles and waited.

I didn't have to wait long; I'd just leaned my head back and closed my eyes when I heard footsteps behind me.

"I'm here," Kevin said.

As he stepped down into the spa, I moved over to give him room on my seat. But he chose to sit across from me instead, and I tried not to feel slighted that he'd wanted distance from me.

He settled in, closed his eyes, and softly groaned as the jets did their work. "I missed this."

I didn't reply, just studied him in the muted lighting. He'd left his long dark hair unbound, and the wet ends stuck to his shoulders.

"Stop it," he said, playfully, without opening his eyes. "How many times do I have to tell you not to stare at me?"

He knew me so well.

"It doesn't matter, I'll never stop. You're beautiful."

One corner of his mouth quirked as he lifted his head and looked at me. "I could change my appearance if it would help. How about an ugly old man? Just say the word."

I laughed. "No thanks. I prefer you just as you are."

"Me too." He closed his eyes again. "It's so much easier."

After a moment, I sighed. "We need to talk."

"Yeah." He sighed, then straightened and gave me his full attention.

"I know you're upset with me," I began. "What can I do to change that?"

"Don't go ahead with your plan."

"You know I can't do that."

He was silent for a moment, then he sighed again and moved to sit next to me. His hand found mine under the water. "Look, I get it. I really do. And under other circumstances, it'd be a great plan. But I just can't shake the feeling this'll end badly." He met my gaze. "For you. Maybe for all of us."

"I promise I will take every precaution I possibly can."

He snorted. "Like you did with the brushfire?"

"You're never going to let me live that down, are you?" I shook my head. "I learned from that experience. Hell, every disaster I've gone to since, I've cloaked myself in invisibility. That experience is what makes me want to be more careful."

He studied me for a moment, then his hand squeezed mine. "If the worst happens and the mob comes for you, they'll have to go through me first. I hope you know that."

"It won't come to that," I insisted. "We'll leave if things turn to shit. Like maybe we'll go to your world. Or Ida's. Someplace they can't follow."

"Promise?" The naked fear and longing in his voice pulled at my heart.

"Promise."

He leaned close and kissed me gently. "I'll hold you to it, you know."

Oh, I knew he would. "You'd better."

His lips quirked, then he cocked his head, studying me. "You've changed."

"Is that good or bad?"

He didn't hesitate. "Oh, definitely good."

"Whew." I smiled. "You had me worried there for a second."

He squeezed my hand again. "I like you like this. More confident. Assertive. I mean, you've always been that, but somehow now you're just... I don't know. *More*. But without being bossy or bitchy."

I swallowed the lump in my throat. "Thank you. That means a lot to me."

We sat in companionable silence for a few moments, just relaxing together, something we didn't seem to do much anymore.

I wondered if I should tell him. About the baby. It wouldn't be fair to Arddhu—I should tell them both at the same time—and I hadn't had it confirmed by the doctor yet, but the sudden urge grew so strong I couldn't resist it.

Instead, he broke the silence. "I've been meaning to ask you something. How did you put out the brush fire? I couldn't tell from the videos."

Hmm. How much to tell him? What if he asked how I learned to do elemental magick? I'd sworn to Loki I wouldn't tell anyone what he'd taught me. Anyone meant *anyone*, even my Consorts.

In the end, I kept it simple.

"I asked it to stop."

"What?" He stared at me. "You... connected to an element? Directly?"

I nodded. "And then I asked Water to wet the ground so Fire couldn't come back."

He just blinked at me for a moment. "That's some next-level shit, you know. Most new-made gods would've followed their first instinct and tried to kill the fire with water from the nearest source, which probably would've drained an entire lake. But using elemental magick... that's pretty impressive, hon."

Thank all the gods he hadn't asked me how I knew to do that.

But just in case he thought of it, I leaned forward and kissed him as a distraction.

Long and hard and full of my love for him.

It was glorious.

After breakfast the next morning, Ogma showed up with the draft script for the video. Together with Anthony, we spent half an hour going through it making changes, and then it was time to record.

Anthony had set up a mini studio in the home office, complete with proper lighting and a backdrop. I'd kept my clothing casual, just jeans and a short-sleeved tee, but decided not to wear my typical ponytail. Instead, I left my hair full and unbound. As for makeup, I didn't use anything other than a bit of magick to hide the battle scars on my face.

The easiest way to show my divinity was with a full glow. Some people would probably think it was some kind of special effect, but I didn't care.

We did a couple of test runs to make sure the equipment functioned properly. While Anthony fiddled with the lighting and camera settings to adjust for my glow, I picked at a cuticle and stared at the wall.

Yes, I was nervous. I'd never done anything like this before. But at least we weren't broadcasting live, so if I flubbed any lines we'd just retake it. As a last resort, Anthony could always edit the video, although I really hoped that wouldn't be necessary.

The fewer cuts, the better. Less chance of humans thinking it was all just a joke.

After conferring with Ogma, Anthony looked at me. "Ready?"

I nodded, and serenity washed over me. All nervousness was gone.

He motioned to me, and I began speaking.

Ten minutes later, we had our video, in a single take.

Somehow, I hadn't fucked up a single word of it.

Anthony gave Ogma a copy of the video on a memory card for safekeeping, and that was that.

CHAPTER FOURTEEN

I n some parts of the world, the spring equinox was celebrated as Ostara, a solemn occasion complete with a full ritual. But in Finn's Cove, it was simply seen as the second of three springtime growing festivals that began with Imbolc in February and ended with Beltaine in May. And because late March was when most farmers sowed barley in their fields, the festival would feature plenty of ale along with the feasting and dancing.

Arddhu, Kevin, and the Morrigan planned to attend with me, but at the last minute Lugh also asked to go with us. We saw no reason to say no, and when he met us after breakfast, it was with a boyish grin of excitement.

We arrived at Ard na Mara in late afternoon, just as the sun dipped toward the horizon. As was normal for whenever I visited Ireland, it was a gorgeous day with clear skies and relatively warm temperatures. A gentle sea breeze made the tall grass and early blooming wildflowers in the meadow dance and sway hypnotically.

A quick check of my wards told me they were just as I'd left them, intact and secure. While we were here, though, I wanted to look in on the garden.

"Can you guys give me a minute?" I asked. "I'll be right back."

The garden gate, which used to squeal mercilessly, now opened smoothly and silently. The beds were tidy and well-kept, with no visible weeds. The herbs were beginning to blossom, and everything was thriving.

Donal was taking excellent care of it. He deserved a raise, and I'd make sure he'd have it in his next payment.

After I returned to the patio, Lugh gushed, "What a lovely little place you have here."

"Thanks." I smiled wistfully. "I don't get to spend as much time here as I'd like to. Maybe that'll change after I finish healing Earth."

"What would you do here that you cannot do at The Hacienda?" Arddhu asked.

"Tend the garden. Make some potions. Maybe tinker with Maggie's old brewing equipment. Hang out on the beach. Get a boat and learn to sail. Just... stuff."

"Chill," Kevin nodded, "in other words."

"Yeah." That was the perfect way to put it.

"Well," the Morrigan said, "by the time Earth is fully healed, you'll deserve a break."

Realistically, by then I'd probably be waddling around with a huge belly unable to do any of the stuff I'd just mentioned, but I kept that to myself. Instead, I checked the position of the sun and said, "We should get going. I'm sure everyone's at the green by now."

Lugh grinned. "They will all be very surprised to see me."

I studied him for a moment, wondering if this was a good time to ask why Finn's Cove celebrated the autumn harvest festival as Lammas instead of Lughnasadh. Then again, that could be a touchy subject, so I decided it could wait.

The five of us formed a little procession on the path through the woods, with Kevin and I leading, followed by Lugh, and Arddhu and the Morrigan behind.

Lugh's head was on a swivel. "I don't think I've ever been through these woods. Then again, it's been so long, I'm not sure I'd recognize them anyway."

We approached Mike's cottage, and as I remembered my first walk through these woods—during my first visit to Finn's Cove almost two years ago—I felt a twinge of bittersweet sadness.

Then I noticed the cottage had new occupants.

A heavily pregnant young woman knelt along the walkway to the front door, tending the flowerbeds, while a young man on a ladder repainted the second-story window trim. When he climbed down the ladder and turned toward the woman, I recognized him as Donal.

Ah, so that's who Garrett had given the cottage to.

Warm happiness spread through me. The unpleasant fruits of Mike's betrayal and death had been transformed into a convenient blessing for the young couple.

I called out as we drew near, using the greeting I'd learned from Mike on that first visit. "'Lo, Donal. Blessings of the equinox on you."

He turned and grinned at me. "'Lo, Lady. Blessings to You as well." He helped the woman get to her feet, then introduced her. "This is my wife, Megan."

I smiled warmly. "I'm very pleased to meet you, Megan."

"'Tis an honor, Lady," Megan said as she curtsied.

I'd never actually been curtsied to before, so I wasn't sure how to respond. I decided just to ignore it and introduce my companions.

Donal was impressed to meet the Morrigan and Arddhu, and respectful toward Kevin. But when I introduced Lugh, his eyes widened and he gaped at him, forgetting all propriety.

"The Shining One, himself?" he whispered.

"Aye, 'tis." Lugh grinned and stood just a bit taller. "In the flesh, as they say."

Donal gazed at Lugh with awe. "I'd heard the Túatha had been set free, but I didna believe it."

"We're staying in our own realm for now, but we'll return to Eire soon. Shh, don't tell anyone," Lugh added with a wink.

"Oh no, sir, I wouldna dare." He stared at Lugh for another moment in silent adoration, and it grew uncomfortable.

Time to change the subject.

"I'm so happy you two moved in here," I said. "Do you need anything?"

Donal shook himself out of his daze. "No, Lady, the village is taking very good care of us. We wouldna even be here now if not for Your generosity, and You have our deepest gratitude."

I smiled warmly at Megan. "When is the baby due?"

"By the summer solstice, Lady."

I glanced again at her belly, so large and round. There was no way she had three more months to go. Then again, I didn't know much about pregnancies. For now.

"Ah, so you only have a little while to go."

She nodded, glanced up at Donal, who was at least a foot taller, then shyly asked me, "Could You... could You bless the child, Lady? It'd mean ever so much to us."

"Of course." I stepped close and gently laid my hands on Megan's firm belly. As I gave my blessing, the twin lives nestled within sent me a tentative yet sweet greeting.

Oh. That explained why she was so big, there were two babes, a boy and a girl. Donal and Megan didn't seem to know, which was curious. Why hadn't her doctor mentioned it? Well, I kept it to myself. Let it remain a surprise. As I stepped back, Megan thanked me.

"Will you be attending the festival?" I asked.

"Yes, Lady," Donal replied. "We'll be along shortly. I just need to finish up the trim on that last window before we go." He paused then added, "Michael's personal things have been packed up and taken to Your cottage, Lady."

Ah, yes. I remembered now. Only a couple of weeks ago, I'd received a call from Garrett with the request for five minutes' worth of access through my wards so his guys could deliver Mike's things.

"Great. I'll go through them when I have time." He seemed to want to say more, but was reluctant. "Is something wrong?"

He glanced at Megan before he replied. "I'm not sure. When we first arrived here, the back door had been forced open. Michael's things had already been removed, and nothing inside seemed amiss, but it was strange, all the same."

"Ah, but things *were* amiss." Megan glanced at him then met my gaze steadily. "All the cupboards were left open, and some floorboards had been pulled up. There were even holes in the walls. The place was a fair mess."

Hmm. Sounded like someone had been looking for something. Something that could be sitting in my cottage right now. "Did you call the police?"

Donal nodded. "The chief came out, took a good look, and wrote up a report, but since nothing was taken—we hadn't moved in yet, you see, so the place was empty—he just asked Garrett to provide additional funds to repair the damages."

I frowned, thinking.

Why hadn't Mike put up any wards? Then again, maybe he had, but they'd expired when he'd died, leaving the cottage unprotected.

Maybe the intruder had known there wouldn't be any wards when he—or she—had broken in. Or maybe they'd just been lucky.

Whatever the item was, it was either in with Mike's stuff—and protected by my wards—or it'd been hidden under the floorboards and taken by the intruder.

"I wonder what they were looking for," I mused aloud. "And if they found it."

"I've no idea, Lady, but it was strange enough that I thought You should know."

"Thank you for telling me." I sighed; I was getting too distracted by the details. "We'll see you both at the festival."

We took our leave and continued on our way.

After a few minutes of quietly walking, Kevin said, "I wonder what he was hiding."

"Who? Donal?"

"No. Mike."

"Oh. Yeah, me too." Maybe it'd be worth it to look through his things, see what was there.

"We should go through his stuff," the Morrigan said.

I smiled at her over my shoulder. "That's just what I was thinking."

"This is all very unusual," Arddhu said. "Perhaps Michael was involved in something he should not have been."

"Like trafficking stolen goods?" Lugh asked. "Or drugs?" Since he was the only one of us who hadn't known Mike, he didn't realize how ridiculous his questions sounded.

Then again, how much did we really know about Mike? I would've never guessed he'd betray us with Ida. Until it happened.

"I suppose anything's possible," I admitted.

By now we'd reached the bridge, but Pete wasn't out and about. At first I was disappointed, but it was probably a good thing since Lugh was with us. He'd been pretty upset when he'd heard we'd freed the Túatha.

As we passed the newly-sown fields beside the road to the village, the Morrigan cleared her throat. "Dee, you should glow."

Shit. I'd forgotten. I thanked her and adjusted the shield I kept in place to allow a soft glow. Nothing too bright or garish for the evening's festivities. "How's this?"

"Perfect," she replied.

When we reached the village green, I stopped and gazed at it with wonder. I'd never seen it decorated so beautifully, virtually transformed into a colorful and cheerful space. Each table was swathed in pastel ribbons and floral garlands. Bright floral arrangements were everywhere, and even the normally plain hay bales were draped in garlands of pretty wildflowers.

The central bonfire was the same as always, already lit and burning bright.

On one side of the green stood fantastical sculptures made entirely of flowers and ribbons. One was a huge rabbit, another a decorated egg. A real-looking tree, a beautiful maiden, a galloping stallion, and a few others completed the ensemble, which seemed to be entries for a contest. Each was unique and impressive; damn good thing I hadn't been asked to judge.

The villagers were warm and friendly toward me, but they pretty much lost their shit as soon as they realized it was Lugh with us.

"Look, it's the Shining One."

"The Shining One is here."

"The Shining One has returned."

They murmured and stared, but seemed too shy to approach him.

Of course, Lugh soaked it all up with a wide, joyful grin.

Then, Garrett rushed out of the crowd and headed straight toward Lugh. They clasped arms and embraced. "It is so good to see you here, Brother," Garrett said. "It has been far too long."

"Aye, Brother, it has." Lugh's eyes shone with tears.

Someone pushed a mug of ale into my hand, but when I turned to look, no one was anywhere near me.

Strange.

The villagers had crowded around Lugh now, and nobody paid any attention to me. I sniffed the mug's contents, but if it had anything other than ale in it, I couldn't smell it. Intuition told me not to drink it, so I poured it onto the grass as an offering to Earth and tossed the wooden mug into the bonfire.

"Smart move," Kevin murmured.

"Did you see who it was?"

"Nope. I looked around at the same time you did, but it was like they'd vanished into thin air."

"Weird."

"Not necessarily," the Morrigan said quietly. "We know of at least three individuals who want you gone. There could be others. Even here, in this sleepy little village. And invisibility spells are easy to get, if you know who to ask."

A shiver of unease crept up my spine as I glanced around suspiciously, wondering if Ares, Athena, or Kali were working with anyone here at Finn's Cove. But for once, nobody was even looking at me because Lugh was the center of attention for the villagers. He soaked it up and radiated with youthfulness and joy.

Garrett extricated himself from the throng and approached me with a smile. "Blessed Equinox, Lady."

"Blessed Equinox to you, as well."

After he greeted Arddhu, the Morrigan, and Kevin, he returned his attention to me. "I have a very special brew for You to try. I'd love to know what You think of it." He led me to the drink station and nodded to the attendant, who filled two cups and handed them over.

I took a sip and closed my eyes to savor the flavors without any distraction.

Warm sunshine, fresh green growing things, blooming meadows, and rich fertile soil were all somehow contained in that ale.

"Garrett, this is spectacular. I taste all the things of Spring in this cup, and you never cease to amaze me."

He grinned and took a long swallow. "I must admit, it is pretty good."

I snorted. "Oh, it's way better than just *pretty good*, my friend."

"I have some news. Do You have a moment?"

"Of course."

We strolled as he spoke. "Donal and his wife Megan have made Michael's cottage their own, thanks to You."

"Yes, I spoke to them on our way here." I glanced around, but no one was within earshot. "He also said the place was broken into before they moved in. Any ideas on who?"

He shook his head. "No, and it pisses me off—begging Your pardon—that someone here right now may be the culprit." He glanced around, then studied me for a moment. "I don't suppose You have any idea what he—or she—was looking for?"

"Not a clue." I took a sip of my ale. "But as far as Donal and Megan go, I'm glad they're the couple you chose. He's taken very good care of my cottage over the past couple of years."

"He's a good lad." Garrett nodded. "Honest, hard-working, and smart. His father expects Donal to take over the market when he retires in a few years. And Megan is a good match for him. She's been assisting the doctor, but with the little one on the way soon, I doubt she'll be working much longer."

"As soon as I get back to Arizona, I'll make sure Donal gets a nice big raise. He's more than earned it."

He smiled. "Much appreciated, Lady. Right now You're his only source of income."

"I understand." We were almost back to my companions. "Was there anything else?"

"No. I'll keep You posted if I hear anything about... the other thing."

"Likewise."

We parted, and I rejoined my family. Arddhu and Kevin stood off to the side, talking quietly, leaving the Morrigan to watch as Lugh wandered off to bask in the glow of attention from a group of young women.

Another young woman approached. "My Lady, would You bless the food, please?"

"Of course."

Just as I'd done at Imbolc, I spread my hands over the food tables and gave my blessing, then did the same at the drink station. There, the attendant winked at me and handed me another cup of ale. I grinned back, remembering how he'd flirted with me at the first festival I'd ever attended at Finn's Cove.

It seemed like a lifetime ago.

As I made my way back to my family, the trio of musicians tucked into the corner of the green began to warm up with their instruments. The sun had dipped below the trees, and now two gentlemen lit the torches around the green to chase away the gathering shadows.

Just as I reached Kevin's side, I felt the cold touch of unfriendly eyes and used my magick to search for the source.

There: someone stood in the darkness beyond the torchlight. Using a tendril of elemental power, I asked the nearby torch to flare brighter, and got a glimpse of a clean-shaven face that seemed vaguely familiar.

"Anyone else notice that guy over there?" I asked.

"The one staring at you?" Kevin replied.

"Yeah. I swear I've seen him before but I can't place where."

"I've noticed he's been staying away from the light," the Morrigan said. "I can go and have a little chat with him."

"If I am not mistaken," Arddhu said, "that is who Michael spoke to on Mabon."

Now that he'd said it, I remembered, too.

"You're right," Kevin agreed. "That's the same guy."

Now, with all four of us staring at him, he turned away.

"Maybe I should go and talk to him," I mused.

"Not alone, you aren't," Kevin warned.

I sighed. "He might tell me more if I'm alone."

Before I took a single step, however, the man began making his way toward us across the green. When he was close enough for my glow to illuminate his face, I studied him.

He seemed young; his dark hair was in a modern cut, the one with tousled waves on top but trimmed short on the sides. He wore plain, nondescript clothing.

The stranger stopped in front of me and bowed his head respectfully. "Blessed Ostara to You, Lady." His voice had the same hint of Irish accent that'd also been in Mike's, and I was pleasantly surprised he'd addressed me with the proper reverence.

"And to you as well," I responded politely.

He hesitated. "May I have a private word?"

"You may speak to me here." I kept my voice formal.

He glanced at the others surrounding me. "I'd rather not."

"Then have a good evening." I shrugged and turned away in dismissal.

"Wait. Please." Now his voice held a note of desperation.

I faced him, but remained silent.

He took a step closer, and Kevin immediately put an arm around my waist.

The man noticed. "I mean no harm. My name is Fergus. I am a friend of Mike's. Or was, I suppose I should say. We... uh... worked together a long time ago."

My witchy-sense said he told the truth, but it didn't make sense because Mike had been much older. Then again, looks could be deceiving.

I cocked my head. "Was that before or after he went berserk?"

He seemed surprised I knew that story. Randy had told me about a mission he and Mike had been on, long before I'd met either of them, when Mike had almost killed everyone. He'd lost control of his wolf, Randy had said.

"Before," Fergus finally answered. "We were childhood friends."

"Funny. He never mentioned you. Not even once."

"I'm not surprised. I brought back bad memories for him."

This was getting more and more interesting. "How so?"

He sighed with impatience. "Look, I'd rather not get into all that right now. I only came to ask a question, then I'll leave."

I raised a brow. "I'd actually rather you *did* get into it."

He clenched his jaw. "I know You inherited his property. I just need to know if You have a certain item of jewelry."

I let him shift uncomfortably under my gaze while I thought of my answer. Sure, I could lie, but what would be the point? I'd get more information by telling the truth. So I replied, "I'm not sure. I haven't seen his things."

"Oh." He blinked. "Well, see, Mike promised me something. A... a ring."

"What sort of ring? What does it look like?"

Fergus seemed like he didn't want to answer that at all, and I was starting to lose my patience.

"How will I know if it's the ring you were promised if I don't know what it looks like?"

"Maybe I should look for it myself. That way You don't have to bother. Just let me know where his things are."

That did it. I lost my patience, and now I did lie. "Dude, everything was boxed up and shipped to Arizona. Right now, it's somewhere between here and there, and even *I* don't know exactly where."

He ran a hand through his hair, like Mike used to do, then dug into a pocket and handed me a worn, dog-eared card. "When it gets there, please let me know. I'll be on the very next flight out. The ring is very special to me, and I'd be very grateful to have it."

I slipped the card into my jeans pocket without looking at it. "You broke into Mike's cottage, didn't you? Maybe I should call the cops instead of you."

He took a menacing step forward and snapped, "Don't be a bitch about this."

Immediately, Arddhu, Kevin, and the Morrigan surrounded me.

"Watch your mouth," Kevin growled.

"Do not dare disrespect the Goddess," Arddhu warned.

The Morrigan just snarled at him.

"Whoa." Fergus backpedaled and held his hands up in surrender. "Sorry. Didn't mean to ruffle any feathers." He met my gaze again, and spoke with forced politeness. "Please consider contacting me when You receive the items." Without waiting for a reply, he quickly turned and left, and a moment later had vanished into the darkness beyond the green.

"What an asshole," Kevin said.

Now I was curious. I pulled his card out of my pocket for a closer look, but it only had his name, Fergus O'Farrell, and a phone number. No company, no address, no social media, nothing. Who in the world gets business cards printed with just their name and phone number? So weird.

"Well," I said, "now we know who broke into Mike's cottage, and why."

"Do you have any idea what kind of ring he's talking about?" the Morrigan asked.

"Not a clue. But we'll get our answer when we go through Mike's stuff."

CHAPTER FIFTEEN

W E HAD A bite to eat and enjoyed the music for a while, but I couldn't get my mind off the encounter with Fergus. What sort of ring had Mike promised him? He'd gotten so defensive when I'd started asking questions, and that seemed suspicious as hell.

What else would I find in Mike's stuff?

The Morrigan was the first of us to say something.

"Why aren't we all at the cottage going through those boxes?" she asked.

"Good question," I said. Then, looking at Arddhu and Kevin, I added, "Um, unless either of you want to stay?"

"I agree our time here would be better served searching Michael's belongings," Arddhu replied.

"Oh, thank the gods," Kevin breathed. "I thought I was the only one wanting to do that."

We hadn't seen Donal and Megan yet, but I didn't think they'd be too disappointed not to see us here. I caught sight of Lugh chatting with a pretty young lady gazing up at him with pure adoration. Kevin went over to him to tell him where we were going, and came back alone.

"He said he'll meet us at the cottage in a couple of hours or so." Kevin shrugged. "I guess he's having too much fun here to want to go through boxes."

I was absolutely fine with that.

On the way to Ard na Mara, the slivered moon didn't give much light on the path through the woods, so Kevin conjured a ball of light to guide us. As we walked we didn't talk much; I supposed we were each lost in our own thoughts.

Childhood friends, Fergus had said. Mike hadn't told me anything about a close friend from his childhood, but as it'd turned out he hadn't told me about a lot of things. A search of Maggie's memories for anything about Fergus only found a single vague reference to a small, quiet boy who'd been sent away to boarding school just before Mike had moved in with Maggie.

That wasn't much to go on, and it didn't confirm a close relationship.

We entered the cottage through the back door, and when I turned on the kitchen light, I saw five medium-sized boxes stacked neatly against the cupboard under the sink. Each were labeled with the room they'd been taken from. Although I didn't question Garrett's integrity, under the circumstances it'd be foolish not to check for spells or booby-traps, so I quickly scanned them and confirmed they were all clean.

Each of us took a box and sat at the kitchen table.

"We don't know what that ring looks like," Kevin said. "So I'd recommend looking for anything unusual."

"Right," I agreed.

My box was marked *living room*.

I recognized some of the stuff from my one visit to Mike's house almost two years ago: magazines, a couple of small flashlights, and an old, chipped ashtray. Other stuff I'd never seen before, like the framed, dusty photographs of an older couple. Checking Maggie's memories, I confirmed they were Mike's caretakers who'd died when he was young. Before we'd found out his real parents had been Maggie and her Assistant, Stuart, he'd referred to them as his parents.

What a bombshell that'd been. Mike had lived with Maggie for years, thinking she was only a sweet and kind older lady. Through the firm, he'd worked with Stuart, never knowing he was his father.

I shook my head to clear the memories, and set the photos aside.

Next, I pulled a couple of spiral notebooks from the box and flipped through the first. It looked like notes from our alliance meetings, pages and pages of agenda items and discussion in his neat handwriting. But in between, I found snippets of a more personal nature, almost like a journal.

I stopped to read something among the notes from our last alliance meeting.

I don't know how much more I can take. She really gets on my nerves. The only good thing is she's letting me call the shots. But for how long? When she realizes how much power she has, that'll all end. And then my hopes and dreams will be ashes.

What. The. Hell.

I flipped through a few more pages. Among the notes from a mission post-mortem, I found a short passage. Surrounded by sinister doodles of an open, screaming mouth, the words were barely legible.

Gods, what a BITCH. I FUCKING HATE HER.

Holy shit. I never knew he'd hated me so much, and my face grew warm with embarrassment.

That day of the battle, when I'd found out how angry he'd been and that he'd betrayed me... not even then had I known he'd despised me.

So why'd he leave me everything? All his stuff, and his cottage?

Wait.

Oh.

Of course.

He'd known I'd find these notebooks and read them.

He'd *wanted* me to.

What an asshole.

I didn't want to read any more of it. I didn't need to. Tossing the notebooks on the floor with disgust, I dug into the box again and found a small box. The kind jewelry came in.

For just a second, I got excited.

Had I found the ring?

But no, the box was empty.

Next: an envelope of credit card receipts, mostly for food and drink from Garrett's Pub and groceries from Conway's Market. Another envelope, this one larger, with photos of Stuart. The firm must've sent it after he died.

Next came a couple of dog-eared paperbacks. From the worn, lurid covers, they seemed to be crime novels or mysteries.

"Check this out," the Morrigan said. She had the box marked *bedroom*, and now she held up an open box, showing us the tarnished silver pendant inside, strung onto a new-looking leather cord. The pendant was a triskele in a triangle.

That symbol looked familiar. Where had I seen it before?

Oh. That was the same symbol Ida had left at the scene of Tyr's murder. Her calling card, Arddhu had said.

"Ida gave him a gift," Kevin spat.

"But from the cord, it looks like he never wore it," I pointed out.

"I wonder why not," the Morrigan mused, careful to keep her fingers away from the pendant. "Maybe she'd wanted to protect him on the day of the battle."

"There aren't any spells or anything on it," Kevin said. "So it wasn't protection magick."

"Maybe it was only supposed to identify him," I said. "So Cromm's army wouldn't kill him by mistake. So why didn't he wear it?"

"Perhaps he did not wish to be saved," Arddhu softly said, and resumed digging in his box.

I actually hadn't thought of that. Had he expected to be killed on the battlefield, or had he expected me to kill him?

The Morrigan closed the pendant's box and set it aside, and the rest of us got back to our boxes.

"Oh hey," Kevin said, a moment later. "Looks like Fergus wasn't lying after all."

From the box labeled *second bedroom*, he showed us what he'd found: a framed photo of Mike and Fergus. It'd once been in color, but years of exposure to sunlight had faded it to almost colorless. The boys were about ten years old, short hair messy from wind or play, and their arms around each other. They looked directly at the camera with wide, gap-toothed grins. In the background, fishing boats dotted the harbor of Finn's Cove.

I already knew from checking Maggie's memories earlier: she hadn't been the photographer.

"Okay," I said. "So he told the truth about being childhood friends with Mike. He could be lying about everything else, like Mike promising him a ring."

"Good point." Kevin placed the photo on the kitchen table, near the pendant found by the Morrigan.

Again, we returned to our boxes.

I pulled out a large manila envelope and dumped the contents onto the table to sort through. High school and college diplomas. Copies of university transcripts. Certificates of completion for various special skills courses, and a bunch of other documents relating to education. I slid them all back into the envelope and dropped it on the floor with the notebooks.

Nothing else in my box seemed interesting. Maybe he'd taken his valuables to Scottsdale. Maybe that's where his jewelry was.

"Ooh, here's something," Kevin said. "But it's locked."

Again, we all raised our heads to look. In other circumstances it would've been comical.

He shook the small fireproof box, and something rattled inside. But when he murmured an unlocking spell, it didn't open.

"Let's look for the key," the Morrigan said.

A moment later, Arddhu produced a keyring from the box marked *kitchen*. Kevin tried the smaller ones among the dozen or so keys, but none of them worked in the lock.

"Shit," he said.

We continued looking, but none of us found any more keys.

Frustrating.

I put everything back into my box and pushed it away to make room for the last box, marked *closet*. Unfortunately, it only had photo albums in it.

One small album held photos of Maggie; another seemed to be his school and class photos for each grade through high school. In most of them, he'd been a nerdy-looking boy with neat short hair and an uncomfortable smile.

Another album was mostly photos of his parents, plus a few with a small girl I didn't recognize. Maybe a cousin who visited from time to time? She couldn't be a sister; he'd never mentioned one. But Maggie's memories weren't any help here, either.

The last album held Mike's baby and toddler photos. I assumed it'd belonged to his caretaker parents. I flipped through idly; he'd been a cute kid. I found three more photos taken with Fergus. In each, they hugged and smiled at the camera, which reinforced the story that they'd been close at the time.

I sighed, repacked the box, and straightened my aching back. "Nothing here except for a few more photos of Mike with Fergus."

The Morrigan also sat back in her chair and rubbed at her neck. "Nothing else in mine."

"I found nothing of interest," Arddhu shook his head.

Kevin closed the flaps on his box. "Nothing here either."

"He must've taken his jewelry to The Hacienda," I mused. "Maybe that's where the key to this box is, too."

Tired and discouraged, we restacked the boxes against the cupboards. As I stretched my stiff muscles, I stared at the boxes. What the hell was I supposed to do with all this shit?

Maybe I could just burn it. Or use my magick to make it gone.

In the silence, a loud, annoying jangle startled me. It took me a moment to realize it was the ancient rotary-dial phone on the sideboard.

I answered it on the second ring.

"Lady?" Donal's voice sounded strained. "Could You come over, please? We're home. At the cottage."

My heart jumped in my throat. "Is Megan okay?"

"Yes, but..." A tiny hesitation. "Just, please come."

"I'll be right there." I hung up and turned to the others. "It was Donal. He wants me to come over."

"You're not going alone," Kevin said, and the others quickly agreed.

I opened my mouth to argue, then thought better of it. Whatever the problem was, these guys might be able to help.

It took us less than five minutes to get to the cottage.

Donal answered the door and quickly ushered us inside. "Come downstairs with me."

I'd been inside this cottage only once, but I remembered the general layout. We followed him to the kitchen, then down the stairs.

Just like mine, the cellar was relatively small with a bare-bulb light fixture, walls of stone, and a low ceiling. But unlike mine, the floor was a jumble of rotted wood planks and hard-packed dirt. Small sections of new concrete began at one side, and a blue plastic tarp covered a large area off to the other.

Megan sat in a folding chair near the tarp, nervously picking at a loose thread on the hem of her shirt. Her dark eyes seemed huge in her too-pale face. She nodded to us in greeting, but didn't rise.

"I've been renovating," Donal explained. "Taking the old rotted wood out, leveling the hard-packed dirt, and putting down a concrete base floor. Eventually, tile will go over the concrete."

While he'd spoken, Megan's gaze darted to the tarp and away, again and again.

Donal sighed. "We didn't stay long at the festival—sorry we didn't see You, Lady—and after we came back, I thought I'd work on another section before bed. So I pulled off some more boards, and... well... I found this." He pulled the tarp away. "We haven't touched it."

In a shallow hole, roughly three feet by three feet, lay the remains of a small body, curled into a fetal position with the skull at an odd angle. The bones held no flesh, so they must've been there for quite some time. Long strands of matted blonde hair were caked with dirt, and the tattered remains of clothing—what looked like a flowered dress—were filthy and crusted with dark blotches.

I really hoped those blotches weren't blood.

The remains seemed to be those of a little girl.

"Oh, no," I murmured, and knelt beside the hole. For a moment I flashed back to when I'd knelt in the cellar of Maggie's cottage and become the Keeper, almost two years ago.

"Careful," Kevin warned. "Don't touch anything. Whoever it is might've been cursed."

I didn't need to. Using only my magick, I probed the skeletal remains. Immediately, a horrible sense of *wrongness* washed over me.

Pain. Fear. Horror. Corruption.

Miserable suffering.

I took a deep breath, determined to continue, and pushed those sensations away so I could concentrate better.

Definitely a young girl, maybe five or six years old. Her neck had been broken, but not before unspeakable things had been done to her. Her poor little body had been damaged so badly it'd been a wonder the blood loss alone hadn't killed her.

I closed my eyes and fought against the bile that rose in my throat. A moment later, when I reopened them, my vision was blurred with tears.

What kind of fucking monster had sexually and physically abused a little girl before snapping her neck and burying her here, in a fucking cellar? And, who was she, this little thing who'd suffered so?

Mike had told me this cottage had been in his family for generations; so did this happen before or after he was born?

The urge for answers was strong, but I also had to be respectful and make sure her spirit was laid to rest first and foremost.

Without hesitation, I used my power to cross the veil into the Otherworld.

On that other plane of existence, the cellar was just a dim backdrop filled with gloom and bone-chilling cold. The girl's spirit-self hovered above her body, and shadows swirled around her as if they were alive.

Due to her broken neck, her head lolled on her shoulder as she stared at me with wide eyes, looking more like a hunted animal than a restless spirit. Her once-golden hair was hopelessly tangled and matted into a bushy aura around her head, and her skin was ashen underneath the dirt and old blood.

Despite the dark circles under her blue eyes and the ugly bruising on her slim neck, she was pretty. Her pink flowered dress was torn and covered in the dark blotches of old blood, just as it was on her physical body. Her skinny arms and legs, also bruised, were smeared with grime, and her bare feet were caked with muck.

As I studied the girl, I realized the shadows dancing around her body were her own powerful emotions made visible. There was pain, yes; but also betrayal, loathing, misery, and hopelessness.

The air was so thick with it all, it was almost enough to choke the air from my lungs.

I kept my voice soft and non-threatening. My sudden appearance alone had startled her more than enough. "Hello."

She continued to stare at me in silence.

"I've come to help you."

"No one can help me." Her voice was so small, so pitiful, it broke my heart.

"Well, I can. I'm the Goddess."

She just blinked at me, so I tried a different tactic.

"What's your name?"

She took so long to answer, I thought she wouldn't, but finally she said, "Jenny."

I smiled my warmest, friendliest smile. "I'm very pleased to meet you, Jenny. I'm Deirdre. But you can call me Dee."

Frustratingly, she just continued to stare.

"How old are you, Jenny?"

"Six and a half."

Now came the tricky part. "How long have you been down here?"

"Forever." The word came out in an endless tormented sigh.

Shit. Although I understood the anguish in her answer, it wasn't helpful. How could I find out who she was if I didn't know how long she'd been buried here? Maybe I could try something else. "Who left you down here in the dark?"

She became highly agitated then; her body trembled and her eyes darted around, frantically searching the corners of the cellar. "Papa," she whispered.

I forced my voice to stay calm and even. "Is he the one who hurt you?"

Her gaze fixed on mine as she nodded, and her tears left pale trails on her smudged cheeks.

"Where was your mother when he hurt you?"

"Sick."

"Did you have brothers or sisters?"

She simply nodded.

This was nerve-wracking. "Sisters?"

She shook her head.

"Brothers, then?"

Again, she shook her head.

Confused, I was about to ask for clarification when she said, "Just one brother. Michael."

Aha. That was what I needed.

And now I could see the resemblance to the girl in the photos I'd seen among his things just a bit ago.

I thought I knew enough to piece the story together. Jenny's parents had been Mike's caretaker parents, except of course he'd thought they were his real parents back then. Her father had viciously raped, beaten, and murdered her, breaking her neck before burying her body down here.

But where had Mike been during all this, and why hadn't he protected Jenny? Unless she'd been his older sister, and he'd been too young to do anything meaningful about it.

"Is he your big brother or little brother?" I asked.

"I don't know." She shrugged, which made her head roll grotesquely. Her face screwed up, as if thinking. "He's bigger than me."

Probably older brother, then. "Where was he when your father hurt you?"

"Away."

This was maddening, but I forced myself to stay patient. Getting angry with her wouldn't help, even as my insides were roiling with disgust, pity, and rage.

"Away at school?" I guessed.

She nodded.

So the asshole had probably made sure Mike wasn't around to stop him. And poor little Jenny had probably been too afraid to tell him about it when he came home from school.

If I assumed Mike had been no older than ten or so, Jenny had probably died about twenty-five years ago.

Okay. Now I really only needed to know one last thing.

"After your father put you down here, did you ever see or talk to your brother?"

"Only once." She hesitated, and more tears fell. "He was a grownup. When I said his name, he ran away and never came back."

I could almost see it: he'd probably come down here for something, heard her call out to him, and freaked. Of course, I was curious as to when that'd happened, but I didn't need to know.

Had he known she'd been buried here? Had he known she'd been hanging around here because she hadn't moved on after her death?

Had he known what her father had done to her?

I took a deep breath. She'd crossed the veil, but stayed attached to this place for whatever reason. I needed to fix that.

Ever so slowly, I rose to my feet and held out my hand. "Come with me, Jenny. Let's leave this awful place."

"No." She shook her head—no small feat, with a snapped neck—and her eyes were wide and panicked again. "I can't. Papa told me to stay here."

Oh, no. So that's why she was still here. What a bastard.

"It doesn't matter what he told you. I'm the Goddess and I overrule him."

She blinked, and tears fell again. "He said he'd hurt me. Even worse than the last time."

"No, Jenny. He can't hurt you ever again."

"Promise?" The hope on her face broke my heart all over again.

I nodded solemnly. "I promise."

She seemed to think about it. "But if I leave... what if Michael comes looking for me? How will he find me?"

Shit. This was getting more complicated.

I couldn't tell her he'd never come looking for her because I'd killed him. And I sure as hell couldn't tell her she'd see him again where she was going, because I didn't think he'd be there. I didn't know for sure, though; I wouldn't know until we got there.

It seemed simpler to lie. As much as I hated it, what choice did I have? "I'll tell him where to find you."

Again, she thought it over, and when her eyes studied me, they seemed older somehow.

I opened both arms to her and waited.

Hesitatingly, inch by inch, she floated toward me until she was close enough. Slowly, so I wouldn't scare her, I drew her gently against me, folding my arms around her small bony frame. After a moment, she fit herself against me as if she wanted to be part of me, and at last she relaxed.

Her body shook with the sobs.

I didn't know how long I stood there, holding her, and sending waves of comfort into her thin body.

As long as I needed to.

Finally, sniffling and hiccupping, she pulled away slightly and took a last look around. "We can really go away from here?"

"Yep." I nodded. "I think you've been here long enough, don't you?"

She gazed up at me, tears shimmering on her lashes. "Yes."

"Okay, then. Hang on tight, 'cause here we go."

She held on as I once again tapped into the Goddess power within me and traveled to where she belonged: a place of rest and recovery.

A safe place for her to stay until she was ready to rejoin the world of the living.

Above us, the sun played hide and seek with elephants and dogs and butterflies made of puffy white clouds, against a robin's-egg blue sky. Kids of all ages ran and played, giggling or shrieking in joy as they chased each other on the softest green grass, among huge trees made for climbing, and surrounded by pretty flowers in every color of the rainbow.

And even some colors I'd never seen before.

Dogs of all ages, sizes, and breeds, tails wagging in joy, chased each other and the children, playing with balls, frisbees, and toys of all kinds.

As soon as I set Jenny on her feet, her appearance changed. Now, she was clean and unblemished, the dark circles under her eyes gone. Her flowered dress was spotless and crisp; white ankle socks with lace trim and shiny black Mary Janes were on her feet. Her golden hair fell straight and untangled and shone in the sun.

Her dark miasma of emotions had vanished.

Best of all, she had no trouble holding her head up, because her neck was no longer broken.

She gazed around in wonder, but when a girl ran past with a burst of loud laughter, Jenny flinched and clung to me desperately.

"Where are we?" She'd spoken so quietly, I'd barely heard her with all the joyful noise around us.

"This is your new home for a while. It's a very safe place. No one will hurt you here."

Another girl about Jenny's age, her russet hair in pigtails and face liberally sprinkled with freckles, approached with a friendly smile. Her bright white sneakers matched her tee shirt, and her red pants matched the dress on the doll she carried. "Lady, who have You brought?"

I blinked at her for a moment. How had she known? "This is Jenny."

"I'm Sarah." She beamed at Jenny. "Would you like to play with my doll? Her name is Susie." Unhesitatingly, she offered her beautiful doll.

Jenny looked up at me. "Can I?"

"Of course." I smiled at her. "Now it's time for me to say goodbye, because I have to go back to my friends."

"Wait. No." She'd begun to panic again. "I'm afraid."

"Don't be afraid, Jenny." Sarah took a step closer, still offering her doll. "We're all friends here. We have lots of toys, and ice cream whenever we want. And nobody hurts us, or yells at us, or takes our food away." She grinned. "This is heaven for kids like us."

Jenny glanced from Sarah to me, biting her lip indecisively, and I nodded encouragingly. "Go on. Go with Sarah. You're free now."

"I'm... free?" Slowly, achingly, the fear was fading from her face. Once again, hope filled her eyes.

"Yes," I said, firmly. "You are free."

She smiled then, a dazzling smile that brought a lump to my throat. She released my hand and took the doll. Sarah drew her away, but after only a few steps, Jenny stopped to look back at me.

"Thank You, Lady," she said. "Please tell my brother Michael I'm okay."

"I will," I promised. As I watched her go with Sarah, I swallowed that lump in my throat and took a deep breath.

Some distance away, the two girls settled under a spreading oak tree, and a large puppy bounded up to lick Jenny's face. Her sweet laughter rang out, and I turned to leave.

Then I cocked my head; there was one more thing I had to do before I could return to the land of the living.

Again using my power, I searched for Mike's spirit-self, and in a heartbeat I was transported from a world of light to a world of dark.

This desolate, lonely landscape was nothing like the beautiful place I'd just left. The sky was an angry, deep purple, with occasional streaks of a sickly green lightning. No soft grass here; no, this stuff was nasty and dead, just like the bare blackened trees.

The bitter wind carried the sound of someone crying, and its intense anguish washed over me in a wave. I slowly turned, seeking the source.

There: a pale lump was curled under a nearby tree. The physical form didn't look familiar, but I recognized Mike's spirit-self. He was naked, just as he'd been when I'd killed him at last year's battle. His entire body shook as he sobbed uncontrollably with his head buried in the arms he'd wrapped around his knees.

This part wasn't gonna be easy.

I took a deep breath, steeled myself, and slowly approached. The crispy grass crunched under my feet.

"Hello, Mike." I'd kept my voice soft.

"Go away," he croaked, voice muffled. He hadn't looked up or moved, and I grimaced at the filth and open sores covering his pale skin.

"I will. But first, I bring a message from Jenny."

A moment later he stirred and lifted his face toward me.

Somehow, I managed not to gasp. His eyes were gone, as if they'd been torn out, leaving only black-crusted empty sockets. Had he clawed his own eyes out? I shuddered.

"Jenny? That's impossible."

Ah, so he *had* known she'd died.

"No, it's not. I just came from helping her to move on. She asked me to tell you she's okay."

His mouth worked for a moment, then his head cocked to one side. "Wait. It can't be. *Dee?*"

I nodded, then realized he wouldn't see that. "Yes. It's me."

"What—how are you here? In this hellish place?"

I answered simply: "I'm the Goddess."

Of all the reactions I expected, wild hooting laughter sure wasn't one of them.

It'd started as a snort, progressed to a chuckle, then to full-on hysterics. I shifted uncomfortably as it continued for far too long, and I wondered if he'd lost his sanity.

"Oh, oh, you've got to be *shitting* me," he finally gasped out.

What the hell could I say to that? Nothing. So I remained silent.

He was still grinning madly, his face turned up to me, but he managed to calm himself a bit. "What happened to Ida?"

"She was stripped of her power and banished."

He cackled. "Oh, that's just rich. It's just too perfect."

The sudden caw of a raven in the branches above, disturbingly loud in this windswept desolation, had an immediate and profound effect on him.

Protecting his head with his scarred arms, he whimpered pitifully and trembled violently. "No, please, no more," he begged, but I didn't think it was to me he spoke.

I glanced up, searching the branches, but didn't see anything, and again wondered if he'd lost his mind.

Seeing him like this was rough. Sure, the sting of his betrayal still hurt—even after all these months—but I wouldn't have wished this kind of suffering on anyone.

Well, I'd done what I'd promised. It was time to go.

I cleared my throat. "Goodbye."

"Wait." He lifted a hand toward me. "Jenny. Is she..." His hand flapped, vaguely indicating the surrounding hellscape.

No. She wasn't in a place like this, and never would be. This was his own private hell, even if he hadn't realized it.

But I wouldn't tell him any of that.

"She's safe," I said. "She's with other children like her. She's playing with friends in a place with warm sunshine and lots of ice cream."

"Oh. That's good, then." His face screwed up as he resumed crying.

It was so strange to see tears fall from empty eye sockets, and I shuddered again.

I hesitated; should I or shouldn't I? If I didn't, I'd never know for sure, and I'd probably never get this chance again because after I left here, I'd never come back.

"She told me what happened, Mike. While you were at school and her mother was sick. Her father hurt her. Badly. And then he killed her."

He nodded, and a bit of the man I used to think he was, long ago, emerged as he spoke calmly and clearly. "I was away at school when I got word that Mother had died. By the time I got home for the funeral, Jenny had gone missing. Father said the search parties had given up looking. One night about a week after the funeral, he got shitfaced and let slip there'd been an accident. That Jenny was dead." Rage flared briefly on his face. "After more booze, he started raging. Said she'd been a horrible brat who'd deserved what she got, and that he wouldn't miss her.

"I knew he was lying. She'd never been a brat. She'd been sweet and kind and innocent. But after he'd raged about her, I just knew there hadn't been any accident. No, he'd killed her." He wiped at his tears but smeared the filth instead, then continued. "So I waited until he finished the rest of the whiskey and passed out. Then I took the big kitchen knife—I had to hold it in both hands—and stabbed him in the chest, over and over, until he stopped breathing."

Oh gods. "How old were you?"

"Ten." He leaned back against the tree trunk and splayed his legs, and I quickly looked away. "That's when Maggie came into my life. Somehow she got his death ruled accidental. She took care of everything, including me. Of course, last year we found out she was my real mother. And Stuart was my real father." His lips twisted. "But for a long time, I felt terrible for what I'd done. I really thought I'd killed my own father."

Shit. I had to tell him. He needed to know the rest of it.

"We... we found Jenny's body. In the cellar of your cottage, under the floorboards. She... she'd been..." I cleared my throat. "Horribly abused. Sexually. And beaten. Her neck was broken."

Mike's face crumpled for a moment before rage took over again. "Then I'm glad I killed him. But he should've had worse. He deserved to suffer."

"Yes, he did. But that was a long time ago, and right now the most important thing is: Jenny's at peace."

After a moment, he sighed and nodded. Then, he seemed to come to a decision. He struggled to kneel and lifted his face to me. "Tell me, Lady: will I ever be at peace?" He'd addressed me formally, with a great deal more respect than he'd ever shown me while he was alive.

I hesitated, thinking it over.

As the Goddess, yes, I could grant him peace. But was it too soon? Did he truly deserve it after only a few months of punishment? I glanced around at this place; it was his own version of hell, so it held terrors designed especially for him. Terrors that were meaningless to me.

The raven cawed again. Mike's entire body flinched but he remained kneeling, and I took a closer look at the wounds on his face and body.

They looked like they'd been inflicted by a beak.

Maybe the raven?

Again, I looked up. It took a moment, but I finally found it: a black body against the even blacker branches. The raven's head cocked to one side, and now an intelligent yellow eye met my gaze.

"*You may, if You wish.*" The voice in my mind was rough, as if it wasn't often used.

So it was my decision, then, to grant peace.

Or not.

Still, I thought it over.

If I granted him peace, his immediate suffering would end, but he'd still need an extended period of atonement and contemplation before he'd be ready to rejoin the world of the living.

Then again, if I didn't grant it, he'd continue to suffer and slowly lose his mind. He might even become irredeemable.

It came down to this: did he deserve mercy?

I studied Mike for a moment longer. He hadn't moved the entire time, just quietly knelt, waiting for my decision.

So be it.

Decision made, I looked up at the raven and nodded once. It dipped its beak once, in reply.

I stepped forward and placed my hand on top of Mike's head. "Be at peace."

He sighed then, a long drawn-out sound of immense relief.

And as I stepped back, his wounds were healed, eyes restored.

"Thank You, Lady." He blinked at me in a mixture of awe, gratitude, and admiration. Then he faded to nothingness and was gone. I was left alone in this hellscape with only the raven.

Once again, I met its gaze. "Blessings to you."

"*Blessings, Lady*," it replied, and it, too, disappeared.

Suddenly, I was back in the cellar, surrounded by my worried friends and the chaos of their frantic questions.

"I'm okay, I'm okay," I insisted.

"Oh, thank the gods," Kevin said. "You scared us all half to death."

"I'll explain everything in a minute." I held up a hand to stop any further comments, then looked over at Donal and Megan. "She's at peace now."

"Thank You, Lady," she breathed.

"Give me a minute to take care of this." Using magickal fire, I burned Jenny's remains. The blue flames destroyed everything without giving off any heat, and left nothing behind, not even ashes. I stood. "Donal, I need salt."

He quickly went upstairs and returned a moment later with a brand-new canister of pure Irish sea salt.

Perfect.

I used the entire container, sprinkling it in a thick layer over the dirt. After another quick probe to make sure the miasma of dark emotions was truly gone, I nodded in satisfaction and handed the empty container to Donal.

He blinked at it for a moment, then asked, "Lady, can You tell us what happened?"

"Let's go upstairs first. I need to sit. And I really could use a stiff drink."

We settled in the living room and Donal brought a bottle of whiskey, five glasses, and a cup of herbal tea for Megan.

Only a couple of years ago, I'd hated the harshness of whiskey as it burned my throat, and only drank beer, wine, and mead. Since then, though, I'd learned there were times when nothing else would do.

This was one of those times, and I hardly noticed the burn at all.

Before Donal had even taken his seat, I'd downed my whiskey and held the glass out for a refill. Thank all the gods, my hand didn't shake.

Donal refilled my glass, and I told them about Jenny.

By the time I was done, Megan's cheeks were wet, and the guys looked like they, too, would cry. The Morrigan looked angry enough to kill someone.

"I wonder what happened when Mike came back from school and found his sister missing," Kevin mused.

"That's the next part of the story." I took a long drink, repeated what Mike had told me, then took another long drink.

"Wow." Kevin shook his head. "That's a helluva tale."

"Yeah," I agreed.

Believing he'd killed his own father for so many years had probably affected Mike much more than he'd realized. It'd probably festered and added to his general state of being fucked up toward the end.

Maybe I could've helped him if I'd known earlier.

"It was very well done, helping Jenny to move on," Arddhu said.

"I really didn't feel like I had much choice," I admitted. "Gods, that poor girl. I just *had* to help her."

"And what about Mike?" the Morrigan asked, dark eyes sharp on me. "Was he suffering for what he did?"

"Yes."

She held my gaze. "Did you release him?"

I couldn't lie. "Yes."

She studied me for a moment longer, then nodded. "I won't ask for details. I trust your judgment."

In the subdued silence that followed, Donal leaned forward and placed his empty glass on the coffee table. "Thank You, Lady. We just didn't know what to do when we found that body. We'll all rest easy now." He put his arm around Megan's shoulders and drew her close. She smiled up at him, one hand on her belly.

I got the hint; it was time to go.

While everyone else finished up their drinks, I took a moment to set wards over the property, including an automatic exception for anyone invited by Garrett, Donal, or Megan.

As I stood, I explained what I'd just done, and added, "I hope you know you can always go to Ard na Mara if you need to. You and Megan both are welcome there."

Donal bowed his head. "Thank You, Lady. That is very thoughtful."

We took our leave, returning to Ard na Mara to wait for Lugh.

None of us spoke on the way. The others were probably just as lost in thought over poor little Jenny as I was.

What a tragic family history. And since Mike had been the last, they were all gone now.

We'd all been sitting at the kitchen table for only a few minutes when Lugh's boisterous singing reached us from the forest path.

"He sounds hammered," Kevin said.

The Morrigan smirked. "Knowing him, he most certainly is."

And then he was there, coming through the back door like a whirlwind, almost taking the door off the hinges.

"Oh, what a *fantastic* evening," he crowed. "The women. The food. The dancing. And the drink. Just fabulous. And to top it all off, the village has decided to rename the autumn harvest festival to Lughnasadh. How cool is that?" His grin was huge, and he almost glowed with excitement.

"That is wonderful news, indeed," Arddhu said.

The Morrigan shrugged. "It's only as it should be."

"But why did they call it Lammas in the first place," I asked, "when the rest of Ireland calls it Lughnasadh?"

Lugh's smile vanished and he looked away. "I don't want to talk about it."

Shit. I hadn't meant to be a buzzkill.

"Time to go home," Kevin said, grabbing the locked box.

Arddhu opened the portal and we stepped through to The Hacienda's living room, where the early afternoon sun streamed through the window-wall.

Lugh left before any of us could tell him all he'd missed with Jenny and Mike. The Morrigan, wanting to check in with Reshep, left shortly after.

As for me, I just wanted to curl up in bed and snuggle in the comforting arms of one or both of my Consorts.

What a helluva day.

CHAPTER SIXTEEN

T HE TIME HAD finally come for Operation Clean Sweep, but for some reason I was more nervous than I thought I'd be. It wasn't because I doubted myself or my ability. No, I knew I had the power to do this.

More likely, it was because this was one of the biggest things I'd ever done, and the aftermath was going to be a huge fucking deal.

The butterflies in my stomach were having a dogfight.

Arddhu, Kevin, the Morrigan, Ogma, and Anthony were with me in the living room. A glass of mead for each of us sat waiting on the coffee table. Not for toasting a successful operation, but for a bit of fortification, should we need it.

I'd already had a large swallow. So far, it hadn't helped my nerves.

Maybe I should've poured myself some whiskey instead.

The television was tuned to an all-news station, but the sound was muted. We'd use it to monitor media reports in the aftermath.

Also on the coffee table was a laptop, ready for releasing the video I'd recorded last week. A few weeks ago, Ogma had created a basic social media presence for me called *The Keeper Goddess*, with an account on the three most popular platforms. Either he or Anthony would post the video on all the accounts, and then they'd monitor the reaction.

Now, I held the list of targets in my shaking hands, took a deep breath, and looked at each of the others. "Ready, everyone?"

Kevin looked miserable—he still wasn't a fan of this—but he nodded along with the rest.

"Okay. Here we go."

I studied each name on the list of targets, and used my magick to find his or her exact location. Some slept peacefully. Others were in the shower, on the toilet, playing golf, eating a meal, or working. A few were in the middle of sex with spouses or lovers. One played catch with his young son in the backyard, and I faltered for a moment.

But only for a moment; it didn't matter. It couldn't. The majority of us had agreed on this course of action, and I had to continue. Besides, bad people still had kids and families.

I steeled myself and continued down the list until I held each target firmly in my mind.

I closed my eyes to concentrate better. For each target, I randomly chose either sudden cardiac death or ruptured blood vessels in the brain.

In the space of about two heartbeats, all the targets had been neutralized. It was over.

Well, that part of it, at least.

"Done." I drank half my mead in one swallow and wondered when my hands would stop shaking, or when the butterflies in my stomach would knock it off.

Kevin turned up the volume on the television, and we all stared at the screen. We didn't have to wait long for the first reports to start coming in. The sudden deaths of the local and regional targets were first. They'd been the ones playing golf or working. Then the national reports came in from other time zones, and the anchor frowned. It was becoming obvious these deaths were more than a coincidence.

Within the hour, the coverage had become chaotic as international reports were added to the rest.

"When should we post the video?" Anthony asked.

"In just a few more minutes," Ogma replied, not taking his eyes from the television.

I tried to relax and stay unaffected at the growing panic and confusion on the screen, but it was almost impossible. I told myself to remember this was for the greater good. For the survival of humans and the planet.

"Okay, let's do it now," Ogma said, just as a political analyst began speaking on the screen.

Anthony leaned forward and pressed a couple of keystrokes, then looked at me. "Done."

As I watched the television, I caught myself chewing the inside of my cheek and forced myself to stop. I took another long drink of my mead and set the empty glass on the coffee table.

My hands were still shaking.

Others, too, had drained their glasses. Kevin took a moment to refill them, and I murmured my thanks.

Ogma and Anthony stared at the laptop, and I assumed they were watching the reaction to the video on the three major social media networks.

"It's going to go viral," Ogma said, again not taking his eyes from the screen. "It's already had over ten thousand views. Clocking in at about a thousand views per second now."

Less than five minutes later, the anchor interrupted the political analyst, who'd been blaming the deaths on either the FBI or aliens.

"We have some breaking news," the anchor said, breathlessly. "A video has been posted online by an individual or group calling themselves The Keeper Goddess. They've claimed responsibility for the deaths reported around the world. We can share it with you now."

My face filled the screen. Seeing myself, larger than life, made my heart skip a beat. In the video, I gazed directly into the camera—and every viewer's eyes—for a silent moment, then began speaking. I'd altered my voice to make it sound more like what I'd thought a Goddess's voice should sound like: several different tones resonating at once. The overall effect of that and my bright glow made me seem like some otherworldly being.

"I am the Keeper of the Sphere and Goddess of Earth. Some of you may recognize me from videos taken when I helped with an Arizona brushfire a few weeks ago. Since then, I've also intervened in other climate events around the world, and saved many lives. And, I've been healing the damage to the planet, cleaning the air, water, and soil of toxins. Some of you may even have noticed a difference.

"But progress has been slow, in no small part due to ninety-nine individuals whose global business empires have been killing the planet for the past fifty years. These vast corporations are the dirtiest and greediest of those involved in gas and oil extraction and refining, coal mining, and plastics and chemical manufacturing. Their operations have destroyed valuable resources, poisoned our air and water, and contaminated our soil with cancerous substances.

"Therefore, let it be hereby known by all the peoples of the planet that I, Goddess of Earth, judged these individuals guilty of crimes against Earth, sentenced them to death for those crimes, and executed them accordingly."

With no emotion, I recited the names of the targets.

"I have authorized others to work with these corporations to convert the worst of the facilities into clean energy operations. It is my fervent hope that together, we can cease all harm to the planet, which will reduce the extreme weather events occurring so frequently.

"Each of you must be a steward of the Earth and do your part to heal the planet. Invest in and promote companies that develop clean, renewable energy. Cease exploitation of the natural resources of the planet. Recycle, reuse, and reduce your waste.

"I am the Goddess of Earth, and the Keeper of the Sphere. Protect the Earth, and you will enjoy my blessings for health, prosperity, and happiness." Now my eyes flashed. "Harm the Earth, and you will suffer my wrath."

After a moment of stern silence, the video ended.

The screen returned to the anchor, who blinked at the camera for a moment, utterly speechless. "Well, that was quite the... uh... statement," he finally commented before quickly returning to the political analyst sitting with him to ask his opinion.

Kevin shut off the television. "I don't think we need to hear any more."

I glanced around the room. "Well, what do you all think? Too harsh?"

Ogma had helped craft the statement, but no one other than he and Anthony had heard it until now.

Arddhu seemed lost in thought and didn't reply.

"I'm actually a little bit jealous." The Morrigan smirked. "I thought it was well written and well done."

Ogma and Anthony were still staring at the laptop screen, and didn't comment.

Kevin grimaced. He looked like he wanted to vomit. "I've still got a really bad feeling about this."

Arddhu finally blinked and met my gaze. "It was a strong statement, yes. But not harsh. I, too, believe it was well done. But what truly matters most right now is the opinion of the people, is it not?"

"Over five million views on the video now," Anthony said without looking up from the laptop. "And you've got over a million new followers, too."

Holy shit.

Was I an internet celebrity now?

CHAPTER SEVENTEEN

FOR THE FIRST time since I'd started the healing sessions for Earth, I felt like my work wouldn't be almost immediately undone. With the remaining targets removed, both the firm and the Túatha were working with the facilities to convert them to clean energy. Maybe the constant onslaught of environmental damage would finally end.

Sure, it'd only been a day since Operation Clean Sweep, but I was optimistic.

I headed outside on yet another beautiful morning in Arizona. On the patch of soft grass just beyond the patio, I stood and breathed in the desert air for a moment, then got to work.

First, I sent my blessings and healing energy as far down into Earth as I could, and kept it up for about fifteen minutes. I sensed rather than felt the healing picked up and spread through the soil further away by the Túatha. Next, I did the same with the air, to clean and purify it, again for another fifteen minutes, and again the Túatha spread it as far as possible. Finally, I reached out to the nearby Salt River and sent healing into the water for fifteen minutes, and the Túatha spread it to all the waters of the Earth.

Weak and shaky, I sat on the grass and rested, tapping into my energy reserves.

"You okay?" Kevin asked as he sat next to me.

"Yeah. I just finished a healing session."

"I thought so. The Earthsong is louder."

"Really?" I frowned. "Why can't I hear it?"

He shrugged. "I'm not sure. Maybe because you're still partly human."

"Humans can't hear it?"

"Not usually, no."

"But the Native American delegation said some of their elders can."

He shrugged again. "Most humans aren't connected to the Earth the same way First Nations are."

"So I'm not connected to the Earth either?" Ugh. That'd come out more petulant than I'd expected.

"Dee." He studied me. "C'mon. Is it really that important to you?"

I had a lot of other things to worry about, actually. "Not really." A moment later, I added, "It'd just be nice, is all."

"Close your eyes." He took both my hands in his. "And listen."

I didn't hear anything other than birds tweeting, but just as I opened my mouth to say so, I heard it.

A deep steady hum, joined by several tones in higher registers, all blending together in an ethereal, otherworldly sound that raised the hair on the back of my neck.

"Oh," I whispered. "It's beautiful."

"Yes, it is."

Intensely beautiful. So much so, tears stung my eyes.

I blinked them away and met Kevin's gaze. "Thank you."

He smiled. "You are very welcome."

I sighed. "Forty-five minutes of solid healing, and it only fixed an area about the size of Arizona. Even with the Túatha helping, it's still going too slow."

"I meant to ask before. What exactly are they doing?"

"They're boosting my healing. So when I send the energy out—into the soil, the air, and water—they sort of pick it up and spread it."

"Like a wi-fi extender," he said.

"Okay. Yeah. Something like that." I nodded. "They're also using their magick to clean the air and water in far-away places. I mean, they're leaving the healing to me, but doing what they can, and we're definitely doing more than I could do alone." I paused. "But I really thought it'd go quicker by now."

He snorted. "You thought you could heal the entire planet in a day?"

He'd made it sound so ridiculous, I had to laugh. "No, but... well, it's not getting any easier."

"Patience, love. It didn't get this bad overnight, and it'll take more than a few healing sessions to fix it."

I picked at the grass. "I do get impatient, don't I?"

He snorted again. "Understatement of the century."

I blew a raspberry at him. "Thanks a lot."

"But seriously," he continued. "Removing the targets was never going to impact how much environmental damage happens on a daily basis. It was more of a statement than anything else. What'll really matter will be converting the facilities, and that'll take some time." He paused. "I thought you knew that."

I sighed. "Yeah, I know. It's just... frustrating."

"Oh, hon." He pulled me close. "It'll happen. I know it seems like it's been forever, but it really hasn't. And you've made such a big difference already. You're just too close to see it."

"I suppose." I yawned, still so tired from the healing session.

We sat quietly for a moment, then he said, "By the way, the public reaction to Operation Clean Sweep is running about fifty-fifty."

"Shit." I had to do better than half positive and half negative. "I need better numbers. Should I do another video?"

"Maybe." He shrugged. "But Ogma and I were thinking you should interact with your followers more. He doesn't want to answer any of the gazillion direct messages or replies on the accounts because he doesn't want to impersonate you. But the continued silence isn't helping. People want answers."

The mere thought of sitting and reading through thousands of posts and messages every day was daunting. But to write replies to all those posts and messages made me want to vomit.

Or maybe that was just the pregnancy.

"I'd rather just do another video," I complained.

He laughed. "Think of it as answering prayers. You don't mind those, right? This wouldn't be much different. Just answer some questions, or thank someone who's said something nice. You don't have to make a full-time job of it. Just maybe an hour or so, every other day." He studied me for a moment. "You've got lots of fans, you know. You should take advantage of it."

Fans? Me? "How many are we talking about?"

"As of this morning, roughly ten million on each account."

My jaw dropped. I'd expected a lot less. "Holy shit."

He nodded. "That's exactly what I said."

"But if the reaction is split fifty-fifty, doesn't that mean I have the same amount who aren't fans?"

He shook his head. "Not really. You asked about the public reaction, so that includes media and other entities. Among just your social media followers, you probably have about a million who are bots and trolls. Ogma and Anthony are looking at software that could automatically flag and block those. So the rest of the non-fan category are real people that you have a chance of winning over. That's why we think if you engage with them and let them get to know you, it could help boost your ratings."

I sighed.

Ratings. Fans. Bots and trolls.

It all made sense, but this was probably my least favorite part of the whole thing so far. Ogma and I had talked about it, of course, but I'd just put off thinking about it too deeply.

Sort of how I'd been putting off making that doctor appointment I needed to make.

I'd never been such a procrastinator like this.

"Okay," I finally said, and yawned. "In a little bit, I'll go inside and give it a go. Anything else I should know?"

"Not really." He grimaced. "I'm just worried. Yes, still. I keep trying to game this out, be prepared for whatever might happen, but I keep thinking I'm missing something." He paused. "I really think it's just a matter of time until the Feds come. Especially after yesterday. What it means, long-term, is probably increased scrutiny on all of us. Maybe even surveillance. We could be targets of paramilitary forces. So we should probably discuss it at next week's Council meeting."

"You should mention all this to Randy. He could beef up our security, maybe prepare for any potential attacks." I glanced at the sky, but of course my wards were invisible. "And I'll double the wards. Just in case."

"Sounds good," he agreed. "I'll talk to him in a bit."

"And remember, if it really gets bad, we'll just go to Ard na Mara."

"Ida's world would be better."

He'd mentioned that before. "You really think things could get so bad we'd have to leave Earth completely?"

He shrugged but didn't look at me. "No way to tell. Humans are unpredictable at best and barbaric at worst. Anything can happen."

Although I saw his point, I could argue the gods were just as unpredictable and barbaric.

"We also need to go through Mike's stuff here," he added. "See if we can find that damned ring Fergus talked about. And a key to the locked box."

Shit. I'd forgotten all about that.

"Soon." I yawned, still exhausted from the healing session. Even replenishing my energy hadn't helped. I really wanted to go back to bed.

He frowned. "Are you feeling okay?"

Oh, how I wanted to tell him. But I couldn't. Not yet.

Remembering the trick Loki had shown me to avoid lie detection, I cloaked my words carefully. "I've been tired, that's all. It's probably just the transition to deity. Plus all the energy I've been using with the healing sessions."

He hadn't taken his gaze from me. "Maybe you should see a doctor. Just to be sure it's not something else. Something bad."

I blinked at him.

Of course. He'd just given me a perfect excuse. Now I wouldn't have to hide it from them.

"You're right. I'll do that. The firm has doctors I can see so nobody will freak out at my wonky bloodwork."

He laughed. "Good point."

I rested my head on his shoulder, and he held me closer. We sat in the warm Arizona sunshine for a bit longer, and it was nice.

Actually, way nicer than just *nice*.

I loved these quieter moments with him, and I hoped they didn't stop after the baby came.

Once again, we were having the Council meeting in the green space I'd created. For the first week of April, the weather was still gorgeous, with cloudless blue skies and relatively mild temperatures. It wouldn't be long, though, until we hit triple digits. Then, I'd activate the climate control system I'd designed.

We'd invited the full Council this time, so all the ambassadors were expected to attend. I was curious what everyone's reactions would be to the healing I'd done since the last meeting. I'd really stepped it up, doing multiple sessions every day, and I estimated about a tenth of Earth's total surface was healed.

Still a long way to go, but it wasn't exactly insignificant.

Daphne was the first to greet me. Tears shimmered in her pale blue eyes. "Oh, my Lady, I have the most wonderful news: more of our sisters have awakened since last we spoke, and now only a few yet remain in hibernation."

"That's fantastic." With a little luck, the rest of those poor dryads would wake shortly. "I'm doing as much as I can, as fast as I can, but I have to rest between healing sessions. It's taking longer than I'd thought."

She smiled warmly. "We understand. Truly. And please, let us know if we can assist You in any way."

"I will."

Alanna and Ferris were next.

"Lady, the other sprites are downright giddy at their cleaner environments," Ferris said in his gravelly voice. "They asked me to tell You they are deeply grateful."

"That's great," I said. "I'm so glad."

Alanna also reported great joy among her kind. "We faery are also deeply grateful, Lady," she squeaked. "There has been much celebration."

"I am so happy to hear it," I said.

The Túatha arrived next.

Manannan stood motionless, eyes unfocused and head tilted as if he were listening to something. A single tear slowly rolled down his pale cheek.

"What's wrong?" I asked.

"It's the Earthsong," Lugh replied. "It's much louder here than anywhere else."

"It is quite beautiful," Manannan whispered, then his eyes focused on me. "Well done, Lady. I look forward to the day Earth is fully healed." He bowed his head to me and left for the bar with the Dagda and Lugh.

"It is truly glorious," Ogma said. "Earth is already much healthier than even just a moon past." He paused before continuing. "My Lady, we must discuss a few things after this meeting. Every day, I receive more and more requests for media interviews. So far, You have not granted a single one. This cannot continue."

He'd referred to my official website, a major part of what he and Anthony called my *branding* as The Keeper Goddess. Both of them were listed as the main contacts for all media inquiries. The site had a few photos, a short biographical writeup, the video I'd released, and links to all the social media accounts. It was professional and classy, with artwork that matched the social media headers. So far, I'd refused to start a blog. I just didn't have the time for it right now. Maybe after Earth was healed, and things settled down a bit.

As far as media interviews went, I hated the thought of taking precious time away from healing the planet to trot out in a dog-and-pony show.

"How many interviews are we talking about?"

"No less than five requests just in the past few days. We're up to thirty now, and they're getting very insistent."

Yikes.

I sighed. "Okay. We'll work out a schedule after this meeting."

"Excellent." He headed to the bar to join the others.

I glanced around for a mental headcount, wondering who we were still waiting for.

Reshep had snuck in, probably while I'd been speaking with Ogma. Now, he and the Morrigan stood close together, talking.

Randy was with Anthony, Kevin, and Arddhu.

Good. Everyone was here. I'd give them a few more minutes to chat and catch up before I called the meeting to order.

The Morrigan had broken off speaking with Reshep and approached. "Well?" she asked.

"Well what?"

She kept her voice low. "I'm assuming you took the test."

Oh. *That.*

She actually hadn't been around for the past week or so, spending some quality time with Reshep. I hadn't had a chance to update her.

"Yeah." I spoke just as quietly, even though no one else was within earshot. "Positive."

She nodded. "I'd assumed so. Let me know if you need my help again."

I smiled. "Thanks. I will."

"So what's next?"

I shrugged. "Make a doctor appointment."

One brow lifted. "Are you sure that's wise?"

"It'll be fine. I'll be seeing a doctor recommended by the firm. Besides, I don't have much choice. There are some things I can't find out on my own."

"Really? Like what?"

"Like how far along I am."

Now her other brow lifted. "You mean you don't know?"

"No, I—" I broke off as Kevin approached.

"I think we're ready to start," he said.

I nodded, and called the meeting to order.

After everyone was settled, I began. "Thank you all for coming. First, a quick update on what's happened since our last meeting.

"As we'd agreed, last week I eliminated the remaining targets. We'd already recorded a video, which was released shortly after. Since then, we've been carefully tracking and analyzing the public response. Ogma, can you give us an update on that?"

Ogma nodded and glanced at his notes. "At first, the public response was split almost evenly between positive and negative. Then Dee began interacting with humans on her social media accounts, and there was an immediate positive effect. Popular opinion on The Keeper Goddess is now at eighty-three point six percent positive, which is actually phenomenal." He met my gaze and smiled. "That's thanks to Your naturally warm and friendly demeanor. It's almost as if You were born for this."

I snorted and shook my head. "I'm sure it'll just be a matter of time before the trolls attack."

I didn't realize my poor choice of words until Manannan leapt from his seat and glanced around wildly. The rest of the Túatha, knowing what I referred to, didn't react at all.

It sort of reminded me of how Arddhu used to be, and with a shock I realized even he'd known what I'd meant.

"No, no," I quickly reassured Manannan. "Not *real* trolls. It's an American slang term for humans who verbally attack others on social media."

"Oh. Of course." Somewhat embarrassed, he sat down again.

"Thanks for that, Ogma," I continued. "Now, I'd like to give an update on the healing sessions for Earth.

"I've done several sessions every day, and although it's going slower than I expected, I think Earth is about ten or fifteen percent healed, thanks in no small part to the magickal boost from the Túatha." I nodded my thanks to the Dagda, and he smiled in return. "As some of you mentioned to me earlier, the Earthsong seems to be getting louder, which I believe is a good indicator of progress. If I had to guess, I'd say we're on track for the planet to be fully healed by the end of the year, at the very latest."

"That is commendable," the Dagda said. "But if I may, I'd like to ask when my people can return to Eire."

Hmm. Good question. Although he and his people spent quite a bit of time on Earth, they still resided in the temporary realm they'd created after we'd freed them in December.

It'd been four months. He deserved an answer.

"I'm not sure," I replied. "It's an island, and I don't think there's enough room for all of you plus all the humans who currently live there. And between erosion and sea-level rise, it's probably even smaller now than it was when you last lived there. I don't think the people of Ireland would appreciate it if you kicked them all out, either. So although I do understand you and your people's frustration, we're probably going to need a bit more time to figure this out."

"Wait," Lugh said. "Why do we have to stay on Eire? Why can't we just go wherever we wish? I, for one, have become accustomed to this place, this *Arizona*. I'd like to settle here."

The Dagda stared at him. "You no longer wish to stay with your own people?"

Lugh shrugged. "It's a different world now than when we were here last. It's a *bigger* world. There's more room for us to spread out."

Actually, the size of the planet hadn't changed, only their conception of it. But it probably wouldn't be helpful if I pointed that out.

"Besides," Ogma added, "some of us rather like the warmer climates."

"And drier," Manannan said.

I blinked at him. Since when did the Lord of the Sea actually like a dry climate?

The Dagda shook his head, but seemed resigned to his people being scattered all over the planet. "So be it," he said. "My people shall be free to live wherever they wish."

"I'm glad that's settled." It was a lot easier to spread thousands of new residents around the globe than to try and squeeze them into an already-occupied island they'd called home, once upon a time.

"It is not settled," the Dagda said. "We have not determined *when* my people can return."

He was nothing if not persistent.

"I don't see why they can't return at any time," I said. "As long as they do it orderly and not all at once. The last thing we need is panic among the humans when they see thousands of aliens pouring through a portal."

Then I noticed Daphne's stricken expression, and remembered there was some history there, as well as with the troll-kind.

Time to nip that in the bud.

"Actually, there's one more thing." I met and held the Dagda's gaze. "Under no circumstances are any of your people to harm anything on this planet. Not humans, not other magickal beings. Not a plant or tree. Not any animals, not even a bunny rabbit. Is that clear?"

"What are You implying, Lady?" His voice was low and menacing, and his multi-colored eyes swirled, making it difficult to maintain eye contact.

"I'm not implying anything. I know that your people hunted the trolls almost to extinction in Ireland. And I also know your people harmed other magickal beings. You must swear to never do anything like that ever again, or I'll banish you myself."

For a moment, I thought he was going to argue or lash out. His jaw clenched and unclenched as he and I stared at each other.

Then he took a deep breath and inclined his head politely. "As You wish, Lady. You have my word that my people will not harm any living creature on Earth, so long as we live on it."

"Not good enough," I said. "Swear it."

His nostrils flared in anger, but again he was polite. "By stone, by sea, by sky, I hereby swear neither I nor my people will harm a single living creature on Earth."

I turned it over in my mind, searching for a loophole, but I couldn't find one. Finally, I nodded. "Thank you." I glanced around. "Does anyone have anything to add?"

No one did, so I continued. "Now, we need to discuss Ares, Athena, and Kali. Reshep, do you have an update on the South Asia situation?"

"Yes. The whispers of war have escalated into cross-border skirmishes and localized attacks with explosive devices. It has become extremely volatile. I can only assume Ares is behind it, but I still have found no proof."

"I checked with the firm on that," Anthony interjected. "They haven't been able to confirm Ares is behind the hostilities, either. But, for what it's worth, I agree with you. I think it's him."

"Or maybe it's all three of them," the Morrigan added. "After all, they're all gods of war."

"And yet, only the Olympians visited Asgard," Lugh pointed out. "So I don't think Kali is involved."

They'd all had good points. "Anthony, have the firm's spies located Ares and Athena on Olympia yet?"

He shook his head. "There's been a few brief sightings, but those two seem to stay one step ahead."

Shit. "Maybe I need to visit those two countries in South Asia and see if I can calm them down."

"I don't think that's a good idea," Ogma said. "At least, not until after you grant some interviews with international media. Right now, you'd only be seen as a meddling American."

Damn. Good point.

"Right." I sighed and rubbed my forehead. "Anyone have anything they'd like to discuss?"

Lugh spoke. "We need to plan the next diplomatic delegation. Unfortunately, Marisha-Ten's pantheon still hasn't responded to my inquiries." He turned to Anthony. "Did the firm have any luck contacting them?"

He shook his head. "They haven't responded to our inquiries, either." He paused before continuing. "I had a long conversation with Marisha-Ten, once. Their realm is called Takamagahara. Just like Asgard, it's accessible from Earth by a bridge, called Ama-no-uki-hashi, or the Floating Bridge of Heaven." He glanced around the table. "Maybe something's wrong with their communication system. Maybe we should send a representative, in person, instead."

Lugh nodded. "I have some free time coming up. I could probably give it a try."

I asked, "Any other business?"

Kevin spoke. "I wanted to mention what'll probably happen now that the last of the targets have been eliminated." He sighed. "We can probably expect some increased scrutiny from law enforcement. Definitely more general attention, at the least. And, we can't rule out retaliation from domestic terrorist groups." He turned to the Dagda. "Your people who have brick-and-mortar businesses, like shops and restaurants, should be on alert for anything out of the ordinary."

The Dagda nodded. "They already are, but I will let them know they must be even more vigilant."

"Anything else?" I asked again. When no one spoke up, I said, "I now call this meeting adjourned. Please help yourselves to the refreshments."

As everyone headed toward the food, I slumped in my seat, exhausted. This damn pregnancy was annoying.

Ogma approached. "Can we meet now, Lady?"

My stomach took that moment to growl loudly. "I really need to have something to eat first. We'll talk after that."

"Yes, of course."

But I hadn't taken three steps toward the food before the Morrigan intercepted me. "That was good news, that your popularity has risen immensely."

I smiled wryly. "Yeah, but I think it also means I shouldn't go on any more field trips. At least not any time soon. I'd get mobbed."

"Sure you can." She grinned mischievously. "Just change your appearance. You could even be a man."

"Are you saying you want to go on another adventure?"

"I'd love to. Besides, we never did go dancing at the clubs like you said we would."

Oh gods. I'd completely forgotten I'd ever mentioned doing that.

It'd be absolute chaos. And probably more fun than I deserved to have.

I laughed. "Let's wait until things calm down a bit, like after Earth is healed. We'll go out on the town and celebrate."

Of course, by that time I'd probably have the baby, and I'd either not be able to go out or I'd beg for the opportunity to be among adults.

One brow lifted. "Oh, so you're promising this? Just like you promised a weekly get-together with your security team last year?"

Shit. Just another thing I'd completely forgotten about. It was a wonder they didn't hate me by now.

"Gee, thanks for reminding me of that and making me feel like shit."

She snorted. "I'm sure they've forgiven you." Her sharp gaze pierced me to the core. "I, on the other hand, will *never* forgive you if you don't keep this promise. I'll hunt you down and make you do something you really hate."

I shivered with apprehension. She'd scare the living shit out of anyone with that look. Probably had, many times, in fact.

It took everything in me to not show fear or back down.

"And what would that be?" I'd asked the question, but really didn't want to know her answer.

She leaned closer, eyes sparkling with mischief. "I'll make you drink fermented goat's milk."

With that, the scary Morrigan was gone, and my dear sister goddess had returned.

"Gross." I grimaced. "I'll keep my promise. Somehow."

She threw her head back and laughed so loud, she drew startled glances. "I thought so."

Oh gods, she was something, and I really did love her.

CHAPTER EIGHTEEN

AFTER MEETING WITH Ogma and setting up a busy schedule for media interviews over the next couple of weeks, I holed up in my suite for some much-needed down time.

And privacy.

I sat on my bed with the tablet I'd received for my birthday, reading an online article titled *So You Think You're Pregnant.* So far, I'd done the first two things on the list: take a home pregnancy test and keep my mouth shut about it.

Well, sort of, on the second. Only Nat and the Morrigan knew. Oh, and Loki. And the firm.

Okay, so maybe I couldn't say I'd kept my mouth shut.

The next item on the to-do list was to contact the OB/GYN for an appointment and be prepared to give the date of my last period.

I ran a hand through my hair in frustration. I had no idea when my last period was. Somehow, I'd lost track, which wasn't like me.

Then again, there'd been an awful lot of shit going on over the past few months. Maybe it'd been bound to happen eventually.

"Dee?" Kevin's voice on the other side of my door was hesitant. "You okay?"

"Yeah," I called. "You need something?"

"Did you want to go through Mike's stuff?"

Hell yes, I did.

"Coming," I said, and shut off my tablet.

He'd brought the box of Mike's stuff from the garage to the living room, and the locked box from Ard na Mara waited on the coffee table.

We sat cross-legged on the floor next to each other, and he removed the box lid.

The top item was Mike's tablet. It didn't power up, so the battery probably just needed a recharge. I set it aside while Kevin pulled out a couple of paperback novels and flipped through them to check for notes or scraps of paper.

The next item was a small wooden box—the type usually found on a man's dresser—that held an odd assortment of buttons, safety pins, and screws. Two broken keychain fobs, but no keys.

Kevin frowned at the wallet in his hand. "Why's this here? Wouldn't it have been on him?"

"Huh. What's in it?"

He checked the compartments. "Credit cards... a towing service card... some business cards... and a couple of shopper's loyalty cards. No driver's license or debit card."

"Maybe he took those two with him. He would've needed his license to board the plane to Ireland. And obviously he needed to access money, so he took his debit card." I shook my head. "But it's really weird that he only took those but left his wallet."

"We're finding out he did a *lot* of weird shit." He tossed the wallet onto the growing pile of stuff on the floor.

He wasn't exactly wrong. It seemed as if I'd learned more about Mike since he'd died than I ever had when he was alive.

Next was the small album filled with photos of Maggie and Stuart. I'd originally found it in her things and given it to Mike after we discovered Stuart was his birth father. I flipped through it, but no notes had been tucked between the pages.

"Oh, hello," Kevin said. "What's this?"

He held up a small key attached to a plain keychain, then inserted it into the lock on the box.

It clicked open, and we exchanged a glance before he lifted the lid to reveal a velvety pouch inside.

"Go ahead," I murmured.

He untied the drawstring and shook an object onto his palm, then immediately let it fall to the carpet with a curse, rubbing his hand against his pants leg.

"What's wrong?" I asked.

What a strange reaction to—I peered at the object—just a man's ring. A single dark red polished stone nearly glowed in its setting on a simple, wide gold band.

Then, whispers crowded my brain in an unrecognizable language. I'd understand them if I just...

Kevin grabbed my hand.

I blinked at him in confusion.

"No." His voice was sharp and seemed too loud. "Don't touch it."

"Why? What is it?"

He hadn't let go of my hand, and when he met my gaze, I recognized fear in his eyes. "It's the Ring of Ur," he said with a shudder.

The what? I'd never heard of it, and a search of the memories of the prior Keepers proved fruitless.

Using my enhanced vision, I studied the ring. Faint markings on the band were all that was left of some kind of engraving. It was so worn I couldn't tell if the markings had been script or a geometric design. The surface of the stone itself had a carving, but I couldn't make it out. I'd need to hold it under a bright light at just the right angle.

As I continued to study it, the whispers grew louder. Wait. I... could... almost...

"*Don't touch it*," Kevin snapped, and yanked my other hand away.

I shook my head to clear it. I must've reached toward the ring again, but I hadn't even been aware of it.

This thing was dangerous.

Letting go of my hands, Kevin opened the velvet bag and used one of the paperbacks to carefully scoop the ring back inside. He tied the drawstring and put it back into the box, closing it with a snap.

Only then did he take a deep, shaky breath and let it out.

"Tell me about this ring," I said.

He waited so long to reply, I almost thought he wouldn't.

"Supposedly, it was created by a dark wizard in ancient Sumer, thousands and thousands of years ago. Entire civilizations went to war to possess it, and some were even destroyed over it." He shook his head. "But how the hell did *Mike* end up with it?"

Not for the first time, I wished I had Ida's memories, like I had of the prior Keepers. "Maybe Ida gave it to him. We know he was working for her."

"That wouldn't make sense." He ran a hand through his hair. "If she'd had it, she never would've given it away. She would've used it. And none of us would be here right now."

"Why? What does it do, exactly?"

"If the wearer is mortal, it basically makes him—or her—a god. If the wearer is immortal, it grants ultimate power. Victory over any foe. Untold wealth. Invincibility. And true immortality." He hesitated, then added, "But all at the cost of the wearer's sanity."

Holy shit. An unstoppable deity who was also insane?

This ring was incredibly dangerous.

I glanced at the box. Thankfully, the whispers had stopped the minute the ring had been locked inside.

"Maybe someone else had given it to Mike," I mused. "Maybe he was supposed to pass it on to someone."

"Like Cromm? Or Malsumis?"

I nodded.

"But then why didn't he have it at the battle? Why leave it in a locked box in Ireland? With the key here?"

I shrugged. "Maybe he changed his mind."

He shook his head. "If he did, the key would've been in Ireland, too."

Shit. He was right. What a puzzle.

Then I remembered Fergus. "Well, Fergus said he'd been promised a ring. If this is it, he probably expects to become Mr. All Powerful."

"Or maybe Fergus was going to give it to someone else," Kevin mused. "Like Ares. Or Athena. Or Kali."

"Oh gods, if he's been working with one of them..." I shivered, imagining any one of them with this ring and completely insane. They'd be ruthless and unstoppable in destroying anything and everything. "But even if he isn't, we can't let it fall into the wrong hands."

"I know." He locked the box, then stared at the key. "So what the hell do we do with it? If we bury it, someone will eventually find it."

"Can it be destroyed?"

"If it could be, I'm pretty sure it would've been destroyed by now." He shrugged. "We could always give it a shot, I guess."

Before I could reply, Anthony interrupted. "We have a problem. The FBI is here."

"Oh, shit." I turned to Kevin. "We don't have time to do anything right now."

"Right," he agreed, then murmured something. "I just put some strong protection spells on it. Can you send it deep underground for now? Meantime, I'll stash the key and get all this stuff cleaned up."

I ported the box so deep beneath the Earth's surface, no human would ever find it. Just in case we couldn't get back to it for a while, since I had no idea what was going to happen with the FBI.

Anthony shifted impatiently. "Dee, we have to let them in."

Oh. The wards.

Shit.

I quickly modified them. "Done."

He radioed the front gate, then turned back to me. "Answer truthfully, but don't volunteer any information. Answer only the questions they ask, and try to stick to just a simple yes or no." After I nodded, he added, "I'll get the door."

Kevin had finished putting all of Mike's stuff back into the box. "I'll take this to the garage. Call me if you need me." He gave me a quick kiss. "And don't forget to glow."

"Thanks." I smiled half-heartedly as my nerves began to frazzle. He was right, though; I needed to show I was divine at first sight.

I set the glow level at medium. Not bright enough to blind anyone, but more than enough to prove I wasn't exactly human. I glanced down at my shorts and tee shirt, and smoothed out the wrinkles. Should I change into a Goddess gown for the full effect?

Nah. Fuck it. As the Morrigan often pointed out, I was a thoroughly modern Goddess.

I sat on the sofa, then after a moment I moved to a chair. The empty coffee table reminded me about refreshments, so I ported the pitcher of lemonade from the fridge, some glasses, and a tray, then arranged it all on the table. It'd have to do.

From the door, Anthony said, "Just breathe. I'll be here with you the whole time."

I nodded and took a deep breath to calm myself.

But why the hell was I nervous? I was the motherfucking *Goddess of Earth*. I had nothing to be nervous about. So I lifted my chin, sat up straighter, and prepared to show these agents what dealing with a real live Goddess was like.

Anthony opened the front door to low voices, then footsteps.

"Dee, this is Agent Park and Agent Wells. Agents, this is Deirdre Connor, Keeper of the Sphere and Goddess of Earth."

Agent Park was a middle-aged paunchy man with thick curly dark hair, dark brown eyes, and light brown skin. Agent Wells was a slender woman with short auburn hair, blue-gray eyes, and rosy pink skin. Both wore dark suits, although Park also wore a tie that was slightly loosened, and both were sweaty from the heat outside.

"Agents." I smiled politely and offered my hand. After the briefest hesitation, they each shook it. Afterward, Wells glanced at her hand, as if she'd expected to see glitter or something, and I had to bite the inside of my cheek to keep from bursting out in nervous laughter.

"Ma'am," Park said. Both he and Wells flipped open their leather credential carriers and waved them in my general direction. "We're special agents with the Federal Bureau of Investigation, Phoenix branch. We'd like to ask you a few questions about the video you posted and the events that preceded it."

"Of course. Please, sit. Would either of you like some lemonade? It was made fresh just this morning."

They glanced at each other and sat on the sofa, and Anthony sat in the chair across from me.

"I'd love some," Park said.

"Yes, please," Wells nodded. "It's already a hot one out there."

Yes, it was. We'd set a record high temperature at ninety-eight degrees, and it was only early April. This summer would probably be a real scorcher. We locals liked to call it Summer on the Face of the Sun.

Ice tinkled gently as I poured four glasses and handed them out. I sat and waited patiently as they each took a polite sip.

"This is delicious," Wells said. She took another, longer sip, then carefully set her glass on the provided coaster.

I smiled. "Brianna, my executive chef, will be very pleased to hear that."

Park also set his glass down and glanced around with professional interest. He cleared his throat, flipped open a small notebook, and clicked a ball-point pen. Total old-school style. "Nice place you've got here. How long have you had it?"

"Thank you. Almost two years."

He wrote something. "You used to be an accountant, isn't that right?"

"Yes."

Wells interrupted, glancing around pointedly. "I wasn't aware accounting paid so well. Unless maybe you embezzled from your previous employer?" She'd said it so casually, it was almost comical.

I knew she was trying to get an emotional reaction from me, and I wouldn't give it to her. "No, it doesn't pay well. No, I didn't embezzle from my former employer. I inherited my wealth." I smiled my best fuck-you smile. "But I'm sure you already knew that."

Park glanced at his notebook. "From a relative by the name of Margaret Sullivan, is that correct?"

"Yes."

"Ms. Sullivan was a citizen of Ireland, correct?"

"Yes." So far this was easy. Just confirming facts. I started to relax.

"From the records we reviewed," Wells interrupted again, "you received quite a substantial amount of money from her estate. Where did she get so much money?"

Anthony spoke up. "I'll answer that, as Ms. Connor's legal representative and administrator." Both agents turned toward him.

"Investments, Agents. Lucrative investments held over a very long period of time, since Ms. Sullivan was an advanced age when she passed."

Wells immediately countered. "You have bank statements to back that up? Showing the date of initial investment, the rate of return, and such?"

Anthony nodded. "Of course. I'll request them from our office in Cork."

"I'm sorry, what's the name of your office?" Park asked politely.

I was tempted to say, *what? You don't know that already?* But since I was only supposed to answer the questions I was asked, I kept my mouth shut.

"O'Shaughnessy, Mayo, and York," Anthony replied. "Solicitors and Attorneys at Law. Licensed to practice in most countries, and all fifty states."

Park made another note. "So, just to be clear, you are here in your official capacity? As Ms. Connor's attorney?"

Anthony nodded. "Yes."

"Convenient," Wells muttered.

Ah. So *that's* what this was: the old good cop, bad cop trope. Wells was obviously the bad, with Park acting the good cop. I wondered if they traded roles from time to time, or stayed consistent.

"Getting back to your inheritance," Park continued. "So you used it and bought this place a couple of years ago. Quit your accounting job. What did you do then?"

"I became Keeper of the Sphere."

He blinked. "What's a Keeper of the Sphere?"

I lifted my left arm and showed off my bracelet. Anu obligingly glowed pale blue, then white. "The Sphere is an ancient artifact, which I protect."

"Protect from what?" Wells asked. "Or who?"

"Whomever—or whatever—would seek to harm it or take its power for themselves."

"And just who would that be, exactly?" she pushed.

I shrugged. "Other deities, other humans."

"Power?" Park frowned at my bracelet. "What kind of power does it have?"

"With the Sphere, I can manipulate energy and matter. I can heal injuries, and teleport."

Both agents blinked at me in utter silence for a moment.

"But then last year," I continued, "I also became the Goddess of Earth. So now I have even more power. As you can see," I indicated my glowing body with a graceful wave of my hand.

"And just how did you become Goddess of Earth?" Wells asked, with a smirk.

It was obvious she thought I was completely nuts. It was surprising she hadn't used air quotes when she'd repeated my title.

"Anu—that's the name of the Sphere—stripped the power from the prior Goddess—whose name was Ida—and gave it to me." I shrugged again. "So now, I'm not exactly human anymore. I'm deity."

The agents shared a quick glance.

"Have you had a recent mental health evaluation, by chance?" Park asked.

Of course they thought I was delusional. In hindsight, I should've expected this reaction.

"Would you care for a simple demonstration of my power?"

"Dee, I wouldn't recommend doing anything harmful," Anthony warned.

"I wouldn't dream of it. Just something to show I am who I say I am."

The agents exchanged another glance.

"Sure," Park said, flippantly. "Why not? Show us something you can do that the average person can't."

Hmm. What could I do?

Ah. That should do it.

I used my magick to raise the pitcher of lemonade and refill everyone's glasses, and didn't spill a drop. The agents watched closely, then Park smiled. "Neat trick. Did you put something in the lemonade to make us susceptible to suggestion?"

Not good enough? Okay, then.

I made my corporeal body fade until it was gone, appearing invisible to them.

"Where'd she go?" Wells asked.

"I'm still here." I smirked as Wells flinched, then let my body return to normal appearance.

Well, normal for *me*, anyway. I still glowed.

"Parlor tricks," Wells scoffed.

But Park stared at me. "What else can you do, Ms. Connor?"

I met his gaze and thought for a moment. What else could I do to show them? Oh, fuck it. Time to end this stupid game. "I can kill someone—or a bunch of someones—on the other side of the planet with just a thought."

"Dee." Anthony sighed.

I shrugged. "C'mon, we all know that's really why they're here." To Agent Park, I said, "Yes, it was me. I executed all ninety-nine enemies of Earth, just like I said I did on the video I posted."

"And exactly how did you do that?" Wells asked, her eyes sharp on me.

"It was random. Some were heart failure, others were strokes. Last year, I beheaded them with my sword."

Park and Wells exchanged another glance.

"So, just to be clear, Ms. Connor," Park said. "You do realize you confessed to the murder of ninety-nine people?"

My anger spiked. "You do realize those ninety-nine people were destroying the planet, right? They were *horrible* humans. They caused untold suffering and pain—and not just to the creatures of the environments they destroyed. *People* have suffered and died, too, because of the poisons those companies released into the air and water. Thousands of kids with birth defects. Millions of people with incurable cancer." I stopped to take a breath, realized I was almost shouting, and calmed myself. "I could go on and on, but I think you get the point."

Wells shook her head. "Doesn't matter. We don't have vigilante justice in this country. We have rule of law."

I snorted. "I'm not vigilante justice, Agent. I'm the Goddess of Earth. I am *above* your rule of law."

Anthony sighed again, louder this time.

The agents exchanged another glance, then Wells stood and retrieved a flexible restraint from somewhere in her suit. "Ms. Connor, you are under arrest for domestic and international terrorism." She took a step closer to me, and Park stood to give support to his partner.

Anthony had also stood. "Now, hold on just a minute—"

The next few minutes seemed to happen in slow motion for me.

I ported to just behind Wells and snatched the restraint from her at double normal speed. I bound their wrists together, then yanked on the restraint and ported back to my chair. From there, I watched them fall backward onto the sofa, in a tangle of limbs.

Honestly, I could've done much, much worse to them. But I hoped this would send the message not to fuck with me.

"I'm truly sorry." I forced my expression to match my words even though I wasn't the least bit sorry. "But I can't let you do that. I'm on a mission to heal Earth, and nothing will stop me from that."

The agents had righted themselves, and Wells removed the restraint. "It seems we have a problem, then."

"I'd say you do." I leaned forward conversationally. "Don't you see? My job is to take care of the whole planet, and everything—every*one*—on it. To do that, I can't be bothered with petty human laws."

"So you'll just eliminate anyone who gets in your way?" Park asked. "Is that it?"

I almost said no, then reconsidered. How else could I possibly hope to get my point across to these two?

I shrugged. "Pretty much."

"*Oh dear lord please let us get out of here alive.*"

For a moment, I thought it'd been spoken aloud, but no. It'd been a prayer from Wells. But why had I heard it? She'd prayed to her own god, not to me. So I shouldn't have heard it.

It needed answering nonetheless.

"My job includes taking care of both of you, too," I said. "So no, Agent Wells. You don't need to worry. Of course you will both *get out of here alive*."

She stared at me in disbelief, then her expression hardened. "More parlor tricks?"

"No." I sighed. "I heard your prayer. I hear prayers all the time. For healing, for money, for love, for a million things. And I answer as many as I can."

"*Lady, help us please.*"

I cocked my head and concentrated on where that one had come from.

"In fact, there's another right now, coming from an accident on the northbound Pima freeway." I paused as the details came to me. "A semi just lost control and took out three cars. People are dying." I stood. "So if you'll excuse me for a moment, I have work to do."

Without waiting for a reply, I ported to the accident site, less than twenty miles away.

It was ugly. Bits of twisted metal and broken glass were scattered everywhere. Traffic had already backed up for miles, and first responders hadn't arrived yet on the scene. I knew it'd take them a while to get through the backup, so I got moving.

At the first vehicle, the windshield glass was cracked and shattered around a large jagged hole. An appalling amount of blood covered the front seat and dashboard, but the driver, a young woman, was alive. I quickly healed her head injury and the lacerations on her face and arms, then helped her get into the back seat, where her toddler was still strapped into his carrier. Thankfully, he was safe and unhurt.

At the second vehicle, the older male driver was already dead and I couldn't help him. But I healed the older female passenger's broken legs and helped her from the vehicle before moving on to the third vehicle. The two shocked humans inside weren't injured, but they just stared at me uncomprehendingly when I tried to remove them from the SUV. Impatient, I used magick to break the restraints, then ported them to the others on the side of the road.

The driver of the eighteen-wheeler was also unhurt, but he'd had a mild heart attack—which had caused him to lose control of the vehicle— and now sat inside, trembling and weeping. He wouldn't answer my questions or acknowledge my presence, and I shrugged, continuing on. Then I stopped, considered, and returned. Rising up so I could reach through the open window, I placed my hand on his head and sent healing to his heart. As another gift, I gave him comfort and peace.

Then I moved on, looking for more injured people, especially the one who'd prayed for my help.

The gathered bystanders stared at me, and more than a few had been recording the whole thing, probably as soon as I'd shown up.

Just fucking great. Another bunch of videos to go viral. Hopefully I could use them to my advantage.

I didn't see anyone else injured, but to be on the safe side, I boosted my voice and called out, "Is there anyone else hurt?"

"Here," a weak voice croaked from the other side of the road, hidden behind some thick scrub bushes.

I was there in a flash.

A young woman in shorts and a tank top lay in a pile of broken glass and debris, bleeding from multiple cuts on her face and body. She must've been the one who'd gone through the windshield of the first vehicle, and landed wrong. Sharp bone protruded from her forearm.

She was lucky to be alive.

"You came," she whispered, blue eyes bright on me. "I prayed to You."

I took a closer look at her head. A deep slash on her forehead bled profusely, and it was a nasty wound. Fresh blood covered her face and the front of her tank.

"I heard you." I crouched down and healed her head injury first, then her broken arm, before working on the rest of her wounds. The whole time, I was dimly aware of others nearby, watching.

When I finished, I helped her into a sitting position.

"You healed me." She stared wide-eyed at her arm, then at me. "Thank You, Lady."

"I'm glad I was able to get here in time to help." I paused, thinking of the one I hadn't been able to save. "I may not be able to get to everyone all over the planet right away, but I'm doing my best."

"You're The Keeper Goddess, aren't You?" someone asked.

I turned toward the voice, and realized it was one of the people filming me.

"Yes," I confirmed. "But please, just call me Dee."

I stood and helped the young woman to her feet. "And now, if you'll excuse me, I have to go. I'm actually in the middle of being interrogated by the FBI."

A burst of laughter broke out as I ported home.

Neither agent had moved from the sofa, and now they blinked at me as I reappeared, casually sat in my chair, and drank some of my lemonade.

Too bad it wasn't whiskey.

Park stared at my shirt, and when I looked down to see what he was looking at, I grimaced. My clean white tee shirt now had several smudges of bright fresh blood.

"Yes, it was bad," I said as he met my gaze. "But I healed three people. Head injuries, broken arms and legs, and lots of cuts. Couldn't help the man who was already dead, though. My power can only do so much."

Anthony clicked on the television and raised the volume so we could hear the breaking news.

"... initial reports state three vehicles and a semi were involved in the accident, but only one death is reported at this time. In a bizarre coincidence, Frank, one of our videographers, was caught in the traffic jam and has been on the scene, so he's been able to give us some first-hand reports. First responders have just arrived." The announcer took a piece of paper from someone off-camera. "He has some interesting footage for us. Apparently, The Keeper Goddess was on the scene. Witnesses say she healed three people of serious injuries, then disappeared. We'll go ahead and show you the video now."

As it played, I watched the agents stare at the screen. Their faces plainly showed their shock and disbelief as they saw me appear and disappear around the accident site, healing people.

I understood what they were feeling. It was a helluva lot to take in all at once. I'd had almost two years to adjust to it, but in the space of only a few minutes, these two agents—who probably only dealt with cold hard facts and black-and white truths—had just learned that magick, real deities, and inhuman abilities really existed. Everything they'd ever thought they'd known about the world had just changed.

And there was nothing black and white about magick; it was all fuzzy and shades of gray.

"You two still think I'm nuts?" I asked softly.

"And now, if you'll excuse me, I have to go. I'm actually in the middle of being interrogated by the FBI." My voice and the bystanders' laughter came from the television speaker before Anthony shut it off.

Wells turned toward me and snapped, "This is *not* an interrogation. Believe me, if it were, you'd know it."

Oh, for fuck's sake. Of all the things to get worked up about... I just looked at her and didn't say a word.

Park seemed to be thinking it all through. After a moment, his voice was soft. "So you can heal injuries. What about diseases? Like cancer, for example."

"I haven't tried it yet, but I don't see why not." It couldn't be that much different than the arthritis I'd healed for Sani not too long ago.

Although I still wasn't sure exactly how I'd done that.

Wells put a hand on his arm. "Joe, don't do this to yourself. She's fake. She *has* to be." She turned to me, eyes flashing in anger. "Don't you dare give him false hope."

"I wouldn't dream of it," I said. To him, I asked, "Will you let me try?"

After only the briefest hesitation, he nodded. "Please."

But when I went to sit beside him, Wells wouldn't budge. She just stared at me with furious defiance.

"Excuse me," I said.

"Cora, please," Park said.

Wells huffed, finally got up, and sat in my vacated chair.

I sat close to Park. "What kind of cancer is it? And where is it?"

He swallowed visibly, fidgeting with his notebook and not looking at me. "Prostate. Stage three."

Fairly advanced, then.

I took a deep breath, laid my hand on his, and closed my eyes to better concentrate as I probed the affected area, looking for the cancer cells. After a moment, I'd found them: darker, larger, and less uniform than the healthy cells elsewhere. Targeting them directly, I sent my healing energy into each to transform it into a normal cell.

He gasped, but I didn't stop. Couldn't stop; I was nowhere near done.

"Joe?" Wells' voice was sharp with alarm.

"I'm fine," he replied. "It just feels really weird. Like the heat of the sun, except *inside* me. Deep inside."

"Shh." At this point, I didn't need the distraction of their conversation. This was delicate work, and I couldn't miss a single cell, or the cancer would return.

I don't know how long I was at it, but after I'd transformed all the cancerous cells and scanned the area to make sure I hadn't missed any, I sent a bit more general healing energy through the rest of his body to fix the other health issues I'd found. Ones he probably didn't even know about yet because they were just beginning.

"Okay, that does it." I opened my eyes and pulled away, stifling a yawn of exhaustion. "When's your next doctor appointment?"

He cautiously met my gaze. "Thursday afternoon."

"Let me know how it goes. Depending on what your doc says, I may need to do another session."

"Will do." He took a card out of his pocket and handed it over. "As for the rest, we'll be in touch." He stood and began walking toward the front door, with Wells following. Abruptly, he stopped and turned back. "I have to ask. If you really are a... a Goddess, why now? Why after so much death? You could've stopped so many tragedies. Pandemics. Nine-eleven. Afghanistan and Iraq. Ukraine. Or even Vietnam. Korea. Et cetera, et cetera, et cetera."

"I'm new," I replied softly. "The last Goddess of Earth didn't do her job and was removed. I'm her replacement."

"Oh." He blinked at me while Wells simply frowned, as if trying to puzzle something out, then he shook his head. "We'll see ourselves out."

They finally left, and I collapsed on the sofa. Had I ever been this tired before? This utterly exhausted? I was more drained than I'd ever felt in my entire life.

"Dee? Are you okay?" Anthony was immediately at my side, brow furrowed in concern.

"Yeah. I just need to rest."

What a fucking past couple of days it'd been. First, the Council meeting, then the Ring of Ur, then the FBI, the accident, and all the healing.

All on top of being pregnant.

Which reminded me... I needed to make that fucking appointment.

"Is there anything I can do?" Anthony asked.

I shook my head. "I'm just not going to move for a while." I curled up on the sofa, and was already drifting off when he gently covered me with a lightweight throw.

CHAPTER NINETEEN

T HE LOCAL OB/GYN, Doctor Sarah Wood-Smith, had been highly recommended by the firm. On the internet, she had rave reviews and all her patients seemed to love her. They said she was highly professional, knowledgeable, and friendly.

And I'd bet not a single one of those patients knew she also worked with a powerful global organization that was affiliated with magick, gods, and goddesses.

When I called for an appointment, the scheduler said there was a two-month wait list for new patients. But that changed as soon as I gave my name for the cancellation list.

"Oh, Ms. Connor, we've been expecting your call," the scheduler said. "We have an immediate opening for you, if you're available this afternoon."

"Sure."

But as Nat drove me, I was nervous.

The last time I'd been to a doctor was in my late teens, when my parents were still alive. After I'd moved away to college, and after they died, I never seemed to need medical care. I hadn't kept up with my regular preventative screenings, and I'd never had anything worse than an occasional common cold.

I didn't think I had a fear of doctors, but I felt just a bit like I had when the FBI had shown up.

The receptionist handed me a pen and a clipboard with several pages attached. "These are our standard new patient forms." She smiled apologetically. "If we'd had more time, they could've been completed online. But we do understand the... ah... unique circumstances of Your visit today."

I'd heard the unmistakable note of reverence in her voice. "It's no problem."

She hadn't stopped smiling. "Some of the questions won't apply to You, so feel free to just skip those."

I nodded and sat in the reception area next to Nat, then began working my way through the forms.

The first page was basic stuff: name, address, birthdate, marital status, employment.

I snorted.

"What?" Nat asked.

"Marital status. There's only single, married, divorced, widowed. Nothing for two Consorts."

"Write it in that little empty space there."

I looked at her with one brow raised. "I think I'll just check the single box, since it's legally correct."

She grinned. "But it's not as much fun."

I shook my head, but couldn't help smiling. I liked this side of Nat, and I wanted to see more of it.

So, I decided to keep playing this little game with her.

The next page was medications, allergies, and medical history. "Do you think my human-to-deity transition is a current medical condition?"

Now it was Nat's turn to snort, and I bit my lip to keep from laughing.

"No, I don't think so," she murmured.

"Prior surgeries. Well, half my arm was cut off, but then it grew back when I became the Goddess. Does that count?"

We both snickered, and I couldn't help but notice we were starting to attract attention from others in the reception area.

The entire next section asked my family history. No, no siblings. No, no living relatives. "Shit."

"What?

"They want to know the cause of death for my parents."

She met my gaze. "Weren't they in an accident?"

"No. They were murdered."

She shrugged. "Put that down, then. It's not like the firm doesn't know, anyway."

Why the hell not? I wrote *murdered*, then flipped the page. "Look at this crazy shit here."

She peered at the form. "That's standard for a first-time OB/GYN appointment, Dee."

They asked for the details of my gynecological history and sexual activity, and I skipped most of it, simply noting I was in a committed polygamous relationship.

Naturally, they asked the date of my last period, which I didn't know. I wrote *not sure*.

The last couple of pages were just privacy policies and such, and then I was done. I returned everything to the receptionist, who then asked for my driver's license and insurance card to scan into the system.

"No insurance. I'm paying cash," I said as I dug out my license and handed it over.

"Of course." She smiled and scanned my license, then returned it to me. "It'll be just a few minutes."

As I turned away, she began scanning in the forms I'd completed.

I didn't have to wait long.

A door opened. "Ms. Connor?"

"See you in a bit," I said to Nat, and followed the smiling medical assistant down a hall and to a weight scale. After weigh-in, we proceeded to the exam room, where she took my vitals—temperature, blood pressure, pulse—and apparently they were normal since no alarms beeped. Then I was left to wait on the cushioned exam table.

I glanced around the small room, and had the sudden memory of sitting on an exam table when I was a child and had my booster shots for school.

Things hadn't changed much since then.

The little counter with a tiny sink and bottle of antibacterial soap had the same clear canisters of cotton balls and swabs I remembered seeing back then. On the wall, a box of blue exam gloves was in a clear plastic holder. A wall poster showed detailed diagrams of female genitalia, while another showed instructions for breast self-exams.

Every time I shifted position, even the tiniest bit, the paper cover on the exam table crackled. It seemed loud in the quiet room, where the only other noise was the soft *whoosh* of the air conditioner.

For a moment, I stared down at the shiny metal stirrups bolted to the table before looking away. They seemed medieval, somehow.

After about ten minutes or so, there was a knock on the door and it opened.

Doctor Wood-Smith didn't seem much older than me, and she had a friendly, welcoming smile. Her ash blonde hair brushed her shoulders, and her stylish eyeglass frames complimented her triangular face. The barest hint of rose-tinted lipstick was a splash of color against her pale skin.

"So pleased to meet you, Ms. Connor," she said, extending her hand. "It's not every day we have the Goddess visit our office."

"I'm sure." I couldn't help but smile in return.

She sat on the swivel stool beside the small counter.

"So," she began. "You told our scheduler You believe You might be pregnant."

I nodded. "I took two home pregnancy tests, and both were positive." I thought it better not to mention it'd also been confirmed by Loki and Anu.

"Any idea how far along You might be?"

"Not really. My best guess for my last period is maybe two months ago." I grimaced. "I'm sorry I can't be more accurate. I've just been so busy lately."

She nodded. "Putting out brush fires, dealing with natural disasters around the world, healing accident victims, and answering prayers, from what I understand. Well then, first things first. We'll confirm Your pregnancy with both a urine and a blood test." She smiled apologetically. "It's standard medical practice."

"I understand."

The doctor left and the medical assistant came back with a cup. She showed me to the restroom, where I provided the requested urine. Then I was taken to the in-house lab, where the technician took a vial of blood. Finally, I was escorted back to the exam room.

This time, I only waited five minutes.

Doctor Wood-Smith knocked and entered, and sat again on the stool. "Your urine shows You are definitely pregnant," she said. "The blood test takes a few hours, but I have no doubt it'll also confirm the positive result." She studied me with head cocked, and her eyes softened with warmth and compassion. "This is technically none of my business, and You don't have to answer if You don't want to, but Your mental health is just as important as Your physical health. Is this good news or bad news for You?"

"I... I'm not sure. I mean, I hadn't planned on having kids, but I hadn't *not* planned on having any, either."

"So it's more of a surprise, then."

I nodded. "Yeah."

"Okay, so now to Your physical health: how've You been feeling lately?"

"I get tired a lot more easily than I used to, but I haven't really noticed anything else. I mean, I'm not any more or less hungry than I was before, and I haven't had any of the typical symptoms I've read about. I don't get sick in the morning and I haven't gained much weight. That sort of thing."

"Those are common symptoms, but not every person experiences them. It's probably still early yet, so You could still see some symptoms show up. Watch for mood swings, breast tenderness, and lower back pain."

"Okay." Some things to look forward to, I supposed. "So what's next?"

"We'll schedule a sonogram, which will help me determine how far along You are. That'll be at the imaging facility just down the street. After that, You'll come back in so we can discuss the images and what You'll need to know to make Your decision."

I frowned. "My decision?"

"To either continue or discontinue Your pregnancy." Stated matter-of-factly.

Oh. *That*. To be honest, I hadn't even thought of *not* keeping it.

"I've already made that decision. I'll definitely continue."

"That's good to know." She reached into a drawer and pulled out several foil-wrapped packets. "Here are some prenatal vitamins I want You to start taking. That should be enough to last until Your next visit."

I took them and sent them to my pocket universe.

She blinked at me, then smiled. "So, congratulations and we'll talk soon. In the meantime, if You have any questions, feel free to call." She'd pulled out a business card from her pocket and now handed it to me. "My mobile is on the bottom."

"Thank you, Doctor." I returned her smile. "I just might take you up on that."

"I'd be honored." She opened the door and showed me to the exit.

In the reception area, Nat got up and walked with me. "How'd it go?"

"Okay, I guess. I need to schedule a sonogram."

She studied me cautiously. "So, they confirmed it?"

"Yep."

She whooped and fist-pumped the air, and I just blinked at her. But when she threw her arms around me, I was even more confused.

I'd never seen her like this.

"Oh, this is so *exciting*," she gushed. "I'll be Auntie Nat." She pulled away, huge grin fading. "Oh. I should probably ask if you're keeping it, huh?"

"Yeah, I'm keeping it. But I don't want to tell anyone else until I know how far along I am." Except for Arddhu and Kevin. I should probably let them know as soon as possible, since it was official now.

I just wouldn't mention how I originally found out.

"You got it. Mum's the word." She grinned again. "But you've got to promise me I get first dibs on babysitting."

"Sure." I had to grin at her enthusiasm, and again, I realized how much I liked this side of her.

All the way home, she chattered about her nieces and nephews, and I just couldn't believe how different she was. In the almost two years I'd known her, I'd never seen her this talkative.

Finally realizing I wasn't adding much to her mostly one-sided conversation, Nat turned to me. "Which room are you going to turn into a nursery? Can I go with you to pick out the furniture? And clothes? Ooh—I hope it's a girl so we can her get the cutest little dresses."

If Loki was right—and he'd been right so far—I'd have a girl. But I couldn't tell her that.

"Whoa, slow down," I laughed. "I promise you'll be part of everything. But I need to tell the guys and find out how far along I am first."

"Oh. Yeah." Pulling into the garage, she nodded. "That'd probably be a good idea."

But as she opened her door, I put a hand on her arm. "Thank you for being here for me. I hope you know how much I appreciate you."

She grinned again. "You're welcome. Remember, I'll be Auntie Nat."

I laughed and shook my head. "I won't forget."

We went our separate ways, she to the guest house that served as security headquarters, and me to the kitchen for something to drink while I thought about how to tell the guys.

Brianna glanced up from peeling and chopping vegetables for dinner. "Are you hungry? You want me to make you something?"

"Nah." I shook my head. "Just stopped by for some of that ridiculously delicious lemonade you've been making lately."

She grinned as I grabbed a tall glass from the cupboard and poured a glass. "I'm glad you like it."

After I put the pitcher back in the fridge, I sat at the island and took a long drink. "Do you know where everyone is?"

She nodded. "Kevin's got another class of Túatha. E-commerce and digital payment methods, I think, for their websites."

He had such a natural affinity for anything computers or internet, I'd originally asked him to be my social media director. But he'd politely declined, citing how busy he was with the classes. And, with Anthony and Ogma in that role instead, it'd worked out.

"And Arddhu is still away?" He'd been spending a lot of time getting ready for his Wild Hunt. I'd had no idea it needed so much planning. Then again, it'd been quite some time since his last one. He probably had to find a whole new team of horses and hounds.

She nodded as she continued chopping vegetables. "And the Morrigan is taking a nap."

Gods. A nap sounded awesome right now. That doctor appointment had worn me out. At this rate, by the last trimester I wouldn't be able to do anything more than lay in bed.

"Great. Thanks." I moved to the living room, where I drank my lemonade and looked out the window-wall. The backyard was gorgeous, but it was already sweltering out there. The pool would be the perfect temperature—it always was—but I didn't really feel like it.

No, that wasn't it.

I was just too tired to do anything right now.

But prayers needed answering, and then I had to think about how to tell the guys they were going to be fathers.

Some time later, I'd just finished answering prayers when Anthony and Reshep found me. "We have news," Anthony said, then sat in the chair opposite.

"Lady." Reshep greeted me with a half-bow, then sat on the sofa. "I have received confirmation that Ares and Athena have completed their new realm. And, unfortunately, there are several deities planning to join them."

Shit. "Already? That probably means they're going to be putting the rest of their plans into place."

"Most likely," Anthony agreed.

"Do we know which deities?" I asked Reshep.

He nodded. "Mostly lesser-known gods, or the last stragglers of dying pantheons. None we've been in contact with."

"Hold on," Anthony said, frowning. "Why would they want to populate this new realm of theirs with deities from Earth? I thought they hated everything about this place."

Reshep shrugged. "Who can know the minds of Olympians?"

Something bothered me. A little detail. "You haven't mentioned Kali. Isn't she still with them?"

Reshep met my gaze. "I am not sure. None of my informants have mentioned her. Only Ares and Athena."

Hmm. Where was Kali? Had there been some kind of falling-out between her and the Olympians? Or was I overthinking it? Maybe it was just something simple, like she'd been busy doing something else.

Oh.

What if it wasn't Ares who was stirring things up in South Asia? What if it was Kali?

Anthony interrupted my thoughts. "I'll schedule a Council meeting for next week."

I nodded, and thanked Reshep for the update. They left together, and I resumed my train of thought.

Thinking back to everything Loki and Reshep had said over the past month or so, there wasn't a single time anyone mentioned Kali sharing in the rule of that new realm of the Olympians. Knowing how ambitious they were, they probably only wanted it for themselves. So they'd probably ditched her somewhere along the way.

Or worse: maybe they'd killed her. As I'd learned last year, gods were only immortal as long as they kept their heads attached. Sure, Kali was extremely powerful, but if they'd waited until she was asleep or otherwise vulnerable... well, I wouldn't be surprised.

However, if she was still alive, maybe there was an opportunity for me to win her back to our side. Especially if they'd all turned against each other.

I just had to find her.

My thoughts scattered as Arddhu fairly bounded into the room with excitement. "My Lady," he greeted me.

"Hello, love," I replied. I'd never seen him so enthusiastic, and it made me smile.

He bent for a quick kiss that lingered and turned into a passionate, longing embrace that left me breathless. When we broke away, his dark eyes smoldered with desire.

But now just wasn't the time for sex.

Hoping to distract him, I asked, "How's everything going for the Hunt?"

It seemed to work. He sat on the sofa nearby. "Quite well. I am training a new pack of hounds, and they will be ready by Solstice."

"That's great." I smiled again.

Now Kevin came through the panel of the window-wall.

"Guys, the Túatha have some fantastic ideas for web businesses that I think we should invest in." He, too, bent for a kiss.

"Sounds like something we should discuss with Anthony," I said. "By the way, I have some news." I quickly briefed them on the update from

Reshep. "Anthony is scheduling a Council meeting for next week," I finished.

"Good," Arddhu nodded. "We will need to discuss our next steps for all three of them." He studied me for a moment. "How are you feeling? You seem tired."

"I am." Now seemed like as good a time as any to spill my other news, I supposed. And just thinking about it made my heart rate speed up. I couldn't believe I was nervous. "And I've seen a doctor about it," I added, then hesitated. I wished I'd had a bit more time to come up with the right words.

Then again, did it really matter?

"I... I'm pregnant."

For just a moment, they both just stared at me. Then they began excitedly talking at once.

"This is wonderful news," Arddhu said.

"Oh wow, Dee," Kevin said.

I held up a hand. "Before either of you ask, I have no idea which of you is the biological father, so as far as I'm concerned you're both the father. And I don't know yet how far along I am. I won't know until next week or so."

As one, they both rushed to hug me.

"This calls for a celebration drink." Kevin ported the Polish mead and three glasses from the bar, then poured for each of us. He raised his glass. "Here's to being parents."

We all drank, and again I was thankful I could still drink. Alcohol would never again affect me like it did a human.

Kevin couldn't stop grinning like a loon, but Arddhu still seemed to be in a bit of shock, just staring at me silently with wide eyes.

"This changes everything," Kevin said.

"No it doesn't," I protested.

"Yes, it does," Arddhu said. "We will need additional security."

"What? Why?"

Kevin answered. "When word gets out that the new Goddess of Earth is pregnant by either Cernunnos or Bricriu, it could be perceived as a threat."

"To who?" I was still confused.

"To any deity who is not our ally," Arddhu replied.

I couldn't worry about that now. There was way too much other shit to worry about. "We'll take precautions. I'm not too concerned."

"We'll have to get a nanny," Kevin said.

"Yes," Arddhu agreed. "Other servants, too."

"And tutors," Kevin added.

"Guys, stop." I set my glass down. "There'll be plenty of time for all that. It's really early yet. Probably only a few weeks or so. In the meantime, I still have healing sessions to do, and prayers to answer. We still have to shut down the developing war in South Asia. And we still need to deal with Ares, Athena, and Kali. So please, just stop."

I took a deep breath and realized I was even more exhausted now.

"Of course," Kevin soothed. "Even if the baby develops faster than a normal human, we still have plenty of time to find a nanny and the proper tutors."

Wait. What? "Develops faster?"

Arddhu nodded. "The condition of pregnancy is much different for immortals than it is for humans. It is not unknown for the child of a deity to fully mature within an accelerated time period, such as six months or less, and it is actually quite common for Goddesses to give birth only a month or two after conception. Sometimes, to a fully-formed adult deity, I might add."

I blinked at him, utterly at a loss for words. At no time had I given any thought to the possibility that my divinity could affect the length of my pregnancy. I'd just assumed it'd last nine months.

"Actually, not just Goddesses," Kevin added. "Zeus supposedly birthed Athena, fully-grown and in her armor, right from his *head*."

"Let's hope that won't happen to me."

Kevin laughed. "It'd be weird, that's for sure."

I had a feeling my pregnancy would be weird enough. I didn't need any more weirdness.

CHAPTER TWENTY

THE IMAGING LAB had called to schedule my sonogram, and my appointment was set for two days' time. I had to admit, I was curious to find out how old the fetus was. Especially since my stomach seemed to have a bit more roundness to it than normal.

Or maybe that was just my imagination. According to the web article I'd read, it was way too soon to see external changes like that.

But there were plenty of other changes I'd noticed.

It seemed I was so tired all the time now. Between my healing sessions for Earth, I needed to rest more often and for much longer.

One evening, I burst into tears during a mediocre television commercial for adopting shelter animals. I hardly ever cried, so poor Arddhu and Kevin immediately went into high alert, thinking something was seriously wrong—which, of course, only made the tears fall even harder.

Thank the gods Brianna had been nearby. Somehow, she'd understood what was happening and came to the rescue. First, she calmed the guys with a brief explanation of hormone issues causing emotional upheaval. Then, she brought me a box of facial tissues and a mug of soothing herbal tea.

She also made sure I had healthy snacks available in the fridge whenever I wanted them—which was often these days. Back when I'd first started my transformation to deity, my appetite had waned, but now it seemed I was constantly hungry.

Thankfully, I still didn't have any nausea or morning sickness. Maybe I'd be lucky and never experience either.

Otherwise, my days had settled into a new routine: breakfast, tai chi, heal Earth, rest for an hour, answer prayers, rest, lunch, heal Earth, rest, post on social media, answer prayers, rest, heal Earth, rest, then dinner.

Unless I heard an urgent prayer, I usually took evenings off, and did some light reading, relaxed in the pool, or watched a movie with the guys.

Normal, pre-Goddess stuff.

Kevin and Arddhu had begged me not to port to disaster sites anymore, and after a contentious discussion, I finally agreed. Not because I thought it was dangerous, but I'd realized I didn't need to physically port to the actual site anymore. Instead, I sat comfortably in the living room or by the pool, closed my eyes, and used my power to steer hurricanes from coastlines or tornadoes from inhabited areas. In fact, I'd discovered it was remarkably easy to keep buildings from toppling during earthquakes, or to extinguish brush fires threatening lives halfway around the world.

I supposed it meant I was getting stronger. More powerful.

Or maybe I was just getting smarter.

Oddly, I hadn't had the smoke and ash nightmare in quite some time. Maybe it meant something had happened to avert that possible future.

I still needed to know what Kali was up to, so I decided to make my own divination pool. Years ago, I'd purchased a shallow obsidian bowl from the annual gem and mineral show in Tucson, but it'd ended up collecting dust on my dresser. It'd be much more useful as my own Seer's Mirror.

One night, I filled the bowl with water and ported it to the patch of soft grass in the backyard. The evening was warm, without even the slightest breeze, which allowed the three-quarter moon to reflect perfectly in the water's surface.

I knelt beside the bowl and gazed into it with one thought: *show me where Kali is.*

A moment later, a scene formed on the still water, obliterating the moon's reflection.

Seedy motel room. Queen-sized bed, sagging in the middle, and covered with a quilted bedspread in a hideous mosaic pattern of rust, orange, brown, and yellow. The carpet, stained and threadbare near the foot of the bed, was a faded burnt orange that contrasted with the dingy mustard walls.

Kali paced back and forth, gesturing and waving her arms. Her mouth moved, but I hadn't been given the privilege of hearing any sound.

Abruptly, she stopped and turned toward me. She seemed to look straight at me, and my heart skipped a beat.

Then, a tall blonde person appeared and walked toward Kali. Kali spoke, then whirled away. The blonde turned, and I got a full-face view of Athena, her features twisted in fury.

They faced each other again, and the argument intensified.

Kali grew taller by at least two feet, head almost brushing the ceiling. Her skin turned blue, and she sprouted her multiple arms, complete with weapons.

It was a nasty argument if she'd assumed her battle guise.

Athena put her hands up in a warding-off gesture and stepped backward, then edged out of view. Kali bared her dagger teeth, but didn't make any attempt to follow Athena.

Then Kali slumped a bit, and returned to her normal sweet grandmotherly form. She sat on the bed and put her face in her hands.

The scene faded, then a new scene began.

Kali walked alone on the scruffy shoulder of a desolate two-lane road with cracked and broken pavement. Desert landscape stretched for miles on either side, with bushy mesquite trees, tall saguaros, spiky yucca, and assorted blooming wildflowers amongst the nondescript brush. An occasional dry wash or narrow dirt road snaked off into the distance. She kept her head down and face hidden behind her long dark hair as she plodded on, never missing a step as she kicked a large rock out of her way once or twice.

In the near distance, a green road sign appeared:

$$\text{Florence} \quad 23$$
$$\text{Phoenix} \quad 87$$

A moment later, the scene faded. The water became still once again, and the moon's reflection returned.

I let out the breath I hadn't realized I'd been holding, sat back on my heels, and analyzed the vision.

Kali and Athena had probably argued about her being excluded from the Olympians' new realm, which would explain why Kali wasn't with the other two anymore.

I wasn't familiar with the road she was on, but she was obviously on her way here, to Scottsdale. If she walked the whole way it'd probably take her a couple more days. But if she hitched a ride or rented a car in Florence, it'd take a lot less time.

So, I could expect her to show up soon.

And that was as far as I got, because I was too exhausted to think anymore. Too tired to port, I emptied the obsidian bowl and walked to my suite for some rest.

In the middle of lunch with Arddhu and Kevin the next day, Nat hailed from the gatehouse.

Kali had arrived, and requested an audience with me.

I'd forgotten to mention the vision to either of the guys, so they were both surprised at this development.

"Kali?" Arddhu asked. "Here?"

Kevin frowned and chewed his food thoughtfully.

"Let her in," I replied to Nat, and quickly modified the wards to allow Kali to enter the property. But when I stood and the guys made to follow, I shook my head. "Stay here, please. I'll be fine meeting her alone."

"It could be a trick," Kevin warned. "Maybe she's just a distraction while Ares and Athena mount an attack."

"She's not here for that. My gut tells me she's here for forgiveness."

They stared at me as I turned and left.

I stood outside the front door and watched the white sedan come up the drive. She parked under the porte cochere, got out, and took a hesitant step toward me.

I greeted her with a nod, waiting to see how she responded.

She took another step forward, fell to her knees, and touched her forehead to the hot pavement. "Greetings, my Lady, Keeper of the Sphere, and Great Goddess of Earth."

I answered as formally as she'd addressed me. "You may rise, Kali, Goddess of Wisdom and Death, and state your business."

"My business..." She rose to her feet smoothly, but kept her head down. "I have come to beg forgiveness. I was blinded by lust for power. I know now what I did was wrong. Although I deserve any punishment You see fit to deliver, I have hope Your heart will be merciful and lenient."

My witchy-sense detected the truth in her words and gave validation to my gut feeling. "Tell me: if you were in my place, what punishment would you impose?"

"Death." She met my eyes steadily. "It is the only option for a traitor."

I held her gaze for a silent moment, and noticed her struggle to not fidget. Finally, I shook my head. "Come. Walk with me." I led her beyond the backyard, toward the green space I'd created for the Council meetings.

"Believe it or not, I don't consider you a traitor," I said. "You haven't taken any action against me or my Council. At least, not that I know of." I gave her a meaningful glance.

"No, Lady, I haven't." *Unlike Ares and Athena*, I heard unspoken.

Again, my witchy-sense told me she spoke true.

We crossed the little bridge and reached the beautiful oasis in the middle of the desert. I'd activated the climate control, so it was blessedly cool.

"Oh," she gasped, eyes wide with wonder. "You created this? This paradise?"

"Yeah." At the table, I stopped and glanced around, proud of what I'd created.

"I have also heard the Earthsong," she said, with awe. "It grows louder by the day." She paused to study me. "You truly are healing Earth."

"Did you think I couldn't?" I asked mildly.

"No, that's not..." She blinked. "I—we—thought You *wouldn't*." Her mouth twisted. "I believed the lies of the Olympians. They said You would be just as bad as Ida. That You would abuse the power of the Goddess for Your own gain." She shook her head. "I believed them. I really thought

You'd simply continue as Ida had, ignoring the needs of Earth and all her inhabitants."

I gestured for her to sit, and took my own seat. "That's what's called *projection*. They accused me of what they, themselves, would've done." I took a deep breath. "But if either of them had taken the power of the Goddess, none of us would be here right now. They would've killed us all, and you know it."

She nodded. "It is what all tyrants do: as soon as they come to power, they remove their opposition. It is what we—I—expected You to do. We thought You would immediately remove us and any others who oppose You."

"And yet, all three of you have remained free and unharmed these past several months."

"Yes." She shook her head again. "I confess, You are not what I expected."

"Oh? And what did you expect?"

She looked away and didn't reply.

"It's okay," I said. "You can be honest and speak your mind."

After a moment, she met my gaze. "In the beginning, I thought You were a rich, spoiled American who was weak and insipid. But as I came to know You better, during the Alliance meetings and then the battle later, I realized how wrong I'd been. You were—*are*—intelligent, competent, and much stronger than You look."

"Thanks."

"But You also have some serious weaknesses," she went on. "You have a soft heart and are too generous, for example." She hesitated, not meeting my eyes as she added, "And You are too trusting."

"Too trusting?" I lifted a brow. "Is that your way of telling me that you're here to kill me? Or to distract me so Ares and Athena can kill me?"

She blinked at me. "No, of course not. But while You heal Earth, those two plot and scheme to remove You, take Your power, and destroy Earth."

I snorted. "Oh, I know."

She frowned. "Then why haven't You stopped them?"

"Because I have other priorities at the moment."

She shook her head. "Healing Earth can wait, my Lady. You must stop them first, or there will be no Earth to heal."

"You think that's all I'm doing?" I scoffed. "But look. They won't succeed. I know all about their plans. The realm they've created, the deities they're taking with them, and the war Ares is starting in South Asia."

Again, she shook her head. "It is not just a war between two small adversaries. It is the war to end Earth. As we speak, other countries are choosing sides, and they all have nuclear missiles. Even if only one missile is launched, others will follow, until there is nothing left but a smoking remnant of dead rock floating in the darkness of space."

Shit. That seemed a bit extreme.

Then, my nightmares flashed in my mind: ash and smoke. Burnt buildings... and bodies.

So many bodies.

Okay, this was way worse than we'd thought.

"It's mostly Ares," she added. "He's the warmonger. I think Athena would be satisfied to simply leave. But Ares is hungry for war. He always has been. Not a strategic or territorial war, but a pointless one, purely for widespread death and destruction. Immense suffering. Ugly cruelty. Rivers of blood and gore."

It seemed strange for a Goddess of Death to speak so derisively of it. Then again, maybe she'd seen enough in her long lifetime to warrant it.

"I understand. I'll move them up in my priority list. I don't suppose you know exactly where they are? Or at least, where he is?"

She shook her head. "I left them over a week ago. At that time, they were at Athena's palace on Olympus. But Athena found me at a cheap motel near Tucson. If she guessed I was coming here, they would've moved somewhere else by now."

Hopefully soon, we'd know something more concrete from the firm's spies on Olympus. "As far as the warheads go, I'll see what I can do about disabling them. Or at least making them all disappear. That should put a stop to a nuclear war."

Her eyes widened. "That it would."

"In the meantime, we need to decide what to do with you."

She hung her head. "I defer to whatever punishment You deem fit, my Lady."

Although it was tempting, I didn't think it was my decision alone. Her actions hadn't threatened only me, but the entire Alliance.

"Tell you what," I said. "Come back in two days. We're having a Council meeting, and I'd like the others to hear your petition before a final decision is made."

She visibly swallowed. "Yes, my Lady. I will return in two days."

"Great. Around nine-thirty in the morning, please." I stood, signaling our discussion was over for now.

At her vehicle, I said, "By the way, you have my permission to use the portal instead of walking or renting a car to get here."

She stared at me, eyes wide in alarm.

Oops. I probably shouldn't have let that slip.

Then again, if it made me seem more powerful, what was the harm?

"Thank You, my Lady," she replied softly, then got into her vehicle and drove off.

Arddhu and Kevin were still in the kitchen where I'd left them, as if they'd been waiting for me.

"So," I said, leaning back against the counter. "I was right. She wanted forgiveness."

"Did you give it?" Arddhu asked.

"I don't feel that's my decision alone, so I told her to come back for the Council meeting and present her case to everyone."

He nodded. "That is wise. Those of us who were Allies will wish to speak with her."

"There's more," I said, and briefed them on the threat of global nuclear war. "So I'll have to deal with Ares sooner than I'd planned. Right after I figure out how to disarm all the world's nuclear warheads."

"Whoa." Kevin's eyebrows shot up. "That'll piss off a lot of countries."

"I know, but it can't be helped. I can't think of any quicker way to avoid total nuclear annihilation, can you?"

"Good point," he said. "Any idea how you're going to do it?"

I shook my head. "Not yet. Maybe I can look for some kind of energy signature and just—I don't know—wipe it out."

"Be careful," he warned. "There are a lot of nuclear power plants still out there, generating electricity all over the world. You won't want to wipe those out, too."

"Shit." I sighed. "I guess I'll have to do some internet research, somehow get smart on the differences between weapons and power plants so I can target just the weapons."

"If you want, I can try to hack into the government's database. Find out where all the missile silos and submarines are."

Holy shit. I couldn't believe he'd just offered to do a criminal act.

"I'm not sure even our government knows the location of every single weapon in the entire world. Plus, that's really top-secret stuff, so you'd be in big trouble hacking into a system like that." I shook my head. "No, I'll figure it out."

He nodded and for once, didn't argue. "Well, let me know if there's anything I can do to help."

I smiled. "I will. Thanks."

Excusing myself, I holed up in my suite with my laptop, and slid down a rabbit hole of research.

Some of the technical documentation I read was decades old, but the basics seemed to still be relevant. After a couple of hours, as a practical application of what I'd read, I sent my consciousness far to the west of Phoenix, to the Palo Verde Nuclear Generating Station. I studied it closely, and noted that the amount of enriched uranium present matched what I'd read was commonly used for standard nuclear power generation. Because the reactor was currently operating, it emitted a relatively small, yet characteristic amount of gamma radiation as a useful signature.

Next, I went to what was arguably the most famous weapons facility known: Los Alamos National Lab in New Mexico. Once again, I studied it closely, noting the higher amount of uranium present, along with plutonium. No weapons were currently in use or being tested, so I didn't detect any gamma radiation at all.

So after a couple more hours, I thought I had a usable formula for the differences between nuclear power and weapons technologies.

I took a short break, used the bathroom, stretched my stiff muscles, and began the next step.

Assuming a nuclear warhead would have a large amount of uranium and plutonium present but no gamma radiation, I sent my consciousness out further, to locate any nearby areas that fit my theory.

Bingo.

Several sites, scattered in sparsely populated areas of Washington State, Nevada, Colorado, and Texas, had the expected results. Comparing those locations to an internet map of known missile sites, my theory was confirmed further.

Okay. So my formula for detecting weapons seemed sound.

At least for the United States.

Would it still be true for other countries?

And what about other types of weapons systems? Nuclear warships. Submarines. Portable missile systems. Were there any nuclear-capable unmanned drones? Would my theory hold for them, too?

Taking a deep breath, I set aside those questions for now, and thought how I could best accomplish my goal: to simultaneously disarm all nuclear weapons worldwide.

The weapons were constructed of complex materials, so I couldn't just ask an element for help, like I had with the brush fire and other natural disasters.

And there were probably way too many weapons for me to disable each one individually. It'd take too long.

Besides, even if I could figure out how to disable or disarm them, humans would probably just fix them.

No, I needed to take them out of their hands entirely.

But where in the world could I stash probably hundreds of thousands of nuclear weapons so no one could get at them? And what was the proper storage environment so they wouldn't break down and harm Earth?

Hmm.

Unless I *didn't* stash them here.

What if I sent them all into their own pocket dimension? I could even seal it off to make sure no one would ever be able to find them and use them. And I wouldn't have to worry about finding a place big enough to store them, or causing any harm to Earth over time.

It seemed a brilliant solution.

At least, I couldn't think of any downside.

So I got comfortable and closed my eyes to concentrate better. Beginning with the biggest missiles at the sites I'd identified, I ported them from their silos and bunkers to a new pocket universe.

After I finished with the United States, I scanned the entire country to make sure I'd gotten all of the weapons. Then, I repeated the process for the rest of the world, country by country.

That took longer, and was more complicated.

In some, the technology was much older, and the amounts of uranium were much higher than I'd expected, way off from my proven theory. But the gamma radiation signature was there, so I tagged those as power plants and skipped over them in favor of the other sites—the ones with plutonium and no gamma. Again, I ported them to the pocket universe and scanned to make sure I'd gotten all the large and medium-sized weapons.

I took a short break to stretch, then realized I was extremely thirsty. I ported a bottle of water from the fridge and drank half of it in one go.

Next, I scanned for the smaller weapons. The ones installed on ships, submarines, and aircraft.

Ooh, tricky: some of those ships and subs were nuclear-powered.

Carefully, I segregated the weapons from the power generating systems and made sure to only port the weapons to the pocket universe. Once again, some of the tech in other countries was older and the signatures were off, and once or twice I had to send my consciousness to the location to double-check before porting the stuff.

Thank the gods no alarm systems could detect the presence of an incorporeal consciousness.

I saved the most complicated stuff for last: the small tactical nukes and suitcase bombs that terrorists used. The signature on those items was almost the same as for nuclear medical technology, like CT machines. So I took extra time to modify my formula for much smaller amounts of the two components and scanned an area suspected for terrorist activity.

There. Found it. I studied the stockpile of small weapons, memorized their unique signature before porting them, then applied that signature to an ever-expanding global search.

Confident I'd ported all of them, I took a deep breath, stretched again, and drank the rest of my water.

Then I did a final scan of every square mile of the planet to make sure I hadn't missed any. I found a few stragglers and ported them, and was just about to celebrate a job well done when I remembered there were armed satellites in orbit.

Ugh. More than a dozen had nuclear warheads.

After I took care of those, I ran one last scan.

Finally.

Earth was clean. I'd gotten them all. But it'd taken almost an entire eight hours to do it.

Of course, the defense departments—and terrorists—of the world would probably want my head on a platter when they found out what I'd done, but it'd been the most expedient way to prevent a nuclear war. I'd just have to make them understand, somehow.

I stretched again, and couldn't stifle a yawn. I was exhausted.

Getting more comfy in bed, I thought over next steps. Should I remove the stockpiles of plutonium and uranium, too? So nobody could make any more weapons any time soon?

No, I couldn't. The power plants and medical tech manufacturers would need some of that.

Shit. I didn't want to make any more of a negative impact than I'd already done, so maybe I should leave the supplies alone for now.

Now there was no doubt. I really needed to deal with Ares next. But my sonogram was in the morning, and the Council meeting was the day after that. And I still had to find out exactly where on Olympus he was hiding.

So he'd have to wait a couple more days.

And right now, I needed a nice long sleep.

CHAPTER TWENTY-ONE

I N THE MORNING, I slept in, and it was glorious. After all, it wasn't often I got a chance to do it, and I'd needed the extra rest after expending so much energy removing all the nuclear weapons from Earth.

After a quick shower, I dressed and headed out to the kitchen for breakfast, where Brianna was just putting the finishing touches on scrambled eggs, fried ham steak, and buttered toast. The delicious aroma made my mouth water.

The Morrigan looked up from her mobile phone and smiled. "Morning."

"Morning," I replied as I sat at the kitchen island. I'd expected to see Nat, since she was going with me to the sonogram appointment.

"Nat isn't feeling well," the Morrigan said, as if answering my unspoken question. "She said she ate some bad leftovers last night. So you get me instead."

"Okay, great."

Brianna set a full plate and a steaming mug of coffee in front of each of us, and I smiled my thanks to her before digging in.

Thirty minutes or so later, we were on our way to the testing facility, not far from the OB/GYN's office.

The Morrigan insisted on coming into the room with me, since she was interested in the technology. I didn't mind, but I couldn't really get excited about the test. I'd been instructed to keep my bladder full, so it was incredibly uncomfortable to lie down on the exam table. But then she took my hand in hers, which was unexpectedly soothing, and it helped make everything more bearable.

The technician spread cold, sticky gel on my abdomen and positioned the wand, then pressed buttons to take pictures of the fetus growing inside me.

The Morrigan watched the process with rapt fascination, and it made me smile.

"Here you go," the tech said, and swiveled the monitor toward me.

Although I used my enhanced vision, I couldn't really make out a damn thing. It was all a mass of black, white, and gray splotches that formed and reformed every few seconds.

"Such a wee thing," the Morrigan murmured, and squeezed my hand.

"She won't be a wee thing for much longer," the technician said with a smile. "She'll grow and develop fast starting in this second trimester."

What? Did she just say what I thought she said? I was over *three months* pregnant? Impossible.

"I'm sorry," I said. "Could you repeat that? The age, I mean?"

"She's about sixteen weeks," she replied, not taking her eyes from the monitor while continuing to click the button and move the wand.

Four months? I was four months along? Holy shit. I'd thought I was still in the first month.

Then the other thing she'd said hit me: she'd said *she.*

Yet again, Loki's prediction was proven correct. I hadn't really doubted him, but it was another thing entirely to actually hear it from a medical professional.

I really was going to have a daughter.

So why did I suddenly feel like crying?

"Okay, all done," the technician said, and handed me a foil-wrapped wipe. "You can use this to clean off the gel. Bathroom's right through that doorway. I'll send the file to your doctor's office." Not waiting for any questions, she turned and left.

Ignoring the tears that threatened, I busied myself by cleaning off the sticky gel as best I could—I'd need more than just that single tiny alcohol wipe to really do the job—and pulled my pants back up, then hit the bathroom to relieve my impatient bladder.

"That was really neat," the Morrigan said as we headed back to the SUV. "I'd bet Kevin would've been fascinated with that machine."

I nodded; he definitely would've. But my mind was stuck on what the technician had said.

How could I possibly be that much further along? I'd honestly expected to be just a little over a month or so, not *four months*. Only a month ago, Loki had said my pregnancy was early yet. How could I have gone from that to this so soon?

"Okay, out with it." The Morrigan had interrupted my thoughts. "What's wrong?"

"Nothing." I sighed. "Well, except for I just can't believe I'm this far along."

I felt her gaze on me as I made a left turn. "I can. Remember, you're the Goddess. You're not going to have a normal nine-month gestation period."

Yeah, Arddhu and Kevin had said the same thing.

"In fact," she added, "your pregnancy might only last another month or two. On the other hand, you could give birth in a year. You need to prepare for any possibility."

Shit. If I only had another month, I wasn't ready.

"But I still have so much to do before the baby's born," I pointed out. "Stuff I won't be able to do while taking care of a newborn."

"Don't worry. We'll help. Arddhu, Kevin, all of us. We won't let you do this alone." After a moment, she asked, "What are you going to tell your human doctor?"

As I pulled into the driveway, Joe opened the gate. I waved and drove through. "She works for the firm, so she already knows I'm the Goddess."

"Ah, so she won't be surprised."

"Right."

"What about the birth itself? Will it be modern, in a hospital?"

"I don't know yet. I haven't really given it much thought."

"There's still time to decide." She grinned. "Congratulations, by the way. A daughter. That's wonderful."

I pulled the SUV into the garage and smiled in return. "Yeah. It is." My smile faded as I had another thought. "But it sucks she's going to grow up never knowing her grandmother or grandfather."

We both got out and shut the doors.

"But she'll have two dads, a fantastic mom, and me, as a fantastic aunt." She grinned again.

When she put it that way...

Two dads, one divine and the other a demi-god.

One aunt who's the Goddess of Battlefield Death, and another who's a kick-ass member of a security team.

And the Goddess of Earth for a mom.

Pretty impressive family, I had to admit.

"You know," the Morrigan said. "I can't wait to see Arddhu try to change a diaper. I think we should record it for posterity."

I raised a brow. "He's never had any children of his own?"

She shook her head. "Ida didn't want any competition for his attention."

Wow. What a bitch she'd been.

"Well, this one will be a little princess, that's for sure," I said, not wanting to think about Ida. "Probably spoiled rotten."

Her eyes twinkled merrily as she laughed. "Oh, don't doubt that for a second."

She went her way, and I went mine: to the living room, where I got comfy on the sofa and started answering the prayers that'd piled up over the last day or so.

The morning of the Council meeting, we gathered once again at the green space I'd created. After everyone had taken their seats, I gave a quick update on my visit with Kali, pointing out she'd be presenting herself shortly.

I also explained what I'd done with the world's nuclear weapons. The Dagda couldn't hide his surprise—and seemed a bit impressed, too.

"That was well done, Lady," he said. "You are quickly becoming quite the competent Goddess."

"Thank you." I smiled at him in gratitude. "Next, I'll be paying a visit to the Olympians. Ares must be dealt with. And by association, Athena."

"Do we know where they are, then?" Reshep asked.

Anthony shook his head. "Still only brief sightings reported by our spies. It's like they know they're being watched."

I sighed, fighting my impatience. Maybe I could try using my Seer's Mirror.

Anthony's handheld radio squawked to life. He stepped away to reply, and returned a moment later. "She's here. Kali, I mean."

We all watched her approach, accompanied by Nat, who'd been stationed at the portal as escort.

Again, Kali was in her kindly grandmother guise. It didn't fool me, though. I knew if she wanted to attack, she could transform into a fearsome and highly effective warrior in mere seconds.

For just a moment, I tensed, wondering if I'd made a grave mistake. What if she really *was* here to attack us?

Kali halted several feet away and repeated the actions of her first visit: on her knees, she touched her forehead to the soft grass.

"Greetings, my Lady, Keeper of the Sphere, and Great Goddess of Earth."

"Greetings, Kali, Goddess of Wisdom and Death. You may rise and state your business."

She rose to her feet and glanced around the table. Her gaze skimmed over the Túatha, Anthony, and Kevin, dismissing them in favor of Arddhu, Reshep, and the Morrigan. She nodded respectfully to them before returning her gaze to me.

"I have come to beg forgiveness of You and Your Council."

Dagda cleared his throat. "Lady, perhaps those of us who were not Your allies before You became Goddess of Earth should not take part in this discussion. It was before our time, as the humans say." The rest of the Túatha, along with the ambassadors, nodded in agreement.

He had a good point.

"Agreed," I said. "Let's adjourn this meeting. Thank you all for attending. Those of you who were in the old Alliance, please stay."

Anthony joined the group of ambassadors and Túatha leaving the green space.

"You can take a seat now," I said to Kali.

She chose the exact center of the empty seats, as if careful not to get too close to any of us.

"May I have some water, please?" she asked.

"Of course." I ported a bottle of water from the beverage station to the table in front of Kali. While she took a long drink, I turned to the others. "So. What do you guys think about forgiving Kali?"

Arddhu replied first. "She has been a formidable ally in the past. I believe she could be again. I would agree to forgiveness and reinstatement, provided she gives us certain assurances."

"What kind of assurances?" she asked.

"We'll discuss those in a moment," I said, then turned to the others. "What about the rest of you?"

"I, too, would agree," Reshep said. "But only if one of the assurances is that she has no further contact with the Olympians. We do not want them to know too much about our Council."

"There is no chance of that," Kali snapped. "I left them for a reason. And I will not be returning."

"Why did you leave?" Kevin asked.

"We had a serious disagreement," she replied. "I didn't want to be part of any plan to destroy Earth. But neither of them would listen to reason. So early one morning, I left them."

"And you came here," the Morrigan added.

"Yes," she nodded. "I wasn't sure there was enough time to stop their idiotic plan, but I had to try."

The Morrigan leaned forward and rested her folded arms on the table. "But you were happy enough to be part of their plans up to that point."

She hesitated before replying, then lifted her chin. "I was blinded by lust for power. I believed their lies even though I should've known better. I have already asked the Lady for forgiveness for my folly."

"What sort of lies?" Reshep asked.

Kali turned toward him and ticked them off her fingers like a list. "The Lady would be just as bad a Goddess as Ida was, if not worse. She didn't care about Earth, only about having the power. Anu had betrayed us all, and wouldn't hesitate to do it again. And finally, that you were all working together to eliminate the gods."

What a bunch of crap. How could she have possibly believed that bullshit?

"Anu only did what she thought was right," Kevin said, quietly.

"Yes." Kali nodded to him, then her gaze slid to mine. "And I am very glad she did. It sickens me to think how close we came to either Ares or Athena stealing Ida's power in that brief moment that it lingered before flowing to You."

The Morrigan cocked her head to one side. "Why should we trust you?"

Kali opened her mouth to speak, stopped, then shrugged. "I can give no good answer to that question. If our situations were reversed, I would've already executed anyone who'd done what I have."

The Morrigan's grin was feral. "If it'd been my decision, I would've already taken your head."

I shook my head. "Which is exactly what Ares and Athena expect us to do. But we can't eliminate all the deities who don't agree with us."

"True." The Morrigan studied Kali for a moment, then added, "I, too, am satisfied, and vote yes on reinstatement."

That left Kevin. I turned to him with raised brows, but his gaze was on Kali.

"What do we gain by letting you live?" he asked.

"Maybe nothing." Again, she shrugged. "But if I am dead, how could I possibly aid you?"

"I'm not sure you can," he said. "You think you're useful to us, but I have my doubts."

I'd just opened my mouth to repeat what I'd said to the Morrigan when Kali laughed bitterly.

"Well, it's possible I may never get the chance to be useful. After all, I'm as good as dead if either Ares or Athena find me." Her gaze slid to mine once again. "Unless You offer me Your protection."

I leaned back in my seat and thought it over.

How useful could Kali be? It wasn't like we really needed a Goddess of Death hanging around. On the other hand, maybe her wisdom would come in handy to help de-escalate the war Ares had instigated in South Asia. After all, they'd probably just use guns instead of nuclear weapons.

But if it came to an all-out war between us and the Olympians, we could use Kali's help.

Honestly, I couldn't see a downside to keeping her around for a while. At least until we knew one way or another.

"Dee," Kevin warned quietly. "We need to talk about this."

I turned to him. "What's there to talk about? I think we've all basically agreed to grant forgiveness and reinstatement. Extending my protection would only be logical."

"Not all of us." He shook his head. "I haven't agreed."

"Why not?"

He glanced at Kali before answering. "I don't trust her."

"Who said I did?" I asked.

He blinked at me. "I thought—but you—"

I leaned closer and spoke quietly. "Just because we agree to certain conditions and reinstatement doesn't mean she's regained our trust. We'll just take it a step at a time."

He nodded. "I can deal with that."

I straightened, turned toward Kali, and spoke with authority. "Kali, Goddess of Wisdom and Death, do you vow to protect Earth and all its inhabitants, even other deities with whom you have been enemies in the past? And do you swear to do so, on your life?"

"Yes," she said. "I hereby swear, on my life, to protect Earth and all its inhabitants, including other deities."

"And do you swear to obey me in all things?"

"I swear to obey You in all things."

"And do you vow to never attempt to harm anyone again, unless it is a direct command from me?"

"I will never attempt harm to anyone unless You command it."

I nodded once. "Then yes, I will protect you from the Olympians. And you are hereby reinstated to the status of ally to this Council. If you continue to prove yourself trustworthy, we will discuss the possibility of you joining the Council as a full member."

She took a deep, shaky breath and let it out. "Thank You." She glanced at the others. "Thank you all. I will give you no cause to regret your generosity. I vow it."

With that done, now I had to figure out the best way to protect her.

If I kept her here at The Hacienda, the wards and security team would help keep her safe and out of trouble. But there weren't any rooms available in the main house, and the guest house was occupied by the security team.

Hmm. Why not create another guest house? It didn't have to be anything fancy. Why not use the power I had?

I closed my eyes and sent my consciousness out to find a good spot on the property, not too far from the existing buildings but far enough for privacy. There, I created a comfortable and cozy two bedroom, two bath guest house. The final touches were electricity, plumbing, air conditioning, furniture, dishes, towels, and all the everyday basics.

Outside the house, I created a small back patio with a garden of shady trees and flowering plants. As an afterthought, I added a soothing fountain.

I opened my eyes to everyone watching me with concern.

"I'm fine," I assured them, then told Kali about the guest house. "You'll be safe there," I finished. "As long as you stay within the fence line, you'll be protected by my wards and security team. But if you stray outside of my property, you're on your own."

Kali bowed her head. "My Lady, I am truly blessed by Your kindness. I am deeply indebted to You."

Nat had remained just outside of hearing range. Now, I called her over.

"Could you please show Kali to her new home? It's off to the east a few hundred yards."

She nodded, waited for Kali to join her, then escorted her.

"You created an entire dwelling just now?" Arddhu asked.

I nodded, stifling a yawn.

"You look tired," Kevin pointed out.

I nodded again. "Yeah, I'm exhausted. I'm going to go lie down for a bit."

A terrifying wall of flames, devastating everything in its path.

Bodies lay everywhere, some blackened beyond recognition.

Distant screaming and hopeless crying.

Fire and ash raining from the sky.

I jerked awake, choking on smoke and trembling. It took a moment to realize it wasn't real. I was home, in my own bed. There was no fire. No smoke.

The air conditioner on my sweat-soaked skin made me shiver, and I drew the covers up to get warm while I caught my breath and tried to slow my heart beat.

Dammit. Just when I'd thought the nightmare was gone, it'd come back. Hadn't it been a warning for the threat of nuclear war? What else could cause that much destruction to our world?

The buzz of my mobile phone interrupted my thoughts.

"Ms. Connor? This is Ann, with Doctor Wood-Smith's office. We've received the results of your ultrasound, and the doctor would like you to come in to discuss them. There's been a cancellation for later this afternoon, can you make it?"

These guys with their short-notice appointments were annoying.

After getting the details, I agreed to the appointment and hung up, then got out of bed. Some cold water splashed on my face helped me to feel a bit better.

I found Anthony and Kevin in the living room, watching the news. I watched the screen for a moment, to see what was going on.

Lots of frantic reports from lots of frantic countries, wondering where all their nukes had gone. Current popular theories ran the gamut from highly professional thieves to, of course, aliens.

It was *always* aliens with some people.

I shook my head and went to the kitchen, where Brianna had already started fixing something for me to eat. I gave her a quick update on Kali and where she was staying. "Could you include her in your meal planning?" I finished.

"Way ahead of you." She smiled. "I've already got her stocked up on some quick meals she can fix for herself, and I've invited her to join us here for dinner this evening."

Honestly, Brianna had been such a blessing from her very first day.

I thanked her as she set the chicken salad sandwich in front of me, and my stomach rumbled appreciatively.

Just as I'd started eating, the Morrigan entered the kitchen.

"Ah, there's our Sleeping Beauty," she grinned. "Feel better?"

I nodded as I chewed and swallowed. "I really needed that. It must be the pregnancy, making me so tired all the time."

"Probably." She sat on the stool to my right. "When do you get the ultrasound results?"

"Later today. The doc had a cancellation."

She raised a brow. "And I'm going with you, right?"

"Sure, if you want."

"Oh, I definitely want."

"Can I come too?" Kevin asked, and sat to my left. The television was off, and Anthony stood off to one side looking at his mobile phone.

"I don't see why not. Where's Arddhu? Maybe he'd like to come."

The Morrigan shook her head. "He's off doing his pre-Hunt stuff. I haven't seen him since the meeting earlier."

I shrugged and swallowed the last bite of my sandwich. "Well, I'm sure the doc will give me a copy of the imaging. I'll make sure he sees it."

"I've been meaning to ask you," Kevin began. "Are you still having those nightmares? The ones with smoke and ash?"

"As a matter of fact, I had one earlier, just before I got up. Why?"

He frowned. "Trying to figure out how all the pieces fit."

Yeah. I knew the feeling.

Anthony cleared his throat quietly. "If you have a moment, I have a quick update."

"Sure." I turned to face him.

"Our spies have identified a pattern with Ares and Athena. They move between several places, staying for one or two days at each. Soon, we should be able to predict where they'll be with greater confidence."

"That's great news."

He flashed a smile, then left for his weekly meeting with the security team.

"So what's the plan for when we find them?" Kevin asked.

"I'll try talking to them first."

"What if they attack as soon as we show up?"

"Not we. *Me*. I'm going alone." They both loudly objected at the same time, but I'd expected that. "Look, guys, if a bunch of us show up, they'll be on the defensive right away and it'd ruin any hope of a peaceful resolution."

"You can't fight both of them alone," the Morrigan said. "Not in your condition."

The rage that spiked in me so suddenly actually scared me.

I'd read pregnancy could cause waves of emotion, and I'd already experienced my share of crying at stupid shit like television commercials.

But I hadn't been this angry in a long time, and I clenched my jaw against the nasty response that threatened to burst free.

Whatever she saw on my face alarmed her. "Dee, you're glowing red."

Oh. Yeah, that was bad.

I closed my eyes and forced myself to calm down, taking deep breaths. After a moment, I returned to normal.

"Please tell me you aren't seriously going there alone. At least take one of us with you. Either Kevin or myself."

"I'll be fine. Trust me."

Kevin sighed. "Arddhu will be pissed as hell when he finds out."

"I wish you guys would stop treating me with kid gloves. Look, I'm the Goddess of Earth. This is my job."

The Morrigan shook her head. "Then I hope you'll wear some armor."

"Of course I will." I rested a hand on each of their shoulders. "I need to answer some prayers before the doc appointment. I'll meet you both back here when it's time to go."

This time, the doctor entered the exam room so quickly, I'd barely paged through half of the magazine a prior patient had left behind.

"Hello again, Ms. Connor." Doctor Wood-Smith smiled as she closed the door, file folder in hand. "What did You think of seeing Your baby on the monitor?"

Normally, I would've asked her to not be so formal in addressing me with reverence, but I decided to let it go.

I'd have to get used to it someday.

"To be honest, I didn't really see much of anything that looked like a baby. Just a lot of splotches."

She nodded. "That's actually quite common. But maybe this 3D rendering will be better." She handed me the folder with a flourish, as if it were a birthday present or something valuable.

I flipped it open and almost gasped at the relatively clear picture of my daughter.

My daughter.

Her eyes were closed and a tiny fist rested in front of a rosebud mouth. She was beautiful.

In that moment, the room seemed to shift around me, and I blinked back tears.

"From the imaging," the doctor continued, "You're about sixteen weeks along. That would put the due date sometime in late September. I'm afraid that's the best estimate we have at this point, since You don't have the date of Your last period. Although every fetus is unique, they all have common characteristics at specific development stages, and we use those to calculate due dates and the biological sex of the fetus." She paused. "I've been told You know You're having a girl."

I couldn't take my eyes from the image. The more I studied it, the more detail I noticed: the bump of a nose, the curl of an ear, the tiny nails in the perfect fingers and toes, and the winding umbilical cord that connected my daughter to me.

"Ms. Connor?"

"Oh." I raised my head to meet her gaze. "Sorry. Yes, I know I'm having a daughter." I knew the image would continue to distract me, so I closed the folder but couldn't seem to let it go. "Can I keep this?"

"Of course. I printed it out just for You."

I smiled. "Thank you."

"And how have You been feeling?" she asked. "Any new symptoms?"

"Nothing really new that I can think of. I'm still tired almost all the time. I go from not being hungry to ravenous in seconds. But I had that even before. Before I got pregnant, I mean. I guess it's a normal part of my body's transition to deity. Eventually, I won't need to eat at all. My body will just sustain itself. Same thing with sleeping. Eventually, I won't need it. But right now, I think I'm sleeping more than I ever have."

I stopped abruptly, realizing I'd been babbling.

"That's fascinating." The doctor's eyes had been fixed on me with intense interest. "I'd love to hear more about this transition, when we have the time." She flashed a quick grin. "I don't often get the opportunity to speak to a real, live deity. Especially one in transition from human to divine."

"I'll bet."

"As far as Your health goes, I'm very glad You're eating and sleeping regularly. Your divine body might not need it, but Your baby does. She'll need as much nourishment as You can give her, and lots of sleep will also help Your remaining human cells stay healthy and regenerate as they're supposed to. We'll do some bloodwork today to make sure Your nutrition levels are good and Your blood looks normal." Her grin was lopsided. "Well, as normal as possible, under the circumstances. Anything else?"

I shrugged. "Just other normal stuff. Breast tenderness and a bit of weight gain. I think my belly is getting rounder, too."

She nodded. "That would be normal for this stage of pregnancy. Any questions or concerns about the next stage?"

"Not really. I've done some reading on the internet, so I have a pretty good idea of what to expect."

"Great Just remember to stick to reputable websites." She set her tablet aside. "Now, hop up on the table for me. I want to do a quick exam for the record."

Awkwardly, I lay back on the exam table and unzipped my jeans.

My belly just about popped out, and I hadn't realized how constricting my jeans had been. In fact, it was definitely rounder than it'd been only this morning.

The doctor seemed to realize how big I was, too; she frowned at my abdomen, then consulted her tablet. "Your weight at check-in must be wrong. According to this, You've only gained five pounds." She pointedly looked at my belly again. "But that's more than five pounds."

"I wouldn't be surprised, from all the eating I've been doing."

"This'll feel cold." She took the stethoscope from around her neck and pressed it to my abdomen. She listened, moved it, frowned, moved it again and listened, all while frowning.

My heart leapt into my throat. *What's wrong with my daughter?*

"Is something wrong?" I couldn't keep the alarm from my voice.

"No, no," she smiled distractedly. "Just hearing a very strong heartbeat." She continued listening, then winced and pulled the earpieces off. "Ouch."

"What happened?"

She laughed. "Your baby just kicked at my scope. That usually happens around twenty weeks, so either Your girl is also a goddess, or we might be way off on our gestational estimate." She made notes on her tablet. Without looking at me, she added, "You can close up Your jeans and sit in the chair again."

"Okay." I zipped up my jeans, grateful they had lots of stretch. Sure, I could adjust them with magick, but maybe that was one of the reasons I was so tired all the time. Maybe I should only use magick when it was absolutely necessary, at least until the baby was born.

She continued tapping on her tablet for a moment, then flashed another rueful smile. "I've adjusted Your due date to sometime in mid to late August. I'm sorry for any inconvenience."

"It's probably not your fault since it's not a normal pregnancy. In fact, the Morrigan told me I could deliver anywhere between a month to a year."

"The Morrigan?" Her eyes were sharp on mine. "The Irish Goddess of Battlefield Death?"

I nodded, but decided not to tell her that same goddess was waiting for me in the reception area. As was an Irish demi-god.

"You have some very powerful friends."

Again, I just nodded. She didn't know the half of it.

"Well, keep me posted on any issues You have." She'd taken more of the prenatal vitamin sample packets out of the drawer and now handed them to me. "We'll schedule another ultrasound for about a month from now, just to check on the baby's development and see if we can nail down that due date for You. In the meantime, let's go do that bloodwork."

I sent the vitamins to my pocket universe and headed to the in-house lab, with the file folder tucked against my chest. I just didn't want to let it go.

Afterward, I met the Morrigan and Kevin in the reception area.

"So, are you both ready for this?" I asked them as we headed to the parking lot. Not waiting for a reply, I flipped open the file folder and showed them the image.

They both stopped in the hallway and stared at it, speechless.

"I'm due sometime in August, but that'll probably change since none of us really know how long I'll actually be pregnant."

The Morrigan met my gaze. "So the doc doesn't know any more than we do because of your transition to deity."

"Nope."

She smirked. "Told you so."

"It—wait, is it a he or a she?" Kevin asked. "Or is it too soon for that?"

I smiled. "She's a girl."

He blinked at me, then stared at the picture again. "Hello, little princess," he murmured.

I almost started crying right there in the facility's hallway.

Damn hormones.

Shaking my head, I cleared the lump from my throat and said, "Let's go home and hail Arddhu. I want him to see this, too."

As soon as we walked into the house, I used my mental communication link to ask Arddhu to come home, then waited at the kitchen island with the Morrigan and Kevin.

I placed the image on the granite and the three of us couldn't keep our eyes off it.

"It's fantastic technology," Kevin said. "I wish I'd been there to see the machine in use."

The Morrigan smirked as her gaze met mine. "Told ya."

I'd just opened my mouth to reply when Arddhu arrived through the panel in the window-wall.

"What is wrong?" His voice was strained, and I immediately felt horrible for worrying him.

"Nothing," I reassured him. "I just thought you'd like an update on the baby." I gestured to the ultrasound picture. "She's a girl."

For a long moment, he simply stared at it, utterly transfixed. Then, he lightly traced the baby's features with the tip of a finger.

"This is truly amazing. It appears realistic, so life-like." He raised his eyes to mine. "How much longer until she is born?"

"Your guess is as good as mine. At the time of that picture, she was about five months. But she seems to be developing at the rate of about a month every week or so." I shrugged. "So, maybe another couple of weeks?"

His eyes lit up and he beamed at me. "She is divine, like her mother."

"Holy shit," Kevin said, gaze dropping to my swelled abdomen. "Two weeks? That soon?"

It was the Morrigan who replied. "Maybe, maybe not. Development could slow at this point, or accelerate even more."

How did the Irish Goddess of Battlefield Death know so much about pregnancy and babies?

Kevin grinned. "Then I think we need to go shopping. And get that nursery set up."

"Uh-uh." I shook my head. "I need a nap. So go ahead without me. Tell Anthony you need to use the household card, and have fun with it. Surprise me."

His grin widened. "You may regret giving us free rein like this."

"Probably." I laughed, then kissed him. "But I can't wait to see what you find. Just don't buy out the whole store."

Over the next couple of days, I took some time for myself. For the first time in months, I relaxed in the pool and somehow managed not to feel guilty about it.

Beltaine was approaching rapidly, and so was the delivery date for my daughter. I felt as big as a house, was uncomfortably hot all the time, with a constant lower back ache. Even wearing a bra hurt. I didn't think I'd be giving birth in two months. It really did feel more like two weeks.

On one hand, I was absolutely terrified, but on the other, I couldn't wait for it all to be over.

Just the day before, Kevin had led me to the room we'd chosen as a nursery. Although Arddhu had spent a lot of time away, getting things ready for his Wild Hunt, he'd pitched in with Kevin and the Morrigan to decorate.

They'd done a fantastic job.

I'd stood in the middle of the room—surrounded by baby furniture, at least a hundred stuffed animals and dolls, and an explosion of pink and cream on the walls and floor—and cried. Everything was ready for whenever our little princess decided it was time to leave the cradle of my body.

That was one of the only times lately I saw Kevin. He was incredibly busy now that the Túatha had finished moving back to Earth from their temporary realm. They needed almost constant advanced technology classes in the VIP tent, preparing for their new business ventures. Kali, too, had decided to learn the internet and computers, so Kevin held separate, beginner-level sessions just for her.

The Morrigan, too, was busy—spending a lot of time with Reshep. I didn't begrudge her a moment of it. I didn't know how long either of them had been without a special someone, but I was truly happy they'd paired up.

In between moments of down time, I'd been just as busy as ever. Over the past couple of days, I'd extinguished six wildfires in four Western states, helped with a massive brushfire in Australia, removed floodwaters in two Midwestern states, and assisted with search and rescue efforts after a magnitude seven earthquake hit Japan.

Then I'd also worked with the element of water to diffuse the resulting tsunami.

I stubbornly refused to consider the possibility we'd moved past the point of no return, or that all the healing I did wouldn't matter in the long run. No, it'd just take longer than I'd originally thought.

Ogma and I had done several media interviews using teleconferencing software, and they seemed to raise my social media popularity even more than the viral videos had. We figured that was why prayers had increased significantly, which forced me to cut back on responding to posts and messages. Poor Anthony and Ogma had to pick up the slack, but they swore they didn't mind.

"Sorry to bother you." Anthony stood at the pool's edge; I'd been so lost in my thoughts I hadn't even heard him approach. "Agent Park of the FBI is back. And this time he's brought along a couple of friends from NASA and DoE. They're waiting at the front gate."

Shit. NASA? Department of Energy? What the hell did they want?

"Okay," I sighed. I left the pool, magickally drying myself off and changing into comfortable shorts and a maternity top as I headed toward the house. The last thing I did was make sure I glowed properly.

"Um, wards?" Anthony reminded me.

Shit. I quickly modified the wards to allow the visitors entry, and we slipped through a panel in the window-wall into the living room.

I quickly ported refreshments from the kitchen and sat in a chair. A moment later, Anthony greeted the visitors at the front door and escorted them inside.

Agent Park stared at my huge belly with an almost comical expression of disbelief. "Wow. You didn't look pregnant last time I was here," he muttered, then flushed. "Uh, sorry, didn't mean for it to come out sounding like that."

I smiled. "No worries, Agent. I knew what you meant. And you're absolutely right, I sure didn't. This"—I waved a hand at my belly—"sort of popped out only a couple of weeks ago. Just part of being a deity, I guess."

He blinked at me for another moment, then shook his head. "Well, congratulations. But before we get started on the reason for our visit, I just wanted to say something. My doc can't believe it. It took two visits and lots of tests, but it's been confirmed: all traces of the cancer are gone. So, thank You."

I heard the unmistakable new reverence in his voice, and blinked away unexpected tears. "I'm very happy for you."

One of the other gentlemen cleared his throat and shifted impatiently, and Park immediately became businesslike.

"Right. Down to it, then. This is Bob Burns, from the Department of Energy's National Nuclear Security Administration." Burns was probably in his late forties, short and stocky with thick curly black hair, unnaturally pale skin that probably hadn't seen sun in weeks, and striking gray-blue eyes.

Park continued, "And this is Frank Cox from the Planetary Defense Coordination Office of NASA." Cox was a younger man, maybe late thirties, tall and muscular like an athlete, with ashy blonde hair and green eyes, full reddish beard, and ruddy complexion.

"As a Special Agent," Park added, "I'm here as the official FBI liaison for national security personnel."

Nuclear security.

National security.

Hmm. They must be here to discuss the nukes I'd removed from Earth. Then again, what would nukes have to do with planetary defense and NASA? Unless it was about the satellites I'd disarmed.

Yeah, that was probably it. This was about the nukes.

Anthony sat in the chair across from me, leaving the couch for the two visitors, who hadn't stopped staring at me since they'd arrived. Seeing we needed another chair for Park, I quickly created one. Park took it in stride, simply sitting and making himself comfortable, but the newcomers' wide eyes and blatant astonishment almost made me laugh.

Instead, I pasted a pleasant smile on my face and said, "Please help yourselves to fresh lemonade and cookies."

Burns shook his head and got right to it. "What we're about to tell you is highly classified. You've been granted special access clearance on orders from the president himself. However, you do not have authorization to discuss anything that follows with anyone else. Not even a spouse or family member." He turned to Anthony. "Sir, you'll have to leave. You're not cleared."

"He's my legal representative," I said. "He stays."

"He's not cleared," Burns stubbornly repeated.

I shrugged and started to get up. "Then this meeting is over."

"Wait," Cox said, and while I got comfortable again, he leaned over and murmured in Burns' ear for a moment. Burns clenched his jaw, but nodded and met my eyes. "Fine. He has temporary clearance. Now, do you both understand and agree to the conditions I mentioned?"

"Yes," I said, and Anthony echoed me.

Burns cleared his throat, took a deep breath, and continued. "NNSA and NASA are partners in Planetary Defense, which identifies and tracks potential hazardous objects within our solar system. In the past few days, we've identified an interstellar object approaching from beyond our sun. It is moving at high speed, with a trajectory expected to impact Earth. Best estimates are roughly six to eight weeks from today." He paused, then leaned forward. His direct gaze was disconcerting. "Normally, this kind of information is made public immediately. However, due to national security concerns, the president has ordered a delay in the release. Other countries, of course, are also involved, so it's only a matter of time before word gets out. That's why it's imperative that you do whatever you can, as soon as possible."

I stared at him, at a complete loss for words. So this wasn't about the nukes, after all? Then I got stuck on—what was it he'd said? An interstellar object? Did he mean a spaceship?

"Aliens?" I asked, only half joking.

"No. It's a previously unknown asteroid."

Just what the hell was I supposed to do about it?

Wait—the president himself knew about me? And thought I could help?

My brain seemed as thick as molasses.

I took a deep breath and backed up a bit. "You said you just noticed it a few days ago. Don't you guys have some kind of early detection system?"

"Normally, yes," Cox replied. "If it'd come from just about any other direction, we would've seen it months or maybe even years ago. But this one was lost in the sun's glare. We just didn't see it until we noticed a weird reflection where one wasn't supposed to be."

Shit. That seemed really bad. How could an asteroid sneak up on us like this?

"Can't you just, uh, blast it with a laser or something?"

Burns shook his head. "We don't have lasers in space, like some science fiction movie. We do have a planetary defense system—or rather, we used to. It's no longer functioning, and we suspect it's been disarmed. Or stolen, just like all the other nuclear weapons from all over the planet." His gaze and tone of voice sharpened. "You wouldn't happen to know anything about that, would you?"

Oops.

My cheeks burned, but I wasn't going to let him intimidate me. I lifted my chin. "As a matter of fact, yes, I do. There was a credible threat of imminent nuclear war, and I did what I had to do to prevent it."

"To protect the planet," Burns said, with heavy sarcasm.

I nodded.

"Some protector you are," he spat. "You've left us defenseless."

I bit back the nasty comment I wanted to make. "Isn't that a bit dramatic? Can't you just launch a rocket at the damn thing and knock it off course or something?"

"Someone's watched too many Hollywood movies." Burns shook his head, but hadn't taken his gaze from mine. "It doesn't work that way. And besides, a complicated mission like that would take months, and we don't have that much time."

I sighed. "What do you expect me to do about it?"

"For starters, you could put back what you stole."

If only it were that simple. "I'm sorry. I don't think I can. I... I'm not sure I know exactly which ones came out of which satellite system."

He blinked at me. "Then we have a problem, Ms. Connor."

That was an understatement, and not just about the nukes.

I changed tactics. "How big is this thing? Maybe it'll just burn up in the atmosphere."

"We wouldn't be here if that were the case."

I just held his gaze and waited for him to answer my question.

It took him a moment to realize what I was waiting for, and then he sighed. "It's a little less than half a mile wide."

Was that big or small as far as asteroids went? I realized it'd been a stupid question to begin with. I knew next to nothing about any of this shit.

"What are we talking about here? I mean, what's the magnitude? Mass extinction of the whole planet, or devastation of a small rural town?"

"Well, it depends on a lot of factors that we just don't know yet, such as composition, angle and point of entry, and speed at moment of impact. But in general, an ocean impact would probably cause a tsunami, earthquakes, possibly spawn a hurricane. And the super-heated water would have consequences that could last for decades.

"A land impact would be much worse. Fireballs, earthquakes, radiation, debris in the atmosphere, and an impact crater. If it strikes a high-density population zone, significant destruction and loss of life. Even a low-density population zone would see significant destruction. For example, if it hit the wheat belt, the loss of viable crops could last for decades, and cause food shortages, widespread hunger, malnutrition. That sort of thing." He took a breath and continued. "Worst case, it hits New York City, Los Angeles, Delhi, Beijing, or any number of big cities with a lot of people. The death and destruction would be catastrophic."

We stared at each other for a moment while I processed everything he'd just told me.

It was a helluva lot to process.

So.

Probably not a mass extinction event, and not a planet killer, but nevertheless a life killer and nasty-ass disaster.

But I still wasn't sure what the hell I was supposed to do about it.

"Look. I'm Goddess of Earth, not the universe. This thing isn't part of the planet, so I don't know what you—or the president—expect me to do."

Cox replied this time. "The president is asking you personally to assist in deflecting the asteroid away from Earth. As the Goddess of Earth, you have publicly stated your job is to protect the planet. So, he expects you to do exactly that."

"Which is only fair," Burns added testily. "Since it was you who disarmed us to begin with."

I clenched my jaw and bit back the caustic retort that he deserved.

To think better, I closed my eyes.

How the hell would I know how to deflect an asteroid? I'd always sucked at science stuff, so I had absolutely no clue here. Maybe I could just aim a stream of power at it? Then again, exactly where would I aim? Every time I'd ever used my power, I'd had to either visualize the target—as in teleporting—or send my consciousness to it—as in diverting hurricanes or tornadoes a thousand miles away.

But I'd never tried to affect a target that was traveling in space, millions of miles from me.

My frustration turned to anger.

As if I didn't have enough going on, now I had to deal with a fucking *asteroid*? When was I supposed to fit this in, between the daily natural disasters, the increasing frequency of prayers needing answering, and dealing with Ares?

And what about the healing sessions? How the hell could I continue healing Earth if part of it was just going to end up being destroyed in a few weeks?

Then there was my pregnancy. I was a whole lot more than sixteen weeks pregnant and exhausted all the time. And from the look of my expanding abdomen, probably ready to give birth any time now.

What a fucking shitshow.

"Ma'am?" Cox prompted. "What shall I tell the president?"

Reluctantly, I opened my eyes and turned to Anthony. "What do you think? What am I supposed to do with this?"

He cleared his throat. "I'm assuming that since you're being asked to step in, they don't have any other viable options." Pointedly, he turned to the other two.

Burns showed no reaction whatsoever. "I can neither confirm nor deny that statement."

Anthony returned his gaze to me and spoke softly. "I don't see how you have much of a choice."

He was right, of course. I *didn't* have a choice. As Goddess of Earth, it was my duty to protect the planet.

No matter what.

My anger had fizzled, with resignation taking its place.

"Fine," I sighed, rubbing my temple. "Tell him I'll do what I can."

"Thank you, ma'am." Cox nodded and stood. "There's a briefing in two days. Nine in the morning, sharp. Roosevelt Room."

"Roosevelt Room? Where's that?"

He blinked at me. "The White House." Before I could say anything, he added, "And yes, the president will be there."

Well, shit. This briefing must be a pretty big deal, then.

He handed me a business card. "In the meantime, you can reach me at the second number if you have any questions." He turned to leave, hesitated, then turned back. "Good luck," he added in a softer tone.

Burns just nodded curtly at me and followed Cox to the door, but Agent Park seemed apologetic. "I have confidence in You. You'll find a way."

Anthony closed the door behind them.

Covering my face with my hands, I collapsed in the chair. I wanted to cry. Or scream.

Or both.

How the hell could I focus on saving the planet when I could have a baby at any time?

And the kicker was, I wasn't supposed to tell anyone else about it. How the hell was that supposed to work when I didn't know the first thing about how to deflect an asteroid?

Well, fuck it. I'd have to ask for help. There was no way I could do this alone.

They'd just have to deal with it.

CHAPTER TWENTY–TWO

A NTHONY AND I had sequestered ourselves in the office for privacy. I'd even surrounded the room with a sound shield so no one could hear us, just in case, even though everyone was still off doing their own thing.

"You know I have to ask for help," I said. "I can't do this alone."

He sighed. "They were very clear. We can't tell anyone else."

"I don't even know what I'm supposed to do. I don't know how to stop or deflect an asteroid. I don't know if I have enough power to do it by myself. And I sure as hell don't know if whatever I do will just end up making it worse."

I was so frustrated, I wanted to punch something. Which was totally unlike me.

He frowned, but didn't respond.

"You know, they never even said what they've already tried. Or even if they've tried anything. Obviously, if they have, it didn't work. Otherwise they wouldn't be asking me. But I still need to know what they've tried, so I don't duplicate their efforts and waste time. I need a lot more information before I can do anything."

"I'm sure you'll find out everything you need to know at the briefing."

Right. The briefing. At the White House. With the project team and the president. They'd better not expect me to have a solution by then, because I'll only have questions.

Wait. It was in *two days*? "Shit. That's the morning of Beltaine Eve. I need to be in Finn's Cove by sundown for the ritual."

He didn't seem concerned. "You'll have plenty of time. The briefing probably won't last longer than a couple of hours."

I calculated the time difference for Ireland in my head, and figured as long as I ported to Ard na Mara by noon Arizona time, I should be good.

But it was going to be a busy couple of days, and I'd be fighting exhaustion the whole time.

"It'll be okay," he assured me. "You'll see."

He sounded so confident, but I wasn't convinced.

"I need to think," I said. "Catch you later?"

He nodded, and I dropped the sound shield before we went our separate ways.

Sometimes I did my best thinking outside in the fresh air, especially now that it was cleaner and fresher than it'd been in decades. So I headed outside, past the resort-like backyard and into the desert beyond, thinking through my limited options.

Assuming I could direct my power over such a vast distance, maybe I could blow up the asteroid. But that'd risk the fragments turning into a thousand mini-asteroids, and probably wasn't a good idea.

Again, assuming I could sustain a stream of power long enough, maybe I could push it off course, like the president wanted. But it was somewhere between the Earth and sun, and moving fast, they'd said. How was I supposed to aim and hold a powerful blast accurately? And what if it ended up colliding with one of the other planets nearby? Or even the moon?

No, there was just too much unknown for that option to be viable.

Hmm. What if I ported to the asteroid and then pushed it off course? Then again, I'd never tried to port to a moving object before, let alone something so far away.

But I was getting way ahead of myself. I didn't even know if I *could* port to space.

I glanced up at the clear blue sky. Why not give it a shot?

My first attempt got me high enough to clearly see the curvature of Earth and the distant clouds scudding below. The air was thin, but I was still able to pull enough oxygen into my lungs to breathe. This was probably airline-cruising altitude.

I tried again from there, and this time I could see the star-strewn darkness of space above me, and the hazy blue atmosphere below me. But I gasped, not finding any oxygen to breathe, and almost blacked out. I quickly returned home and collapsed on the soft patch of green grass, light-headed and panting.

Thank the gods no one had seen me. I'd never hear the end of it if they had.

The baby kicked me. *Hard.* I winced and rested my hand on my belly. "Sorry, little one. Yes, it was stupid. I won't do it again. Promise."

"*Deirdre, You must stop.*" Anu's voice was sharper than I'd ever heard it before. "*You are Goddess of Earth, not the Universe. You cannot travel beyond its boundaries.*"

Yeah. Because I still needed to breathe. "*But what if I had a space suit and a tank of oxygen—*"

"*No, Deirdre. You cannot leave Earth or the realms connected to it.*"

What? I couldn't leave Earth?

"*Not even in a space ship?*"

"*No. You would die.*"

Shit. If my brain wasn't still molasses, I would've asked her *before* I tried anything so stupid. I could've seriously hurt myself. And my baby.

"*Thank you for telling me, Anu.*"

"*Much love, Deirdre.*"

I sighed. I knew there'd been constraints on Ida, so it made sense for me to have some limits, too. But it narrowed my options in this case, and I couldn't think of anything else I could try with such limited information. It'd have to wait until after the briefing.

Until then, I needed to recover and I had prayers to answer.

And I had a lot to think about.

At dinner, Reshep and Kali joined Arddhu, Kevin, the Morrigan, and I for a tasty chicken pesto pasta dish that Brianna had worked on almost all day.

But my mind kept drifting, and it was next to impossible to keep the news of the asteroid or the upcoming briefing from slipping out. My family deserved to know the truth—especially since I'd probably need their help—but it was too soon for Reshep and Kali to know anything.

Of course, Kevin was the one who noticed I was preoccupied. Somehow he always noticed things like that before anyone else did. Almost as if it were a sixth sense or something. Part of his magick, maybe.

"Everything okay?" He'd asked it quietly, but everyone else immediately stopped talking and waited to hear my reply.

"Sure," I lied, hoping he wouldn't detect the lie. "Why wouldn't it be?"

"You just seem like you're a million miles away."

I shrugged. "Just thinking about everything."

"Is the babe okay?" The Morrigan asked.

"Yep." I continued eating and hoped they'd go back to their own conversations.

No such luck.

"That reminds me," Reshep said. "Morrigan told me the news. Congratulations."

"Such wonderful news. It's always a blessing to welcome a little one to the world." Kali smiled warmly, reinforcing her grandmotherly guise. "Is this Your first?"

My mouth was full, so I just nodded.

Kali turned toward Arddhu then Kevin. "You both must be so proud."

Arddhu smiled. "Indeed, we are."

Kevin hadn't been sidetracked. He still studied me closely. "Did something happen that we should know about?"

Pretending I was still chewing, I shook my head and just continued to eat. After a moment, the conversation around me resumed and Kevin finally returned his attention to his food.

After the briefing, when I had the answers to my questions. That's when I'd tell my family.

I just had to stay busy between now and then, and hope I didn't slip up and mention it accidentally.

The morning of the White House briefing had arrived, and I spent a bit more time than usual fussing with my appearance. After all, it wasn't every day that I got to meet the President of the United States.

On the other hand, this briefing was basically just a project team meeting—although for one helluva project—and I'd had plenty of those back in my accounting days. So I went with my go-to outfit from that time: a tailored navy blue suit.

Unfortunately, it only accentuated my huge belly and didn't exactly present the professional appearance I'd expected, so I scrapped that idea.

Then, distracted, I studied my belly in the mirror and frowned. In just the past two days alone, it seemed like I'd progressed another two months in my pregnancy. At this rate, I didn't think I had another two weeks left. I could deliver any day now, and that terrified me just as much as it fed my impatience to get it over with as soon as possible. I was really tired of carrying the extra weight, having near-constant lower back pain, breast swelling and tenderness, never-ending exhaustion, and the countless other aspects of pregnancy.

I shook my head. I had to focus on the task at hand: getting dressed.

Maybe I could do glamor magick and hide my pregnancy completely? Nah. That seemed silly. Besides, Burns and Cox had already seen me fully pregnant, and I really didn't care what anyone thought.

So. To hell with looking professional.

I was the Goddess of Earth, and I was pregnant. Why should I hide either? Why shouldn't I look like the Goddess I was?

I chose a flowing, life-of-its own, diaphanous Goddess gown in the palest shade of blue, with pretty flowers embroidered around the scoop neckline. Then, I set my glow at a stronger than average level, to drive home the point.

First impressions, and all that.

Next, I applied a bit of magickal makeup, just enough to conceal the facial scars from last year's battle with Mike, and to cover the dark circles under my eyes. Then, I put my hair up, into a Goddess-worthy style I'd seen years ago in some old movie about Greek mythology.

Lastly, I studied my appearance in the mirror and grinned. I looked otherworldly and divine, and no one would doubt who or what I was.

Fifteen minutes before nine, I thought *Roosevelt Room at the White House,* and ported.

Then all hell broke loose.

I'd almost collided with a burly guy who carried a cup of coffee in one hand and a half-eaten pastry in the other. "Hey, watch it," he yelped, and barely avoided spilling hot coffee on both of us.

There was a lot of swearing, and somebody screamed.

A loud crash behind me, like someone must've dropped something. I flinched and hoped it wasn't an expensive piece of computer equipment.

With dismay, I glanced around the room but saw no familiar faces. Instead, thirty-odd strangers stared at me with various expressions of shock, surprise, or annoyance. More than a few gazes dropped to my huge belly, and I couldn't help but feel self-conscious.

Maybe I shouldn't have ported into an already-occupied space.

Oops.

Oh well, the damage was done. Now it was time to deal with the consequences.

"Hi." I cleared my throat and lifted my chin. "Deirdre Connor. Keeper of the Sphere and Goddess of Earth. I was invited to this briefing."

Then the door burst open and four men in dark suits, earpieces, and firearms rushed in. They quickly aimed their pistols at me, and I shielded myself immediately. I didn't think bullets could kill me, but I couldn't say the same for my unborn daughter. I didn't want to take the chance of her getting hit.

"Intruder located," one of the men said, apparently speaking into a concealed communication device. The other three watched me closely, bodies tensed as if ready to spring into action at any moment and tackle me, like I was a terrorist or something.

Most likely, they were either White House security or Secret Service, and I felt even more embarrassed. Dammit. I should've realized something like this would happen.

I wouldn't make the same mistake again.

"It's okay, Bruce. She's on the team."

I turned toward the familiar voice with a smile of gratitude. Burns had stepped forward from somewhere.

Bruce, the security guy, hesitated briefly before holstering his firearm with a sigh, and the others followed suit.

"She still needs to be scanned and badged," Bruce said.

Burns met my gaze with a raised brow. "Do you mind?"

"No, of course not." I dropped the shield and lifted my arms away from my body. "Scan away."

Bruce reached into a pocket and removed what appeared to be a small metal detector. As he slowly moved it up one side of my body and down the other, I watched the green light flicker once or twice, but it didn't blink or change color. And it never beeped, which I assumed was a good thing.

After all, I wasn't armed with anything other than my wits and my power.

He frowned and repeated the scan, spending extra time around my protruding abdomen, as if he thought I'd hidden a cache of weapons in there.

"When are you due?" he asked casually, not taking his eyes off the device.

"A couple of weeks, more or less."

Finally, he straightened and put the device back in his pocket. From a different pocket, he removed an object and offered it to me.

"Wear this visitor badge at all times while you are on the premises. Surrender it to the project lead when you leave." He paused while I slipped the lanyard over my head, then continued in a gruffer tone. "And from now on, use the goddamned door like a normal person. We can't have anyone just popping around here willy-nilly."

For some reason, it hit me as really funny, and I bit down hard on the inside of my lip, but it was no use. The nervous laugh escaped anyway.

"Gotcha," I said, voice uneven. "No popping around willy-nilly." Maybe I'd even start using that phrase myself. *Now, don't go popping around here willy-nilly.* Or maybe, *I'll just pop around willy-nilly.* Kevin would probably love it.

Bruce narrowed his eyes for a moment as I struggled to contain my laughter and ended up with a snort instead. Disgusted, he shook his head, turned, and left with his team.

"You shouldn't piss off Secret Service, you know," Burns said.

"Sorry." I wasn't, not really, but I didn't care. *Popping around willy-nilly* was still funny.

Cox caught my eye and nodded politely from the other side of the room, but then I was approached by a handsome middle-aged gentleman with an extended hand.

"Welcome, Ms. Connor. I'm John Simmons, project leader."

"Thank you." I smiled wryly as we shook hands. "Sorry for the disturbance. I should've known better."

He flashed a smile. "Well, you certainly made a grand entrance." He introduced me all around, but there was no way I'd ever remember everyone's names, so I didn't bother trying.

Too bad the power of the Goddess didn't include perfect memory.

The seats around the large oblong table filled up quickly, leaving the rest of the attendees to either stand or sit in the handful of chairs placed along the wall. It seemed almost everyone had already helped themselves to the selection of hot beverages and pastries spread out on the long, narrow credenza.

I shook my head and politely declined the offered refreshments, and Simmons directed me to one of the last remaining seats at the table. I sank into the chair and bit back a grateful sigh. My backache was getting worse, and by now I really couldn't wait for this pregnancy to be over.

"Do we call you Deirdre, the Keeper Goddess, or Your Highness?" a young man at the other end of the room asked.

I wasn't sure if he was joking or not, but I shrugged. "Dee is fine."

"No," Simmons corrected as he took his seat nearby. "Everyone will address her as Ms. Connor." He glanced around. "Looks like we're only waiting on the president, but he should be here any minute."

Some rustling as a few attendees got a last-minute pastry or coffee before sitting. Just as I wondered if I should shut off my glow for the rest of the meeting, there was movement at the doorway and a voice I'd only heard on television until now.

324

"Sorry I'm late, John. Had to stop at the men's room on the way."

My heart skipped a beat as Samuel Jackson entered the room and took the last empty seat, only a couple of spots away from me.

Holy shit. I was actually in the same room as the President of the United States.

Jackson smiled in greeting at several attendees, and then made eye contact with me. He nodded once, respectfully. "Ms. Connor, I appreciate you coming on such short notice."

"Mr. President," I replied, equally respectful. "It's an honor, sir."

So far, no one here had shown any reverence while addressing me, but I wasn't surprised. Most likely, none of them truly believed I was a deity, and I wasn't sure if I could change their minds.

Someone—maybe another Secret Service agent—had closed the door and now stood in front of it, as if to prevent us from leaving.

Or, maybe it was to keep someone from entering.

Yeah, that was probably it. No need to get paranoid.

Simmons began the briefing without further delay. "Good morning, Mr. President. We have the updated coordinates for the object, unofficially named Eris, for the Greek Goddess of Chaos." After a few keystrokes on his laptop, the screen on the left-side wall came to life and displayed an animated computer-generated diagram of the solar system.

The attendees seated on the table's left side, including the president, swiveled their chairs to briefly study the diagram, and I followed suit.

Near the large yellow sphere labeled *Sun*, a small red dot blinked rapidly. A curved white line plotted the object's trajectory, which directly intercepted Earth's orbit.

The president swiveled back around. "Any change to the impact date estimate?"

"Not at this time," Simmons replied. "It's still six to eight weeks."

Jackson nodded, then turned to me. "I assume you know why you're here. Any questions?"

"Yes." He'd wasted no time getting right to the point, and I appreciated it. "First, what's been done so far?"

Simmons leaned back in his chair. "Not a damn thing."

"What?" I blinked at him. "Why not?"

"What'd you expect?" someone asked. "We'd land a mining crew on it and set off explosives?"

There were a few chuckles at that, and my cheeks burned.

"Well, yeah." It'd sounded like a good idea to me, although it seemed vaguely familiar, for some reason.

"Evans, that's enough." Simmons sighed and shook his head, then turned to me. "This isn't a Hollywood movie, Ms. Connor. We don't have that kind of technology, and our available mitigation efforts are limited due to the time constraint. So let me take a minute to explain why we haven't done anything.

"First, we don't have enough time to launch a propulsion device for a slow-push or slow-pull effort. And even if we did, Eris is too big for either of those methods to be effective.

"Second, our nuclear-based targeting satellites are non-operational, and we don't have enough time to repair and test them.

"Lastly, a kinetic impactor device also isn't useful in this situation, because it'd require a launch that we don't have time for. And before you ask, the reason we don't have enough time is because all our current tech is designed to deploy months or even years in advance. We don't have anything designed for quick mitigation."

Although he'd answered a few of my questions—and some I hadn't even known to ask—I had a few more.

"Thanks for that overview." I leaned forward. "For argument's sake, let's say I have the ability to blow up Eris. What would happen?"

It was Cox who replied. "The object is currently traveling at approximately forty kilometers per second. If it exploded, it'd most likely fracture into thousands of smaller fragments that would travel in various directions. Many would probably continue toward Earth, but at increased speed due to the added force of the explosion. Even a relatively small fragment—say, about the size of a basketball—could result in extensive impact damage. But if hundreds or thousands of fragments impact the planet, we'd have to multiply the impact damage by that number." He paused to take a breath. Or maybe it was for dramatic effect, I wasn't sure. "In short, the potential damage could be much, much worse."

At least he'd given me the courtesy of a polite explanation, instead of just a snarky remark. In the awkward silence that followed, I desperately tried to think of something to say that wouldn't sound ridiculously stupid.

"Let me put it another way." A woman—I couldn't remember her name—said. "Do you remember hearing about that big explosion over Russia several years ago?" I shook my head and she continued. "A meteor only sixty feet in diameter exploded less than fifteen miles over Chelyabinsk, a relatively good-sized city. That aerial explosion had the force of thirty atomic bombs. It completely destroyed hundreds of buildings and injured over a thousand people. Now imagine thousands of fragments, ranging in size from a baseball to a large house, raining down on the planet." She paused, holding my gaze. "The destruction could be catastrophic."

Although Cox had said basically the same thing, her information gave me a better visualization for the scale of damage to expect, and I nodded my thanks.

"I see." And I did; I now clearly understood that blowing it up wasn't an option.

But what if I used my power to push it off course?

"*No, Deirdre.*" Anu said, with a hint of impatience. "*I have already told You: You are the Goddess of Earth, not of the Universe. Your power does not extend beyond the planet and its attached realms. You cannot affect this object in any way. Not until it reaches the planet.*"

"*Gratitude, Anu.*" So. That was that.

I rubbed my temple while I considered any remaining options.

Since I couldn't affect anything beyond the planet, what could I do here? Could I throw all my power at it just before impact, and hope to push it away? That seemed awfully risky.

What would make more sense is if I could cover the Earth with some sort of shield. Something that would make the asteroid disintegrate on contact.

I'd need a lot more information—and a way to test the theory way before impact date—before I could hope to try it.

"Ms. Connor?" The president's voice interrupted my thoughts.

"Yes, sir?"

"I've heard you have considerable power. What some call *magick*. So why can't you just"—he waved his hands around—"magick it away?"

He seemed to be sincere, so I decided to be honest instead of sarcastic.

"No. I can't. I'm sorry."

In the stunned silence, someone's stomach loudly growled.

His brows lowered. "Can't, or won't?"

"Look." I sighed, leaned forward, and rested my arms on the table. "I'm the Goddess of Earth. Not of the solar system or universe. My power doesn't go beyond the planet and any realms attached to it."

He blinked at me and slowly repeated my words. "Realms attached to it."

I nodded. "Asgard is one. There are others."

"Wait. You're saying Asgard really exists?" It was the woman who'd mentioned the meteor over Russia.

"Yes." I nodded again. "I've been there just in the past couple of months. It's beautiful. And the Æsir are allies of mine."

The president cleared his throat. "Getting back to business here. So are you telling me you can't do anything about this asteroid?"

"I didn't say that. I was thinking of creating a shield."

His eyes narrowed thoughtfully. "Around the entire planet?"

I nodded.

"But that means we'll just be sitting ducks, waiting for it to get here," someone protested.

"And hope she doesn't fail us," someone else said.

"Knock it off," Simmons said, glancing around the room. "All of you. Just knock it off. In case you haven't noticed, we're running out of options."

"Besides," Burns said. "If her power only works here on Earth, a shield makes perfect sense." He turned to the president. "But I strongly recommend we do a press release and get out in front of this. The people have a right to know about the asteroid."

"You're right." Jackson sighed. "People should have as much time to prepare as possible, and we've only got six weeks to save lives. So while she's working on a planetary shield, we can put our disaster plans in motion. Open up some old bomb shelters and work with other countries to stockpile food and medicine. I'll get the communications team started on it."

"What if we just escape to one of those other realms she mentioned earlier?" a young guy asked with a laugh, and a few others joined in.

I didn't laugh. I stared at him, thinking.

It was actually a brilliant idea. Not an existing realm, no.

But a new one.

"Thank you," I told him. "That's actually a fantastic idea. I could create a sanctuary realm for everyone to go to, as a sort of contingency plan just in case the shield doesn't work. If it does work, everyone could just... come right back."

"Why can't we just go to Asgard?" someone asked. "I think that'd be pretty cool."

I shook my head. "Not an option. It's not big enough. And I don't think they'd appreciate an entire planet's worth of refugees invading their realm."

"Would this sanctuary realm be big enough for the entire population of Earth?" the President asked.

"I can make it as big as necessary."

"What if the worst happens," a woman asked. "And the entire planet is destroyed? Wouldn't that affect this sanctuary?"

"Not if it's not connected to Earth." My mind had already raced ahead. "After everyone goes through the portal, I'd cut off the connection, like snipping an umbilical cord. No matter what happened to Earth after that, the sanctuary realm wouldn't be affected."

"But would everyone—and future generations—be safe? Forever?" the woman persisted.

"Absolutely. Obviously, I don't have the details yet. But I'll make sure it has everything necessary for everyone's comfort and security."

"I like it." The president leaned forward. "Tell me more."

Hadn't he been listening? I didn't have more to tell him. Not yet. "Let me work on it and get back to you."

"*Us*," Simmons corrected. "Get back to us. We all need to be kept in the loop on this."

"Of course."

"Great," the president said, "we finally have a plan. You'll create this sanctuary realm and a planetary shield. My office will handle informing the public. The project team will continue to monitor the asteroid and apprise us of any significant changes." He glanced around the table. "Is that about it?"

"Yes, sir." Simmons turned to me and slid a business card across the table. "You'll be doing a lot of heavy lifting on this. Here's my direct number if you have any questions."

I sent the card to my pocket universe without thinking, and felt the intense stares of several of the attendees. They'd seen it vanish before their eyes, and even though it was such a mundane use of my power, maybe now they'd have a bit more respect for me.

"I'll definitely be in touch," I told Simmons. "First, I'll need to create a prototype Earth and asteroid, then come up with the right shield configuration. For all that, I'll need some of the technical information your team has gathered."

Burns responded. "We've got some specific data and calculations you'll probably find useful." He opened the file folder in front of him and flipped through it, then pulled a couple of sheets out. He slid the folder across the table to me. "This'll get you started. For anything else, you already have my direct number."

I sent the folder to my pocket universe, and now even more of the attendees stared at me.

It was Cox who finally asked. "So, um, where did that stuff go? The business card and the folder, I mean?"

"To a pocket universe. I use it sort of like a briefcase, for temporary storage." I sure as hell wasn't going to tell them I'd stored the world's nukes in another pocket universe.

He blinked. "That's... fascinating."

"One more thing," Simmons interjected. "We want a tour of the sanctuary realm well before impact date."

"Of course." I smiled and pointed at the guy who'd given me the idea. "And you should probably give him a raise. It was an awesome idea."

Amid the burst of laughter and quiet conversation around the table, the president wasted no time leaving.

Urgent prayers reached me, and I took a moment to respond.

It was another wildfire in Australia. Quickly, I sent part of my consciousness to the scene and asked the Fire element there to go to sleep. It reluctantly complied, and the flames extinguished. Next, I healed the injured wild animals and humans, and ensured the situation was resolved before bringing that part of my consciousness back to the room.

Glancing around, it seemed no one had noticed my momentary lapse of attention as they began to disperse.

Simmons remained seated, his expression grave. "Ms. Connor, I hope I don't need to tell you how critical this is. We need that sanctuary and shield as soon as possible. If that damn asteroid keeps speeding up, our impact date might need to move up as well."

"I do understand the urgency." I slipped off the lanyard with the visitor badge and placed it on the table. "I'll get right on it."

He nodded, and I ported away without getting up from my chair.

CHAPTER TWENTY-THREE

I'D PORTED DIRECTLY to my suite at The Hacienda, where I changed into comfy clothes, dropped the glamor on my scars, shook out my hair, and shuttered my glow. After I splashed water on my face, I had to sit on the toilet lid to rest for a moment.

My lower back ached more than it ever had, and now I had the start of a headache, too. I was exhausted from that briefing. I really just wanted to sleep for a few hours.

Or days.

But it was time to talk to my family about the asteroid, secrecy be damned.

I took a deep breath to steady myself and left my suite.

In the kitchen, Arddhu, Kevin, and the Morrigan had just finished breakfast.

"Hey guys." I sat on an empty stool and shook my head in response to the unspoken question in Brianna's eyes. I'd eat a little later, after I said what I needed to.

"Where've you been?" Kevin asked, eyes sharp on me. "We looked everywhere."

"That's what I'm here to talk to you all about. I was at a briefing at the White House, with NASA and the president."

Kevin's eyes widened. "No shit?"

"No shit." The smell of food from their plates suddenly turned my stomach, and I stood abruptly. "Let's go sit in the living room." As if she'd read my mind, Brianna quickly cleared the plates and began cleaning up.

As we got settled, the Morrigan said, "This seems serious."

"It is." I took another deep breath, then got to it. "There's no easy way to say this, so I'm just going to say it. An asteroid is headed for Earth. The president saw my videos and assumed I could stop it from hitting the planet, so now it's my job to save the world. Literally." I laughed nervously, but all three of them just stared at me, and the silence stretched uncomfortably.

"It's between Earth and the sun right now," I added softly. "Preliminary estimates put impact at roughly six to eight weeks, although that could change. They said it's speeding up."

"Wait a minute," Kevin said. "Why isn't this all over the news or the internet?"

"It will be, eventually. The president wanted to talk to me first to see what I could do. At first, I thought maybe I could push it off course, but my power doesn't extend beyond Earth and any realms attached to it." I sure as hell wasn't going to mention my failed attempt to port to space.

Arddhu frowned. "You know this for certain? That you cannot affect the path of this asteroid?"

I nodded. "Anu told me."

"How much damage are we talking about?" Kevin asked.

"It probably won't be an extinction-level event. But it could still do a lot of damage, especially if it hits someplace with a dense population, like New York City or China. Even if it hits a less populated area, the long-term effects could be planet-wide."

"Not just Earth," Arddhu said. "Anything that would damage the planet that severely could also affect the realms connected to it."

"I'm not sure I agree with you on that," the Morrigan said. "Meteors have hit Earth hundreds of times over the millennia, and some of them were extremely destructive. But Asgard never even felt a thing."

"I think it depends on the magnitude," Kevin said. "I mean, if Asgard had been around at the time of the dinosaurs, at the very least they would've known something big had happened on Earth. More likely, some type of kinetic energy blast or shockwave would've traveled through the connection. There would've been some damage."

"Possibly," she conceded. To me, she asked, "So what's the plan? I'm assuming you have one."

"Sure do." I nodded again. "First, I'm going to create a sanctuary realm for everyone to go to. Then, I'm going to put a shield around the planet to mitigate the impact. If the shield works, everyone just comes back afterward. If it doesn't, well, at least everyone has a safe place to live while I heal the damage."

"Wait a minute," Kevin said. "Won't this sanctuary realm be just as vulnerable as, say, Asgard?"

"Not if I disconnect it from Earth just before impact."

"Yeah." He nodded thoughtfully. "Okay."

I looked at the three of them. They were all so calm. "Why aren't any of you more worried about this?"

The Morrigan shrugged. "Gods don't panic."

Oh.

I shifted in my chair, trying to relieve the backache, but it didn't do a damn thing to stop the constant throbbing. I glanced at the clock.; it was still early yet. As Anthony had said, the briefing had taken less than two hours. I had plenty of time before I had to start getting ready for the Beltaine ritual at Finn's Cove. In the meantime, my bed was calling to me.

To wrap up the discussion, I said, "Anyway, I wanted to let you guys know what was going on. I plan to start working on the sanctuary realm as soon as we get back from Ireland."

"Will you also continue the healing sessions?" Arddhu asked.

"Yeah." Like a human body, Earth would have the best chance of recovering from extensive damage if it was as healthy as possible. "For as long as I can."

"You are doing too much." He eyed my huge belly and frowned. "Under the circumstances, we should forgo the Sacred Union tonight."

"Normally," Kevin said, "I'd disagree because of how important it is to the people. Y'know, the symbolic union of God and Goddess with the land, which they haven't experienced lately. But I have to admit, because of how far along you are, it could be dangerous."

Channeling the massive energy required for the Sacred Union could affect the baby, and I was glad we weren't going to take any chances. They'd get no argument from me on this.

"Right," I agreed. "We'll just do the ritual and the feast, then come home. I'll probably be too tired for anything else anyway. I need a nap now, as a matter of fact."

The Morrigan's eyes were sharp. "Still exhausted all the time?"

"Yeah. And my back is killing me." Before Arddhu could question the phrase, I added, "I mean, it's just constantly hurting now."

"When is your next doctor appointment?" she asked.

"Not for another two weeks. But look at me. I look like I'm going to deliver any day now. I'd only be about half-way through this pregnancy if it were normal."

She smirked. "You can probably thank Arddhu's wild forest magick for that. It does tend to have a chaotic effect on growth."

"Very true." Arddhu chuckled. "I once grew an entire forest in little more than an eyeblink."

Shit. No wonder this pregnancy was so accelerated.

"Great. *Now* you tell me. Anyway, I'm going to go take that nap now. See you guys later."

Smoke and ash.

Fire and screams.

I woke with a start, heart racing and covered in sweat.

Again.

I was beyond sick and tired of that goddamned nightmare. I'd taken care of the nukes. Why the hell was I still—

Wait.

I sat up in bed and stared at nothing while the scenes replayed in my head.

It seemed so obvious now.

The nightmare was about the *asteroid*, not nuclear war.

Which meant it wasn't a nightmare at all, but a vision of the future.

A prophecy.

Fuck.

But why did I only see it while sleeping? Why hadn't I seen it in my Seer's Mirror, like a proper divination vision?

Maybe it wasn't a prophecy after all. Besides, Loki had said visions only showed one possibility for the future. This wasn't definite.

I could change this outcome. I knew I could.

I just had to make sure the sanctuary realm and the planetary shield worked flawlessly.

But that'd have to wait. I had to get through Beltaine first.

Beltaine was one of the most important days in the Wheel of the Year, heralding the light half of the year and the warmth of summer. Its opposite was Samhain, which ushered in the dark half of the year and the chill of winter.

Beltaine was joyous, focused on fertility, life, and growth; Samhain was solemn, and dealt with honoring the ancestors, death, and hibernation.

This would be my first Beltaine as both the Keeper and the Goddess, and I wanted to make a good impression.

My stomach growled loudly in my quiet room.

"Okay, okay," I muttered. "Food first."

When I entered the kitchen, Brianna slid a plate across the granite island without a word.

Obediently, I sat on a stool. The chicken salad sandwich smelled delicious, and the fresh-baked bread was still warm from the oven. She'd even included a handful of my favorite potato chips.

"I fucking love you," I blurted, then took a bite.

She smiled and winked at me as she started cleaning up. "Nah. You just love my food."

Mouth full of sandwich, I shook my head. "No, I really love *you*, too."

Still smiling, she left me to my lunch.

Where was everyone else? I sent out a few probes to find out.

Kevin was back in the VIP tent, teaching another class.

The Morrigan was in her room, snuggling with Reshep.

Arddhu wasn't around, so he must've gone off-world again, still preparing for his Wild Hunt.

My family.

A warm glow filled me, then I burst into tears for no apparent reason.

Damn this hormonal bullshit. I'd never been so emotional in my entire life.

Shaking my head, I wiped my face and finished my lunch. Then, unsure of what to do until it was time to get ready for the ritual, I sat down again and stared out the window-wall at my backyard paradise, not seeing any of it as I thought about the asteroid.

I'd expected to finish healing the planet, continue to answer prayers, and raise my daughter. Now, everything had changed because of one fucking rock flying through space.

It'd just been one thing after another ever since Mike had knocked on my door almost two years ago. Crisis after crisis after crisis.

It was so frustrating. And exhausting.

"Feel better?" the Morrigan asked, entering the kitchen alone. She'd already dressed for Beltaine, into black pants and a black sleeveless top with red trim.

I don't think I'd ever seen her in anything other than black.

"Yep." I smiled to cover the lie. I really didn't feel better. Just thinking about everything had raised my heart rate and blood pressure.

"Liar," she said as she sat on the stool next to me. "What's wrong?"

Did I really want to get into all of it right now?

"I keep having the nightmare." The words were out before I'd even thought about saying them.

"The smoke and ash one?"

I nodded. "But then I was thinking. It's not really a nightmare. It's more like a vision. Or a prophecy, maybe. About the asteroid hitting Earth and causing mass destruction." Which would mean my shield would fail, but I wasn't ready to talk about that just yet.

"I wouldn't really call it a prophecy." She frowned. "You can still change the outcome."

"Semantics." I shrugged. "Anyway, now it makes sense why I'm still having it even after I took care of the nukes. It was never about a nuclear war. It was about the asteroid. I just didn't know about it yet."

"Well, I'm glad you figured it out." She rested her arm on the granite and changed the subject. "So when are we leaving for Finn's Cove?"

"As soon as Arddhu gets here, I guess."

She eyed my comfy clothes. "You're not going like *that*, are you?"

"No. Of course not. I'll change right before we leave."

"Into what?"

From Maggie's memories, she'd worn a beautiful summery sundress. But that wouldn't work for me; I'd look ridiculous with my massive belly. And I sure as hell didn't want to wear heels. My back hurt enough already.

"You have no idea, do you?" the Morrigan asked.

I shook my head.

"Well, whatever you wear, don't hide your pregnancy. A big part of Beltaine is fertility, and that's you, right now. The people need to see it. They need to see you, in all your pregnant glory."

She had a good point.

I stood and changed my comfy shorts and tee shirt into a calf-length stretchy lace dress in sky blue, lined in dark blue satin, with a sash of the same dark blue tied at my upper waist. The neckline was a modest scoop in the front but a deep vee in the back, and the unlined sleeves were elbow-length. For a final touch, I added dark blue satin flats.

It was comfortable, but pretty and feminine.

"How's this?" I turned in a circle.

"I love it." She nodded her approval. "It's classy, divine, and shows off your fertility."

She pointedly looked at my hair, but didn't say a word. She didn't need to; I got the hint.

"Hold on." I magicked my long locks into a classic updo, with tiny blue flowers tucked in. "Better?"

"Much." She smiled. "Now, don't forget—"

"—to glow," I finished. "Yes, I know."

"Perfect."

I didn't bother with any magickal makeup; the villagers had seen my scars before.

"Ready to go?" Kevin asked as he came through the panel in the window-wall. He'd already changed into what he called his feasting garb: dark green tunic embroidered with gold Celtic knotwork, and darker green trousers. He'd left his long dark hair unbound except for the small warrior braids at each temple.

It was always a good look for him, so handsome and elegant.

"Where's Arddhu?" I asked.

"He was right behind me," Kevin turned to look. "Oh, there he is. He's just outside."

The three of us went out to meet him. He was dressed simply, in a loose linen shirt and relaxed trousers. I knew he wanted to transform into the Horned God at Ard na Mara.

Arddhu's eyes lit up when he saw me. "You look beautiful."

"Thank you, my love." We kissed, then he opened the portal and we went through.

The sun hung low in the sky, about thirty minutes from setting. We'd timed our arrival perfectly.

I took a moment to close my eyes and inhale the sea air. Sweet music surrounded me: crickets in the meadow, birds in the trees, and underneath it all was the bass of crashing waves on the beach.

"Gods, I never get tired of this place." I sighed and opened my eyes.

"You should probably take a break sometime soon," Kevin suggested.

"I really want a vacation, but there's too much to do and too little time to do it."

Then, we grew silent. It was time.

As we watched, Arddhu transformed into his Cernunnos aspect.

His antlers, normally two-inch stubs, grew to a towering, powerful rack adorned with yellow hawthorn flowers and fresh ivy. His long sable locks were wild, forming a tangled aura around his head and shoulders. His torso was bare, and his tattoos seemed to shift and move in the dying light of the day.

Sometimes, I forgot what a fucking gorgeous man he was.

No. He wasn't a man. He was truly a God.

His dark brown eyes fixed on mine. "Shall we go?" His voice had deepened, and I shivered.

Arddhu and I led our little group on the path through the woods. Unlike at Lammas or Samhain, the villagers wouldn't be escorting us.

We hadn't gone more than a dozen yards when Kevin asked, "Okay, which one of you is doing that?"

My gaze followed where he'd pointed.

Along the path, blue yellow, and white wildflowers pushed up through the fronds of ferns and debris of the forest floor, blossoming into fullness almost immediately.

"It must be you," I said to Arddhu.

"It is not me." He shook his head. "It is You."

No way.

"Remember," the Morrigan said. "You're the epitome of fertility right now."

As we continued on the path, the wildflower petals unfolded as we passed by. Deeper in the forest beyond, the rowan and hawthorn trees bloomed in a profusion of cream and yellow, and the breeze lifted the petals to scatter on the path, giving the forest a dreamy, romantic feel. Even the canopy of oak and ash trees above us had burst out in fresh green leaves, and now almost completely obscured the lavender hues of the twilight sky.

The entire forest had come to life.

If it really was me doing all this, I had no idea *how* I was doing it.

"The Goddess of Earth bestows Beltaine blessings on the land," the Morrigan intoned.

I didn't reply; I had no words.

We continued on the path.

Donal's cottage was dark except for a dim porch light; he and Megan were probably already at the village green.

At the bridge over the creek, I didn't see Pete. Although that wasn't exactly unusual, at this point I hadn't seen him in months. I hoped all was well with him and Petunia.

We reached the village green just as the sun set. Again, perfect timing.

Torchlight danced in the gentle breeze, and every surface was adorned with hawthorn blossoms and vibrant greenery, including the food tables. The very air was sweetly perfumed from so many flowers.

The waiting villagers immediately saw us. After a moment of shocked silence, they reacted to my obvious pregnancy with cheers and pure unbridled joy.

Once again, the Morrigan had been absolutely correct; they'd needed to see me in all my big-bellied glory.

Maura, the village elderwoman, stepped forward with a broad grin and moist eyes, and nodded to me. She took one of my hands, then one of Arddhu's, and began her song.

> Oh Great Goddess,
> We offer our praise to You.
> Bestow Your abundance upon us,
> On our fields, our flocks, and our wombs.
>
> Hail, Cernunnos, great Horned God.
> We offer our praise to You.
> Bestow Your protection upon us,
> On our homes, our shops, and our food.
>
> The light has now returned,
> Our world is green and abloom.
> Tonight the fires shall burn,
> 'Neath the bright glow of the moon.

During the song, Maura had led us toward the twin unlit bonfires.

Thank goodness I'd kept the memories of all the prior Keepers after I'd become the Goddess of Earth; Maggie's had shown me my role for tonight, and what to expect.

If only it'd worked the same way when I'd received Ida's power, and also received her memories. There was so much I didn't know about being the Goddess.

Then again, she'd been a shitty goddess, so it was probably just as well I hadn't.

No modern tools were allowed to light the sacred needfire. Only the traditional and ancient method of wheel and spindle could be used to light this special fire.

Maura released our hands, took the tools from an assistant, and passed them to Arddhu. To me, she gave a handful of dried grasses. Another assistant placed a soft cushion on the ground.

The entire village green was silent as everyone watched and waited.

Arddhu helped me to kneel on the cushion, then joined me. He inserted the spindle into the hole in the wheel, and spun the spindle in a blur of movement. In moments, a thin tendril of smoke rose. I leaned close and gently blew on it to give it life, then carefully fed the dried grasses to the tiny fire.

In another moment we had a flame big enough for the next step. Arddhu rose to his feet and helped me to rise, and an assistant passed a thin strip of wood to each of us. We lit them from the sacred needfire, then each of us used our strip of wood to ignite one of the bonfires. The path between them was just wide enough for driving livestock through, for the ancient blessing.

The bonfires roared after a few moments, and we stepped aside.

The cattle and sheep were led forward, necks and horns adorned with festive flower garlands. As the livestock tenders guided the animals in single file through the two fires, Arddhu raised his hands and began chanting.

> The sacred Beltaine fires are lit.
> May their light and heat
> Bless each of these creatures
> And grant them My protection.
> All who travel through
> Will be safe and strong
> Throughout the year.

It took quite a while to lead all the livestock through, and although a few of the sheep bleated loudly, none of the animals freaked out at the fires or tried to run away.

While I waited impatiently, I really tried not to think of how badly my back hurt and how much I wanted to sit down. I failed miserably, and even sending a wave of healing energy through my body didn't help.

After the livestock blessing was finished, Maura sang another song to begin the handfasting ritual.

> Come, all ye young lovers,
> Who wish to join together.
> Come, all ye beloveds,
> With a cord or ribbon to tether.
> Come and be handfast,
> All to speak your vow.
> Come and be handfast,
> By the Lord and Lady now.

Arddhu and I moved to the center of the green and waited as four young couples shyly came forward to line up. I began with the youngest-looking couple on the left, and smiled warmly at them. With trembling hands, the woman offered me the red silken cord they'd chosen.

"Hold now each other's hand," I chanted. "To show your consent across the land." The couple complied, and I began wrapping the cord around their joined hands. "To each other now, speak your most sincere vow."

The woman went first. "My beloved, I promise to love you, honor you, and respect you. I wish to share in your joy, your pain, your dreams, and your burdens. From now until I die."

Surprised, I paused wrapping the cord for a moment. Handfastings for such young couples were usually only for the traditional year and a day. To make a lifelong vow at such a young age was either wise or folly.

The man repeated the vow, and I finished wrapping the cord.

Arddhu and I laid our hands on the couple's bound hands, and spoke our blessing together. "With our blessing, under the moon and stars above, you are now bound together, in peace and love."

The couple grinned and moved off to rejoin their friends and families, and we moved on to the next couple.

We performed the ceremony three more times, and then the handfastings were done.

Gods, my back and legs ached.

Only two things left to do before I could sit and rest.

Next was the fertility rite.

Several women of child-bearing age gathered in a loose circle around me. I raised my hands and sang.

> As the seeds begin to sprout
> And the grass turns green,
> As the warm wind blows
> And the days grow long,
> As the sun shines bright
> Across the verdant land,
> So now do I bestow
> Upon each of thee
> Rich and ripe fertility.

To grant my blessing, I made my way around the circle and pressed my palms against each woman's belly for a moment. For those who had medical issues preventing conception, I took that moment to heal them. For the others, I simply blessed them. Each woman thanked me, and some eyed my bulging belly with wide grins. Their joy at being so blessed by a very pregnant Goddess was almost palpable.

Finally, the rite was done.

Oh how I wanted to sit down. But not yet.

It was time for the last task: to bless the feast.

Traditionally, the Beltaine feast had always been cooked on the bonfire. But in a nod to modernity—and in the interest of many hungry bellies—this food had already been prepared in the community kitchens and brought here for serving.

At each table of food, I held my hands above the warming trays and gave my blessing. My back throbbed so much, it was hard work not to rush through. The last was the drink station, with its many barrels of ale and crates of wine and liquor.

Then, finally, I could sit.

As I made my way to our reserved table, the villagers immediately began celebrating.

I sank into my chair with a groan, and my stomach growled loudly. Arddhu sat next to me, Kevin left to fetch food and drink, and the Morrigan wandered off.

"Are you well?" Arddhu asked. His antlers had returned to their normal stubs now that the ritual was over.

"I'm just really tired. And all that walking and standing made my backache worse."

"Will you eat?" he asked.

"Absolutely." My stomach growled again. "I'm starving."

The musical trio in the corner had already started playing a lively tune, and some folks formed a dance circle.

A ruckus over at the bonfires drew my attention, and I had to smile. A few young studs loudly goaded each other into leaping the raging flames, which also caught the eyes of the pretty girls. As I watched, a boy approached a girl, and she nodded. Smiling, they joined the circle dance.

More than a few of them would sneak off later; it was a Beltaine tradition, after all. And not just for the young, either. Plenty of the oldsters were openly flirting, too.

Nothing like a fertility festival to encourage getting frisky with someone. If I hadn't felt like shit, I would've joined in that circle dance.

I also knew that much later, each of the villagers would take a piece of wood from the bonfires to light their own hearth fire with. That tradition spread the blessings of Beltaine throughout the village and beyond.

Arddhu placed his hand on my arm. "Garrett is coming this way."

We watched him bring two cups.

"Beltaine Blessings, Lady, Great One."

I smiled. "Beltaine Blessings to you, as well."

He offered a cup to me. "Have You tasted the ale yet? It's a new recipe, called the Beltaine Blonde."

"No, I haven't." I took a sip and tasted warm sunshine, blossoms of all kinds, and fresh honey. "Oh, this is lovely." I paused after a glance around. "Is everything okay with Donal and Megan? I don't see either of them here tonight."

Garrett nodded. "They went to Cork City earlier today. She's in hospital and has probably had the baby by now." He shook his head. "She's of the modern sort, wanting a hospital and all that. I s'pose we'll need to talk about building one here. Midwifery isn't good enough for the young folk anymore."

Well, I sure wouldn't tell him I was also the modern sort, with my OB/GYN in Scottsdale, fancy ultrasound imaging, and plans for a hospital birth.

Then the server at the drink station called for help with a malfunctioning keg, and Garrett quickly took his leave.

My thoughts turned to Megan. Her labor must've come early. Back in March, she'd said she wasn't due until the Solstice. Maybe the gestation period for twins was shorter than normal? I sent a quick probe her way, and it came back with good news: she had delivered healthy twins, and everyone was doing fine.

My stomach growled again; even the little bit of energy I'd just used for the probe left me drained. I pulled more from my reserves and wondered what was taking Kevin so long getting the food. I'd probably pass out before he got back.

And where the hell had the Morrigan disappeared to?

Shit. I was getting cranky. Between the back pain, overall discomfort, exhaustion, and hunger, I didn't know how much more I would last.

"You seem distracted," Arddhu said. "Are you not feeling better with this rest?"

"Not really," I admitted. "And I'm wondering what the hell is taking Kevin so long."

He seemed even more concerned. "It has only been a few minutes."

Really? It'd seemed much longer. Like at least half an hour.

"I have been meaning to tell you," he continued. "All is ready for the Hunt, but I have decided to wait until the Summer Solstice."

"Why?"

"The unique energies of the Solstice are useful for my purposes, and I wish to harness those energies."

I did the calculation in my head and frowned. The Solstice was within the asteroid impact window of six to eight weeks. "That's cutting it a little close."

He shrugged. "It will have to suffice. I will not choose an ordinary day for something so important." He squeezed my arm. "And I am eternally grateful to you for allowing me to perform the Hunt again."

"It's the least I can do for my beloved Consort."

Kevin finally returned. Somehow he balanced two fully-loaded plates on his right arm, and gripped two cups of ale in his left hand. Arddhu left to get his own.

"Sorry it took so long," Kevin said as he set everything on the table. "I ran into that guy again. What's his name? Fergus?"

Shit. I'd forgotten all about him and the Ring of Ur thing. "Really? What did he want?"

"He wanted to know if we found the ring he asked about. I told him we haven't finished going through all of Mike's stuff yet. He seemed disappointed, but didn't push it, and took off."

"So, you lied." I smiled at him. "Thank you."

He shrugged. "I didn't want him bothering you." He leaned closer and quietly added, "By the way, we still have to do something about that ring."

"I know. But first, I need to deal with Ares and Athena, the asteroid, and have the baby." I stared at my belly, which seemed to have swelled even more just in the past hour. No wonder my back hurt so much. "Not necessarily in that order."

"True. As far as the food goes, I wasn't sure what you wanted, so I got you a little bit of everything."

"Thanks. It all looks delicious." My plate held roasted pork medallions with apple chutney, oatcakes with honey and berries, fresh veggies, and herbed beef tips in a rich mushroom sauce.

Arddhu returned with his food, and the Morrigan wasn't far behind, although with only a drink. While the rest of us ate, she sat and wistfully watched more young men leap the bonfire.

"Ah, to be young," she said. "For a minute, I thought about joining them."

Kevin grinned at her. "I dare you."

She raised a brow. "Don't tempt me."

"If you do it, I'll do it."

She grinned right back at him. "You're not making it very hard to say no."

It actually sounded like it'd be a lot of fun to watch. I'd just opened my mouth to say so when a sharp pain sliced through my belly, strong enough to force a gasp from me. My fork clattered onto my plate.

"What is wrong?" Arddhu asked.

"Is it the baby?" the Morrigan asked.

Kevin stared at me, his fork halfway to his mouth.

"I'm not sure," I said as another pain hit. "Pain in my belly."

Shit. Was the baby coming *here*? *Now*? I wasn't ready, and I hadn't brought my go-bag with me, full of all the stuff I'd need for a hospital stay.

But there was no hospital here. And it wasn't like I couldn't just magick whatever I needed.

An even sharper pain ripped through me, and I tried to breathe the way I'd seen in a video. Wait. Was that wetness between my legs? Gods, I hoped it wasn't blood.

Another pain drew an involuntary moan, and I squeezed my eyes shut.

"We must get her to the cottage," Arddhu said.

"I can port us," Kevin said. "If someone gives me a power boost."

"Me," the Morrigan offered. "Take it from me."

Someone grabbed my hand, and then we were in my bedroom at the cottage. I didn't even make it to my bed; I doubled over in the middle of the room and groaned again.

"We should have asked if the village midwife was available." Arddhu's voice was tight with tension.

"There's a doctor in the village," Kevin said. "But he's also the veterinarian." He shook his head. "Shit. I could've ported us back to Scottsdale instead. Closer to the hospital. I wasn't thinking."

"No time," the Morrigan snapped. "Baby's coming *now*." And to my surprise—and gratitude—she smoothly and effortlessly took control of the situation.

As I groaned from another stab of pain, I was dimly aware of her removing my dress and draping a soft throw around my shoulders.

"Take off your shoes," she said.

Trying to focus on my breathing, I impatiently waved them away into thin air.

To Kevin, she said, "We'll need some hot water and washcloths." He raced out of the room.

"What can I do?" Arddhu asked.

"Find some clean towels and extra sheets."

I hadn't let go of her arm, and now another pain ripped through me. Arddhu returned with a pile of linens.

"Keep her steady," she told him, and he supported me with his strong arms while she spread the towels and sheets in a thick layer on the floor nearby.

I frowned at the bed. Why hadn't she put the towels and sheets on it?

"We'll do this the old way." She must've seen where I'd looked. "Now, get over here. Squat down and let me feel where the baby is." To Arddhu, she said, "Help her."

Still a bit confused, I followed her instructions. It was probably considered a high honor to have the assistance of the Goddess of Battlefield Death in delivering a baby, and if I weren't in so much pain I'd probably have a good laugh at the irony.

Then again, how the fuck did the Chooser of the Slain know so much about childbirth?

Arddhu helped hold me steady as I squatted and tried to ignore the awkwardness of having her hand so far up inside me.

As another wave of pain came, it stopped being important.

Was it my imagination, or was the pain getting stronger and more frequent? My stomach rolled over, and I prayed the food I'd eaten would stay down.

"I can just feel the crown," she said. "We've got a ways to go."

Crown? Oh. Top of the head. Right.

I wished I'd read more about this phase of pregnancy. Somehow I'd thought I'd have more time.

Still trying to maintain steady breathing, my legs began shaking from holding the squat position for so long. Thank the gods for Arddhu's strength. Then Kevin was there, wiping my sweaty face with a blessedly cool wet cloth, and I could've kissed him in gratitude.

Wait. When did he get back?

"Okay, up you go, time to walk around," the Morrigan said.

I held on to her like a frail crone as we paced the room, carefully avoiding the chairs and other obstacles until Kevin impatiently waved his hand and shoved them aside with his magick.

Another wave of pain hit, and I doubled over.

Walk. Pain. Walk. Squat so the Morrigan could check progress. Then doing it all over again. On and on it went, seeming to drag on forever. At this point, time became a meaningless construct.

Between the intensifying spasms in my belly, waves of nausea, and utter exhaustion, I was completely lost in a haze of pain.

And people really went through this multiple times? Sheer lunacy.

Once, after checking progress, the Morrigan said, "Keep holding her steady, guys. We're heading into the final stage."

Final stage? Thank the gods.

Drops of sweat fell from limp strands of hair that'd come loose from my updo, and I didn't know what had happened to the throw, but my shoulders were now bare. I was naked but I didn't give a shit. I just wanted it all over with.

On each side of me, Arddhu and Kevin held me firmly. Without them, I would've simply been a sweaty mess on the pile of towels and sheets. Even though I had to bite my tongue—and taste blood—to keep from screaming at them that this was all their fault. Especially Arddhu, with his fucking wild forest magick.

Then the pain grew worse.

Way worse.

Something was ripping me apart inside, and I screamed.

"Push," the Morrigan said. "And keep pushing until I tell you to stop."

Huh? Push what? How? Nothing made sense. My brain was mush.

Luckily, instinct took over.

PROPHECY

A lifetime later, something inside me gave way and it felt like all my internal organs were vomited from my vagina.

My head hung from exhaustion, which was the only reason I saw the tiny, wet, red thing land in the Morrigan's waiting hands. Just a glimpse, though, because my vision was growing dim from being split in two.

Wait—how did a kitten get in here? The poor thing was mewling pitifully.

Oh. That was *me*, making that pathetic sound.

Why was I still in so much pain?

Things happened in flashes: the Morrigan cutting the umbilical cord; Kevin using magick to seal and heal the cut while somehow keeping me from collapsing; the Morrigan tenderly cleaning the bodily fluids from the baby.

The little thing never made a sound.

Unlike her mother, whose mewling cries had become moans.

More pain.

"Push again," the Morrigan said.

What? Why? Oh gods, please don't let it be twins. Another one would kill me at this point.

No, it couldn't be. There'd only been one fetus on the ultrasound, and there'd only been one heartbeat.

Then another sensation of something leaving my body, and a bloody mass with a long cord plopped onto the towel beneath me.

Oh. That was the placenta.

Finally, I could breathe again. And my brain seemed to be working again. I was beyond exhausted, and incredibly sore, but at least I didn't feel like I was being ripped apart anymore.

Only Kevin's arms held me now. Arddhu held a tiny pink thing in his arms as the Morrigan came near.

She cleaned me as gently as she could, but it still stung. Then she and Kevin helped me rise, and I was grateful for their help. I didn't think I could do it by myself. My legs were so weak and shaky, they had to half-carry me to the bed, where Kevin placed extra pillows behind me and kissed my forehead.

"Congratulations, love," he murmured. "She's beautiful, just like you."

"*Deirdre, please accept my gift of healing,*" Anu said.

Her warmth and light filled me, and the pain was immediately gone. She'd also given me an energy boost, so although I was still tired, I wasn't exhausted anymore. Tears stung my eyes at her kindness.

"*Thank you, Anu. Much love.*"

"*Much love, Deirdre. And congratulations on the birth of Your daughter.*"

My daughter.

A lump formed in my throat, and I looked up in time to see the Morrigan bring the babe to me.

As she placed the blanket-wrapped bundle in my arms, she spoke formally. "Deirdre Connor, Keeper of the Sphere, Lady of the Cove, and Great Goddess of Earth: I present Your daughter."

My daughter.

Her eyes held all the colors of those of her parents: the blue of mine, emerald green of Kevin, and warm brown of Arddhu. All swirled together in a kaleidoscope.

How could that be?

As I stared at her in wonder, she gazed at me unblinkingly. Somehow I couldn't help but feel she was measuring me. Assessing me. Judging me.

Was I worthy?

After a long moment of intense eye contact, she blinked, waved one tiny fist and cooed, then smiled at me.

Oh. I must've passed.

Yes, I was worthy.

Now I absorbed all the other details: the soft dark fuzz covering her head, her tiny perfect nose, her peaches-and-cream skin, and her rosebud mouth.

I couldn't resist leaning over and nuzzling her, inhaling her unique scent. She giggled, then used both of her small hands to bring my closest breast to her mouth. She latched on and began sucking greedily, one tiny hand pressed against my skin, and closed her eyes.

In that moment, I fell deeply, hopelessly, in love.

"She is beautiful, just like her mother," Arddhu murmured from my right.

"Have you picked a name yet?" Kevin asked from my left. "I know in the past, babies weren't given a name until they were older, but these days people choose a name even before the babies are born."

Unable to take my eyes from my new princess, I just shook my head. "Not yet. I thought I had more time before I had to start thinking of a name."

"You still have time." The Morrigan sat on the edge of the bed near my feet. "Don't rush it. The right name will come to you."

I tore my gaze away from my beautiful girl and lifted my head to look at each of them.

"Thank you. All of you." My eyes filled with tears. I blinked, and my vision cleared. "In case you didn't know it before, I want you all to know it now: you are my family. *We* are a family."

The Morrigan brushed tears away impatiently. "Of course we are."

A sudden strong need gripped me, and before I even knew what I was going to say, the words left my mouth.

"If something happens to me, I want each of you to promise me, right here and now, that you'll take care of this little girl." Kevin started to object, but I shook my head and talked over him with steel in my voice. "*Promise me.*"

One by one, they promised, and the strange urge left me as soon as it'd come. My gaze returned to the babe in my arms, and I relaxed. She left the nipple and belched delicately, making us all laugh. She blinked slowly, as if ready for sleep, but not yet, I thought.

There was something I had to do.

"Arddhu, Great One, Beloved Consort, come and hold your daughter." I offered her to him, and he held her close, rocking her, cooing at her, and kissing the top of her head.

Seeing her in his arms, so well loved, almost brought me to tears again.

He returned her to me, and once again, I offered her up. "Kevin, Beloved Consort, come and hold your daughter."

Kevin wasn't as natural holding her as Arddhu had been. He was almost too careful, as if she were a precious crystal object that would shatter if handled. But he gazed at his daughter with such wonder and deep love, my heart felt as if it would burst.

He passed her back to me, and I offered her again. "The Morrigan, Goddess of Battlefield Death and Chooser of the Slain, come and hold your niece."

She took the babe and held her, breathed in her scent, and smiled as she looked down at her.

Then Kevin and Arddhu moved to surround the Morrigan, and this time I let the tears fall freely as I quietly watched the three of them fuss over our little princess.

The world might be rushing headlong into catastrophe, but for this brief moment in time, all was perfect.

And maybe, just maybe, everything would turn out fine.

CHAPTER TWENTY-FOUR

W E RETURNED HOME to Scottsdale the next morning. At first, I worried if the portal would hurt a newborn baby, but the Morrigan assured me all would be well. Nestled in my arms, my daughter thought the whole thing was loads of fun. She giggled and cooed as I stepped through the portal behind Arddhu. Even so, I used my magick to run a quick scan afterward, and confirmed she'd had no ill effects.

"Told you," the Morrigan teased. "But you're not the first to worry. It's normal to be a bit overprotective with a first child."

Although it was reassuring to know my concerns were normal, I didn't want to become overbearing.

That first day passed in a blur.

Of course, everyone on the security team had to come and see my new daughter and fuss over her. Some even brought gifts: soft blankets in shades of pink and cream, darling little dresses with frothy lace and cute bows, lots of diapers, and a zoo of plush animals.

Nat was overjoyed with the little one, cooing at her and tickling her tummy to make her giggle. "One thing's for sure," she said, "you can tell just by looking at her that she's not exactly human. Those eyes are incredible."

Her kaleidoscope eyes reminded me of the multicolored eyes of the Túatha, and how difficult it was to maintain eye contact with them.

The guys on the security team were more reserved, and almost seemed a bit awkward in the presence of an infant. I wasn't too concerned; they'd relax soon enough.

Kali quickly overcame her surprise that I'd already given birth, and was warm and grandmotherly. She softly sang ancient lullabies as she held my little princess, and generously offered to help care for the babe whenever I needed a break.

Brianna immediately began planning highly nutritious pureed meals, and making a list of all the supplies she'd need.

"It could be months before she's ready to eat solid food," I pointed out.

I didn't mention it could also only happen in a matter of days.

Brianna laughed. "Of course. I know she'll be on your milk for quite some time yet. I'm just doing the prep work for now."

The baby slept a lot, was hungry almost constantly when awake, and was astonishingly prolific with poop and pee. And it didn't take long for me to realize I knew next to nothing about babies.

Again, the Morrigan was indispensable, patiently explaining how to do everything. With her guidance, I quickly learned how to properly care for my daughter.

I'd just finished changing her diaper—again—when I decided to ask the one question that'd been on my mind the most.

"How does the Goddess of Battlefield Death know so much about babies and childbirth?"

She shrugged, pretending intense interest in refolding a neat stack of diapers. "I've been around a lot of new mothers. You just pick things up after a while."

My witchy-sense said she hadn't lied, but I didn't think it was the whole truth. I let it go anyway. There was obviously more to her than she let on, but it wasn't my business if she didn't want to tell me about it.

Besides, I didn't want to annoy her.

"Time for a nap, I think." My daughter's eyes fought to stay open, so I tucked her into the cradle and rocked it. I'd cloaked it in protection spells earlier, along with most everything else in the nursery.

"Catch up with you later, then." The Morrigan left, quietly closing the door behind her.

Next to the cradle was a plush recliner—a thoughtful addition. I sat in it and set the cradle to rocking, then looked around at the nursery.

Although I'd seen it a couple of days ago, this was my first real good look at everything.

The room had been repainted, turning plain vanilla walls into a colorful forest complete with hundreds of playful critters. The cradle was old-fashioned solid wood, and matched the dresser, crib, and changing table. A cute mobile hung over the crib, with iridescent dragonflies and butterflies in every color of the rainbow gently turning in the air currents from the ceiling vent. The drawers beneath the changing table were stocked with diapers and wipes, and the dresser was filled with baby clothes.

And, of course, hundreds of stuffed animals were everywhere: atop the dresser, in the crib, on the changing table, and in the corner hammock, suspended from the ceiling.

There was even one in her cradle.

Wait.

That pink giraffe snuggled next to my daughter hadn't been there a minute ago.

I'd probably dozed off. Someone had probably come in to check on the baby, and had put it in there.

Yeah, that's probably what'd happened.

My babe was sleeping peacefully now, and my eyelids felt heavy. Well, why not take a nap? I fumbled for a moment, not finding a handle to recline the chair, but then I found a button. Ah, it was motorized.

My last thought as I fully reclined and closed my eyes was how spoiled I was.

"Dee, time to wake up."

Kevin's voice.

"Okay," I mumbled.

"Reshep is here. There's news."

I opened my eyes, blinked a couple of times, then brought the recliner back to a sitting position. Kevin stood nearby, holding our little princess, who was fussing.

"She's probably hungry," I said. "Give me just a minute."

He handed her to me, and I gave her a nipple.

"What news?" I asked while she nursed greedily. I hoped it was good news.

"They found Ares and Athena."

Oh. That was fantastic news, actually.

"Hand me that cloth, would you please?" I draped it over myself for privacy, then stood. "Okay, let's go."

As soon as I entered the living room, Reshep stood. "My Lady, happiest congratulations on the birth of Your daughter."

"Thank you." That reminded me: I had to pick a name for her. *Soon.* "Tell me."

He grinned. "The firm's spies have sent word. Ares and Athena. We have their location."

"Where are they?"

"At a small villa on Olympus, only a short distance from their own palaces."

"Where, exactly?" As he did so, the baby stopped feeding. I fixed my clothing and gave her to Kevin. "Could you please change her and take care of her? It's time to pay them a visit."

"Not alone, you're not," Kevin protested. He'd draped the cloth over his shoulder and now pat her back to encourage any air to release.

"Oh yes, I am." I wasn't stupid, though; I quickly transformed my comfy clothing into armor. Similar to the catsuit Mike had given me back when I was the Keeper, this armor covered me from neck to toe and would protect me against any human weapons, such as bullets or blades. But the added protection spells and shielding would make me impervious to most magick, too.

For just a moment, I thought about taking my sword. But no, I didn't want to walk in armed if there was a good chance I could resolve this peacefully. It'd send the wrong message. Besides, I could always access it from my pocket universe if I needed it.

"I really don't think this is a good idea," Kevin said. "Although I'm glad you're armored."

"I'll be fine," I insisted. "They can't hurt me."

358

Then I ported to the location of the villa on Olympus, and arrived near its front entrance.

It wasn't exactly a small villa, but it was much smaller than a palace.

Two shadows stepped out from the massive bougainvillea shrub nearby, and I tensed, ready to counterattack. Then the shadows became two human males in dark tactical clothing and sunglasses. They nodded respectfully and holstered their pistols.

"Ms. Connor," one softly said in greeting. "We're your backup."

Ah, they were from the firm. No wonder they'd been hiding in the bougainvillea—their dark clothing made them way too conspicuous among all the beige stucco and white marble surrounding us.

As did my own dark-colored armor.

"I don't need any," I assured them both. "I'll take it from here."

"Ma'am, we're under orders," the other one said.

"I'm a higher authority, and I just overrode your orders. I'm going in alone."

The two men glanced at each other, then shrugged.

"Yes, ma'am," the first one said. "We'll be here if you need us."

That'd have to do.

I nodded and turned away to study my surroundings.

A number of dilapidated villas were scattered along the narrow cobbled street, which led to two enormous palaces built into the slopes of the looming mountain. Unlike the villas, the palaces gleamed bright white in the hot sun, appearing well-maintained and currently occupied. Each had multiple fluted columns and wide steps leading to magnificent gilded double doors.

The sky above was such a pale blue it was almost white. No birds sang, no insects buzzed, no dogs barked. The trees along the street were scraggly, and the flowering shrubs were covered in dead blossoms.

A sudden gust of wind came through, and I jumped at a loud noise nearby.

Oh. It'd just been a door or gate, banging in the wind.

I half-expected to see a tumbleweed blowing down the ancient street.

The place gave me the creeps, and I put another layer of protective shielding over my entire body, just in case.

If each realm reflected its gods, what did that say about Ares and Athena? Olympus was desolate and pitiful, not the beautiful shining realm I'd expected. They'd seemed so dazzling and noble when I'd first met them over a year ago.

But they'd also been arrogant. I couldn't forget that.

Turning toward the villa, I studied what was visible from this distance. It seemed just as broken-down as the rest of the buildings nearby. The outer wall's stucco was patchy, and the underlying stonework near the entrance door was crumbling to dust.

Interesting, that the Olympians would rather hide in this decaying building instead of their gleaming palaces up the street.

Taking a deep breath, I approached the villa's entrance and scanned for protection spells or wards, but found none.

What I did find was a glamor spell. Ah, so this desolation was just a mirage? Even more interesting.

I used my magick to push the door, and it swung open silently. Beyond was a large paved courtyard with a surprising amount of healthy green growing things.

Slowly, I crossed the threshold, continuing to check for spells or magickal traps. Again, I found none.

Keeping close to the wall, I looked around. The courtyard was deserted but well-kept, a far cry from the decrepit appearance given by the glamor spell. Not a single paver was missing or out of place. A large fountain burbled at the far end, seemingly the only happy thing in this desolate realm. Potted trees and blooming shrubs were everywhere and thriving, proving someone was around to tend them.

The villa's two levels wrapped around three sides of the courtyard. Marble columns supported the covered balcony of the upper floor, where more potted plants continued the garden atmosphere.

I took three steps toward the fountain, and a booming voice echoed on the ancient stone walls.

"Stop where you are. You are not welcome here."

Ares. It sounded like he was somewhere to my right. Maybe near that open doorway up on the second floor?

Boosting my voice so it, too, boomed, I replied. "Noble Ares, God of War. Wise Athena, Goddess of Battle Strategy. Please allow me to plead for peace on behalf of the planet Earth."

"Fuck your peace, *Thief of Power*," Athena screamed.

Holy shit. She didn't sound like the cool, calm Athena I'd known in all the Alliance meetings last year. She sounded... unhinged.

Keeping my hands clearly visible, I took two more steps into the courtyard. No attack came. "Please. This will take only a few moments of your time. And what harm is there in just talking?"

My enhanced hearing heard murmurs as they spoke quietly, but wasn't able to make out the words. Athena's voice rose in anger, but it was garbled, as if her mouth was covered.

A moment later, Ares called out. "Speak, then."

Oh hell no. There was no way I was going to yell back and forth like this. "Let us sit together and talk, like civilized people. I will not shout what I've come to say."

More arguing, then a single sharp word was spoken, followed by a rustle and footsteps.

I'd guessed right. Ares appeared in the open doorway upstairs, then he stood in the shade of the balcony for a moment, studying me. Or maybe he was making sure I'd come alone. Then he proceeded to the staircase in the far corner.

As he approached, I tensed, ready for an attack. But he wore no weapons or armor, only a short white tunic belted at the waist and plain leather sandals. It seemed odd to see the Greek God of War without his armor.

"My sister does not trust you and will wait for you to spring your trap." His eyes searched behind me before meeting mine. "I fear no trap, even though I, too, do not trust you." Now he took in my armor and snorted derisively. "If you are only here to talk, why have you come dressed for battle?"

I shrugged. "I wasn't sure if I'd have to defend myself. And don't even try to say you wouldn't have done the same."

A flicker of respect showed in his eyes. "You are correct. If our situations were reversed, of course I would be in full armor." Now his gaze narrowed. "And fully armed."

"I am unarmed, but fully shielded." I gestured at my armor. "However, if you'd prefer, I can change into something else."

"I care not what clothing you wear. Although, I would not mind if you wore none at all." He leered almost comically.

Same old Ares. Such a horny old goat. And an asshole.

"Not an option." I glanced around, knowing Athena was hiding somewhere close enough to listen. "What happened to the old laws of hospitality? You'd truly leave a tired and thirsty guest standing out here in the blazing sun?"

He studied me for a moment then sighed. "We still abide by the ancient laws." He motioned for me to accompany him. "This way."

I followed him through the courtyard, past the fountain, into a pleasantly cool room that was small but richly appointed. Marble floors and columns gleamed bright white, and colorful tapestries of hunting scenes hung on the walls. Velvet-covered couches and ornate golden tables were arranged for dining or casual sitting. The space was well-lit by just the natural light streaming from the courtyard.

Ares indicated for me to sit on one of the couches, and he sat on another opposite me. He clapped his hands twice, and a servant appeared with a laden tray in her shaky hands. She kept her eyes downcast as she placed the tray on the table between us, then quickly disappeared into the shadows.

"Idiot," Ares muttered. "She didn't even mix and pour. So hard to find good help these days." Reluctantly, he poured some wine then water into a large bowl, then filled two golden goblets with the mixture. He offered one to me and raised the other. "To truth and honor."

I echoed the toast, took a polite sip, and set the goblet on the table. It was quite a good wine, actually, and I appreciated that its strength had been tempered with the water. "Thank you for your hospitality. I'll get right to the point: I have come to offer a truce."

Of course Athena was listening; I could sense it.

"A truce." He snorted. "We have no need of a truce."

He leaned to one side, spreading his legs wide enough to clearly show his genitals. It reminded me of a nature show I'd watched once, where male gorillas basically did the same thing as an intimidation tactic.

Instead of letting it unnerve me, I boldly stared at his privates for a moment, keeping my expression carefully blank. Then I met his gaze unflinchingly. "I think you do. From what I understand, you and Athena plan on leaving Earth and taking whichever gods want to go with you. You want to destroy Earth and any realm connected to it. But what of Olympus? Do you truly wish the treasure of Olympus to be destroyed, never to be enjoyed again?"

He didn't seem surprised I wasn't intimidated. He shrugged off my argument. "We will take whatever is valuable with us. The rest is just stone and metal."

"Really? Just stone and metal?"

"Well, there are some mosaics in the palace of Zeus that we would not be able to take with us. But we do not really want them, anyway." He shrugged again, then narrowed his eyes. "But you seem to know an awful lot about our plans. That fucking bitch traitor Kali told you, didn't she?"

"She told me some, but you and Athena haven't exactly been discreet in your discussions with other deities."

If he knew I was talking about Odin, he didn't say so.

"You cannot stop us from leaving." He drank from his goblet.

"Of course not. You are free to leave and take any who wish to leave with you. No one will stop you, follow you, or attack your world. You have my word on that. All I ask in return is that you leave Earth and all its realms in peace."

"Peace," he spat. "Humans are a disease. Wherever they go, they cause ruin and chaos. There is no hope of peace on that planet. You are deluding yourself."

"I disagree. In fact, I'm going to fix it."

"Oh?" He raised a brow. "How?"

Dammit. I wished he hadn't asked that. I hadn't worked that part out yet.

"I'm not sure," I admitted. After he snorted, I added, "Hey, I'm being honest here. I could've told you some made-up bullshit, but I didn't." My voice had risen; I took a deep breath and forced myself to calm. "I'm just saying, I'm still working on it. But I do think I can fix it."

"Your honesty is commendable. It has always been one of your most redeeming qualities. But once again, we do not need your truce. We don't need Earth. So why should either of us care enough to spare it?"

He had a good point. I hadn't expected him to be this well-spoken, actually. I'd only known him as a hot-head who didn't spend his time thinking if he could be fighting instead. Or fucking. He was notorious for enjoying carnal desires.

Hmm. What would sway him? I could go one of two ways right now: either I could use a carrot, or a stick. I decided to try a carrot first.

"What's it worth to you? I mean, what would you require in return for leaving Earth in peace?"

"Power." No hesitation in his reply. "Give me the power of the Goddess."

"I'm sorry, but that's impossible. I need it to heal the Earth."

"No, you don't. Get your friends to help you instead."

Should I mention the asteroid? My instincts said no. So, I'd have stay vague and speak in generalities. "They can't. Only I can protect the Earth from threats like nuclear war and asteroids."

He rolled his eyes. "Fine. Then give me the Sphere."

"That's also impossible." This time I didn't even think twice about telling a bald-faced lie. "The Sphere can only be commanded by a woman."

No one commanded her, but I had to speak in terms he'd understand. *Forgive me, Anu.*

His eyes narrowed. "So, give it to Athena, then."

He was quick, I'd give him that. "Sorry, I can't do that, either. The Sphere is sentient. I cannot force Anu to attach herself to anyone. And she won't leave me of her own free will." I sure as hell wasn't going to tell him Anu would leave me if I died.

"How unfortunate." He tapped a finger impatiently against the side of his goblet. "Since you are unwilling to meet any of my requirements, I believe our negotiations are over."

I sighed. "There must be something else. Something that is within my power to give."

He refilled his goblet, then stared at my full goblet.

"Drink. I refuse to speak further unless you drink."

Shit. Fine.

I swallowed quite a bit more than just a sip and set the goblet down. "Satisfied?"

"Not even close." His gaze wandered over my body, but my neck-to-toe armor wouldn't let him see much. "I could go for a fuck, but you'd probably say no."

So predictable. He was almost as bad as Zeus when it came to not keeping it in his pants. Er, beneath his tunic.

"You'd be right," I said. "It's a definite no."

"Too bad. I'm told I'm very, very good." He continued to leer at me with a tiny hint of desperate hope visible in his eyes.

I pretended to think it over, but there was no way I was going to fuck Ares. I could give him a made-up excuse, but for some reason I decided to tell the truth.

"Look." I leaned forward and kept my voice soft. "I'll be honest here. I just had a baby. I'm not ready to have sex with *anyone* right now. Not even my Consorts." I shook my head. "The answer is still no."

His eyes had widened as I spoke, and now he, too, leaned forward, his voice barely over a whisper. "You've had a child?"

Oh shit. I fucked up. Now he had valuable information, and I'd lost whatever slim advantage I'd had just a moment ago.

Fuck. Fuck. Fuck.

But instead of using that information to press me, he stared off into nothing and muttered, "This changes everything."

Huh? How? Why?

Now Ares glanced around furtively and leaned closer. "Follow my lead."

What game was he playing?

He straightened and spoke loudly. "Blow job it is, then. We have a deal. A truce. Let us drink to our agreement."

Before I could open my mouth to reply, Athena rushed into the room, hair disheveled and wide eyes. She, too, wore a short belted tunic and leather sandals, except with lavish gold trim.

"*No*," she screamed. "You don't speak for me. I refuse any deal. No truce. *None*."

"I just did, dear sister." Ares spoke mildly, not taking his eyes from mine.

He suddenly seemed tired.

"*I said no*," she screamed again, making my ears ache.

I almost expected her to stamp her foot, like a child having a tantrum. This wasn't the Athena I knew from last year. What had happened to her calm, strategy-focused demeanor?

"As the male and the head of household in this family," Ares calmly said, "I have the authority to speak for you. And, in fact, I already have. You will heed my words or be punished."

Athena's jaw dropped as she stared at her brother, then she advanced on me with pure hatred in her gaze. "This is *your* doing. You have turned *my own brother* against me."

I stood, ready for anything.

Ares, seemingly unconcerned, corrected her calmly. "Half-brother."

"This isn't over," she spat, never taking her gaze from me. Her hands curled into fists. "Not by a long shot."

"*That's enough.*" Ares slammed his goblet onto the table, stood, and stalked toward her.

Her fury instantly transformed into fear; she cringed, frantically searching for escape, but Ares was too quick. He wrapped one hand around her slender throat and easily lifted her until she dangled in the air. She struggled, kicking out and using both hands to pull at his arm, but to no effect.

Shit. I hadn't wanted any of this. I'd only wanted a truce, and for Earth to be left in peace. *Follow my lead*, he'd told me, but I wasn't exactly sure what I was supposed to do except watch helplessly. Since he was facing away from me, I couldn't read his expression to gain any clues.

Which was probably a good thing, based on the sheer terror on Athena's face.

"*It is over.*" His voice boomed, amplified by all the cold hard marble around us. "You will obey me, or I will do much worse than simply punish you." He spoke slightly softer now, but with just as much cruelty. And he punctuated his words with violent shakes that made her teeth snap together. "Never forget: it is within my right as head of household to execute you for your continued disobedience."

Finally, Athena stopped struggling and went limp. A moment later, Ares released her, and she staggered but didn't fall. The redness on her throat would turn into a nasty bruise later, and I winced in sympathy.

"Forgive me, brother," she croaked with downcast eyes. "I forgot my place."

"Best you remember from now on."

"Yes, brother."

"Now go to your chambers. I demand privacy with my guest. I will know if you disobey me again, and I will not be merciful."

"Yes, brother." Shuddering, she turned and fled without a backward glance, her sandals slapping on the marble.

Ares turned toward me, and his expression of rage melted into tired resignation. His shoulders slumped and he sighed as he motioned for us to sit.

This time, he sat on the couch beside me and refilled his goblet.

"I am sorry you had to witness that," he spoke quietly. "It wasn't pleasant."

"It seemed... harsh."

"It must be. I have no choice. If I had done anything different, she would have taken control of the situation. And that would have been much worse. Believe me." He drank half his wine in one swallow.

I took a healthy swig of mine. "What's wrong with her? It's like she's lost her mind. And why does she hate me so much?"

He shook his head before replying. "It's not you. I mean, it *is* you, but it's not personal." He met my gaze, and I saw the pain there. "Her... illness... is getting worse."

"Illness?"

"For some time now, she's been having hallucinations, terrible headaches, and trouble sleeping. In the beginning, she was still able to function somewhat normally, but then it started to affect her personality. I fear for her sanity."

This was all news to me. "She seemed fine last year."

"She was. This behavior began soon after the battle against Cromm. Headaches and nightmares kept her from sleeping. By the time Ida was banished and you received the power of the Goddess, she was becoming irrational, although outbursts were rare. Now, they're almost constant. She has become impossible to live with, but she is the only family I have left." He sighed heavily. "I cannot abandon her."

Then why the hell had he threatened to execute her? This made absolutely no sense at all.

"I know you are thinking of the threats I said to her. Yes, it is cruel. But it is the only thing she understands now. Believe me, I tried to be pleasant with her. It got me nothing but bruised balls."

"Can't you heal her?"

He shook his head. "I can only heal myself. And she has burned so many bridges, no one was willing to help her. Even the great healers at the Sanctuary of Asklepius refused."

He hadn't asked me. What if...

"Do not fret," he murmured, and patted my knee. "I do not really expect a blow job. I only said that because I knew she was listening. You have your truce."

"Why did you say my baby changed everything?"

He sighed again. "First, because of my honor. I will not knowingly harm a new mother, or a baby god. Second, if she ever found out... well, let's just say she would lose the last of her sanity. I fear she would find a way to either harm you or the child. Or both."

I still didn't understand. "Why?"

He hesitated. "She is unable to bear children. For the past thousand years or so, she has been barren."

I drank more of my wine, then came to a decision. "Let me heal her."

His eyes searched mine. "You truly believe you can?"

"Yes."

"You will never be able to get close enough to her." He shook his head. "Not unless I drug her."

"Then I suggest you do that."

It took a bit more coaxing, but I finally convinced him, and he left to retrieve the necessary herbal mixture. He was gone longer than I expected, but it gave me some time to think uninterrupted.

I didn't know for sure what was wrong with Athena, but it sounded like she'd had some kind of head injury. I'd successfully healed a human with such an injury, so maybe it wouldn't be much different for a deity. I sure hoped it wasn't. I didn't want this to be my first healing failure.

Ares returned, refilled his goblet, then added the powder to the wine, swirling it with his finger to mix it thoroughly.

"I have tried to make it strong enough to take effect in about twenty minutes," he said. "But I am not an expert in these things. If I am wrong, and it does not work, she will try to kill you."

"I'm not worried. I can defend myself."

He nodded. "Well, then. Come upstairs with me. Wait in a nearby room while I deliver it to her."

I followed him up the stairs, but hung back in the shadows as he knocked softly on the door.

"Athena, my sister, I've brought you some wine." He cracked the door, peeked in, and slipped through.

They spoke in low voices, then it was quiet. A moment later, he returned with the empty cup. He closed the door and approached me.

"Now we wait," he whispered, and drew me into a nearby room. It looked like a bedroom, but I didn't think it was his. It was far too neat and tidy. No personal items or clothing anywhere, either. It was probably a guest room.

"We can talk here, but very quietly." He sat on the bench at the foot of the bed, and after a moment's hesitation I sat beside him. "If you are successful in healing her, she will regain her wisdom and honor our agreement. I will stop instigating war among the humans. We will both leave Earth in peace and never bother any of you again."

"What if you stuck around? Helped me make Earth a better place for everyone?"

He shook his head. "We have burned too many bridges for that."

Fair point.

Should I tell him about the asteroid? As I debated, he stood.

"I will go and check on Athena."

I didn't think twenty minutes had passed yet, but I didn't say anything. A moment later, he was at the doorway waving at me to follow.

"She is deep asleep. I may have made the potion a bit strong."

In contrast with the room I'd just seen, Athena's bedroom was pure opulence. The bed itself was massive, larger than anything I'd ever seen. She lay dwarfed in a sea of rich purple silk and satin, looking more like a child in her parents' bed than the ancient goddess she really was.

I wasted no time, stepping close and scanning her. First I looked for skull fractures or any other external damage to her head. Not finding any evidence of an obvious wound, I delved deeper, into her brain.

After several minutes of searching for anomalies, I found a suspect area and zoomed in for a closer look.

A large blood clot, with a few smaller ones, was affecting the nearby brain cells. Comparing them to healthy cells elsewhere, it seemed some had already died.

Shit.

This appeared to be a serious head injury. If I had to guess, the longer it went untreated, the worse it would get. She'd probably continue to deteriorate until she died, but she'd get even more mentally unstable long before then. Being deity instead of human might've been the only thing that'd kept her alive this long.

I wasn't familiar with the specific functions of this part of the brain, but I had to assume this injury was the cause of everything Athena had been going through: the headaches, nightmares, trouble sleeping, and personality changes.

But I wasn't a brain surgeon. This was so much more complicated than when I'd simply targeted the cancer cells in the FBI agent last month, or the concussions in auto accident victims.

Why couldn't the power of the Goddess be all-knowing?

For just a moment, I panicked.

What if, in trying to heal this, I only made it worse? Or what if I accidentally killed her?

"*Deirdre, breathe.*" Anu's voice was soothing. "*You can do this.*"

"*Thank you, Anu.*" I took a deep breath and let it out. "*I don't suppose you know how to fix it?*"

She took so long to answer I thought she wouldn't answer at all.

"*No. I am sorry.*"

It'd been worth a shot.

Forcing myself to calm, I made myself comfortable beside Athena, since I had no idea how long it would take.

First things first. I located the blood vessels that'd been slowly leaking and causing the clots to form, and used my magick to repair them. Next, I removed the clots and cleaned the blood from the area. Now I could get a better look at the dead brain cells.

I gauged the extent of the damage with a gentle probe. Luckily, it didn't seem too widespread. Only the area closest to where the blood vessels had ruptured was affected. I sent healing energy directly to the cells, then tensed as Athena moaned and twitched.

After a moment, she settled, and I breathed again.

Touchy business, this.

I continued to send healing energy to the cells for a few more moments, then paused to evaluate progress.

Shit.

The dead cells were completely unaffected.

But I didn't have time to try and figure out why. I had to keep going. If I couldn't heal dead brain cells, I'd have to remove and replace them.

Carefully, but as quickly as I dared, I removed all the dead cells. Using the closest healthy cell, I replicated it millions of times. As the gap filled with healthy cells, I tried to ignore Athena's spasmodic jerks, and hoped she didn't feel any pain.

Finally, I took a minute to double-check my work.

Now, the affected area didn't look any different than the rest of that brain section, and it was actually difficult to see where I'd made the repair. With a little luck, it'd function completely normal.

I took another deep breath and scanned the rest of her body for other injuries.

No injuries, but there: an anomaly in her reproductive organs that might've been keeping her from getting pregnant. It was a quick fix for my healing power.

I blinked and refocused my eyes from microscopic to normal vision, and stretched the kinks out of my muscles. Only then did I realize my face was dripping with sweat.

As I moved to the nearby chair, I took the offered cloth from Ares and wiped away the sweat.

"Done," I murmured. "I just need a few minutes to rest."

Ares offered me a fresh goblet of watered wine, and I took a sip gratefully, then set it down. I replenished my energy from Anu's reserves, then rested my head against the back of the chair for a moment.

I must've dozed, because a hoarse voice roused me.

"What did you do to me?"

Athena had awakened, and now she stared at me with wide eyes.

"You had a brain injury. I healed it."

She blinked at me, then sat up.

Ares was immediately there to help. "How do you feel?"

"My headache." She touched her head in wonder. "It's gone." She looked up at him. "For the first time in months, I feel no pain." She turned to me. "It seems I owe you a great debt."

I shook my head. "There is no debt. The healing was freely given." I paused, then leaned forward. "Honestly, if I'd known you were suffering all this time, I would've offered to heal you a long time ago."

She stared at me for a moment. "But I've said terrible things. And done terrible things."

"For what it's worth, I think it was the brain injury doing all that."

"But I wanted you *dead*," she wailed, and burst into tears.

"Shh, my sister." Ares sat on the edge of the bed and held her close. "All is well. We will go to our new world and be happy."

Athena looked at me with disbelief. "You would truly let us go after all we've done?"

"Yes." I didn't bring up the agreement I'd made with Ares. Let him tell her about it later, after I'd left.

She closed her eyes for a long moment, then seemed to come to a decision. She pulled away from Ares and got out of bed, then slowly knelt on the floor in front of me with head bowed. "You truly are worthy of the power of the Goddess. I most humbly ask Your forgiveness."

This was unexpected. Then again, one shouldn't underestimate the power of healing an enemy who's been suffering.

"Athena, Goddess of Wisdom and Battle Strategy, you are forgiven." I stood and helped her rise. "Go in peace and good health, and be happy." I kissed her on each cheek and tried to pull away, but she wouldn't let go of my hands.

Tears shimmered in her eyes. "Thank You for Your blessing, Lady."

"You are welcome." I smiled and firmly extricated myself from her grip. "I'll take my leave now." I nodded to Ares. "Be well."

I ported back to The Hacienda's living room.

Everyone was still there, waiting for me, plus Arddhu had returned from off-world.

"Hey guys." I changed my armor for comfy clothes.

At the sound of my voice, my daughter smiled and reached for me with chubby arms, and Kevin handed her over. "She's been changed and had a nap."

"How'd it go?" the Morrigan asked.

I got comfortable in one of the chairs and told them what happened.

"So, just like that, it's over?" Kevin asked.

I nodded, then took a good look at my daughter. Her hair had grown at least three inches just in the past day, and now it was a beautiful auburn that matched my own. She'd also grown quite a bit, and probably doubled her weight.

At this rate, she'd be a toddler in less than a week.

"I am not at all surprised you healed Athena," Arddhu said. "You truly have the heart of the Goddess, and I am proud of you and all you have accomplished."

"A brain injury, all this time." Kali shook her head. "It explains so much, how it started right after the battle, and how she changed before my eyes. I should've realized something like that was the reason."

"Even if you'd known," I pointed out, "what could you have done? Could you have healed her?"

"No." She shook her head again. "Healing is not one of my powers."

"By the way," Reshep said. "The news is reporting that both countries in South Asia have stopped all hostilities. They've resumed peace talks."

"That's great news."

"So, now what?" the Morrigan asked. "Ares and Athena leave for their own world, and we never see them again?"

"Yes to the first, probably yes to the second."

"So, crisis averted," Kevin said. "Everyone lives happily ever after."

If only. "Not really. There's still the asteroid to deal with."

"Shit." Kevin groaned. "Believe it or not, I'd actually forgotten about that."

"Asteroid?" Kali and Reshep asked at the same time.

Oh. That's right. They hadn't known.

I quickly got them up to speed on the asteroid and my plan.

"How long until it arrives?" Reshep asked, frowning.

"Roughly five to seven weeks," I replied.

"If I understood you correctly," he continued, "even if this asteroid does not destroy the planet, it could possibly make it uninhabitable to humans for millennia?"

I nodded.

"Like with the dinosaurs," Kevin said.

"But that's where my plan comes in," I said. "Which reminds me: I need to start working on the sanctuary realm. The project team at NASA wants a tour when it's done, and I'm sure they'll start bugging me any day now."

"Tell me more about this sanctuary realm," Reshep said.

"It'll have climate zones similar to Earth, the same composition of air, and the same features. Oceans, mountains, plains, that sort of thing. When it's done, we'll open portals all over the planet and move as many people as possible to it. Then, if the shield holds, we just bring everyone back. But if it doesn't..." I swallowed. "Well, then they have somewhere else to live. Someplace familiar. And safe."

Reshep slowly nodded, as if thinking it through. "It is a good plan."

Just then, my daughter pulled on my hair, and she wasn't gentle about it.

"Ouch, baby girl. That hurts Mommy." She gazed at me unblinking, and I remembered something important. "You know, I've put it off long enough. She needs a name. Something worthy of her beauty, intelligence, and divinity."

"How about Astrid?" Arddhu asked. "It means *divinely beautiful.*"

Before I could reply, the Morrigan said, "I was thinking Morgan. For *bright one.*"

Kevin laughed. "And I was thinking Kyra. It's Greek for *Lady.*"

Reshep cleared his throat softly. "Ain is Egyptian for *priceless gift.*"

"Devyn means *divine poet,*" Kali added.

Damn. Those were some good names.

But none seemed exactly right.

I hadn't lifted my gaze from my daughter's, and a strange warmth spread through me as a name echoed in my mind.

"Brighid," I said. "It's Irish for *exalted one.*"

"That would be an excellent choice for our little goddess," the Morrigan said.

"Okay. That's her name," I said. "Brighid Astrid Kyra Morgan Ain Devyn Connor. Bree for short." My girl giggle and cooed, then quite obviously nodded her head twice, never taking her gaze from mine. "Hey, did you guys see that?"

"See what?" Kevin asked.

"She just nodded her head. Like she approved of her name."

"She's only a little over a day old," Reshep laughed. "There's no way she understands what we're saying."

Bree turned her head and scowled at him.

Unmistakably.

"Are you sure about that?" I asked.

He shook his head, staring at Bree. "She is remarkable."

"So, Bree it is, then," Arddhu confirmed.

I stood and held my girl high above me. "Before all the Gods and Goddesses, before all the Elements and Gaia Herself, I hereby proclaim this child of the Goddess of Earth and Consorts Arddhu and Kevin is so named

Brighid Astrid Kyra Morgan Ain Devyn Connor." I hugged her to my chest and kissed her forehead. "Bree for short."

And so it was.

CHAPTER TWENTY-FIVE

I N ONLY THE past few days, Bree had continued to grow at an abnormally accelerated rate, and was now quite the handful.

She'd already outgrown all the clothes gifted to her just last week, so I'd had to create a whole new wardrobe using my magick. Her hair fell in soft waves past her shoulders, and seemed to grow an inch every few hours. The fresh baby food Brianna had prepared for her lasted only three days before Bree wanted to eat the same food as the rest of us.

One day, she'd started speaking words. The next, it was complete sentences. She wasn't even a baby anymore; I didn't know that much about kids, but based on her size and development level, I estimated her to be about two or three years old. Her kaleidoscope eyes held a deep wisdom, far beyond her age, that also made her seem much older.

Strange things happened, too. Mostly innocent things, like toys that'd been in the storage hammock in her room suddenly appeared next to her as we sat in the living room.

But then there was the time her stuffed pink giraffe was nowhere to be found. While I'd searched under the sofa and chairs, she'd run to the window-wall, giggling. I'd glanced her way and frowned.

Who the hell was she waving at?

I'd joined her at the window-wall then stared speechless at the huge pink giraffe stomping through the backyard, ruining the oleander and bougainvillea. A moment later, it'd fallen into the pool and thrashed around as if it were really drowning.

Oh no. She'd discovered her magick.

"Bree, put it back. Make it a toy again." The giraffe had found its way out of the pool and headed for the mesquite trees.

"Wanna play." She'd pushed on the glass, then studied the window panels, trying to figure out how to open them.

Oh, hell no. The last thing I'd needed was her running around in the backyard with a giant pink giraffe on the loose.

Thank the gods we didn't have any close neighbors.

"No." I'd scooped her up into my arms. "I said *put it back*."

"No," she'd wailed, kicking and wriggling to be free. "Wanna *play*."

"Stop that this minute," I'd said, then spent several minutes unsuccessfully commanding her to change the giraffe back into a stuffed toy. In the meantime, it'd started munching on the upper leaves of the mesquite trees, making a fine mess of things.

"Fine. I'll do it myself." I'd used my own power to transform the damn thing—which wasn't really *alive*, just animated—back to its normal size and inanimate state, then ported the soggy thing to the laundry room where it could dry out.

I'd set her down and scolded her, "Don't you *ever* do that again."

She'd promptly burst into tears. "Sorry, Mama."

Then, I'd spent the next several minutes explaining to her. "When you want something, you need to ask me first. There are many dangerous things in this world that could hurt you, and it's my job to make sure they don't. I can't do my job if you do things like this."

"I promise." Her eyes had fixed on me. "I won't do it again."

At the rate she was growing and learning, she'd be a teenager in only a few weeks, and that terrified me.

I remembered all too well what I'd been like as a teenager, and I knew damn well I was nowhere near ready to go through any of that as a parent.

But in the meantime, there was a lot of other shit to worry about.

I'd started creating the sanctuary realm, taking my time with the design and perfecting it over the past few days. Because I was Goddess of Earth and not the Universe, as Anu had reminded me more than once, I knew I couldn't create an actual planet with a solar system and everything. So I was content with creating just a realm.

I'd also done a ton of internet research, studying the cycles of the sun and moon, star maps, various climate zones of the planet, and all the species of flora and fauna in each zone. I'd studied geological formations, composition of the atmosphere, and seemingly a million other details.

Now, the time had come to do the actual construction of the realm.

It was a beautiful mid-May morning, and I sat outside on the patch of soft grass. I'd coordinated with everyone to make sure I wouldn't be disturbed while I worked: Bree was with Arddhu, Kevin was teaching Kali in the VIP tent, and the Morrigan and Reshep were spending some alone time.

I took a deep breath of the fresh morning air, closed my eyes to better visualize my work, and began.

I made the realm big enough to hold the current population of Earth, but I really expected about half to actually populate the realm. Everyone probably wouldn't migrate, just like there were always some people who wanted to stay in their homes despite a looming hurricane.

First, I created the lands and seas, making sure to include mountains and valleys, plains and deserts, forests and beaches, and canyons. I used all the best examples of Earth's features and made them appear as they had before the coming of humans, unspoiled and undamaged. After those broad strokes were done, I spent time on smaller details: caves, knolls, creeks and rivers, and rolling hills.

Next, I created a sun and moon, and set them to move across the sky at regular intervals to simulate current Earth periods of night and day. I added blue sky for daytime and the proper oxygenated atmosphere, and watched as wispy clouds began to form. I scattered twinkling stars across the sky for night, remembering to form them into the familiar patterns of Earth constellations. Just for fun, I included a distant comet slowly streaking across the starfield—one that would never be an impact danger.

I filled the realm with all the trees and plants of Earth, except for anything deadly to humans or animals. I took care to ensure the flora was contained in similar ecosystems to Earth's: cactus and mesquite in the deserts; oak, maple, ash, elm, and other trees in some forests but pine and aspen in others; and a myriad of wildflowers everywhere.

I reproduced climate zones as best I could, but it'd be impossible to have the wide variety that Earth had, because I needed to keep everything simple. Since the realm wasn't an actual planet with an orbit or axial tilt like Earth, technically it couldn't have multiple concurrent seasons like Earth did. But I did what I could: winter would have snow and colder temperatures; spring would be rainy and windy; summer would have warm days and lots of sunshine; and fall would be cool, with leaves turning gold, red, and copper, as they should.

Then, I took a look at everything with a more critical eye, and found some things to fix. That mountain range blocked the sun in the nearby valley, so I shortened it. This lake was too small, and that forest too big—on and on it went. Finally, I had to admit I was being too nitpicky and just left it alone.

After all, Earth wasn't perfect either.

By then I had to take a break. My stomach growled, I was extremely thirsty, and my joints had stiffened up from maintaining the same position for too long.

I went inside and found my family in the kitchen, just sitting down to a late lunch. Of course, Brianna had made up a plate for me, too.

"How's it going?" Kevin asked as I joined him, Bree, Arddhu, and the Morrigan at the granite island.

"Good. Basic realm infrastructure is done."

"What is next?" Arddhu asked.

"I need to double-check a few things on the internet, then I can start on the wildlife."

Bree grinned. "Will there be any pink giraffes?"

I had to laugh. "Absolutely not."

"But Mom," she protested. "You're depriving so many other kids of a great experience."

I stared at her, wondering when she'd started to sound so grown up.

"Don't look so serious," she teased. "I'm just kidding."

I locked eyes with Arddhu. "What have you been teaching her?"

"Not him, me," Kevin answered. As we all turned toward him, he looked back at us in bewilderment. "What? *Somebody* had to explain humor to her."

Putting it that way, of course it made sense. Kevin's sense of humor was fully functional, while Arddhu's was... well, it was a work in progress.

"I need to get back to work." I shook my head and finished my food.

"It doesn't have to be finished today," the Morrigan said.

"I know. I just want to get the basics out of the way. Tomorrow I'll work on details."

"Mom, don't make yourself sick," Bree admonished.

"I won't." I gave her a hug and went to my suite, where I got back on the internet and brushed up on wildlife, to make sure I got it right.

Then, I went back to work: smaller fish in the creeks and rivers, bigger ones in the lakes and seas. Deer, antelope, moose, elk, buffalo, reindeer. Birds of all kinds, from hummingbirds to eagles and everything in between. Foxes, coyotes, and wolves. Elephants, giraffes, and hippos. Insects and lizards.

I even made sure I included the necessary predators to keep everything balanced.

But not too many of anything, just a few to start with. They'd reproduce on their own, but at a measured rate.

By then, the sun was setting and I was hungry again. Time to call it a day.

It took another three days of work for me to feel like the realm was ready for my family to see. I couldn't help but grin as I remembered the old Hebrew creation myth of Yahweh creating the world in six days.

I'd created a mini-world in five.

But as I opened the portal for the look-see, I was nervous. I'd gone to the realm myself a few times to tweak something or other, but this was The Big Reveal. What if I'd forgotten something crucial, or included something stupid? What if I lost the respect of my family?

As it turned out, I needn't have worried.

With Bree's hand in mine, I waved Arddhu, Kevin, and the Morrigan through the portal and followed, then stood anxiously waiting for their reactions.

For this trip, I'd chosen to show them early summer in southern Ireland. But it was as it'd been centuries ago: large tracts of thick forest, abundant wildlife, and warm breezes. No pollution, rising sea levels, telephone or power poles, or trash blowing around.

Just a pristine and natural landscape.

Arddhu gazed around in wonder, absolutely speechless.

"Wow, Dee," Kevin breathed. "This is *amazing*."

"I never thought I'd see this again." The Morrigan's eyes were misty. "This is almost exactly how I remember Eire as she was, over five thousand years ago."

Holy shit. I'd actually gotten it right?

I let Bree go so she could explore, and she headed straight for the lush meadow of wildflowers, so unlike what we had at The Hacienda.

Arddhu stepped close, took my hands in his, and kissed me softly. "This is a wondrous place. You have done very well."

I could've burst with happiness. "Wait until you see the rest. There are mountains and beaches, forests and deserts. Trees and plants. All the things of Earth. Except for anything toxic to humans or animals."

Kevin frowned. "But without natural predators, the insects will take over."

"I didn't say there weren't any predators. There are lots of them for every level of life. There's just nothing toxic."

The Morrigan stared up at the blue sky thoughtfully. "What will the weather be like?"

"It'll rain and snow here, but not too much. No flooding, no snow squalls. No hurricanes, tornadoes, or earthquakes. Nothing extreme."

"Paradise," Kevin murmured.

I nodded. "As much as I could make it so, yes."

"Mom, look what I found." Bree ran to me, holding a pretty blue flower with a small bug on it.

"That's a ladybug." I smiled at her. We didn't have many of those in the desert.

"Ladybug," she repeated, and quietly studied the tiny red thing with the black dots. Within a moment, it flew off, and she smiled. "She can fly."

"Yes, she can," I confirmed.

Bree flapped her arms, and rose up into the air. "I can fly, too," she said.

"Bree, no." I grabbed her before she could get too high. "No flying until you're older."

Immediately, she killed her power, and I settled her back onto her feet. "Sorry, Mom," she murmured, eyes averted.

Shit. I hated to keep her from using her power for fun, but until this threat was over and I had more time to spend with her, I just didn't want to take any unnecessary chances that she could get hurt.

I changed the subject with a brighter tone. "So, everyone, what should we call this place? New Earth? Terra? Gaia?"

"New Earth seems... clumsy," Kevin said.

"And Terra is just Latin for Earth," the Morrigan said. "So it's not very original."

"The same is true of Gaia," Arddhu said. "It simply means Earth in Greek."

So much for my ideas.

"What about..." Bree had been deep in thought and now spoke hesitatingly. "Tearmann."

"Ta-ra-man?" I frowned, trying to figure out how my girl had come up with such an obscure name.

Bree nodded, but it was the Morrigan who replied.

"That's *sanctuary* in Irish Gaelic." She stared at Bree with wide eyes.

Wait. How the hell did Bree know Irish Gaelic?

"Where did you hear that word?" I asked her.

She shrugged. "It just popped into my head."

There was absolutely no way a little girl could think of such a word by herself. Well, not a *normal* little girl, anyway.

Arddhu didn't seem too surprised. He gently stroked Bree's cheek with his fingertips. "That is a wonderful name, Bree. Thank you for suggesting it."

Oh, my heart. How she beamed at him.

It reminded me not to be too hard on her. She was remarkable, and deserved to be treated as such. I hugged her, kissed the top of her head, and said, "Well, my vote is for Tearmann."

Arddhu nodded. "Mine as well."

"Mine too." Kevin said.

"And mine," the Morrigan added.

"There we have it," I said, smiling at Bree. "Tearmann it is."

Bree was ecstatic she'd been the one to name the new realm.

"So, what do you think?" I asked everyone. "Is the place good enough to show to the project team?"

"I don't see why not," Kevin said. "I mean, if the rest of the zones are as perfect as this one, they should be knocked on their asses."

"Well, I don't know if I'd call them perfect," I said. "But yeah, I tried to do my best on everything."

"I think they will be very impressed," Arddhu said.

"And if they're not," the Morrigan said with a menacing grin, "tell them to come see me."

Bree hugged my legs and looked up at me. "Mom, they'll love it as much as we do."

Warmth spread through me at my family's approval, followed by a flush of confidence.

I'd nailed it.

We returned to The Hacienda, and I made the call to John Simmons to let him know the sanctuary realm was ready for their tour. We set up the appointment for ten the next morning.

"Uh... how do we get to this realm?" he asked.

The easiest way would be for me to port to where they were and open a portal. "Is there someplace you can get everyone together? Someplace outside, I mean."

"Let's see... hmm... okay, I think I got it. Rock Creek Park, just outside the main entrance. It's just a couple miles north of the White House."

"Okay, I'll meet you there and open a portal to the realm."

With the details worked out, we ended the call.

Kevin eyed me. "You want one of us to come with you?"

"Nah." I shook my head. "I'll be fine."

For the official project team's visit of the sanctuary realm, I didn't wear armor or a Goddess gown, just my normal shorts and tee shirt. I did make sure I glowed a bit, though. Just so they wouldn't forget I wasn't human.

At five minutes to ten in the morning, I ported to the main entrance at Rock Creek Park in Washington, DC.

The team was already there waiting, but the place was otherwise deserted.

As was the president and several Secret Service agents.

Shit.

I hadn't planned on him joining us this time. Now I was even more nervous.

Glancing around, I didn't see Burns or Cox, but I did see Simmons, with only five other team members. Where were the rest?

"Morning," I greeted him. "Is everyone here and ready?"

Simmons nodded. "We're keeping it small for this visit."

"Oh. Okay." I took a deep breath and opened a portal to Tearmann.

The large circle shimmered in the air, with my chosen zone of the mid–Atlantic United States visible beyond.

A few gasps and oohs from the group, but no questions.

I turned to Simmons. "Who's going through first?"

"I will," he said. He approached the portal, then stopped and turned. "What do I do now?"

"Just step through, like a doorway."

He followed my instruction without further hesitation.

The rest of the team were next, until only the president, his security team, and I were left.

"Sir, there's no danger," I assured him.

"It's not that," he murmured. And then I realized why he'd hung back: he was absolutely fascinated with the portal. He stared at the shimmering circle with eyes wide in wonder. "I've never seen anything like this in my life." He turned toward me. "You can go anywhere like this, can't you?"

"Pretty much. Well, except for space or another planet. But yeah, anywhere on Earth."

"Amazing," he murmured. He grinned at his security team. "Let's go, guys. We're actually going to visit another realm."

The first two agents went through, followed by the president. The last two agents motioned for me to go, then followed me.

"I'm just going to close this so nobody else gets nosy," I said, and closed the portal.

Simmons and the project team hadn't gone far.

A couple of them stood nearby, staring around at the scenery or up at the sky. The warm, gentle breeze played with their hair and neckties. Others had walked as far as the top of the nearby hill and turned in a slow circle, taking it all in.

"There are mountains way over there," one said. "I can't believe I can see them from here. The air is so clean, so fresh. It's unbelievable."

Simmons stood among the lush grasses, staring at the ocean in the near distance. "Is that... is that the Atlantic?"

I joined him. "Technically, no. But it's modeled on the Atlantic."

"Everything looks so... pristine. So unspoiled." His voice held more than a touch of awe.

"Yeah. I basically created zones of Earth as they would've been about five thousand years ago."

"Before industrialization," Simmons said, as he watched a small herd of horses run along the beach.

"Yeah."

"Five thousand years ago," the president echoed as he joined us. "So if your planetary shield doesn't work, you expect us to go back to living in the Stone Age." It wasn't a question.

I blinked at him.

When he put it *that* way...

Then I got pissed.

"Look. I'm the Goddess of Earth. I'm not a miracle worker. I can't duplicate cell phone towers and power plants. And to be honest, that's not what Tearmann is all about anyway. It's more of a peaceful, safe place for humans to escape disaster, should it come to that."

He stared at me. "*Ta-ra-man?* Is that what you're calling this place?"

"Yes. It means *sanctuary* in Irish Gaelic. My—uh, my daughter named it."

Now his gaze flicked to my flat belly for a moment, and he frowned. "You had your baby already?"

"Yes. She was born on Beltaine. Um, May first."

"So she's a little over two weeks old, yet she named this place you built. Using Irish Gaelic." His biting sarcasm made me even more pissed.

"It's complicated. She's a divine child, so she's more like around three or four years old now."

"I... see." He shook his head. "Whatever. Back to this place. This Tara-man." He glanced around. "How big is this realm?"

"Big enough to hold the population of Earth. I've created different climate zones, so there's desert, mountain, forest, beach, everything that Earth has."

He nodded. "And this is my territory?"

"Your territory?" I echoed.

"Yes. Is this what would be considered the United States?"

What the... no, I hadn't made any boundaries. Nothing separated any territories for any country on Earth. And I was quickly losing my patience with him, president or not.

"No. There are no territories. It's all just one realm."

He shook his head again. "You really expect everyone on Earth to get along all mixed together here, when we can't even peacefully exist within our own damn neighborhoods?"

I couldn't help it. I was snippy with my reply. "I would hope humans would be thankful that someone had provided a sanctuary for them to survive a potential disaster, and would manage to get along for the greater good."

"Very disappointing, Ms. Connor." His tone was one of thorough disgust. "I've seen enough. Open the damn door so I can get the hell out of here."

Without waiting for a reply, he turned away and gestured to the agents to follow him.

I clenched my jaw and opened the portal without a word, and watched as he and his security detail stepped through.

The project team stayed where they were, enjoying the healthy tranquility.

"What an asshole," I muttered.

"You can't take it personally." Simmons briefly rested a hand on my shoulder. "It's tough for some people to realize they're not as powerful as they thought they were. He's a good guy, but he's been shaken to the core, seeing the power you command. And what you can do with it."

"Did he think I was making it all up? That I'm the Goddess of Earth? Of course I have power." I took a deep breath and slowly released it, to calm myself.

Simmons gestured at our surroundings. "For what it's worth, what you've done here is... well, nothing short of amazing." He paused before continuing. "If you could add some infrastructure, I'm sure he'd appreciate it. It's probably what surprised him the most—how beautiful our world was before we humans made such a mess of it."

"Infrastructure," I repeated.

He nodded. "Roads, bridges, that sort of thing."

He was being surprisingly helpful, and I began to better appreciate his insight.

"Thanks." I flashed a grateful smile. "I'll get to work on bringing Tearmann into this century without losing its... purity."

He nodded, and we turned toward the portal.

"C'mon, everyone," he called. "Let's get back." To me, he said, "By the way, congratulations on the birth of your daughter. First kid?"

"Yeah. Equal parts exhilarating and terrifying."

"That's normal. I have three boys and a girl. The oldest is almost a teenager. You're in for a real rollercoaster ride, and that's with a normal kid." He shook his head. "I can't even imagine one that goes from newborn to three or so in only two weeks."

"It's been a challenge," I admitted. "And she has magickal power of her own. Last week, I had a giant pink stuffed giraffe stomping through my backyard."

"Seriously?" His gaze was sharp.

"Oh yes. *Very* seriously. After it fell into the swimming pool and got itself out, it munched on the mesquite trees."

He stared at me for a moment, and we both burst out laughing. As absurd as that story probably sounded to him, it was even more absurd that it'd actually happened.

He shook his head again. "I think I'll count myself damn lucky I have normal kids."

By now, the other team members had already gone through the portal.

He turned for a final look around and one last deep breath of the pristine air. "It really is beautiful. I wish it could stay just like this."

"Tell you what. I'll hide the infrastructure as much as possible."

He smiled at me. "Sounds great."

We stepped through and I closed the portal. After a final goodbye, I ported home to The Hacienda.

The house was quiet, but a moment later my mobile phone rang. The caller ID showed it was the OB/GYN's office, and I immediately felt guilty for not calling them to let them know I'd already given birth.

"Ms. Connor, you missed your appointment earlier this week," the caller said.

Oops. I'd completely forgotten about it. Now, of course, it was pointless to reschedule it.

"Ms. Connor, is everything all right?"

"Sorry. Yes, everything's fine. Please let the doctor know I had the baby several days ago, and both she and I are fine. I won't need any more appointments."

A brief pause, then she asked, "You're—are you sure?"

"Absolutely sure." We ended the call, and I put it out of my mind.

Wondering where everyone was, I sent out a probe.

Kevin was in the VIP tent with Kali again, for more computer lessons. The Morrigan and Reshep were outside, enjoying the swimming pool. Bree was in the home office with Arddhu, since it was his turn with her lessons.

We'd each agreed to take a subject or two and teach Bree, in lieu of sending her to human school. Arddhu taught history, Kevin taught science and math, and the Morrigan taught reading, language, and literature. Since I didn't have a specialty other than accounting, I helped her with writing and penmanship.

Soon, she'd begin magick lessons, which we'd all take part in.

Right now, I didn't want to interrupt her lessons, but I was too restless to relax, so I decided to get comfortable in the living room and start brainstorming the shield to protect Earth from the asteroid.

How close should it be to the planet's surface? If it was in the upper atmosphere, it might have a better chance of slowing down the asteroid to lessen its impact should the shield fail to stop it completely. But I couldn't put it too far out into space, given my limitations as Goddess of Earth.

Wait. What about all the satellites in orbit? Would they still work if the shield was above them? Or below?

How thick would the shield have to be in order to stop the asteroid? If it was too thick, it could obscure the sun's light, which would impact crops and a whole host of other issues. But if it was too thin, it might not give enough protection.

Shit. I needed more information. A lot more.

Maybe Cox could help.

I called the number on his card, but it went straight to voicemail.

"Um, hi," I recorded. "This is Dee Connor. I'm in the planning stages for the planetary shield, but I have some questions. Technical questions, I mean—"

A click, then: "Ms. Connor, this is Bob Burns. Frank is away from his phone at the moment. Can I help you?"

Maybe. I'd really wanted Cox's NASA expertise, but Burns was on the planetary defense team too, so he might know.

"I hope so. I need to know where I should place the shield so it doesn't interfere with the satellites in orbit."

A pause. "Tell me again about this shield."

"Think of it like a force field around the planet. It won't need any traditional sources of power or anything like that, I'll power it with Earth energy. And if—or when—the asteroid hits the shield, it should just burn to ash, so there won't be any fragments to worry about."

"Ash, huh? You sure about that?"

No, but I wasn't going to tell him that.

"Yeah. So what are the highest and lowest altitudes of the satellites?"

"I'm afraid that's classified information, Ms. Connor."

Shit. "I don't need to know any specifics. Just in general."

"It's still classified. Some of those satellites are black ops. And I shouldn't even have told you that much."

"But I don't need to know what they're doing, just where I can put the shield."

"No."

This was infuriating, and I lost my patience. "Then I can't guarantee they'll still work after I put the shield in place."

"They'd better, or the president will have my hide. And yours, too."

"Look. If I put it too high, it'll probably affect some satellites. If I put it too low, it'll probably affect some other satellites. Pick one, because I won't be the goat on this."

"Fine." He sighed. "I'll get back to you." The line clicked.

What an asshole.

In the meantime, I could at least start working on a prototype. I needed to figure out the shield composition, anyway.

I ported out to an empty patch on my property, far beyond Kali's guest house. Then I created a round object about the size of a basketball and set it to hover several feet off the ground. I enclosed it in a thin protective shield, roughly two inches from the object's surface.

Not exactly the scientific method, but it'd do for a first attempt.

It took me a moment to find a small rock, sort of in proportion to the object I'd created. Boosting my strength, I hurled it at the fake planet.

The rock bounced off and landed a bit too close to my right foot.

Which certainly wasn't the result I wanted.

I adjusted the shield's thickness and position from the object's surface and tried again. This time the rock exploded, showering me with dust and tiny fragments.

Again, not what I wanted.

It took an unknown number of attempts, tweaking the shield over and over, until the rock finally burned to ash on contact.

Good thing, too, because I'd almost run out of suitable rocks in the immediate area.

I retrieved a notebook and pen from my pocket universe, and wrote down the successful combination so I wouldn't forget it. Then I headed back inside to share the news.

Bree had moved on from her history lessons with Arddhu, and was now with Kevin in the home office. I entered the room and stopped, not quite believing my eyes.

My little girl had grown since the last time I'd seen her, about twelve hours prior. Now, she appeared to be about five years old.

"Hi, Mom." She smiled. "Daddy Kevin's showing me how to use the internet."

We'd gone from Mama to Mom already. I raised a brow at Kevin. "No porn."

"What's porn?" she asked.

"Something for when you're older," Kevin smoothly replied.

She grimaced. "You guys always say that. I *am* older."

Oh gods. She sounded like a teenager.

"Well, you have to be a *lot* older," I insisted.

"Yes, Mom."

Kevin and I shared an amused glance, then I changed the subject. "I started testing the planetary shield theory. Just on a small scale. Very small, actually. Anyway, it took a while but I finally got the rock to burn to ash on contact."

"So you proved the theory," he said. "That's great news. What's next?"

"Well, I have to wait for NASA to get back with me on the information I asked for. But in the meantime, I could probably do some larger-scale tests, just to make sure the theory still works."

"It'll work, Mom." Bree's gaze fixed on mine with utter seriousness. "Trust me."

How could she be so confident? I sure as hell wasn't.

"I do trust you." I bent and kissed the top of her head. Her hair smelled like coconut, her favorite shampoo. "I just need to practice a bit. To make sure I don't screw this up."

Again, she met my gaze. "You won't."

I couldn't shake the feeling that she knew something I didn't.

Kevin and I shared another glance. "Do you have visions, honey?" I asked Bree. "Is that how you know?"

She frowned and looked away. "Not really. I mean, I don't *see* anything. It's just a feeling." She paused before adding, "A really strong feeling."

Interesting.

I smiled at her. "I love you, sweet girl." Shit. I'd sounded just like Maggie.

Bree grinned. "I love you too, Mom."

"*Deirdre? Where are you?*" Arddhu asked on our mental communication link.

"*In the home office, with Kevin and Bree. Is everything okay?*"

"*Yes. I am in the living room and wish to speak with you.*"

"*Be right there.*"

To Kevin and Bree, I said, "Arddhu is back and wants to talk. Probably about the Wild Hunt." I turned to leave.

"I want to go, too," Bree said.

"Go where?"

"On the Hunt with Daddy Arddhu."

Like hell she would. "I don't think that's a good idea."

"Why not? He says it's not dangerous. At least not for me. Only for humans. I want to go."

"Not this time."

"You never let me do *anything* fun," she complained. "I never get to go *anywhere*."

Shit. She sounded just like I did when I was about twelve.

"Go," Kevin said to me, then put his hand on her shoulder. "Honey, you're just too young for something like that. Let me explain more about what it really is."

I left him to it and went to the living room, where Arddhu waited on the couch. Compared to how giddy he'd been since beginning preparations for the Hunt, he seemed sad.

"What's up, my love?" I sat next to him.

He caressed my cheek gently. "I was thinking of how little of you I have seen lately." Now he took my hand and raised it to his lips. "And that we have not yet resumed relations after the birthing. Have you become tired of me already?"

Oh gods. I'd been so busy I hadn't even stopped to think about making love with either of my Consorts. And just to make sure he knew I wasn't giving Kevin preferential treatment, I decided to say so.

"Oh, my love, I could never tire of you. *Ever.* I am so sorry I've been neglecting you and Kevin. It hasn't been my intention. I've just been so busy—"

He interrupted me with a soft kiss that quickly turned passionate. I was just about to suggest we move to the bedroom when a cacophony of screams in my head made me flinch and pull away.

"What is wrong?" he asked.

I listened closely and pinpointed the source: Chile. An earthquake—a really big one—had just hit, and thousands of prayers flooded my mind.

"There's been a bad earthquake." I stood. "I'm so sorry. I have to go."

Arddhu sighed but nodded his head. "Go. We will talk later."

Guilt filled me as I ported to Chile, but then the chaos and tragedy wiped everything else from my mind.

CHAPTER TWENTY-SIX

H OURS LATER, I stood in the shower with my eyes closed and just let the hot water cascade over my filthy, exhausted body.

Scenes from the earthquake kept replaying in my mind, and I couldn't stop the tears.

So much destruction.

So much pain and suffering.

So much death.

I hadn't been able to save everyone. Hell, I hadn't even been able to *heal* everyone. There'd been thousands of people buried under the rubble of buildings, and I'd only been able to help the rescue crews find some of the battered bodies.

Aftershocks had shifted the piles of rubble, making them more unstable and pausing any further rescue efforts.

I couldn't help thinking maybe we'd passed the point of no return, and maybe it was already too late for humans to live safely on the planet.

Maybe the sanctuary realm was even more important than I'd thought.

Now, I slowly and methodically cleaned the dirt, blood, and soot from my skin.

But it couldn't clean the guilt and disappointment from my heart and soul.

When I left my suite, Kevin and Bree were in the living room, watching a superhero movie on the big screen. Brianna was busy in the kitchen, making dinner. Arddhu was probably off-world again.

As soon as Bree saw me, she came to me and hugged me.

"Mom." Her voice was muffled against my chest, and I frowned. When had she grown so tall?

"You were gone a long time," she added.

"Yeah." I rubbed her back and smoothed her hair. "It was... pretty bad."

Kevin had shut off the television.

After a moment, Bree said, "It wasn't your fault. You did what you could."

I closed my eyes, but the scenes replayed again. "I always knew I wouldn't be able to save every person every time, but that shit sure doesn't help me feel any better right now."

Now, Kevin's arms wrapped around us both, and I just stood there, drawing comfort from them both.

"Dinner will be ready shortly," Brianna softly called from the kitchen.

Bree pulled away and met my gaze. "I love you."

"I love you too, hon. Now go wash up for dinner."

She nodded and left, but Kevin didn't let me go.

"You look exhausted."

"I am exhausted." I glanced around. "Arddhu off-world again? And where's the Morrigan?"

"Yeah, he's finishing up his plans for the Hunt. The Morrigan's with Reshep in her room."

My stomach growled, loudly. "Oh man, I'm starving."

We sat at the granite island, then Bree came back and sat next to me.

As I ate, I remembered her complaint from earlier, that she never went anywhere or did anything fun. She'd been right, of course. I'd been so busy, I'd neglected her, too.

She'd heard me mention Ard na Mara, but hadn't been there yet. Maybe that'd be a nice little trip for just the two of us.

And I needed a little getaway after Chile.

"Bree, how'd you like to go to Ard na Mara tomorrow morning? Just the two of us."

She grinned. "Oh, yes, please. What should I pack?"

I smiled ruefully. "It'll only be for a few hours." Her grin slipped a bit, and it hurt me to see it. "Tell you what: after this asteroid thing is over, we'll all go someplace for a real vacation." I stopped myself from making it a promise, because who knew what would happen after the asteroid.

"It's okay, Mom. I know you're really busy right now. A short trip to Ard na Mara will be great."

Damn, how I loved this girl.

Smoke and ash. Screams of terror. Death and destruction.

I jerked awake, heart pounding and gasping.

Had it been my regular nightmare, or memories of Chile? At this point, I couldn't really tell.

I'd been so exhausted after dinner, I'd just gone to bed. But my sleep had been restless, and I'd decided to read for a while instead. There'd been a fantasy novel I'd been trying to read for weeks, so I'd snuggled in bed with my tablet, and promptly fell back asleep.

Now, I shook my head. At least I'd had a few hours of rest.

I joined Bree in the kitchen for a quick breakfast.

"Ready to go?" I asked.

She grinned and nodded.

I held her hand and ported us to Ard na Mara.

"That was fun," she said, looking around. "We could go anywhere like that, couldn't we?"

"Yeah." I squeezed her hand, then let it go.

We'd arrived in the late afternoon. The sun was bright overhead, in a beautiful blue cloudless sky. Although the temperature was much cooler than Arizona, it was warm for Ireland.

It was almost perfect.

Was it like this even when I wasn't here? Or was it only perfect as soon as I arrived? Maybe someday I'd find out exactly how I was affecting the weather here.

First, I showed her the cottage, including the cellar, where I explained how I'd become the Keeper.

"So it hurt when you got that?" She pointed at the bracelet on my arm.

"Yeah. But only for a few minutes."

Upstairs, she was suitably impressed with the grand furniture in my bedroom.

"It's just like you're a queen in a castle." She climbed onto my high bed.

"It's not a castle, it's just a cottage." I laughed, then grew serious. "But I haven't been to my palace yet, so who knows? It might be even more luxurious."

"Wait. You have a *palace*?" She stared at me, wide-eyed.

"Sure do. I inherited it from the last Goddess of Earth."

"Then why don't we live there?"

I shrugged. "I like The Hacienda and I love Arizona. It's where I've lived for most of my life. Long before all this," I said as I gestured at our surroundings. "C'mon, let's go down to the beach."

Instead of porting, we walked through the meadow and down the steep steps carved into the cliffside. At the bottom, she ran ahead of me on the path to the beach, between tall grasses and rocks. Once there, she kicked off her sandals and took a few steps into the surf.

"Ooh, it's cold."

"Yeah. The water's always cold here."

She stood ankle-deep for a moment, then took a few more steps.

"Be careful," I warned.

"I will." Then she glanced at me over her shoulder. "I know how to swim, though, so don't worry."

"Since when?" I hadn't taught her; I hadn't had the time. Maybe one of the others had.

"Since... since... forever. I don't know. I've just always known." She shrugged and splashed in the water with her feet, not looking at me.

Huh. That didn't make any sense at all, but I let it go for now.

Soon, probably next week, she'd start magick lessons. Each of us would take a turn and evaluate her natural abilities. Of course, we were all curious about what those natural abilities might be, but at a minimum she could probably do basic energy manipulation. If she'd inherited Arddhu's wild forest magick, he'd help her learn to work with it. Kevin and the Morrigan would teach her defensive magick—and later, when she was a little older, offensive magick too. I planned to work with her on healing, herbs and potions, and whatever else came up.

"Hey, want to see a really cool cave?" I asked.

"Sure." She skipped over to me, stopping on the way to pick up her sandals.

As we walked on the beach, I told her about the blue beads that sometimes washed ashore after storms, and showed her the one I wore on the cord around my neck. For the rest of the way, she was focused on finding an elusive tiny treasure for herself.

At the entrance to the Sanctuary, I formed a ball of light and set it loose to guide us into the dim interior.

"Whoa." Bree's voice echoed in the small chamber. "This is so cool."

"This is the Sanctuary. A safe place for any who come to it."

The phosphorescent veins in the walls and floor glowed, giving the cave an otherworldly feel. Bree studied the clean fire ring for a moment, then moved to the little pool and peered into its depths.

"Are there any fish in here?"

"I've never seen any. It's fresh water, fed from a spring."

"That's unusual, isn't it?" She leveled her serious gaze on me.

"Yeah, I think so."

"Did someone used to live here?" Bree's voice was hushed as she gazed at the hole above us, letting in natural light.

"No, but it's had visitors from time to time."

She sat on the same rock Maggie and I had used during my visit earlier in the year.

"Who's Maggie?"

I blinked at her. "She was the Keeper before me. And also a distant relation."

Bree lightly ran her fingers over the rock surface beside her, frowning. "She's dead?"

"Yes." I took a couple of steps closer. "Why are you asking about her?"

Her gaze met mine again. "I feel her. I can even *smell* her. Cinnamon and vanilla, with a hint of some other spice. I'm not sure what."

"Nutmeg," I offered. We didn't use that spice much, so Bree couldn't know of it. But she'd nailed it; that was *exactly* how I remembered Maggie's essence. Either Maggie had left a bit of herself here at our last visit, or Bree could connect to the other side of the Veil.

My girl was coming into her powers quickly now.

I sat next to her and smoothed her hair. "Your magick is growing. Good thing we're starting your lessons soon."

She leaned against me. "Would Maggie have liked me?"

"Oh, she would've *adored* you. And you'd love her. She was a remarkable woman." I kissed the top of her head. "I'd like you to see another special place now. Ready to go?"

"I guess." She took a final look around. "It's really peaceful here."

"Yes, it is. It really is a sanctuary. Okay, here we go." I held her hand and ported us to the stone circle.

She slowly walked around the outside, gently tracing the symbols on the ancient stones as she went. "This is a very special place," she softly said.

"It's actually a portal. Back before I became the Goddess, this was how I used to travel between The Hacienda and Ard na Mara."

She nodded absently, still studying the stones. "Now you don't need a portal."

"Right." While she continued her way around the circle, I went to the Goddess Well on the other side of the clearing.

The crevices and creases in the stone held even more tiny poppets and tokens than the last time I'd been here. The tree nearby had many newer ribbons and fabric scraps tied onto its branches, and they fluttered in the breeze alongside the older, faded and tattered ones.

It only took a moment to answer all the prayers.

"Humans love you," Bree said from beside me, voice hushed in respect for her surroundings.

"Many do, yes. Seems like there are more of them every day." But there was also a growing contingent who hated me, and they were getting increasingly more vocal.

"Daddy Kevin says it's because you're popular on social media."

"Probably." I was sure those media interviews I'd done a few weeks ago had helped, too. "Are you hungry? Do you want some lunch?"

She side-eyed me. "Since when can you cook?"

My girl knew me well. "Not me, silly. I was thinking of us going to Finn's Cove."

She grinned. "Oh, yeah, let's go. I've heard so much about it."

"Really? From who?"

"*Everybody*." She rolled her eyes. "Daddy Kevin, Daddy Arddhu, and Aunt Morrigan."

Which pretty much *was* everybody, in her world. But that'd be changing soon, as she matured and her mind expanded.

We walked side by side on the path through the woods, and along the way she pointed to different plants and asked what they were. Some, of course, I knew; others I wasn't sure of, and wasn't afraid to say so.

"This is so different from home," she said. "It's so green. So lush."

"That's why I love it almost as much as home."

Donal's place was quiet. Not abandoned, just empty. Maybe they were still in Cork City? I knew Megan and the babies were doing fine, but maybe they'd decided to stay a bit longer since the twins had been born so early.

As we neared the bridge over the creek, Pete scrambled up the bank.

"Oh, Lady, I was hoping to see You. Oh." He'd taken off his hat and now stared at Bree, who was only a few inches taller than him. He was probably fascinated by her multicolored eyes, since they were so unique.

"Pete, I'd like you to meet my daughter, Brighid. Bree for short. Bree, this is Pete. He's a friend of ours."

"Pleased to meet you," Bree politely said.

"Very pleased to meet *you*, milady." Pete looked at me. "She's a beauty just like You, Lady."

"That's sweet of you to say." I smiled and squatted down to his level. "I haven't seen you for a long time. Is everything okay?"

"Oh yes, Lady. Everything is fine. We were off visiting Petunia's family. And she's carrying twins, so I'll bet we're going to have a big family."

He was almost bursting with pride, and I couldn't help but grin in response. "That's wonderful news. Congratulations to you both."

He gazed out at the trees wistfully. "Someday, I hope this forest is filled with my kind, once again." Then he looked at me again. "Which reminds me, could I ask if You've had a chance to speak with the Túatha yet?"

"I sure have, and the Dagda himself gave his word that he and his people will never hurt anyone again. To be honest, a lot of them don't even want to come back here—to Ireland, I mean—and they've also found other things to occupy their time. The world changed while they were gone, and they understand they need to change, too."

He nodded. "I've seen them all over the internet, with their cooking shows and what-not. They're very popular. As are You, too."

"You have the internet?" Bree asked.

Pete grinned. "It's even high-speed."

"Did you take classes with Daddy Kevin?"

Pete blinked. "Um, no. I learned at the library right here in Finn's Cove."

"Libraries are good places to learn, too, I guess," she admitted.

Pete just stared at her, and I wondered what he was thinking.

I changed the subject. "We were just on our way to Garrett's. This is Bree's first trip here."

"I'll not keep You then." He started to bow, then snapped his fingers. "Och, I almost forgot again. Have You decided on Your boon?"

Shit. I'd completely forgotten about those boons he'd offered Mike, Kevin, and me after we'd given him and Petunia an impromptu wedding ceremony last year.

"No, I'm sorry." I just had to ask. "Did Mike ever name his?"

Pete nodded. "Last year. Before... well, before."

He didn't elaborate, and I didn't feel it was proper to ask, so instead I asked, "What about Kevin?"

"No, Lady. I owe him as well."

"I'll let him know. And I'll try to think of something. Will we see you on our way back?"

"Yes, Lady, I'll be here." He bowed to me and nodded to Bree, then turned and scrambled away.

Bree peered into the shadows under the bridge. "Does he actually live under there?"

"No. It's a portal to his world."

"Oh, cool." We continued over the bridge and along the path for a few minutes. She glanced over her shoulder, then asked in a quiet voice, "What is he?"

"He's a troll."

"Wait." She stared at me. "I just met a real, live internet troll?"

I had to bite my lip to keep from laughing. "No, Pete's a *real* troll. The ones on the internet are just mean humans. I'm not really sure why they're called trolls."

"Oh." After a few more minutes, she asked, "What's a boon?"

"It's another word for a favor. Last year, Kevin and I helped him marry another troll named Petunia. So in return, he offered each of us a boon."

A few minutes later, she asked, "Who's Mike?"

She hadn't missed a bit of the conversation.

But... how much to tell? How little?

I decided to stick with the basics.

"He used to be my Assistant when I was the Keeper, back before I became the Goddess. But he—he betrayed me to my enemies."

She gazed up at me. "Did you kill him?"

Her question didn't surprise me. "Yes."

"Good." Just before she turned away, I caught a glimpse of a cold, hard set to her eyes and mouth.

Shit. She was quickly maturing, and I'd bet she'd be a fierce warrior.

Gods, how I loved her, and the woman she was becoming.

Hmm. Should I ask Kurt to train her on weapons, like he'd trained me? Or would that be overkill? On the other hand, both the Morrigan and Kevin were formidable with weapons, so she'd get a good foundation with them.

By now, we'd reached the road that led to Finn's Cove proper, with the harbor and the ocean beyond.

"Oh, that's really pretty," Bree said.

"It almost takes my breath away, each time I see it."

"It's such a quaint little village, too. So picturesque."

Damn. Her vocabulary was increasing exponentially, and she was growing up even as I watched.

At the pub, we chose a table not far from the door to the kitchen, and when Garrett came by, I introduced him to Bree. He seemed to have no trouble focusing intently on her strange eyes.

Then again, he was Túatha, so he was familiar with the even more bizarre eyes of the Dagda, with their numerous pupils and multi-ringed irises.

"Brighid, is it?" He'd pronounced her name the Irish Gaelic way, as *Breed.* "'Tis a fine name, for a fine lady. Welcome to Finn's Cove and my fine establishment, daughter of Deirdre."

She grinned at me as he left. "He's nice."

"Yes, he is."

A moment later, he was back with our drinks: for Bree, a non-alcoholic cider and for me, a pint of Litha Lager. One sip, and I tasted the bright sun, lazy warm days and tepid nights, and all the best things from the height of summer.

"Here y'go, today's special," he said as he placed two plates on the table. "It's new. It's called a Reuben sandwich."

It might've been new for Garrett's Pub, but it was practically a staple at every Irish pub back in the States, something I certainly didn't mention.

But to his credit, the ones I'd had in the States weren't anything like this.

Thin slices of lean corned beef topped with farm-fresh cheese melted to perfection, crispy sauerkraut, and coarse-ground mustard were stuffed between thick slices of hearty fresh-baked rye bread that'd been lightly and perfectly toasted. My sandwich had been cut in half, but Bree's was in quarters. Colorful little frill-topped toothpicks held each section together.

Alongside the sandwiches were fresh-made fries.

"This looks delicious," I said, just as my stomach growled.

"Enjoy." He smiled and left to tend the other customers.

Bree wolfed her food, which told me she'd been more hungry than she'd let on.

"Pretty good, huh?" I asked, between bites.

"*Really* good," she agreed, moving on to her fries. "So, what're you going to tell Pete you want for your boon?"

Good question.

From what I remembered, troll magick was limited. Just like the fairies and nature sprites, trolls had a special connection with nature. They could work with elementals and had the gift of illusion. And, of course, they could grow in size and strength when threatened. But none of that helped me.

When it came right down to it, Pete couldn't give me what I really wanted: an end to worldwide suffering, a healed Earth, or for the asteroid to disappear.

I shook my head. "There isn't a damn thing he can give me that I want."

She chewed on a couple of fries thoughtfully. "Maybe... instead of thinking of what he can *give* to you, think of something he can *do* for you. Like, have him help evacuate all the other trolls to Tearmann."

"That's actually... " I stared at her as I thought it through. "A great idea."

She grinned.

When did she get so damned smart?

A moment later, Garrett came to clear away our dishes. He asked her, "Well, what did you think of your lunch?"

"It was very good. You're a really good cook."

"Thank you." He smiled warmly. "And the cider?"

Her eyes unfocused, became distant. "It made me think of summer. Sunshine and happiness. Puppies playing and kids climbing trees." She blinked, then cocked her head. "It was... magickal."

Garrett and I shared a glance, then he bowed his head. "Thank you, Brighid, daughter of Deirdre."

She excused herself to use the restroom, and he abruptly sat in the empty chair beside me.

"Och, that one's the spittin' image of You. Smart and charming, too. You'll have Your hands full when the boys start calling."

I smiled ruefully. "At this rate, that'll probably only be a couple of weeks from now. She's maturing at an alarming rate. She's not even three weeks old."

He whistled quietly. "Three *weeks*? Well, that's a divine birth for ye, unpredictable. In fact, goddesses have sometimes popped out full-grown adults."

"Unpredictable is right," I said, and sighed. "Sometimes I think she's already a teenager. Or maybe even older, based on some of the stuff she says. She has remarkable insight." Or, they could be visions. We'd have to explore that a bit more.

"She's full to bursting with magick, that one."

I studied him. "You can sense it?"

"Oh, yes. And she'll be a very powerful goddess in her own right. Just You wait and see."

Bree returned from the restroom, and Garrett piled our empty plates together.

"Another round of drinks?" he asked.

"No, we should probably get going," I said. "Send the bill to Anthony?"

"Certainly." He nodded. "It was wonderful to see You again, Lady." He turned to Bree. "And it was a pleasure to meet you, Brighid, daughter of Deirdre."

"It was very nice to meet you, too."

As we left, I felt Garrett's gaze follow us.

Outside, we stood on the sidewalk for a moment, taking in the nearby harbor sights, sounds, and smells.

"I really like it here," she said. "You need to make a Finn's Cove on Tearmann."

Yes, I did. "You're absolutely right. And I will."

As we walked back, I couldn't help but notice the top of her head now was level with my shoulder. Had she really grown another few inches just since we'd arrived here? I shook my head. This was crazy.

We approached the bridge, and Pete appeared from beneath it.

"Well, Lady," he began, hat in hand. "Name Your boon."

I crouched down to his level. "There's an asteroid heading for us, and in a few weeks, Earth might take some really heavy damage. But I've created a sanctuary realm for everyone to escape to, and I'll be putting a shield around the planet, to try to save as much life and environment as possible." As I'd spoken, his eyes had grown wide and his hands had crumpled the brim of his hat anxiously. "When the time comes, I need you to lead all the trolls through a portal to Tearmann—the sanctuary realm. I'll let you know when it's time. But for now, you can't tell anyone. We don't want to cause a panic."

"I... see." He swallowed visibly, then lifted his chin a bit. "You can count on me, Lady."

I smiled. "Great. Thank you."

He frowned again. "What about the other magickal creatures?"

"Others? Oh you mean like fairies and sprites? We've got them covered." Daphne, Alana, and Ferris would take care of their own kind.

He shook his head. "No, Lady, I mean the brownies, kobolds, dwarves, gnomes, goblins, and such."

Shit. By now of course, I knew better than to be surprised that any of those legendary creatures truly existed. But naturally, I hadn't exactly included them in our plans.

"Is there any way you could take care of them, too?"

He nodded. "Of course. Each of our realms connects deep within the Earth. I'll use those pathways to gather everyone." Now he frowned again. "This sanctuary realm, Tearmann... will we have our underground realms there, too?"

Shit. No, I sure hadn't created anything like what he'd just described. I was ashamed to admit I hadn't even thought of it, but I had to own up to it.

"No, I didn't even know about your underground realms until just now. But there's still time. I'll make sure to add them."

He smiled, then. "Lady, thank You for placing Your trust in me. I'll make sure everyone is ready to leave when it's time."

"Thank you, Pete." After a moment's hesitation, I drew him to me in a quick hug. "I'll rest much easier now." I stood, and we farewelled each other.

Bree was uncharacteristically quiet on the way back to the cottage.

"You okay?" I asked.

"Yeah. Just thinking."

At Ard na Mara, I stood with her on the patio for a moment, and took a deep breath of the unique salty-sweet air.

Oh, yes. I'd definitely reproduce this, too, in the sanctuary realm. Someone might need its tranquility someday.

Maybe more than one someones.

"Ready to go home?" I smoothed Bree's hair of the breeze-tossed tangles.

Again, she nodded.

I took her hand and ported us back to The Hacienda, where she immediately hugged me, and I held her close for a long while.

"Thanks, Mom," she finally said. "I really liked that visit."

I smiled at her. "I'm glad. And I'll try to plan other short trips. Maybe some family trips, too."

Her smile seemed a bit sad. "It's okay. I know you're really busy. It can wait."

Not even a minute later, my mobile phone rang, and it was John Simmons from NASA.

"I have the information you requested," he said without preamble. "You might want to write this down. Your planetary shield needs to either be below three hundred kilometers, or above three hundred thirty thousand kilometers. Don't bother asking for any details, because I won't tell you any."

"That's good enough," I assured him. As he'd spoken, I'd pulled my notebook and pen from my pocket universe and jotted down those figures. "Thank you. I'll keep you posted on my progress."

The pieces were falling into place, and with this information I'd be able to scale the shield's distance to the fake planet, and hopefully get a more accurate experiment with some better results.

Then Arddhu and Kevin entered from outside, and we all moved to the living room.

"It was quiet while you were gone," Arddhu told me. Then he asked Bree, "How was Ard na Mara?"

"I really liked it. And I got to meet Pete and Garrett, too."

She spent a few minutes describing the visit, and for me, it reinforced the importance of adding Ard na Mara and Finn's Cove to Tearmann.

When she finished, I turned to Kevin. "By the way, Pete wants to know what your boon is."

"Did you tell him yours?"

"Yeah. And, he told me Mike asked for his last year."

He raised a brow. "That's interesting."

"I thought so, too."

He changed the subject. "What's next on the agenda?"

"First, some more work on Tearmann. Then, because Simmons called me back with the information I needed, I can get back to the experiments with the planetary shield prototype." I sighed. "I have some lost time to make up for."

"It is almost time for dinner," Arddhu said. "Why not take the rest of the day off and rest? Perhaps we could spend some time together."

Oh. That's right. We'd planned on making love, right before the Chilean earthquake had hit.

Shit. Had that been only yesterday? I was losing track.

"Sure," I smiled. "I'd love that."

His look made me warm and tingly all over.

"Are you guys talking about having sex?" Bree asked.

I blinked at her. What? How?

Just how the *hell* did she know about sex already?

No. It was way too soon for having *that* talk.

Wasn't it?

Kevin met my gaze with wide eyes and shook his head, as if to say *don't look at me, I didn't tell her about it.*

"Yes," Arddhu replied, very matter-of-fact. "Your mother and I will make love after dinner."

"Will you have another baby?" She didn't seem concerned, simply curious.

This time, Arddhu deferred to me to answer.

"Probably not just yet," I said. "Maybe later. After the asteroid."

"Oh. Yeah. That'd be smart." She nodded sagely.

"Who's hungry for dinner?" Brianna said, from the kitchen.

I hadn't even seen her enter.

"Me," Kevin said.

"Me too," Bree said.

I was still full from the sandwich at lunch, but I could probably have a few bites. Wait. "Where's the Morrigan?"

"She is resting in her room," Arddhu said. "She said she did not feel well."

That was weird. She never felt sick. "Did she say what was wrong?"

He shook his head. "I asked, but she would not tell me."

"Mom, you have to help her." Bree looked worried, which made me even more worried. What did she know?

"Go," Kevin said.

A moment later, I knocked on the Morrigan's door. "It's Dee. May I come in?"

"Sure." Her voice was muffled.

I entered the dim room and shut the door quietly behind me. My eyes adjusted quickly, but I still had a hard time discerning her form amid the bundle of covers on the bed.

I sat on the edge. "Arddhu said you're not feeling well. What can I do?"

"It's nothing," she mumbled. Slowly, she emerged from the covers and sat up, but I still couldn't see her well. That didn't make sense, because my enhanced vision usually worked better than this.

So I created a ball of soft, gentle light, and set it to hover nearby.

I gasped at the radical change in her appearance. She just sat there, motionless, as I studied her.

Her normal full, long dark hair was thin and dull, and now hung lifeless and grayish. Her cheeks were hollow, making her cheekbones even more prominent than usual. Her eyes had lost their luster, and the dark circles underneath looked like bruises against her extreme paleness. Her skin was dry and papery, with fine wrinkles where before had only been smoothness.

For the first time since I met her, she looked ancient.

I didn't bother asking for permission. I simply scanned her, seeking answers.

My heart ached as I realized the truth of what was before me.

She was fading away. It was the same fate of all deities who were no longer worshipped.

Now I noticed that her physical form was blurred around the edges. Her internal organs—especially her heart—were trying to compensate for the loss of vitality, but it was only a matter of time until they failed. She could even die before she fully faded away.

But I wouldn't let any of that happen. No fucking way.

"What can I do?" I asked again.

She smiled wryly and shrugged. "There's nothing you can do. I'm being forgotten. It had to happen eventually."

"Bullshit." I had another thought. "Does Reshep know about this?"

She shook her head. "No, I sent him home when I felt it coming on. I didn't want him to see me like this." Her indicated her body with one hand.

Shit. I didn't know exactly how I could reverse this, but I had to stop it from getting worse, at least.

"Here. Take some strength from me to tide you over until I can fix this." Again, without waiting for her consent, I grasped her hands and sent some of my essence into her.

Before I'd even sent enough to feel the loss of it, the effect on her was immediate and striking.

Her vitality returned, giving gloss and volume to her hair and shine to her eyes. The dark circles disappeared and her skin plumped up, turning a healthier shade of pale. Her physical form became solid once again.

"I feel much better," she said, voice stronger. "Thank you. But you know it's only temporary. It'll come back. You're only delaying the inevitable."

"Not if I can help it. I'll fix it."

"How? I know of nothing to help a deity who's been abandoned by their followers." She'd spoken the last with bitterness.

"I'm not sure yet. But I'll think of something. I promise."

She smiled, but it was sad. "Maybe it's just time for us old ones to move on."

"Nope. Never. Besides, you don't see Arddhu giving up, do you? Or the Æsir?"

She shook her head again, but didn't argue. "I am in your debt."

"Nah. There's no debt. Now c'mon, it's time for dinner. And there are some folks who've been worried about you."

I waited as she dressed, and then we returned to the living room. Bree threw her arms around the Morrigan and hugged her like she'd never let go. Then Arddhu and Kevin gathered around them in a group hug, and tears stung my eyes.

My family.

We sat at the table for dinner: a savory beef roast that Brianna had been slow-cooking for hours, complete with tender potatoes and carrots, and a splendid cabernet sauvignon.

"The three of us," Arddhu indicated himself, Kevin, and Bree, "have made a decision. "We will visit the palace tomorrow."

"But I need to get back to working on Tearmann and the shield."

"One more day won't make a difference at this point," Kevin said.

"It'll be a family trip," Bree said, repeating my earlier words to her. "We'll all go. You too, Auntie Morrigan."

"A family trip," Kevin echoed quietly, with a note of wonder in his voice.

From what he'd told me of his life over the long years, he hadn't ever had a real family. And although we couldn't be considered anything close to a traditional family, we loved each other all the same.

"Okay," I finally said. "You've all convinced me. Family trip to the palace tomorrow."

CHAPTER TWENTY-SEVEN

S O, AFTER A fantastic family breakfast of omelets the next morning, Arddhu opened a portal to Ida's old realm. Kevin, the Morrigan, Bree, and I went through, followed by Arddhu.

I didn't know what I'd expected, but it wasn't this.

This was a paradise.

The gardens were spectacular, filled with blooms of every color that delicately perfumed the air. Grand marble fountains were everywhere and ranged in style from graceful dolphins to a whimsical peeing boy. Trees laden with figs, pomegranates, apples, and other fruits were surrounded by shrubs neatly trimmed into intricate shapes.

Just beyond the gardens, a small lake sparkled invitingly in the bright sunlight. Further off in the distance, a blue-tinged mountain range rose high above a lush green plain dotted with yellow wildflowers.

I'd never seen anything like it.

Since he knew his way around, Arddhu led us through the gardens on the paved pathways. Everything was well maintained and probably required an entire team of gardeners to keep up such beauty, but not a single living person was in sight. The place seemed as deserted as Olympus had been.

We rounded a screen of tall cypress trees and I stopped in my tracks.

Ida's palace—mine, now—was no longer hidden from view.

I'd seen artists' renderings of the great palaces and temples of Greece and Rome, and this reminded me of those illustrations.

The palace sprawled across a low rise like a replica Parthenon. Tall columns lined the front and sides, and wide steps led to the massive entrance doors that gleamed golden in the sun. The entire façade was brilliant white marble, similar to the palaces I'd seen on Olympus.

"Wow," I breathed. "This is really something."

Arddhu smiled wryly. "Ida always demanded the very best."

"Where is everyone? These gardens can't maintain themselves."

"The servants should still be here," Arddhu said.

"They're probably hiding," Kevin said.

"Why?" The Morrigan asked. "They would've seen Arddhu by now and known all is well."

Bree was uncharacteristically subdued, and slipped her hand in mine as we mounted the steps. Arddhu barely pushed on one of the golden doors, and it swung open easily and soundlessly. Our footsteps echoed on the polished marble of the soaring atrium beyond.

The small pool in the center was spotless, which confirmed that staff was still around to take care of the place. But why hadn't anyone heard us and come to investigate? Where were the security guards?

I shook my head and continued exploring.

The atrium's open roof let in plenty of air and light. A massive, ancient tree shaded the pool when the sun was directly overhead. A fountain at the far end of the pool featured a serene young woman, nude except for an artistic drape of fabric across one shoulder. Water poured from the jug she held in both hands, and the cascade of the water seemed loud in the eerie silence.

In the shade of the roofed perimeter, several couches, chairs, and tables were arranged in intimate conversation groupings, accented by lush potted palms and flowering plants. The second story balcony surrounded all four sides of the atrium, with a balustrade of narrow columns, again in gleaming white marble.

"This way," Arddhu said, leading us toward the wide double doors opposite the entry.

This time, both doors swung open with his touch. Bree still hadn't let go of my hand, and we followed Arddhu into a lavish throne room with more white marble flooring and columns.

Half the walls were covered in colorful frescoes of dryads, naiads, and satyrs frolicking in meadows and forests. The rest had deep red velvet draperies tied with golden cords and tassels in an garish display of pretentiousness.

"My Lady," Arddhu called.

I turned toward his voice and frowned. He stood on the dais, behind a large golden throne with a plush red velvet seat. A smaller, otherwise identical throne was nearby.

With a graceful but formal flourish, he indicated I should sit on the larger throne.

Me? On a throne?

I laughed nervously. "What's going on?"

"It is customary," the Morrigan said.

"Traditional," Kevin added.

"Protocol," Arddhu said.

"Mom—Mother—Lady." Bree stammered at first, but now her voice became smooth and mature. She turned her serious gaze on me. "You must take Your throne."

The divinity in me responded to the divinity in her, and reacted with a flare of power and a muted glow.

Who was I to refuse?

I nodded to her, turned, and strode confidently to my throne. I pivoted to face the room and sat, as gracefully as if I'd done it a thousand times.

I expected Arddhu to sit on the other throne, but no. He stood to my left, and Kevin moved to stand on my right. The Morrigan walked to the smaller throne, then stood behind it.

It was almost as if it'd all been planned.

Or rehearsed.

Bree stood alone at the bottom of the dais, and although she was almost as tall as me now, she seemed so much smaller in that sea of white marble.

Wordlessly, holding my gaze, she began to kneel.

No. It didn't feel right.

"Brighid, take Your throne." My voice echoed in the room; it'd come out a bit louder than I'd expected.

Bree nodded solemnly, took the three steps to the other throne, and sat.

There. *That* was right.

Power thrummed through the floor, the walls, everywhere. I felt it through the soles of my feet.

Just as I opened my mouth to ask *now what*, people began streaming through the open doors.

No, not exactly *people*. True, some were human, but most were deity. Among so many strangers, I saw a few familiar faces: Reshep; all the Túatha, including Garrett; the Æsir and Loki; Kali; and even Ares and Athena. Some smiled, but most were respectfully serious, as if this were a formal occasion. In fact, many were dressed accordingly, in ceremonial armor or similar.

Thinking this was only going to be an informal visit, I'd worn my shorts and tee shirt. Then again, the rest of my family had worn casual clothing, too. But they weren't the center of attention like I was. And it made me feel overly self-conscious.

Six males and three females—all human—lined up and bowed before the dais. They wore matching clothing in light blue, tunics with pants or dresses with golden belts. Some held unfamiliar objects.

An elderly gentleman with bright silver hair and a deeply lined face came forward with one precise step.

"My Lady." His strong voice belied his age. "Goddess of Earth, Queen of Heaven, Divine Mother, Great Goddess of All, welcome home. Your throne has awaited You, as have we, Your humble servants." He gestured to the other humans, who stood with heads bowed. "We look forward to serving You." He stepped back into the line, and another man immediately came forward, bearing a shiny object on a red velvet cushion.

"My Lady, Your crown."

I stared at the thing in stunned silence. I hadn't expected a crown. Hell, I hadn't expected a throne, either.

But oh, was it beautiful. Golden vines were interwoven with finely crafted silver leaves and gem-encrusted flowers.

In the awkwardness of the moment, Arddhu took the crown. As he gently placed it on my head, its heavy burden was almost unbearable. But as it settled on my brow, it weighed nothing at all.

The man stepped back in the line, and another man came forward, this time with a smaller crown. Its design was similarly nature-based, and it, too, was gold, silver, and studded with gemstones.

The Morrigan placed it on Bree's head.

It fit her perfectly, just as mine fit me perfectly.

As if this had all been planned. Whatever *this* was.

Had everyone known about it except for me? It was almost like a surprise party, except on a much higher level.

Another of the palace servants—my new staff, I realized now—stepped forward. This one held a golden wand about three feet long. I accepted it with my right hand and stared in wonder at the terminator: a stunning replica of Earth worked in blue, green, and white glass.

The staff had apparently completed their official duties, and moved off to the right of the dais. Now, the multitude of deities formed an orderly line that looked suspiciously like it'd been rehearsed—but left room at the foot of the dais.

Arddhu and Kevin left their places beside me to descend the steps and to the front of the line. There, each took a knee and bowed his head.

First Arddhu, then Kevin spoke: "I hereby pledge my fealty to Deirdre Connor, Keeper of the Sphere and Goddess of Earth."

They rose, nodded solemnly to Bree, then returned to their places beside my throne. The Morrigan was next with the pledge, and I could only sit, speechless.

Fealty? Just what the *fuck* was going on here?

Anu replied to my unspoken question. "*This is Your coronation. It is protocol.*"

"*Why didn't anyone tell me about this?*"

"*If You had known, You wouldn't have come.*"

She was damn right about that. "*And why is this so important?*"

"*It is traditional for the Goddess to receive Her crown and wand as the formal acceptance of power and authority. And it is protocol for each deity within Your realm of influence to give their oath of loyalty to You.*"

My realm of influence? I gazed out at the sea of faces and realized for the first time just how big my realm really was.

"*Did you have a coronation?*" I asked her.

"*Yes. As did Ida.*"

So, this had been expected of me, and no one had even mentioned it. If I weren't sitting on a throne in front of a thousand deities, I'd show just how pissed I was.

The Túatha were the next to approach the dais, with the Dagda, Ogma, Lugh, and Manannan followed by others I didn't know by name or recognize. Each moved off to the left after giving his or her pledge.

After some time, the line began to dwindle, but then more deities poured through the open doors. Deities I'd never seen before or had known existed patiently waited their turn to vow their loyalty.

To me.

The thought left me gobsmacked.

Now I noticed many had brought gifts, which the palace staff placed to the right of the dais, where the pile soon grew to a small mountain.

This was madness.

Some of the deities didn't have a human form, or a knee or head to bend, but still somehow made their respect known.

Others couldn't form human speech, and instead made odd unintelligible noises as their vow. Somehow, I understood every word.

And yet, I was increasingly uncomfortable with this whole thing. From the beginning, I'd never wanted any of the trappings of being the Goddess. I'd only wanted to be myself, and left alone to do my job.

Now, Reshep approached the dais. His unfettered joy as he knelt and spoke his vow gave me pause.

One glance around the room told me he wasn't the only one so happy to do this, either.

Why?

"*You will see,*" Anu said. "*Be patient.*"

And now came the Asgardians. Odin. Thor. Frigg. And all the Æsir. Even Loki.

I was even more uncomfortable with these ancient gods bowing to me and swearing their loyalty. It made me feel like an imposter.

"*You are not an imposter,*" Anu said, with a touch of impatience. "*You are the Great Goddess of Earth and all her realms.*"

Loki had set aside his trademark sardonic grin and instead showed genuine respect as he approached, knelt, and swore loyalty.

Next were even more Túatha. Shit. Had every single one of them come? It sure looked like it.

After what seemed like hours, the last to come forward were Ares and Athena. Maybe they'd intended it that way, but it could've been bad luck.

Without hesitation, Ares knelt and spoke his oath clearly, with his deep voice echoing in the room despite the mass of bodies. Athena, too, knelt and gave her oath. When she rose, she met and held my gaze with profound respect. Then I saw the shimmer of unshed tears in her eyes, and was even more confused.

"*You must now rise, and speak as their Great Goddess,*" Anu prompted.

What the hell could I possibly say to all these deities, many of whom I'd never even met?

"*You will know,*" Anu assured me.

As I stood, I took a deep breath and slowly let it out. I didn't really know what I was going to say, but when I opened my mouth, the words flowed like a natural spring.

"I pray I am worthy of the loyalty each of you have sworn here today." Now, I met as many of their gazes as I could, including the palace staff. "In return, I swear to each and every one of you that I will fulfill all my duties with strength, wisdom, compassion, and honor. For as long as I live."

As if on cue, a chant began.

> Hail the Goddess.
> Hail the Queen.
> Hail the Mother.
>
> Hail the Daughter.
> Hail the Princess.
> Hail the Maiden.

Twice more the chant reverberated, then stopped abruptly.

A peal of thunder boomed overhead. On my left arm, Anu turned bright white, lighting up the entire throne room and shining on the faces of those nearby.

"*Move the wand to Your left hand,*" Anu instructed, and I complied. Immediately, the replica Earth on the scepter glowed. A moment later, something inside me shifted and fell into place.

Power rose in me, such great power as I'd never felt before. My skin tingled and I could almost feel every cell in my body. The power continued to grow until I thought I'd explode if I didn't set it free.

On pure instinct, I lifted the wand and pointed it at the large circle of flowers carved on the ceiling. Immense power flowed from me into the wand, then to the ceiling in a bright stream of pure energy. The ceiling glowed white for a moment, then a shower of light rained down onto everyone present.

Hands rose to meet the shimmering particles. Shouts of joy rang out here and there, as each deity absorbed the energy I'd released. As I watched, each of them began to glow just as I was. Arddhu, Kevin, and the Morrigan grinned like kids who'd just been given a puppy.

Even the humans—and the palace staff—glowed.

It was glorious.

And Bree... she glowed the brightest of all. Feeling my gaze on her, she turned toward me and grinned. Her multicolored eyes sparkled and shone.

Then it was over.

The energy stopped flowing from the wand, and the sparkles of light stopped falling. For a few more delightful moments, everyone continued to glow before finally fading.

The packed room seemed so much darker now.

Everyone began talking at once, so excited and happy and full of life.

"What happened?" I murmured.

"You gave all of us a bit of your power," Kevin said.

"And it revitalized us," the Morrigan added.

Brows raised, I met her gaze then studied her. She looked younger now, somehow.

She grinned and nodded. "You said you were going to fix it, and you did."

"*All* of us have been rejuvenated," Arddhu said. "I feel as I did when I was young." He, too, looked younger. More vibrant. More alive.

"*Unlike other deities, You are not affected by the nonexistence of worshippers*," Anu explained. "*By giving each deity a part of Your essence, none of them will ever fade away due to being forgotten by humans.*"

Oh.

Oh.

Finally, the pieces clicked into place.

I swallowed the lump in my throat and blinked away the tears. What a wonderful gift I'd given to my family and the others.

No wonder everyone was so giddy.

"*Yes, now You see*," Anu said.

"*Thank you for explaining it to me*," I told her.

A female staff member hesitantly approached the dais. "My Lady, all is ready for the feast."

"Feast?" I echoed.

"It is customary," the Morrigan said.

"Traditional," added Kevin.

"Protocol," Arddhu affirmed.

Of course it was.

Boosting my voice so it could be clearly heard above all the celebrating, I made the announcement. I had to smile at the cheers that followed.

Arddhu, Kevin, the Morrigan, and Bree joined me as we followed the staff member from the throne room. As everyone else fell in behind us, many continued to talk excitedly and I caught a few snippets of conversations.

"... I can't believe how good I feel..."

"... I haven't felt this alive in a thousand years..."

"... She was very generous with Her power..."

"... oh yes, very generous indeed..."

I didn't feel the loss of any of my power. On the contrary, I felt as if it'd been boosted. Maybe that'd been part of the magick of the whole thing?

A staff member led us through the atrium and to another set of double doors, which stood open. An enormous dining hall lay beyond, and as I entered, I looked around in wonder.

Sconces along the walls gave off plenty of light, and although they flickered like torchlight, there was no smoke. Curious, I probed one. It wasn't electric or gas: it was fueled by magick. Intrigued, I probed further and discovered the entire realm was powered by a deep reserve of magick.

Clever.

It hit me like a thunderbolt: I could do something just like this to power the infrastructure and amenities on Tearmann. It should be self-sustaining and limitless, especially since billions of people could be there for an indefinite period of time.

But that was for later. For now, there was this dining hall and the ensuing feast.

Long tables lined the perimeter of the room. Nearby, groups of chairs, couches, and pillows gave guests their choice for reclining or sitting. Naturally, a staff member guided me to the center of the head table, and my Consorts flanked me. Bree took the seat to Arddhu's left, and the Morrigan sat on Kevin's right. She motioned to Reshep to sit beside her, and I had to smile. After he took his seat, I leaned forward to meet his gaze.

"Welcome to the family," I said.

He blinked, then returned my smile. "Thank You."

Ares, Athena, and Kali sat at the nearest table, and I was glad to see they no longer harbored any resentment toward one another.

The Æsir and the Túatha filled the rest of the close spots, and I was impressed—and a little surprised—that no one argued or fought over position.

The staff bustled about, placing countless heavy platters heaped with every imaginable delicacy. A small army of additional staff filled golden goblets with mead, ale, or wine, according to each guest's preference. A harpist sat in the far corner and began playing.

"Mom, you did great," Bree said with a grin. "I'm so proud of you."

"Well, it's not like I knew what was going on. Thanks, guys, for not telling me."

"That was the whole point," Bree said.

"Oh really? So whose idea was this? Yours? Or yours, Arddhu? Maybe it was your idea, Kevin?"

"It was my idea," the Morrigan said.

I blinked at her.

She shrugged. "We all knew you had to do this, but we wouldn't be able to get you to agree. So we didn't ask."

"You're not wrong," I admitted. "Except for one thing: if you'd told me I'd be giving all of you this—this—rejuvenation thing, I would've said yes in a heartbeat."

"But we didn't actually know that part was going to happen," Bree said. "Not for sure."

"So everyone was in on it? Even you?" I asked her.

"Yep." She boldly met my gaze, as if daring me to criticize.

When did she get so mature? She was growing up so fast, she'd be an adult in another month. If even that.

"You know," Kevin began quietly. "You should relax and enjoy this moment. The Coronation of a Great Goddess is a once-in-a-thousand-lifetimes sort of thing. You can bitch at us later."

All true. Besides, what was done was done. "I wasn't really planning on bitching at any of you. I just want to say, for the record, how much I love each and every one of you."

"Gratitude to the Lady," the Morrigan said, and lifted her goblet in a toast. "I feel younger than I have in two thousand years."

"I am full of energy and power," Arddhu added, also raising his goblet. "As I haven't been in centuries."

"I, too, feel young and strong again," Reshep said.

"What about you?" I asked Kevin, who'd gone quiet.

He lifted his goblet. "The effects are different for me, since I'm younger than everybody else. But I feel like I could... run... for days." His sly grin told me he'd really meant *fuck*, and I shivered.

Bree had raised her goblet with the others, but I hadn't noticed what it'd been filled with. "I'm the youngest here, but I feel like I could fly to the moon and back."

I lifted my goblet in response to the rest of them. "To youth, vitality, energy, and power."

We all drank.

I took a moment and glanced around at the celebration taking place in the enormous room. The joy and positive energy was infectious. Everyone was getting along tremendously, as if all the petty disagreements and age-old arguments of these rival deities had been forgotten.

It was amazing.

And over the next several hours, we all stuffed ourselves with exquisite—and, in some cases, unusual—dishes, oohed and aahed at the agile gymnasts who performed, and laughed at the satirical bard's recitations.

I also took the time to surreptitiously study the ancient deities around me. Even though I strongly disliked pomp and ceremony, I clearly understood what this Coronation had meant to them. I'd also noticed they'd elevated me from Goddess of Earth to Great Goddess, and although I hadn't asked for that, apparently it was what they all needed.

But this title change also made me responsible for more than just the Earth and the humans.

I was also responsible for and accountable to each of these deities who'd pledged their loyalty to me. I saw it as a reciprocal relationship.

Then, it hit me: what a brilliant move this Coronation had been, both politically and strategically. After all, we'd need the help of every one of these deities in the coming weeks, when we had to move billions of people from Earth to Tearmann before the asteroid hit.

That fucking asteroid. I'd managed to not think about the damn thing for several hours, but it'd come creeping back into my thoughts.

I shook it off, putting it firmly out of my head so I could bask in the joy as the celebration continued on.

And continue it did, into the wee hours.

And for once, I didn't get tired. Not even a little bit.

CHAPTER TWENTY–EIGHT

S HORTLY AFTER THE feast concluded, we returned to The Hacienda. It was early in the morning yet; unlike Ireland, time at the palace seemed to be synched to that of Arizona. None of us were tired in the least, so Kevin and Bree went to the home office for her regularly-scheduled computer class, and the Morrigan and Reshep headed to her room for some alone time.

I started toward the window-wall to go outside and work on Tearmann—and possibly the planetary shield after that—but Arddhu stopped me.

"I have made a decision and wish to discuss it with you."

That sounded ominous. "Okay."

We sat on the couch in the living room.

"All is ready for the Wild Hunt, and I no longer feel the need to wait until the Solstice. Do I have your approval to conduct the Hunt earlier?"

"Of course. But I thought you said the energies on the Solstice were better for it?"

He smiled. "I am filled with so much vitality from the gift of your life-force, I no longer need the Solstice boost."

Oh.

"I'm really glad, then. Even though I had no idea what I was doing at the time."

He rested his forehead against mine. "Do you forgive us for not telling you ahead of time?"

"There's nothing to forgive." I kissed him softly. "I love you so much."

"And I truly and deeply love you." We kissed again, for a bit longer this time, then pulled away. "I will make the final inspection of my hounds and steeds, choose a date, and return later to advise you of my decision." He paused before continuing. "And perhaps, we could spend some time together."

After he left, I got comfortable on the patch of soft grass near the patio, and began making a few updates to Tearmann.

First, I created duplicates of Ard na Mara and Finn's Cove, in the zone that most resembled Ireland. I also scattered several blue glass beads on the beach. Maybe they'd bring a little brightness to whoever found them someday.

On a whim, I also created a duplicate of the Sanctuary cave. I made sure to include the bioluminescent rock that would make the walls and floor glow in the dark.

Next, I created several mini-realms connected by a warren of passageways under the surface for other magickal creatures, as Pete had mentioned.

Then, I set up a magick reservoir similar to the one I'd seen at the palace. I made it self-sustaining so it could generate virtually unlimited power.

Now it was ready for roads, buildings, and other infrastructure—but I needed to do a bit more internet research before I added all that.

I got up and stretched, then went out to where I'd created the first experiments for the planetary shield. I ditched the small Earth replica and made a new one, this time about the size of a small car. For a touch of realism, I colored it in browns, greens, and blues, with swishes of white for clouds. Then I made it rotate slowly a few feet above the ground, in as close to real Earth rotation as I could get. Next, I created the shield at a proportional thickness, consulted my notes from Simmons' call, and placed the shield a few inches from the globe's surface.

I stood a few yards away and studied my work.

The shield was transparent enough for me to see the fake planet rotating beneath it, but something didn't seem right.

Oh. Maybe the shield should rotate with the planet?

I made it so, then gathered a pile of rocks, each about the size of a baseball.

Using a precise power boost to replicate somewhat realistic velocity, I threw the first rock. It hit the shield and broke apart, sending hundreds of shards falling back to the desert soil.

I frowned. Why hadn't it turned to ash like in my last successful experiment? I'd used the same composition and thickness. Maybe it was the size difference?

I made a slight alteration to the thickness of the shield, got another rock, and tried again.

And got the same fucking result.

Shit. Not good.

Slowly, I walked around the fake planet and shield, studying every detail to figure out what was wrong.

Ah. It was the rotation. My old experiments hadn't used any rotation at all. Essentially, every rock I threw was at a moving target, and my calculations hadn't taken that into consideration.

I wiped the sweat from my face and neck and thought it through.

What if the shield didn't rotate with the planet? What if it just stayed in place, while the Earth rotated beneath?

But no, that wouldn't work. Since the planetary shield would get most of its power directly from Earth, the two had to be connected in multiple places. Those connections meant the shield would have to rotate with the planet.

Somehow, I had to make it work. I just needed to do more calculations.

"How's it going?" Kevin asked.

I'd been so engrossed in my thoughts, I hadn't even heard him approach.

"Not so good." I sighed. "The planetary rotation is causing the asteroid to break up instead of turn to ash."

"Hmm." He picked up one of the rocks and had a go. But just like mine, it broke apart. He stood quietly thinking for a moment, and I let him, since he was so much better with math and numbers than I was. He'd probably figure it out a lot quicker and easier than I would.

A moment later, he tried again, with a slightly different angle. This time the rock disintegrated into a fine, sand-like consistency that hung in the air for a moment before slowly drifting to the ground.

"How about that? Would that work?"

All the dust still hadn't fallen to the ground, but eventually it would because of gravity. In space, without gravity, asteroid dust would just float in place, surrounding the planet and obscuring sunlight.

"It depends. NASA isn't really sure yet about the angle that the asteroid will impact the planet. It could be straight-on, like I've been doing, or it could be at an angle, like you just did. But we won't know until it's too late to make any changes to the shield. So the shield needs to work for any impact angle." I sighed and pointed to the ground under the fake planet. "But there's the problem of the dust. A dust cloud would affect the climate, maybe even throw the planet into a mini ice age. So it's a no on the dust."

"Shit. I forgot about that."

We both grew quiet, thinking. And sweating in the brutal heat.

"You know, the firm might have some people who could help," he said. "They've been a fantastic resource for so many other things, I'd be very surprised if they didn't have experts on astronomy and physics, too."

Why did I keep forgetting about the firm? It was almost like a mental block, and it was so frustrating.

"Good idea. Let's get back to the house, and I'll check with Anthony."

He nodded, and we started back.

"I was wondering about something else," he said. "What happens if we don't stop the asteroid from breaking up into larger fragments? You said the shield will be powered by the Earth itself, so what if we just leave it in place indefinitely? That way, it'll keep the fragments from doing any harm."

"Not necessarily." I shook my head. "Those fragments could interfere with the orbits of the moon or other planets. Or, we could end up with an asteroid belt around the planet, which would cause problems with satellites and space programs. And then, it's possible one or two fragments could break out of orbit and wreak havoc. That'd be bad, too." I paused to walk around a creosote bush. "As for leaving the shield in place indefinitely, that's not a good idea, either. It'd take a helluva lot of energy, and might even drain the Earth completely."

"What if Earth was completely healed? Wouldn't it have enough energy to maintain the shield?"

"Not indefinitely. Besides, there's no way I can completely heal the planet in only a month. Even though the Túatha have been helping to boost my healing, we're still only about half done."

"And how much energy is Tearmann siphoning from you?"

He'd asked it casually, but I could feel his sharp gaze on me.

"None. It's completely self-sustaining."

He stopped walking. "What? How?"

"Everything runs off magickal energy stored in a reservoir. A generator recycles and replenishes the energy constantly, without any effort from me. Sure, I used a lot of energy in the beginning, when I first created everything. But I haven't used any to maintain it. And when I create the infrastructure that the president wants, it'll run off the reservoir."

"That's... brilliant." He blinked, then began walking again. "When do you think it'll be finished?"

"Probably in the next couple of days. I need to do a bit of research first, to make sure I don't miss anything and piss him off again. Plus I don't want to wait until the last minute, since I'll be preoccupied with the shield and portals as the impact date gets closer."

"Makes sense." He grimaced. "It'll be absolute chaos when people find out. I'm amazed someone hasn't already broken the story."

"I know. I really expected some amateur astronomer to see it and blast it all over social media by now." I shook my head. "At the briefing, the president said he wanted to announce it soon, but I haven't heard anything since then. So I don't know."

"He's probably waiting until the infrastructure on Tearmann is done, and they have another look."

"Yeah, maybe."

We were almost to the backyard, and I saw Sam on his rounds nearby. He waved, and I returned the greeting.

"I'll be happy when this is all done." I sighed. "With a little luck, I'll get some time to spend with you guys—my family—until it's time for you all to leave."

Again, he stopped. "What are you talking about? We're not leaving you here alone."

"Of course you are. None of you can do anything to help. And you'll only distract me because I'll be worrying about you instead of taking care of business."

He narrowed his eyes. "You're not planning on doing anything stupid, are you?"

"What? Of course not. What are you even talking about?"

"Sacrificing yourself."

I hadn't thought about that, but would it work?

Unfortunately, I'd hesitated too long, and now Kevin was even more suspicious.

"Dee, please tell me you're not going to sacrifice yourself."

I shook my head and wrapped my arms around him. "Of course not. Look, I just don't want to worry about any of you. I need to know you'll all be safe. Besides, I'll be fine."

He frowned. "How? How do you know that?"

"When we were on Asgard, Loki told me he'd seen a vision of the future. A future where I was living happily, thousands of years from now."

His gaze was steady on mine. "Was it here, on Earth?"

I thought back to what Loki had told me, but he hadn't mentioned it and I hadn't asked. Did it really matter? "He didn't specify."

"Oh, Dee." He brushed a lock of hair from my face. "I've got a bad feeling about this."

I laughed softly. "You *always* have a bad feeling. About *everything*."

After a moment, he laughed, too. "Yeah, I know. But all this time, I thought we were all going to stay and help with the asteroid. Now, you tell me you want us off the planet before you try to save it, all by yourself." He shook his head. "It's insanity."

"No, it's not," I insisted. "Think about it. What in the world did you think any of you could do to help? I mean, seriously?"

He did think about it, for all of a moment. Then he rolled his eyes. "There you go, being all logical."

"Look. It's just a precaution. Just in case the planet becomes severely damaged. I'll need to focus on repairing it without worrying about anyone else. Especially any of you."

"Because we'll be on Tearmann taking care of the humans." Resignation had settled into his voice.

"Exactly. But it'll just be until Earth is ready for everyone to come back."

"And how long will that be? Months? Years? Centuries?"

I laid a hand on his cheek. "I just don't see how I have a choice. And if anyone can do this, it's me."

"Fuck." He pulled me closer. "Don't you fucking *dare* leave us to raise Bree without you." His tone was fierce. Unforgiving.

"I wouldn't dream of it." But he'd brought up a good point, and it wouldn't be a bad idea to talk about it, as a contingency plan. "But I need to say this. If something should happen to keep me from reconnecting and reopening the portal to Tearmann after the asteroid hits, I want you, Arddhu, and the Morrigan to watch over her, protect her, and teach her. You can ask anyone else you trust to help, like Reshep, for example." I swallowed the lump that'd formed in my throat. "All I ask is... if the worst happens, and we're... separated... for a while, don't forget me. Don't let Bree forget me."

His gaze held mine for a moment, pain and fear naked in his. I could only imagine what he saw in mine, beyond the tears I blinked away.

"Never, love." His voice was soft. "*Never.*"

Gods, how I loved this man.

I tugged his head down and kissed him with all the love I felt in my heart, then we just stood there, sweating in the sun and holding each other close for a moment before heading back to the house.

I just had to make sure I didn't fuck up this planetary shield and destroy myself along with the planet, because I was pretty sure he'd never forgive me if I did.

None of my family would.

CHAPTER TWENTY-NINE

I'D ASKED ANTHONY to contact the firm for expert advice on my planetary shield experiments, and he'd promised to have someone call me as soon as possible.

In the meantime, I sat at the kitchen island with Kevin and waited while Brianna prepared lunch. Arddhu, Bree, and the Morrigan had just finished watching a nature show in the living room and now joined us.

Bree had grown even more rapidly since the Coronation, and I wondered if the influx of power had caused it. She was as tall as me now, and seemed to be about sixteen years old.

Had I really given birth to her less than a month ago?

"What happened with the shield experiments?" Arddhu asked.

"Nothing worked. I've asked for help from the firm."

"So you have some free time?" Bree asked.

"Not really." My heart ached at the disappointment in her face. "After lunch, I need to get back to work on Tearmann."

"Why?" the Morrigan asked. "What else needs to be done?"

"Infrastructure. Roads, bridges, houses. Stuff like that."

"Will it have running water?" Bree asked. "Toilets? Electricity?"

"Yep. All that and more."

"What will you use for the power source?" Arddhu asked.

"Magick."

"Yours?" the Morrigan asked.

"No. Tearmann is self-sustaining now. And it'll have a reservoir of power for everyone to tap into."

"Self-sustaining, and renewable," Kevin added. "She's a genius."

"Are you going to make cars, too?" Bree asked.

Hmm. Good question. Humans would need to get around somehow. I hadn't really thought about it, but why not? Just not the gas guzzlers Earth had. And I could also make some mass transit options, too, like buses and trains.

"Not like the cars we have here," I responded. "I'll make vehicles that run on Tearmann's magick so there won't be any pollution or chemicals to worry about."

"You know, if everything runs on magick, the humans will go crazy," Kevin pointed out.

"Why? They won't have to work for any of it. No solar panels to install. No coal to shovel. No power plants to manage. They should love it."

Kevin shook his head. "Humans *hate* having nothing to do."

"I never said they wouldn't have anything to do. They just won't have to work for basic necessities like food, water, shelter, that sort of thing." I sighed. "Speaking of shelter... what kind of houses should I make? I don't want any mansions or palaces, but nobody should live in shacks or hovels either. Something modest but comfortable."

So many decisions yet to make, and I hoped I made the right ones.

The Morrigan nodded in agreement. "Nothing too big or too small. Something just the right size for an average family."

"But you should probably plan on some other types for smaller families," Kevin pointed out.

"Households without children," Arddhu agreed.

"And maybe some apartments," Kevin said. "For people who are single or don't want a house."

I saw the logic in apartments, but I didn't want any tall buildings blocking the scenic views. So, I could make them horizontal instead of vertical. There was plenty of room, so I could spread them out a bit and make sure none were higher than two stories.

"Good afternoon, Lady."

The sudden voice in my head startled me. Then I recognized who'd just contacted me through a mental communication link.

Loki.

"Uh... good afternoon."

"*I humbly request your permission to pass through your wards for a friendly visit.*"

"*Where are you?*"

"*Here. Arizona. Your house.*"

Oh. I'd automatically glanced out the window-wall before realizing how ridiculous that'd been. I modified the wards to allow him in. "*Done.*"

"*Thank you.*"

Loki appeared in the backyard in jeans and a tee shirt, and slowly turned in a circle to take in his surroundings. Seconds later, Nat and Joe appeared with weapons drawn, and Loki raised his hands.

Shit. I quickly opened the panel in the window-wall.

"Guys, it's okay," I called. "He's a friend."

Nat and Joe holstered their weapons with a nod, then returned to their rounds.

Loki approached, smiling his thanks.

"I wasn't expecting you." I held the panel open for him.

"I was just in the neighborhood and thought I'd stop by."

He stepped inside and nodded politely to the others.

"Welcome to The Hacienda, Loki." I gestured with both hands. "My home."

"Is this your first time here?" Bree asked him.

He smiled at Bree. "It is not my first time on Midgard, nor is it my first time in Arizona, but it is my first time visiting this house."

Of course, Brianna had known we'd have a guest for lunch, and set six place settings on the dining table instead of the granite island.

"We were just about to have lunch," I said. "Would you like to join us?"

"I'd be honored."

We sat, and Brianna served a savory pasta dish with sweet Italian sausage and a light marinara sauce topped with fresh-shredded parmesan cheese. Two baskets were heaped with small knots of fresh garlic bread, nestled in cloth napkins to keep them warm.

As Brianna poured wine, Loki smiled at her. "This looks delicious."

She grinned and continued to pour a nice cabernet for each of us, adding a generous amount of water to Bree's.

Surprised to be included with the adults for the first time, Bree stared at the glass for a moment, then sat a little straighter in her chair and lifted her chin.

I bit my lip to keep from grinning.

Between bites, Loki continued speaking with Bree. "And how is Princess Brighid doing? Have you begun to study magick yet?"

My heart warmed a little at his use of her unofficial title.

"No," she said with a sigh. "Mom says I have to wait another week or so."

He nodded sagely. "Mothers can be a pain in the ass sometimes."

I almost choked on my wine, which turned into an embarrassing coughing fit.

Bree's gaze flicked to me, then back to Loki, who smirked. Kevin laughed, but Arddhu and the Morrigan didn't react at all.

For the rest of the meal, we spoke of nothing consequential. Afterward, in the living room, I poured a glass of Polish mead for everyone except Bree.

Wine could be watered down, but doing that to mead should be a criminal offense.

Of course, she sulked, then perked up when Brianna brought her another glass of watered wine. Gods, but she was already so much like a teenager.

After one sip, Loki smiled. "Oh this is delightful. It certainly rivals Odin's best mead."

"It is my favorite," Arddhu said.

Loki leaned back in his chair and asked me, "How are things going with your sanctuary realm?"

"Almost done. Just need to add some stuff the president asked for."

"And how much time until the asteroid arrives?"

I quickly calculated it and swore silently. Where had the time gone? "Two to four weeks."

I needed to get Tearmann finished and get the shield done as soon as possible.

"I see." He frowned. "From what I understand, the current human population of Midgard is over eight billion. And there are thousands of magickal creatures: trolls, goblins, fairies, dryads, and sprites, for example. And there are also several thousand Túatha living here now. How do you plan to move so many bodies in such a short period of time? You probably should've started already."

I stared at him and tried to think of an intelligent response.

Of course, I knew he was absolutely right. It'd take at least three weeks to get that many people moved, and that was only if we started now and had all hands on deck to do it.

Ignoring that issue for now, I answered his other question. "I'll be opening portals all over the planet. The deities and other allies will move everyone through as quickly and efficiently as possible."

He glanced at the others before returning his gaze to me. "And do you plan on saving *all* the humans? Even the murderers, rapists, child molesters, and sex traffickers?"

Oh. That was something else I hadn't given much thought. "I don't know."

He raised a brow. "You don't know?"

"I mean, first of all, how would I separate them out from everyone else? Obviously, I'm not talking about the ones already in prison or awaiting trial."

"Let's say for argument's sake you could segregate them. The question remains: would you migrate them to your peaceful sanctuary realm?"

"I don't know," I repeated testily.

Gods, he could be aggravating. And, he'd made it sound like I was going to allow wolves into a sheepfold or something.

Arddhu cleared his throat. "I could resolve that issue tomorrow night." At Loki's frown, he explained. "For the first time in centuries, I am again performing the Wild Hunt. I could target the mortal vermin of the planet and leave only those of good character free to migrate to Tearmann."

Oh. He'd decided on tomorrow night for the Hunt. So soon. While my brain had stalled on that detail, Loki responded.

"That is an excellent solution," he said. "Perhaps Odin could join you. His last Hunt was also centuries ago. Although his was on Midwinter's Eve and was most likely different from yours, I'm certain that, under the circumstances, he'd be delighted to join you."

Arddhu smiled. "And he would be most welcome. Many deities have asked to accompany me, and I expect it will be quite exciting for us all."

Now my brain had caught up to the rest of the discussion, and I frowned.

Mass murder.

Loki and Arddhu were sitting in my living room, calmly discussing mass murder.

Then again, how was it all that different from when I'd taken out the remaining targets? That, too, had been mass murder.

In my defense, I'd only done one mass killing and it'd been for the good of the planet. These deities had probably done it hundreds of times in the past. And how many times had I been told that deities didn't live by human laws?

But, if I were brutally honest, eliminating all the criminals and nasty people before beginning the migration to Tearmann would solve quite a few problems, maybe even some I hadn't thought of yet. For one thing, I hadn't planned on building any prisons. For another, although I'd made it quite a large realm, it wasn't finite. I was ashamed to admit I hadn't done the most basic of research and looked up the current population of Earth before I'd created Tearmann. So I wasn't exactly sure it'd be big enough to hold over eight billion humans plus the thousands of deities and magickal creatures. Then there were all the animals I'd created. It'd be over capacity before anyone even had any babies.

Then my brain locked onto something else.

I'd murdered, and so had my allies. Would that make us targets of the Hunt? Arddhu had said he'd target mortal vermin, but would any deities also be considered fair game?

I had a lot of questions, but I wanted to wait until after Loki left.

Arddhu had noticed I hadn't being paying attention, and now asked, "Deirdre, do you disagree?"

I shook my head. "Not really. It's just that... well, to Loki's point, Tearmann might not be big enough for everyone, and your idea solves that possible problem."

"I see. I realize now we haven't discussed much of this prior to this moment." He paused before adding, "Iif you wish to join the Hunt, I would be honored."

Me?

Uh, no. Yes, I was curious, but I really needed to finish Tearmann and get moving on the shield experiments.

"As much as I'd love to, I can't."

"I understand. You have much yet to do in a short time period."

"What about me?" Bree asked. "Can I go with you, Daddy Arddhu?"

She'd been so quiet, I'd almost forgotten she was still sitting with us. "I don't think it's a good idea, honey."

"Why not?" she asked.

Arddhu answered. "You are too young. The Wild Hunt is for grown-ups only."

She rolled her eyes dramatically. "I never get to do *anything*."

"I won't be going, either," Kevin told her. "How about we go see a movie?"

"In a real theater?" She'd perked up.

He nodded. "With buttered popcorn and everything."

She grinned. "Deal."

I smiled at Kevin in gratitude.

"One more question," Loki said. "Will you also be asking all the deities to migrate to this Tearmann?"

I nodded. "Ideally, yes. I mean, after I close the portals and sever the connection, it'll be a separate realm, untouched by anything that happens to Earth. So, if Earth is destroyed by the asteroid—or damaged so badly that it can't be healed—everyone will be safe on Tearmann."

"Wait a minute," the Morrigan said. "You never said anything about Earth being destroyed."

"Because I don't expect it to be. But I can't take the chance of any deities remaining on Earth—or in any of the realms attached to it—when the asteroid hits. It's just a precaution."

"There are nine realms full of deities and humans," Loki said. "Surely, you're not thinking of evacuating them all."

"Of course I am. What choice is there?"

"That's insanity." He shook his head. "Of course you have a choice. For example, you could create a temporary connection to Tearmann for each realm, then sever the connections to Earth. Or, simply sever the connections to Earth for each realm. Afterward, reconnect them."

Hmm. Either of those ideas had potential, if they were within my power.

"*Yes, Deirdre,*" Anu said. "*The realms are within Your domain. You may do as Loki has suggested.*"

I thanked her and nodded to Loki. "Great ideas, thanks. I think the simplest would be to just leave all the realms as they are and sever their connections to Earth. That way they'd all be protected from whatever happens here."

"Um, Mom?" Bree's voice was quiet and shaky. "You haven't said anything about all the animals. You're not going to leave them here to suffer and die, are you?"

Shit. I stared at her, realizing I was fucked no matter how I answered.

"Well, I have to, honey. There's just no way we can evacuate all of them, too."

She hadn't taken her gaze from me, and now her eyes filled with tears. "You can't. That's cruel. And it's wrong."

I rubbed my forehead. "Sweetheart, it's an impossible task. We can't move all the humans, plus all the magickal creatures, plus all the animals. We just don't have enough time."

"But you're the Goddess. You can do *anything.*"

If only that were true. "I have limitations, honey. You know that."

One glance at everyone else's frowns told me they were all concerned, too. Even Loki seemed disturbed by the prospect of abandoning all the animals.

Bree just continued to stare at me, and now the tears spilled onto her cheeks. "It's not right, Mom."

Fuck.

She was right, but what could I do? I was running out of options.

And time.

"There is some time yet," Loki reassured her. "We will think of something."

She held his gaze for a long, silent moment, then nodded.

"I will relay your request to Odin," Loki said to Arddhu, then stood. He placed his empty glass on the coffee table and nodded politely to everyone. "I thank you for your hospitality, and we will speak again soon."

He took two steps away, then disappeared in a puff of mist as he ported.

I refilled all the adults' glasses with mead, then took a deep breath. Sometimes it seemed I took two steps forward and one step back with every challenge I faced, and it was discouraging.

I glanced at the Morrigan. "You okay? You've been awfully quiet."

"I apologize. I've been lost in thought." She flashed a quick smile at me, then turned to Arddhu. "I'd like to join the Hunt, if I may."

"Of course." Arddhu seemed pleased. "You are most welcome, old friend."

This seemed like a good time to ask my questions.

"How will you know who to... um, target?" I asked him.

"When the magick of the Hunt begins, it is easy to see into the hearts of the wretched. They are blackened, as if diseased. Greed, cruelty, or hatred makes them so, as do such acts against common decency as we discussed earlier."

Black hearts. Interesting.

"Will all murderers be targeted, then?"

"Not necessarily. Any who have killed in self-defense, for example, will be safe from the culling. As will any others who carried out other acts that human law condemns but are not, in fact, true acts against common decency."

"So, for example, I won't be targeted, even though I murdered almost a hundred people."

"You are correct."

"Will other deities be included, too?" I thought of Malsumis and Cromm, and how despicable they'd been.

He shook his head. "Not typically, no. Deities are usually subject to a different judgment process."

Interesting.

"And what happens to those you target?"

"Their souls are cast into the Void, and their bodies vanish into thin air, as if they never existed."

The bodies would just vanish? Well, wasn't that convenient? Way better than dead bodies piled everywhere, like a horror movie.

Wait. The *void*? I'd never heard of it. "What's the void?"

"It is a place of nothingness. There is no escape or return from the Void."

"It's a bit like the Christian Hell," the Morrigan added. "Except worse, because nothingness is far more terrifying than their concept of fire and brimstone. They won't feel pain, but they also won't feel anything at all. They won't have their senses, memories, or consciousness. And they'll be there for eternity, because the Void will never cease to exist."

I stared at her in horror. My mind couldn't truly comprehend being in nothingness for eternity, unfeeling and unseeing.

"What are the chances of anyone getting sent there by mistake?" I asked.

"That is impossible." Arddhu shook his head. "No one without a blackened heart can be taken in the Hunt."

I thought about Mike. "What if someone did horrible things that made his heart black, but he wants to change? Be better?"

Arddhu frowned. "If he truly wanted to change or be a better person, his heart would not be blackened."

Okay. So, according to that criteria, Mike would've been spared from the Void, if he were still alive.

"What about if someone hasn't done anything really bad yet, but will at some point in the future? Is that heart blackened?"

His frown deepened. "Why are you asking me these questions? Do you have doubts?"

"No, no. I'm just..." I sighed. "I need to understand this completely, because I'm the one who's going to be held responsible for it."

"Shit." Kevin ran a hand through his hair. "You're right. Everyone's going to think you did it."

"I think I can handle any backlash," I assured him. "I just need to know exactly who's going to be targeted, and exactly how this works."

"I understand." Arddhu's frown had cleared. "Normally, there are many whose path changes before a future event, and the event never occurs. There are others, however, whose path will not change, and their heart will already be blackened. If you wish, I can include them in the Hunt."

I nodded. "I think that'd be best." It wouldn't be much of a sanctuary if a person migrated, then raped or murdered someone on Tearmann.

Now, this Hunt made more sense to me, and I was more confident in the decision. Only the worst humans alive—no one with any possibility of redemption—would be taken in the Hunt.

I could live with that.

Just then, my mobile phone rang, and it wasn't a number I recognized. I answered it anyway because I'd been expecting to hear from someone from the firm.

"Hello, Ms. Connor? I'm Tommy—um, Thomas Finch—from the project team. We met at the briefing a few weeks ago. I, um, I was told You need some assistance with the planetary shield calculations?"

I tried to place the name and voice, but drew a blank. "How did you get my number? Who told you to call me?"

A slight hesitation, then he replied, "I'm with the firm, ma'am. Uh, my Lady."

The firm had someone on the project team?

Holy shit. I would've never guessed.

"I'm so sorry, but I don't remember you."

Another slight hesitation, then he laughed nervously. "I, uh, was the one who suggested we migrate to another realm."

Now it clicked. The young guy. Nicely dressed, white shirt and dark tie. Neat, short hair. Clean-shaven. The one I'd said deserved a raise for his brilliant idea.

"Oh. Pleased to meet you, Tommy. Yes, I've been having trouble with my prototypes. Would you be able to come by and help me figure out what's wrong?"

"I'd be honored, Lady."

We agreed to meet the next morning and hung up.

Not even a moment later, my phone rang again, and this time it was John Simmons, the project leader.

"Where we at?" he asked without preamble. "It's almost June, and I haven't heard from you."

"I'm just finishing up the infrastructure that the president requested for the sanctuary realm. I'm still working on the planetary shield." Should I tell him one of the team members would be helping? Nah. I shouldn't blow his cover.

"When will the infrastructure be done?"

"A couple of days, tops."

"Finish by end of day tomorrow," he snapped. "What about the shield? We only have a couple of weeks to go, you know."

"It'll definitely be done before we need it. What's going on? Has something changed on the impact date?"

"No. But the president wants to announce. He's been waiting on you, and he's out of patience."

Shit. Of course he was, just as I'd suspected.

"Tell him to go ahead. Wait—no, tell him to announce in two days."

"Two days? Why in two days?"

"I've got something planned that will have... a significant impact."

"Care to elaborate?"

"Not at this time."

He sighed. "Fine. We'll announce in two days. Be ready to start moving people next week." He hung up.

Shit. He could be so rude when he was stressed.

Then again, so could I.

"Hey guys, I need to finish the infrastructure." I drank the rest of my mead and set the empty glass on the coffee table. "We need to start moving people next week."

"Don't forget about the animals, Mom," Bree said. "We have to figure out how to move them, too."

"It'd be a lot easier if someone could just tell them to go through the portals," I said with a laugh.

The look on Bree's face before she turned away instantly worried me. It was as if she'd just been given a priceless gift.

CHAPTER THIRTY

I T WAS DONE. It'd taken several hours, and I'd had to refer back to the internet more than once for specifics on some details, but Tearmann was finally finished.

For the houses, I'd created only a few different styles and sizes, ranging from modest one-story bungalows to larger two-story homes. I'd even paired local architecture to the zones, such as the central courtyard style in the Mediterranean zone, and the ranch style in the American Southwest zone. In most places, I'd also included neat rows of one- or two-story apartment buildings with all the modern amenities, including lush gardens and sparkling swimming pools.

There were lots of other buildings, too: hospitals, offices, stores, and schools, plus civic buildings like libraries and community centers. Nothing was taller than two stories, and every building had whatever was needed for use on day one. Houses and apartments had furniture, cooking utensils, dishes, drinkware, linens, and appliances. Hospitals had beds, medical equipment, testing and imaging devices, and medications. Shops of all kinds had everything I could think of, from books to nonperishable food. And the schools had desks, sports equipment, musical instruments, and art supplies. I'd even remembered to include computers and communication devices, and I'd also remembered places for pets and their needs: veterinary and grooming facilities and stores for food, toys, and treats.

For short-term food requirements, I'd created warehouses in each zone and filled them with stuff that'd keep for weeks. For the restaurants,

I included instructions on how to create fresh nutritious food from the reservoir of magick.

One of the best parts? They could easily plant gardens to grow everything they needed, and they wouldn't have to slaughter any animals for food.

Not unless Earth became uninhabitable and Tearmann became their permanent home.

Which meant that Bree's idea of moving the animals—wild and domestic—was actually a pretty good one. Should the unthinkable happen or something went wrong, the humans would need more than what the reservoir could provide.

Especially if they reproduced at a high rate.

One of the last things I'd created were the winding roads for travelling between the climate zones, and vehicle warehouses filled with cars and small SUVs that ran on magick. The humans could pick whichever one they wanted for themselves; I'd made enough for one vehicle per house or apartment. I'd also created light rail and buses, and included stations for boarding.

No planes, though. They'd have to do without, or create their own.

There would be no money on Tearmann; I'd created no banks or lending institutions. The humans could work in the stores and offices, doing whatever it was they liked to do to stay busy, but all their basic needs for a short-term stay were taken care of.

Beyond that, they'd have to figure it out on their own.

Now, as I came back to myself, I stood and stretched. I'd been outside, on the patch of grass near the patio, and the sun had just dipped below the mesquite trees. The heat was stifling, at least one hundred twenty degrees with high humidity. The monsoon had started early this year.

Or maybe this was just the new normal, thanks to climate change, despite my numerous healing sessions.

I quickly transformed my sweaty clothing into dry, then headed inside.

Kevin was on his laptop at the granite island. "I was just about to come out and get you before you melted."

I smiled. "It is a bit toasty out there."

"Is the infrastructure complete?" Arddhu asked from the living room, where he and Bree were playing a board game. I noticed the Morrigan wasn't around, which meant she was probably in her room with Reshep again. Those two were almost as bad as a couple of horny teenagers.

And I was beyond thrilled for them.

"Finally. Yes." My stomach growled loudly. "And apparently it's time for dinner."

But Brianna didn't appear in the kitchen to start cooking, and I frowned.

As if reading my thoughts, Kevin explained, "She's at Kali's place. They had a cooking lesson earlier, and she must've been held up."

"Kali is learning how to cook?"

"No, you've got that backwards," Kevin laughed. "Brianna is learning Indian cuisine from Kali."

"I suspect there will be some tasty curries in our near future."

"Sorry I'm late," Brianna burst through the panel in the window-wall. "But I've got a fantastic new recipe for you guys tonight, as long as you don't mind waiting a bit."

"Looking forward to it," I said.

And it was, indeed, a delicious curry.

After breakfast the next morning, Bree began her magick lessons outside with Arddhu and Kevin, while I waited in the kitchen for Tommy to arrive.

But when the time came for Bree's lessons on battle magick with the Morrigan, absolutely nothing would keep me away from watching.

I didn't have to wait long. The gatehouse buzzed to let me know Tommy was here, and I quickly modified the wards to allow him entry. After greeting him at the front door, I escorted him to where I'd been doing my shield experiments.

Tablet in hand, Tommy made a circuit around the rotating fake planet, frowning as he studied it. Tentatively, he placed his hand flat against the shield, then yanked it back. "It's hot," he said.

I glanced up at the sky and shrugged. "It's been out in the sun for a few days."

"Oh." He blinked at me for a moment. "What's it made of? How thick is it?"

I told him, and he made notes on his tablet.

"Can You show me what You've tried so far?"

As I did, he watched closely and made more notes.

"And You want it to burn to ash on contact, correct? Instead of fragments or dust?"

"Ideally, yeah."

He continued typing on his tablet for a few moments, then turned it toward me. "Try this."

I modified the shield using his calculated thickness and composition, then threw another rock.

It, too, turned to dust, just like the last one.

Tommy frowned and studied his tablet. "That should've worked."

"Does it have something to do with the rotation of the planet?" At his sharp glance, I explained, "It worked before I made a more realistic fake planet that rotated. And since the shield is connected to the planet, it rotates, too."

"Hmm." He continued frowning as he turned back to his tablet. "Maybe."

A few more minutes passed, and sweat trickled down my back from the blazing sun overhead. I took a moment and created a shade canopy above us, but Tommy was too engrossed with his tablet to notice.

"Okay." He showed me the tablet screen. "Make this adjustment to the thickness. That should do the trick."

I complied, and picked up another rock from the pile I'd gathered a few days ago. Only four remained after this. I'd have to manufacture more if the experiments continued to be unsuccessful. But I'd have to be careful with that, since any deviation in size or composition would affect the results.

This time, it broke into a thousand fragments.

"That should've worked," Tommy repeated, and stared at the fake planet.

"Now you see what I've been dealing with," I said. "It's been so frustrating."

He nodded absently, still staring at the fake planet. A moment later, his gaze met mine. "This might call for a different decision. As in, which is worse: a thick dust cloud or thousands of fragments?"

"I've already given that some thought." I ran through my opinion on the two options. "So I guess, fragments is the lesser of the two evils in this case," I finished.

"I think You're right. But Simmons may not see it that way."

"Can you help convince him, if it comes to it?"

"Of course, Lady. You can count on the firm for any and all assistance required."

"Thank you." As I walked him back to the house, I asked, "Did they ever give you that raise?"

"They sure did." He grinned. "Um, not NASA, though. The firm. They know who's the boss."

Those words sent my mind reeling.

I'd known the firm, that vast shadowy organization that'd existed for centuries and had operations all over the world, worked on behalf of the Goddess. When I'd first heard of them, of course, that'd been Ida.

But now, they worked for *me*.

For some reason, I hadn't thought of it that way until Tommy had just mentioned it.

And for once, it made me feel good.

"Damn right." I couldn't help but grin back at him. In the backyard, I showed him to the walkway that led to the front of the house, and sent him on his way. Then I changed course and headed to where Bree's magick lessons were taking place.

But I didn't get far before my mobile phone rang. It was Simmons again.

"Okay, the president is set to announce tomorrow morning," he said. "Now, please tell me you have some good news for me."

Shit. I braced myself for more verbal abuse.

"Yes and no. The infrastructure for Tearmann, the sanctuary realm, is finished as promised. Houses, buildings, roads, communications, vehicles, and more."

"Electricity? Sewers? Indoor plumbing?"

"Yes to all of that. And everything's fully stocked, so no one has to bring anything with them other than personal items."

"Fully stocked?" He sounded confused.

"Furniture, linens, food, dishes, that sort of thing."

"Oh. Great. That's actually... pretty great." He paused. "So what's the bad news?"

"It's the planetary shield." I sighed. "In my experiments, I can't get better than fragments or dust. I think dust is worse, so we'll have to go with fragments. To protect the planet, I'll have to keep the shield surrounding the planet indefinitely."

After a few beats of silence, he said, "But that'll keep us from leaving the planet."

"You mean with rockets? Space ships?"

"Yeah. And new satellites."

"Yeah." I nodded even though he couldn't see me. "Nothing in, nothing out. For as long as the asteroid fragments hang around the planet."

"Those fragments could hang around forever. Maybe even in a permanent orbit."

"So I guess the shield will have to stay in place forever."

"Not an option," he snapped. "We have a space program, in case you hadn't noticed."

"Apparently, not anymore," I snapped back.

He took an audible breath and spoke with more calm. "Look. There has to be another way."

"I guess I can see about removing the fragments somehow. After."

"Okay. Keep me posted."

We hung up, and I almost threw my phone into the desert.

If only I could just leave for Tearmann with everyone else. There sure as hell wouldn't be any asteroids to worry about.

I took a deep breath and released it, forcing myself to calm before I continued toward where Bree's magick lessons were taking place. I approached quietly so I wouldn't interrupt or distract.

Arddhu had just closed a portal. "Now, you try."

Bree's lips moved silently as she duplicated the movements Arddhu always made when he opened a portal: palms facing out, hands drawing a clockwise circle in the air three times. A moment later, the air shimmered as a small portal opened.

"Very good, Brighid, well done," Arddhu praised. "And where does this portal lead?" He moved close to peer inside. "Ah, Ard na Mara." He turned and smiled at Bree. "Excellent choice." Then he noticed me, and beckoned me closer. "Our daughter has opened her first portal." His voice was full of pride and love.

"That's fantastic." I grinned at Bree, but really felt like crying. She was growing up so fast. "I'm so proud of you."

She flashed me a grin, then asked Arddhu, "Should I close it now?"

Arddhu nodded, and she complied.

She jumped up and punched the air with a loud, triumphant "*yes.*" She glanced at each of us, unable to hold back her grin. "Now I can go anywhere I want, just like you guys."

I raised a brow at Arddhu, and he took the hint. "Until you are an adult, you must still ask permission."

She was immediately serious. "Of course."

"What else have you learned so far?" I asked.

"How to heal, and how to port without a portal. Later, Daddy Kevin is going to show me some spells, and tomorrow, Auntie Morrigan is going to show me how to fight with magick."

Arddhu added, "Her healing and porting abilities are natural. I suspect we will discover other natural abilities as we continue her training."

I nodded, and smiled again at Bree.

"How did the experiments with Tommy go?" Kevin asked.

My smile faded. "Shitty. No change."

He frowned. "Damn. I'm sorry, Dee."

"We'll just have to deal with fragments." I shrugged. "Maybe I'll figure out a way to zap them into ash. After."

"Mom, the shield will work," Bree said. "I don't know why the experiments aren't working, but I *know* the shield will work."

She sounded so sure. Maybe one of her natural talents was for divination?

"Did you have a vision just now?"

She shook her head. "I haven't *seen* it, I just *know* it." She seemed frustrated. "It's hard to explain. You wouldn't understand."

I almost laughed. She really knew nothing about me, but it wasn't her fault. I really hadn't told her much about my life.

"I get it, Bree. After I became the Keeper, I just *knew* things too, without really knowing *how* I knew. So, yes, I do understand."

"Oh." Her face cleared and she hugged me. "I love you, Mom."

"And I love you. *All* of you," I added, including Arddhu and Kevin.

"We love you, too," Kevin said, at the same time as Arddhu said it.

Arddhu glanced at the sun's position in the sky. "It is time. I must be off." He started away, then stopped and studied me. "Are you certain you do not wish to join the Hunt with me?"

"Absolutely certain. It's not my thing. But I sincerely wish you a most fruitful Hunt."

"Thank You for Your blessing, Lady. I will return on the morrow." He turned and left for the house, to collect the Morrigan.

"Why don't you come with us to the movie?" Kevin asked me. "It's an action flick. Superheroes, I think."

I was too restless to sit still for a movie. "Nah, you two go ahead. Have some daddy-daughter time."

He turned to Bree. "We've got some time before we have to leave. You want to practice some fireballs?"

"Oh, yes, please," she excitedly replied.

"I'll leave you to it, then." I headed back to the house, trying not to feel strange at being left to myself for a change.

By the time I got there, Arddhu and the Morrigan had already departed for the Hunt, and the house was quiet.

Too quiet.

I'd never been in The Hacienda all by myself before. Hard to believe only a year ago it'd been full to bursting with all the allies and their attendants. What a crazy time that'd been. It'd seemed more like a frat party house than my home.

It seemed so long ago, and so much had happened since.

Then again, my life had just been one thing after another for almost two years now. Sure, I'd had a couple of breaks here and there—healing on Arddhu's world after my escape from Cromm, and just recently, my birthday—but I was so ready for a long period of absolutely nothing going on.

Thinking about a nice dip in the pool, I went outside. But when I got to it, I didn't want to get in.

I glanced over to where I'd left Kevin and Bree, but they must've already left for the movie.

In the other direction, that goddamned fake planet slowly rotated, as if taunting me to keep throwing rocks at it in the hopes that one would finally turn to ash on contact.

What was that saying about the definition of insanity? Doing the same thing over and over, but expecting a different result? Something like that.

Nope, not going to give in.

Back inside, in the cool air, I headed to the living room and sat on the couch. I turned on the television and flipped through the channels for a while, then shut it off. Nothing interested me.

Was there anything I'd been putting off? Something I'd been meaning to do but hadn't because of time constraints?

Maybe I could work in the garden at Ard na Mara; I'd always wanted to do that. Maybe even make some potions.

Nah. Not feeling it.

Wandering from room to room without really seeing anything, I wondered what the hell was wrong with me.

And then I stopped cold, realizing what it was: this was *boredom*.

I was bored.

It'd been so long since I'd experienced it, I'd actually forgotten what it felt like.

"Oh, fuck it," I muttered. Grabbing the flask of mead from my bedroom, I ported to the beach at Ard na Mara.

It was early evening there, and a gorgeous one, at that. The coolness was a balm on my hot skin, and as I walked toward the Sanctuary cave, my eyes automatically searched the sand for the elusive blue beads, hoping to find one for Bree.

No such luck.

At the cave, I created a ball of light and entered, watching my step carefully on the uneven rock. Inside, I set the ball to float and sat on one of the rocks around the fire ring.

Someone had been here recently; firewood was arranged neatly in the ring, ready to light.

Using magick, I lit the fire and sat watching as it caught, occasionally taking a sip from the flask.

Staring into the flames, I took a deep breath and released it, relaxing for the first time in days. Weeks, maybe.

Beginning tomorrow, everything would change. There'd be the fallout from the Wild Hunt, and then the migrations would start. It'd be a hectic couple of weeks until the asteroid's expected impact.

Of course, there was always the possibility its trajectory might deviate between now and then, and maybe it'd miss us.

The way my luck seemed to be, though, I highly doubted it.

At least it'd been several days since I'd last had the nightmare. I wasn't sure what'd changed, but maybe it meant the impact wouldn't be so bad. Maybe Bree was right, and the shield would do what it was supposed to do.

Well, why not try to see it? I had a fire, and that was a valid divination method.

I stared at the flames and let my eyes unfocus slightly while holding the thought: show me the asteroid impact.

It took longer than with water divination, but eventually the vision unfolded, and my heart sank.

Earth was on fire. Distant screams could've been human or animal, I really couldn't tell the difference. Fireballs rained from the sky, which was clouded with smoke and ash. As I walked, my feet stumbled on charred debris, and I hoped it wasn't the remains of bodies. I tripped on something big, lost my balance, and accidentally inhaled a lungful of smoke and ash, which caused a terrible coughing fit.

And that's how I came out of the vision: coughing and gagging, my mouth tasting of ash.

After I caught my breath, I took a mouthful of mead, swished it around and spit it out. It helped a bit. Next, I took a nice, long drink, then another for good measure. Thank the gods—and Maggie—the flask was magickal. No matter how much mead I drank, the flask would always stay full.

So. Nothing I'd done so far would change the outcome. Earth would still burn.

But since I hadn't made the shield yet, it might not take that into consideration. Maybe I should check again after I put the shield up.

For now, though, I just sat, drank the mead, and tried not to think at all.

CHAPTER THIRTY-ONE

I RETURNED TO The Hacienda only a few hours after I'd left, and ported directly to my room, where I stowed the flask. I'd only been back a moment when a cacophony of prayers bombarded me, and I knew they were the result of the Wild Hunt. None of them had reached me while I'd been in the Sanctuary cave at Ard na Mara, and it'd given me a period of true peace. Now, I braced myself for the looming aftermath as I left my suite.

Kevin and Bree were in the living room playing a board game, and they both looked up at me as I stopped in my tracks and stared at Kevin.

"What in the world are you wearing?" I asked, all thoughts of the Hunt fading for now. I'd never seen him wear a brown leather jacket—with matching pants—before.

He glanced down at himself sheepishly. "It's a long story."

"I have the time." As I sat in a chair, Bree giggled.

"I made him get a new feasting outfit," she said.

"Watch this." He stood and slowly turned, and the supple leather shimmered as he moved.

Deceptively simple, the outfit consisted of a modern, trim-fitting jacket and tailored pants. As I watched, the color changed from the brown of the couch to bright, sparkling gold. A moment later, it was shiny silver.

"What the hell," I murmured.

Kevin grinned. "It's a special leather that changes color."

I could see that for myself, but I didn't say that. "Where in the world did you get such a thing?"

He sat on the couch again. "After the movie, we went to Finn's Cove for dinner. That's when Bree said my feasting outfit was getting—"

"—old—" Bree interrupted.

"—and maybe I could ask Pete for something—"

"—worthy of a Consort of the Goddess—" Bree interrupted again.

"—so this is what he came up with," Kevin finished.

Of all the things to ask for... I shook my head. "So how does it change color? I mean, do you control it, or does it do it all by itself?"

"I just think it, and it does it," he replied. "But Pete also said if I wanted to, I could let it take over. It could even change with the seasons if I wanted. White in winter, light green in spring, golden green in summer, and reddish orange in fall."

In Ireland, maybe. This part of Arizona didn't have those kinds of seasons. No, we pretty much had only two: Summer on the Face of the Sun, and Regular Summer.

"It works like camouflage," Bree said, with a grin. "Daddy Kevin the Chameleon."

Oh, the visual. How could I not laugh?

"Well, it suits you," I said. "It's very modern and fashionable."

He nudged Bree with his elbow. "That's the same thing she said."

Bree just continued to grin, obviously proud of herself, and in high spirits. It warmed my heart.

Just then, Arddhu arrived, full of radiant energy, with the Morrigan at his side, grinning like a satisfied cat.

"Good Hunt?" I asked.

"No." He bent and kissed me until I was breathless. "It was an *excellent* Hunt."

The Morrigan also looked vibrant, her skin flushed and healthy. "Oh, it was wonderful." She placed a hand on Arddhu's arm. "Thank you for allowing me to take part, Great One."

He grinned boyishly at her. "It was a Hunt for the ages, was it not?" He dropped to one knee beside my chair, serious once again. "Great Goddess, Your planet has been cleansed of its plague of evil."

"How many were taken, do you think?" Based on the noise level in my head, it had to be hundreds of thousands.

456

The Morrigan dropped onto the sofa beside Bree. "A lot more than I expected. I'd say at least three or four billion."

What? Billions? Holy fucking shit.

Kevin became absolutely still, eyes wide with shock.

Bree closed her eyes for a moment, then quietly began putting away the board game.

"That's..." I cleared my throat. "Were there really that many with blackened hearts?"

Arddhu simply nodded. "I must admit, there were many more than I expected, as well."

"That's almost fifty percent of the world's total population," Kevin murmured. "That's *insane*."

I was too ashamed of my next thought to speak it: *well, it'll make the migrations go a lot easier and faster.*

I shook my head.

The fallout on this was going to be bad. Really bad. Shit. Why didn't I have any videos or social media posts ready to go? Maybe I could've mitigated some of the reaction.

On the other hand, with that many gone, maybe not.

Reluctantly, I knew I had to see the reaction. I took a deep breath and ported my tablet from my room, then opened my news feed.

The headlines screamed at me from the account of every news service all over the world.

"Hundreds of thousands have vanished in cataclysmic event in New York City."

"Massive reports of missing persons in Los Angeles area."

"Untold disappearances in the United Kingdom."

"Unprecedented event in Paris."

"Worldwide disappearances have every governmental agency panicking."

I rubbed my forehead as I scrolled through hundreds of headlines. Some were outlandish conspiracy theories, and I shook my head at the idiocy.

"Are aliens responsible for abducting millions of Earth citizens?"

"Bright lights seen in the sky just before thousands disappeared in this Midwestern city."

Why was it always fucking aliens?

"Mom?" Bree's voice seemed loud in the quiet room.

I shut off my tablet and looked up. She'd turned on the television, and now raised the volume.

We all watched the screen in silence.

As the newsman stuttered and stammered through his lines, the right corner of the screen showed footage of people crying and screaming in the streets. Their grief was palpable, and I knew I couldn't ignore the cacophony of suffering in my head much longer, although there seemed to be more curses than prayers at the moment.

I had to focus on something. I needed to *do* something.

"I need to talk to Anthony," I muttered. "And Ogma. We need damage control."

My mobile phone buzzed. It was Park, the FBI agent I'd cured of cancer. I hadn't heard from him lately, but I had a pretty damn good idea why he was calling now.

I almost didn't answer. But that would be irresponsible.

And I was anything but irresponsible.

"Agent Park," I said. "It's good—"

"What did you do? *Just what the fuck did you do?*"

His loud voice made my ear hurt.

Technically, I hadn't done anything, since I hadn't gone on the Hunt. But to say that would also be irresponsible.

"What had to be done. Earth has been cleansed of its evil."

"Evil? What the fuck are you talking about?"

"They were all criminals, Agent Park. Either sentenced and sitting in prison, arrested and waiting for trial, or in the process of committing a crime. And I'm not talking about shoplifting here. I'm talking murder, rape, that sort of thing."

After a beat of silence, his rage practically radiated from my phone. "You're telling me my baby brother was a *criminal*? You're out of your goddamn mind."

Oh. Shit. Now I understood where his anger was coming from: grief. "I'm so sorry, Agent. But yes, he had either already committed a serious crime or was about to. His heart was blackened, and so, he was... taken."

I'd almost said *culled*. That wouldn't have gone over well.

"Blackened?"

"Deities can see into every heart. It's how we—I—knew who was unredeemable."

He was silent for a moment.

"So where are they, then? What did you do with them?"

If I mentioned the Void, I'd have to explain it, and I didn't want to do that. So instead, I told him something he'd understand. "They've been sent to hell."

"So they're dead?"

"Yes." For all intents and purposes, anyway.

"Oh my god," he whispered. "Do the words *mass murder* or *genocide* mean anything to you? Anything at all?"

I stared at the crystal bowl on the coffee table, not wanting to meet anyone's eyes. Kevin had turned off the volume on the television, and now everyone around me was silent, listening to my half of the phone conversation.

"It was necessary, Agent Park. There's only so much room at the sanctuary, and only so much time to get everyone moved."

After a brief silence, he asked, "Sanctuary? What the fuck are you talking about now?"

Shit. He didn't know? No one had told him?

Well, he'd find out now.

"The asteroid, Agent Park. Remember that? Well, I'm putting a shield around the planet to deflect or destroy it, but in case that fails, I've created a sanctuary realm—it's called Tearmann—and everyone will have to start moving there soon. The president is supposed to make the announcement later this morning."

His sigh was loud in my ear. "Still. It doesn't excuse your actions. Some of those criminals deserved better. They deserved a chance to redeem themselves, and you took that away from them."

"No, Agent. These weren't the redeemable ones. These were the ones your justice system would've kept in prison for life, or eventually executed. But we don't *have* eventually, and there would've been no one here to save them if the asteroid hits. This was the expedient way, the merciful way—the *only* way—to deal with the problem."

"You mean to tell me, over half the world's population was unredeemable? Bullshit. Absolute bullshit."

He must've been watching the news reports, too.

"For what it's worth, I also think the toll is high. But it is what it is."

He sighed loudly again. "There's going to be a lot of flak over this. You know that, don't you?"

"Yes, I know. And I'll deal with it. Maybe I'll call a press conference or post a video."

"A *press conference*," he snarled. "A *video* won't help this. I'll tell you right now: you've just destroyed whatever good will you had with most people. If—*when*—you publicly take responsibility for this, they'll be coming for you with pitchforks."

I doubted that, but I didn't say it. "I said I'll deal with it."

"Fine. I wish I'd known this was your plan."

"Why? So you could try and talk me out of it?"

"*Yes*. Of course."

"Look. I'm responsible for all life on the planet, Agent Park. I had to do what's best for everyone."

He snorted. "The needs of the many outweigh the needs of the few?" His voice was heavy with sarcasm.

"Yes, actually. That's *exactly* it." Although it fit the situation perfectly, it was too perfect of a line, like it'd come from a movie or a book.

He didn't give an inch. "I would've thought you, as the so-called Goddess of Earth, would be more concerned about *every* life, not just the ones you care about."

Goddammit. He may have heard me talk, but he hadn't *listened* to a word I'd said. "Well, I'm sorry I've disappointed you. But at least you're alive. And you'll keep on living, thanks to me."

"Whatever." He ended the call.

"That went well," I lied.

"I don't think a press conference is a good idea," Kevin said.

"I don't either. I was just throwing shit out there to try and calm him down."

My phone buzzed again, this time showing an unfamiliar number.

"Hello?" I answered tentatively.

"Please hold for the president of the United States," a stiff, formal voice said.

Great. Just fucking great. From bad to worse.

But at least it meant he wasn't a bad guy, since he was still around, like Park.

A moment later, President Jackson was on the line. "Ms. Connor, it seems we have a problem." His tone was stony, his words clipped.

"Apparently, sir."

"You sure know how to upstage a world leader." He sighed. "I was supposed to be holding a press conference shortly, but instead, I just got off the phone with the Secretary General of the United Nations. You and I have been summoned to New York. The UN Security Council has requested our presence at an emergency meeting. I'm sure it has something to do with the roughly *four point two billion* worldwide disappearances that occurred over the past twelve hours or so." By the time he'd finished, he'd allowed his voice to rise in unbridled anger.

In contrast, I kept my voice calm and even. "Will you still be announcing the asteroid?"

"Yes, but it'll have to wait until after the meeting."

"I understand. When and where?"

"In one hour." He gave me the address, then added, "This isn't a polite request, Ms. Connor. Do not *dare* be late." He hung up without waiting for my reply.

I really had to fight with myself to not throw my phone across the room.

"Who was that?" Kevin asked.

"The president. He and I have to appear before the UN Security Council in New York in an hour." My brain was already working on what I'd say and how I'd say it.

"Will they imprison you?" Arddhu's voice was hushed, his face ashen.

I shook my head. "They could try. But I don't think they have anything that could keep me from porting away. Besides, I'm their last hope to save the planet. Even if they could lock me up, they'd be signing their own death warrant. And I think they know that."

"That's the spirit," the Morrigan said encouragingly. "Don't let them intimidate you."

I glanced at Kevin, wondering why he hadn't said he had a bad feeling about this. His gaze was fixed on the silent television.

Bree came over and hugged me. "Do you want us to go with you?"

Oh fuck no. The absolute last thing I needed was to worry about any of my family being held by the government in retaliation for this.

"No, sweetheart." I smiled at her and hoped it was reassuring. "As much as I'd love for you to see the great city of New York, it's better if you—all of you—stay here. It's safer."

Her gaze held mine, then she nodded solemnly. She probably understood all the things I hadn't said as much as what I had said.

"But you'll be alone," Kevin objected.

"It's fine." I smiled at him, too. "Trust me. I can handle it."

And for once, I felt absolutely confident that I could.

In my suite, I thought about the kind of image I wanted to project for this meeting. If I wore a business suit, even with a modest glow, they'd see me as human and an equal—which could either be good or bad.

On the other hand, if I wore a gown and really amped up my divine appearance with a full glow, they'd have no choice but to see me as the Goddess. Which, again, could either be good or bad.

Shit.

I wish I knew more about what kind of people were on the Security Council. Sure, I could check the internet, but that'd take time I didn't really have.

Fuck it. A Goddess gown was probably the better choice in this case, since I wanted absolutely *no one* to mistake my divine status.

First, I chose a pale blue diaphanous gown that was so light, it floated by itself on the air, as if it were alive. I set my glow bright enough to intimidate, but not blinding. I made my hair much longer and fuller, leaving it unbound to cascade in waves to my lower back.

As a final touch, I ported to my palace and quickly donned my crown. I left the wand there, though; that'd just be theatre.

Only a few minutes later, I ported directly to just outside the entrance to the United Nations Conference building. After what'd happened last time, I'd never again port to an occupied room inside a building.

With my enhanced hearing, the noise of the city around me was almost painfully deafening, and I had to muffle it. The isolation of The Hacienda— and the peacefulness of Ard na Mara—had spoiled me. I'd forgotten what it was like to be in a big city.

No use stalling. It was time to go inside.

I took a deep breath, raised my chin, and pushed open the entrance door.

Immediately, a young gentleman in a gray suit approached me. "Ms. Connor? The Keeper Goddess?" To his credit, he managed to only squint a tiny bit at my bright glow.

"That's me." I gave him a friendly smile, which he didn't return. Instead, he skimmed a wand up one side of me and down the other, obviously checking for weapons. Assuming it was a metal detector, I was surprised my crown didn't set it off.

Apparently, so was he. He blinked, looked at the wand, then at my crown, and shrugged. "Please come with me. I'll escort you to the chamber."

"Torture chamber?" I joked.

Without looking at me, he dryly replied, "Assembly chamber."

Well, I couldn't blame him for not joking with me. This was serious business. He might've even lost a relative or friend to the culling.

The wide double doors opened to an enormous room with pale wooden desks arranged in almost a complete circle. Most of the seats were already occupied, and quite a few of the members turned to watch me enter the room. As I followed my escort, I glanced around at the legendary chamber.

Almost one entire wall was covered with an enormous screen for viewing media, and my heart sank. I hoped they weren't going to play any of my videos. Or worse, news coverage of the Hunt's aftermath. Either of those wouldn't help me plead my case.

Rows of orange seats, which I assumed were designated for visitors, sat mostly empty, thank the gods. I'd almost expected to see hundreds of journalists and photographers ready to document this event.

My escort led me to an end seat, where a translation headset and microphone waited. It also had a nameplate:

Deirdre Connor
"Goddess of Earth"

I bristled at the use of quotation marks, as if my title was illegitimate or illusionary. Well, in a few minutes they'd find out how wrong they were.

I politely thanked my escort and sat, then noticed several seats next to mine were empty, with blank nameplates. Couldn't have anyone sit too close to me, could we?

Seething with anger, I kept my face expressionless and casually scanned the faces around the chamber. President Jackson was about ten seats away from me, in what I assumed was his assigned seat. He met my gaze briefly before turning to an assistant seated behind him. No polite nod, no acknowledgement whatsoever.

The other council members studied me with everything from mild curiosity to intense distaste to simple indifference.

There were no friendly faces here.

So.

That's how this was going to be.

Well, I couldn't really blame them. Their countries had taken heavy losses, and they knew I was obviously at fault. It didn't matter to them that it was justified.

To my right, a pitcher of water and two glasses sat on a large gray coaster. I took a closer look and realized the coaster was actually a cooler, designed to keep the water colder than room temperature.

Neat technology.

In front of me, an old-fashioned brown leather desk pad covered and protected the blonde wood. A thin pad of paper had been inserted into the attached holder on the left side. A pen and pencil set, imprinted with a logo and *UN Security Council*, had been neatly placed beside the notepad.

I was tempted to pick up the pen and fidget with it.

But no. No fidgeting. I needed to project strength, confidence, and calm. So I sat tall and straight in my chair and calmly folded my hands together on the desk in front of me, completely masking my inner turmoil while I waited.

But I didn't wait long.

An older gentleman entered and took his seat across the wide open space between us. In a melodic voice with a pronounced accent, he called the meeting to order and identified himself as Pierre Baudin, the President of the Security Council.

Immediately, he began to question me.

"Ms. Connor, you have referred to yourself as the Goddess of Earth. Do you take responsibility then, for the entire planet and its wellbeing?"

"Yes."

"Please speak directly into the microphone."

I adjusted the microphone and leaned forward a bit. "Yes."

"How, then, do you explain the disappearance of approximately four point two billion inhabitants of Earth?"

"Unfortunately, it was necessary. They were all criminals. Most were already condemned to life in prison, were awaiting the completion of their death sentences, or had been arrested and were waiting for trial. The rest simply hadn't been processed yet."

Murmurs around the room.

"What do you mean, *hadn't been processed yet?*" Baudin frowned, but kept his gaze intent on me despite my bright glow.

"They hadn't made their way through the criminal justice system. They hadn't yet been arrested, tried, and sentenced. But they were guilty, nonetheless."

Louder murmurs now, and Baudin had to call for silence.

"Please explain how you determined this information."

How could I answer that truthfully without implicating Arddhu? To buy some time while I thought it through, I poured myself a glass of water and took a sip. It had absolutely no taste at all.

The easiest thing was to say it was all part of the power of the Goddess.

"One of the aspects of deity is the ability to see into someone's heart and judge them accordingly. So in this case, their hearts were blackened, and so they were... removed."

"To where?"

"Hell, or whatever the cultural equivalent is for those who don't believe in it."

Again, murmurs around the council. This time, Baudin stared at me for a moment before continuing.

"So, to be clear, did you just state that you judged approximately four point two billion people as guilty of crimes, sentenced them to death, and then... sent them to hell?"

"Yes."

"Ms. Connor, you designated yourself as judge, jury, and sentencer for a significant percentage of the population of Earth. Do you truly understand the gravity of your actions?"

"Of course. But it was necessary."

Baudin snapped, "That's the second time you've used that word. Exactly why was it *necessary*, Ms. Connor?"

I hesitated. How much did this council know about the asteroid? The answer to that would determine how I could respond.

I turned toward President Jackson. Using a mental communication link, I asked, "*Do they know about the asteroid? Can I tell the truth here?*"

He whipped his head toward me, eyes wide. I raised a brow, and he blinked, then slowly and clearly nodded.

Okay, then. That helped a lot.

So I cleared my throat and spent the next several minutes explaining the plan, including the planetary shield and its expected effect on the asteroid. Next, I spoke of the sanctuary realm, and emphasized its size was finite, but would be sufficient for a short-term stay as a contingency plan.

Surprisingly, I wasn't interrupted, not even once.

After I finished, Baudin muted his microphone and spoke to the woman next to him for quite some time, while several other council members murmured quietly amongst themselves.

I poured another glass of water and was impressed that my hands didn't shake.

A moment later, Baudin unmuted his microphone. "When will the migration to the sanctuary realm take place?"

Again, I looked to President Jackson for guidance, knowing he'd been planning on announcing that topic at his press conference.

He held a hand up to me, cleared his throat, and addressed Baudin directly. "If I may, Mr. President, I can answer that." He waited until Baudin nodded, then continued. "First, I'd like to mention I'd planned a press conference this morning to announce the incoming asteroid and the details Ms. Connor just spoke of, including the migration plans. However, the other... event... took precedence, and I was forced to delay the press conference.

"To answer your question specifically, we planned to begin migrating people next week. After all, we only have roughly two to four weeks until impact. It'd be best if everyone is moved well before then."

"That doesn't leave much time," Baudin pointed out.

"No, sir, it doesn't."

"What kind of place is this sanctuary?" Baudin asked.

Jackson turned toward me and indicated I should answer.

"Well, it's sort of a simulated Earth," I began. "It's a realm with zones like Earth's major climates. Deserts, mountains, forest, oceans, for example. There is clean air and water, and all the basics for humans to live safely and comfortably for as long as necessary, should the asteroid's impact make Earth uninhabitable.

"I created houses, schools, hospitals, vehicles, and roads. But there are no prisons, banks, factories, or power plants. No coal, electricity, gasoline, or natural gas. Nothing that could pollute the air, water, or soil."

"No power plants?" Baudin echoed. "What powers this realm of yours, then? Magick?" He snorted, and there were more than a few snickers scattered throughout the chamber.

I let them have their fun for only a moment. "Yes. Everything runs on magick."

Now they all just stared at me in silence.

"It was the cleanest power option," I explained. "And it's renewable."

More silence as they continued to stare at me. The need to fidget was almost overwhelming, but instead I took another sip of the tasteless water.

"I see." Baudin seemed to consider everything I'd said, and when he resumed his questions a moment later, he used a softer tone of voice with me.

An hour or so later, I truly felt I'd gained the respect of Baudin and the rest of the council members, and I was certain they'd accepted my divinity as fact.

And we had a solid plan for the migration, which would be handled by the individual nations of the world.

I'd only had one suggestion to add: people had to take their pets with them. No exceptions.

I'd felt bad enough that so many of the humans taken in the Wild Hunt had left their pets behind; I didn't need even more starving doggies or kitties on my conscience.

In final remarks, President Jackson suggested a joint press conference with Baudin, to announce the asteroid and related mitigation efforts. Baudin readily agreed. Then Jackson turned toward me. "I'd also like you to attend, Ms. Connor. To show that we're all united on this effort."

"Of course, sir." I'd noticed the lack of reverence. Maybe I hadn't done enough to convince him.

Baudin gaveled the meeting to closure, and approached Jackson and I. "Ms. Connor, would it be possible for me to visit this sanctuary realm?"

Before I replied, Jackson added, "I'd also like to see the improvements you've made. The infrastructure. We could go after the press conference."

"Of course," I said. "It would be my pleasure."

I don't know how they got the members of the press together on such short notice, but within the hour, everyone was gathered in a smaller conference room near the Assembly Chamber.

Jackson and Baudin stood at separate podiums, with me in between. I didn't feel slighted at not having my own podium. If anyone asked me a question, I could boost my voice well enough to be heard, but the same couldn't be said about the two world leaders.

It went about as well as could be expected.

Jackson introduced me, but advised I wasn't there to answer their questions. I was only there for support and to show solidarity.

Baudin made the actual announcement of the impending asteroid, and the reaction was mostly one of silent shock, with only a few gasps scattered throughout the attendees. No one freaked out, which actually surprised me.

I still wondered how the asteroid's presence had been kept such a secret all this time. Why hadn't some amateur astronomer noticed it? Why hadn't it been all over the internet before now? How'd we get so damn lucky?

Jackson explained the planetary shield and sanctuary realm, and most of the attendees seemed to relax a bit after that.

Baudin detailed the migration plan, and added that the Security Council was responsible for making sure each individual nation had its people ready to migrate at the appropriate time.

Then the press asked their questions.

Some were ridiculously stupid, like the woman from a conspiracy-theory website masquerading as a news site, who asked if the moon's orbit could be changed so it would get hit by the asteroid instead of Earth. To their credit, neither Jackson nor Baudin rolled their eyes or made any snarky remarks.

Overall, both men did great at answering the questions without needing any input from me. The whole thing lasted a little over an hour.

As soon as it was done, Jackson and Baudin headed toward a side door, and I followed them. The three of us stood in a corridor, surrounded by Jackson's Secret Service detail and Baudin's security personnel.

"How does this work?" Baudin seemed a bit nervous. "How do we travel to this sanctuary realm?"

"First, we need to go outside so I can open a portal." Technically, I could open one indoors, but I didn't want to.

"Ah. I see." He beckoned us to follow him to the end of the corridor and through the exit doors, where a small courtyard garden waited. It had green grass, a few mature trees, and some flowering shrubs. "Will this do?"

"Perfectly." I glanced at the small horde of security agents milling nearby. "How many are going with us?"

Jackson called two of his detail over, and Baudin did the same. The rest were instructed to stay and guard the portal, to make sure no unauthorized humans went through while we were there.

I opened the portal to Tearmann, then stepped aside.

"After you, gentlemen."

This time, Jackson went through immediately. Baudin simply stared at the shimmering circle for a moment before slowly stepping through. None of the security personnel hesitated at all.

I'd chosen a different destination location this time, since Jackson had already seen the Atlantic zone replica. Now, it was the Pacific zone replica.

Ocean waves rolled gently onto a sandy beach dotted with palm trees that rustled in the breeze. To our immediate right, a four-lane road led to a distant ridge of snow-capped mountains. On the other side of the road, a small town looked like a movie set, with several stores, a school, a hospital, city administration buildings, and houses. On the far end of town, a medium-sized lot held a couple hundred vehicles gleaming in the sun.

"This is remarkable." Baudin slowly turned in a circle to take it all in.

"What town is this?" Jackson asked, pointing.

"I have no idea. Since it's not an exact replica, I didn't name anything. Humans can call these places whatever they want after they get here."

He was silent for a moment. "Where are the churches?"

"I didn't create any."

His gaze on me was sharp. "Do you expect everyone to worship you? Because I don't think that will go over very well right now."

And then, I lost my patience.

"I don't expect *anyone* to worship me," I snapped. "You humans can build your own damn churches. Use the reservoir of magick I've created and make whatever you fucking want. I've left complete instructions." Without waiting for a response, I walked away.

Gods, he was such a pain in the ass. I almost wished he *had* been culled.

I stared out at the waves and took a deep breath to calm down. It really was beautiful here, and it reminded me of Ard na Mara.

Footsteps halted beside me.

"I'm sorry." Jackson spoke quietly and respectfully. "I'm nitpicking, and I know it. I don't mean to, I'm just stressed. And this morning didn't help."

Did he think he was the only one stressed? I took another deep breath, then turned toward him.

"Look. I know it's not perfect. But it's a good start. And people will need things to do to occupy their time and stay busy. I've provided all the basics and the materials, but it's up to them—and you—to do the rest."

He nodded. "You're right. And it's better than just a good start. This place is amazing." He paused and glanced around. "Sometimes I lose sight of the complexity of what you've done here."

"If I'd had more time, I might've been able to create an exact replica. But, well, there's so much more to do. The shield isn't going to create itself."

"I understand." He met my gaze. "And I've been remiss. I haven't told You how much I appreciate all Your hard work. Thank You for creating this sanctuary realm, and for the shield You're about to put around the planet. We'd be well and truly fucked without You."

I'd noticed the change as he'd spoken: when he'd become reverent toward me. I hadn't expected it from him, but it was long overdue just the same.

"Thank you for saying that, sir. And you are quite welcome." I turned, looking for Baudin, who was in deep discussion with his security detail. "If you've both seen enough for now, I need to get back to work on the shield."

"Of course."

We rejoined Baudin and the security personnel.

"Ms. Connor, this is extraordinary," Baudin enthused. "I do believe we'll all be quite comfortable here."

I nodded. "And, most importantly, you'll all be safe." I paused. "And for what it's worth, I really am sorry about the... the culling. But it truly was necessary."

He studied me for a moment. "I do understand it, now. But you cannot be forgiven."

"I appreciate your understanding, but I don't need anyone's forgiveness."

He nodded once, then turned with Jackson toward the portal. I followed them back through, then closed it. A moment later, I was home, where I immediately changed into my comfy clothes.

My family had been waiting anxiously in the living room. Over the next few minutes, I briefed them on what'd happened.

"Thank all the gods you have returned," Arddhu said, plainly relieved.

"We watched the press conference," the Morrigan added. "It went surprisingly well."

"I thought so, too," I agreed.

"Anthony stopped by," Kevin said. "We told him what happened. He said he'll schedule a full Council meeting as soon as possible."

"Perfect," I smiled. "Thanks."

After a quick bite of some leftovers—Brianna was with Kali again, apparently getting another cooking lesson—I got online and monitored the effects of the culling and press conference.

Unfortunately, it seemed everything had changed.

More humans had turned on me than I'd expected. My social media accounts had quite a few posts calling me disgusting names. Over the next hour or so, I noticed the number of prayers I received slowed to a trickle. My heart ached from breaking the sacred trust between my followers and me.

One by one, the individual nations of the world made their announcements regarding migration plans. I watched Jackson give his on live television, and was pleased when he specifically mentioned the work I'd done on the planetary shield and the sanctuary realm. I smiled when he emphatically stated everyone had to take their pets with them, and actually repeated it three more times throughout the address.

And then, he surprised me by strictly forbidding anyone from bringing firearms or weapons of any kind to Tearmann. All weapons had to be left behind, and if anyone tried to sneak one through any of the portals, they'd be immediately confiscated. I hadn't thought of this, but I quickly realized it was pretty damn smart. They'd have knives for cooking on Tearmann, and they wouldn't need to hunt animals for food, so firearms weren't necessary. And because there wouldn't be any bad humans there, none were needed for self-defense, either.

Finally, he mentioned that all the individual nations of the world were also making the same announcement.

"For the first time in history, we are a unified Earth," he said, and it gave me chills. He finished with: "Remember: the gods will be watching you."

Damn. That'd been a great line. So good, I wished I'd come up with it.

So then, everything changed again, as gratitude poured in from all the humans who realized I'd been the one with the plan to save them.

CHAPTER THIRTY-TWO

I T WAS NOW the beginning of the second week of June, and our full Council meeting was scheduled for later in the morning.

Bree was sleeping in, and everyone else was off doing whatever, so while I waited for the Council meeting, I settled in the living room and answered a hundred or so prayers for healing or comfort. People were still nervous or scared about the upcoming migration, and needed the reassurance I could provide.

Next, I spent half an hour or so checking my social media accounts and posting uplifting messages, and going through my email.

In one important email, I'd finally received something I'd need later this week, when the human migrations to Tearmann were expected to begin. A few days earlier, I'd met virtually with the project team to determine the required number of portals and the best locations. They needed to be scattered all over the world yet conveniently located for every human to get to with minimal effort.

By the time we'd finished plotting the portals on maps, they'd numbered into the tens of thousands.

Those maps had been finalized and attached to an email.

Next week, I'd create a portal at each of the specified locations, and either a deity or a Túatha would be at each and every one of them to keep the migration running smoothly.

Now, I'd just closed my laptop when my mobile phone buzzed.

It was John Simmons.

"We have a bit of good news, for a change," he began. "Eris has slowed. New projections push the expected impact almost two weeks out."

Oh, thank all the gods.

"That's great. But why did it slow down? Is that normal?"

"Yes and no. Usually, foreign bodies speed up, but that's further out in the system. This close in, there's plenty of space debris and microscopic particles to cause the friction necessary to slow its speed. Unfortunately, it also means the trajectory has shifted a bit, just enough for a higher chance of impact."

"Shit."

"Yeah." He paused. "And the shield? When will you, uh, install it?"

"Probably next week."

"Great. After... well, after we all come back, we'll work together on figuring out how to get rid of the fragments."

"Sounds good."

After we hung up, I turned to find Anthony waiting to speak to me.

"Good news?" he asked.

I nodded. "The asteroid has slowed down. We have some extra time, maybe as much as two more weeks."

"That *is* good. On the Council meeting: are you sure you want Ares, Athena, and Kali to attend?"

"Absolutely. We need all hands on deck for the migration, and I won't turn away their help. Besides, Ares and Athena offered their new realm, just in case we need more room for refugees. That could come in handy."

"Okay." He nodded. "I just wanted to double check."

Just as he left, the Morrigan entered and sat on the couch nearby.

"Anything new?" she asked.

I told her about the new estimated impact date, and she flashed a quick grin.

"Well. That's convenient." I nodded, and she studied me for a moment. "This'll be hard for you, you know."

"What will?"

"The migration. Maintaining the shield. Witnessing the impact. Staying behind to heal Earth. All of it."

"I know." I met and held her steady gaze, well aware of what we were both not saying.

"Do they know?" she asked quietly.

"Kevin does. He figured it out right away. I'm not sure either Arddhu or Bree have thought it all the way through."

She nodded. "Kevin's pretty sharp, but so is Bree. Don't be surprised if she's figured it out but just hasn't said anything about it yet."

"Can't sneak much past either of them, that's for sure." I met her gaze again. "I'm counting on you to be Bree's mom until I can join all of you on Tearmann."

"Of course." Again, she studied me. "Are you sure this is the right thing to do? Why don't you just come with us? Let Earth take care of herself. She's survived worse. She'll survive this."

Well, yes. I knew that. Hmm... "*Anu, did you see any asteroid impacts in the past?*"

"*Yes. Many.*"

"*Did you try and stop them?*"

"*No. There was nothing I could do. Like You, my power was limited to the planet.*" After a brief pause, she added, "*I am quite ashamed to admit I did not consider creating a shield, as You plan to do.*"

Oh.

"*I'm sorry, Anu.*"

"*Do not be sorry. It is in the past. You are the future. Much love, Deirdre.*"

"*Much love.*"

"Hello, Earth to Dee." The Morrigan had been watching me with interest. "Where were you just now?"

"Sorry," I said. "Talking to Anu. I know Earth will be fine. The part that worries me the most is that Earth could end up uninhabitable by humans for thousands of years. Maybe even longer."

She shrugged. "So? They'll be fine on Tearmann."

"I know." I sighed. "But to answer your earlier question, I can't just leave. I'm not Goddess of Tearmann. I'm Goddess of Earth, and this planet is my responsibility. It's my job."

"Okay, okay, okay." She held up a hand for me to stop.

"As far as the plan goes, if the shield holds, great. Everyone can just come right back. If it doesn't but Earth only has minor damage, it won't take me long to fix it. And again, everyone can come back." I paused to take a breath. "But if the worst happens... if the shield fails completely and

Earth is too damaged to fix, I'm not stupid. I won't stay. I'll leave for Tearmann as soon as I can."

"Promise?"

"Of course."

"And are you going to tell Arddhu and Bree all this?" Her voice hardened. "Or do you expect *me* to do it, after we're on Tearmann and you don't show up for weeks or months? Maybe even years?"

"Look." I kept my voice steady. "I need to know my family will be safe, no matter what. And I need to stay focused right now. So yes, I'll tell them. But not right now."

Unexpectedly, she stood and pulled me into a close embrace. I breathed in her scent: spicy-sweet, like cinnamon, and blinked away tears. She pulled away after a moment, and unshed tears shimmered in her dark eyes. "Don't you dare sacrifice yourself for this godforsaken planet."

"Now you sound just like Kevin. He's totally convinced that's my real plan." I shook my head. "But it's not. It's just as I've told you."

"I'm serious, Dee."

"So am I. Didn't I just promise you? Not even a minute ago?"

She nodded. "Okay, okay."

"I love you," I blurted. "You're like the sister I always wanted but never had."

"I love you, too." Her grin was sly and lazy. "Good thing you didn't say I was like a mother to you. I would've had to kick your ass."

We were both laughing when Brianna came in.

"You two want some breakfast?" she asked.

"Yes, please," I said. "I'm sorry. It's like I can't even do the simplest meal myself."

"Don't you dare be sorry. It's my job. You've got enough to do." She smiled mischievously. "I didn't think you even knew how to cook."

I laughed. "I actually don't."

It was good to have friends. Especially when the world as you knew it might be ending.

Just as the Morrigan and I finished up breakfast, Bree entered, yawning.

"Morning, sweetie," I greeted her. "We're just about ready to head out to the Council meeting. You know you need to stay here until it's over, right? No porting?"

"Yeah, I know." She studied me for a moment, then added, "But I actually think I should attend, too. Everyone needs to know about the animals migrating."

"Did you find a way to save them?"

She nodded solemnly, and I sighed.

In that case, she was right. "Okay. C'mon, let's go."

As we left through the panel in the window-wall, the Morrigan caught my eye and raised a brow, but I shook my head.

We'd all find out soon enough what Bree had in mind.

Reshep, Arddhu, Anthony, and Kevin were already there. A moment later, Randy arrived with the Túatha, laughing and joking as if best buddies.

Well, thank the gods they were all getting along so well now, unlike earlier in the year.

Kali came from her guest house at almost the same time as Ares and Athena arrived from the portal. The last to arrive were my ambassadors: Daphne, Ferris, and Alana.

Anthony had made several printed copies of the portal location maps, and now he distributed them with the corresponding assignments. The Dagda was the only one to receive a thick stack of maps, since he was responsible for assigning most of the portals to his people, who numbered in the thousands and would be assisting in the migration. Lugh would deliver additional maps to other deities who'd agreed to help.

Next, we reviewed the relatively simple plan.

Tomorrow morning, I'd open all the portals to Tearmann. The Túatha and participating deities would then guide the local humans through the portals in an orderly and efficient manner.

Areas of high population, like large cities, would have multiple portals. Areas with low population would have fewer portals, but no humans would need to travel more than an hour or so to reach any portal.

Each portal would stay open until all the humans in that area had migrated, and it was the responsibility of each portal attendant to confirm his or her area was uninhabited before contacting me via mental communication link to report that the area was clear. Then I'd close the portal and mark it on the master map, and the portal attendant would return to The Hacienda for further assignment, if necessary.

"What if some humans refuse to migrate?" Lugh asked.

"We'll just have to leave them," I said.

Daphne gasped. "You would just leave them to possibly die?"

"Unfortunately, there are always a few humans who refuse to leave their homes. We see it all the time with hurricanes or other natural disasters. I don't know if it's because they think they're invincible, or just in denial about being in danger, but we can't go house to house and forcibly remove people who don't want to leave. We won't have time for that. And we can't sacrifice thousands for only a handful."

"Oh. I see." She nodded slowly.

The next part of the plan was also simple: after each portal attendant returned to The Hacienda, he or she was free to either stay on Earth and assist with other portals, or go to Tearmann to help the humans get settled in.

We expected the migration to take a bit over a full week, which should allow plenty of time for a margin of error.

"The last portal to stay open will be here, at The Hacienda," I said. "I'll only close it after everyone else—including all of you—have migrated. Then, I'll sever the connection between Tearmann and Earth."

"And then what?" the Dagda asked.

"I'll set the shield in place and connect it to Earth for its power. Then I'll monitor the situation at impact and decide whether to stay and heal the damage, or leave immediately and join all of you on Tearmann."

He nodded thoughtfully. "Seems logical."

"What if something happens to you, and you get knocked out or something?" Kevin asked quietly.

"I'll do what I can to have personal shields up, too." I shrugged. "It's all I can do."

"Will you stay here, at The Hacienda?" the Morrigan asked.

I nodded. "I don't see any reason to port to the asteroid impact site. I can do whatever I need to do from here." I glanced around the table. "Any other questions?"

"What about all the other creatures, Lady?" Ferris asked. "The troll-kind, sprites, fairies, and such? Who will migrate them?"

Damn. I should've asked Pete the Troll to attend, since I'd made him responsible for that effort. I hadn't been thinking.

After I explained the arrangement I'd made with him, I added, "I'm so sorry I didn't remember to ask him to come here. Your kind—and the other magickal creatures—are as much a part of this planet as humans are, and I should've done better to make sure I communicated that to all of you."

Daphne, Alana, and Ferris shared a quick glance, then Daphne said, "Lady, we're grateful You remembered us at all. We will contact Pete of Finn's Cove and coordinate the migration of our folk with him."

"Thank you." I swallowed the lump that'd formed in my throat. Sometimes, I truly believed I didn't deserve the honor these creatures gave to me.

I needed to do better.

Once again, I asked if there were any other questions.

After everyone demurred, I turned to Bree. "By now, you have all probably met my daughter, Bree. But if you haven't, it is my honor to introduce Brighid Astrid Kyra Morgan Ain Devyn Connor, Bree for short. She was born on Beltaine and her fathers are Arddhu and Kevin." I paused as the attendees smiled and nodded at her, then continued. "I now yield the meeting to her, to discuss a very important part of the migration."

Bree gave me a shaky smile, cleared her throat, and with a clear, strong voice, she began.

"A couple of weeks ago, when my mom—um, Dee—um, the Goddess—told me about the migration, I asked what would happen to all the animals. She said if I wanted to save them, I'd have to find a way to do it. So, I did. I, um, found a way."

She glanced at Arddhu and the Morrigan, who both nodded for her to continue, tiny smiles on both of their faces.

Hmm. So, they'd known about this.

"A while back," she continued, "I found out I could communicate with animals. So, a couple of days ago, I held a... a meeting with all of them, even the elephants in Africa and the tigers in Asia. And all the birds. And I told them what's happening, that an asteroid is coming. I explained how I wanted to save them." She paused before continuing. "So now, they're all heading toward the portal locations."

I blinked at her. "How do they know where to go?"

"I, um, got a copy of the maps from Anthony and told them this morning. They're all going to their nearest portal location."

So she hadn't been sleeping in, after all.

"When can we expect them?" Reshep asked.

"They should be arriving at each portal location any time now."

"So they'll actually go through first," Kevin said.

She nodded. "That way, they can go and hide on Tearmann and they won't scare the humans."

"But won't they attack them?" Kali asked. "Attack the humans, I mean."

Bree shook her head. "I made them promise to obey the rules."

"Rules?" I didn't know whether to laugh or cry at this point. "What rules?"

"They can't eat anyone, or start any fights. They have to stay calm and well-behaved. And they can't hurt any of the humans or the Tearmann animals."

Oh gods. This girl was going to be the death of me.

"And they all agreed?" I asked.

She nodded. "They all promised."

"But they eat other animals," the Dagda said. "For food. For survival. How will they live?"

She blushed. "I... um... well, in return for their promise, they made me promise to feed them and take care of them."

Again, I was speechless.

"How will you do that?" Lugh asked.

"I've been experimenting, and I think I found a solution. I'll make their food *look* like the animals they normally eat, but it won't be *real* animals."

"Fake animals." Lugh seemed fascinated with Bree.

She nodded, and I could only look at her.

But the more I looked, the more I saw. She was more than just my daughter; she was a young woman now, worried about all the animals she'd promised to save, and nervous about the subdued reaction she was receiving from this Council.

She glanced at me and, catching me watching her, blushed. "Is that okay?"

"Yes." I didn't need to look around the table for confirmation. "And I'm sure it'll be fine with the humans, too."

Her smile was like a ray of sunshine on a cold winter's day.

"Does anyone have any questions?" I asked.

No one did, so I adjourned the meeting and the members headed for the refreshments.

Bree hadn't moved from her seat beside me. "Are you disappointed in me?" Her voice was barely above a whisper.

"No. I'm very, very proud of you."

"Proud?"

"Sure. You identified a problem, worked to find a solution, and made it work. All by yourself."

Now, her smile was wry. "Well, it wasn't *totally* by myself. I had a little help from Daddy Arddhu and Auntie Morrigan."

I raised a brow. "And neither of them said a word to me about this?"

"No, it wasn't like that. I told Daddy Arddhu how I could communicate with the coyotes outside our property walls, and asked him how I could boost the... um, signal... to other animals. So that's what he helped me with."

"And the Morrigan?"

Now, she hesitated. "Well, um, *she* sort of knew. 'Cause I asked her to help me come up with the rules."

Of course she did.

"Well, I'm glad you had some help, since you didn't feel you could ask me."

"Really?"

"Really. But since this whole thing is your idea, it's also your responsibility."

"My responsibility?" Her eyes widened.

"Yep. It's your job to make sure all the animals get through the portals smoothly and don't cause any humans to panic. If you need help, ask for it." I paused, holding her gaze. "But once they're on Tearmann, your job doesn't end with just feeding them. You'll have to make sure they stay out of trouble there, which means figuring out how to monitor them. And discipline them, if necessary."

"Monitor them? All of them?" She blinked at me. "Can I ask for help over there, too?"

"Of course. Maybe you can get other young people involved."

After a brief moment, she grinned. "I can do that." Then her arms were around me in a tight hug. "Thank you, Mom. I won't let you down. I promise. I've got this. You'll see."

I held my girl—now almost a grown woman—and smiled, even as tears formed in my eyes. She'd grown up so fast, and things had been so crazy, I hadn't had time to truly enjoy her infancy or childhood. "I know you will, Bree."

She pulled away, then hesitated. "It'll all be okay. I know it will."

I nodded, ready to believe her. "I love you, sweetie."

"I love you, too, Mom."

And then she was gone, bounding away and ready to take on the world. Who knew? Maybe all the worlds.

CHAPTER THIRTY-THREE

E ARLY THE NEXT morning, the sky was a deep, gorgeous blue, without a single cloud in sight. Unfortunately, the high temperature was expected to break records that'd stood for over a hundred years, and the entire Phoenix Metropolitan area was under a severe heat warning.

There were other areas around the world where the local conditions would be challenging for the migration, too. There wasn't much I could do about that, though, except watch for any threatening weather that could impact our efforts, and divert it if possible.

But there was one other thing I could do: make sure all the portal attendants had plenty of water on hand for the humans.

And for the animals.

Via a mental communication link with everyone, I reminded them of the herds of animals and flocks of birds arriving at each portal, and explained why a large refrigerated container of bottled water had also shown up at each site.

Then, after a quick breakfast, I got comfortable in the living room, which was the command center for the entire migration effort.

Promptly at eight o'clock, I opened all the portals, officially launching the migration.

Since the birds and animals had already gathered at their portal sites, they went through first, as Bree had detailed at yesterday's Council meeting. I stayed out of the whole process, letting her handle it. I didn't even interfere when a scuffle broke out between a grouchy pregnant panther and the portal attendants at a Southeastern Asia site.

Bree, sitting beside me on the couch, handled the whole thing via her communication link with the panther, plus a few comments for me to pass along to the attendants with my own link.

I was even more proud of her.

Throughout the day, the portal attendants kept me updated on how things were going. Of course, some of the first humans through were the world leaders, which didn't surprise me. They'd wanted to help guide their people as they arrived on Tearmann, and I'd agreed it was a good idea.

Finn's Cove was the first area cleared, since it was so small, and so it was the first portal closed. Pete the Troll was off with Daphne, Ferris, and Alana, coordinating the migration of the magickal creatures, but first he'd made sure his wife was safe on Tearmann with the rest of Finn's Cove.

Just after lunch, a problem occurred at one of the Chicago portals. The zoo animals had been late to the portal, since they'd needed help being freed, and a woman had gotten spooked at the parade of lions, tigers, and other animals as they patiently waited to go through the portal with humans. She'd pulled a handgun out of her purse and almost succeeded in firing it before the Túatha portal attendant magicked the pistol away. Bree directly communicated with the animals to keep them all calm, and in the end all was well, as the attendant didn't let the woman pass until after the animals finished going through.

As the day wore on, there were a few other isolated incidents here and there, and more than a few humans who tried to sneak their guns through. The portal attendants did a fantastic job keeping order. To their credit, there was no violence or panic reported at any of the thousands of portal sites.

Having all the unredeemable humans removed in the Wild Hunt had probably helped with that, too, and I realized it'd been a blessing.

Mid-way through the afternoon, I grew bored with just sitting around and monitoring, so I took over on one of the Scottsdale portals. Within the first five minutes, though, I'd had to heal several cases of heat stroke, so I quickly created a cooling canopy over the long line of humans. Underneath, the temperature was twenty degrees cooler—which was still hot, but quite a bit more bearable. I also restocked the bottled water, and many of the humans thanked me as they passed by on their way through the portal.

Being useful, actually *doing* something, raised my spirits a bit.

At nightfall, one of the Túatha arrived to take over, and I ported back to The Hacienda, exhausted and sweaty, but feeling a bit more confident that maybe this whole thing was going to work, after all.

The next several days passed in a blur. All over the world, humans—and more than a few late-arriving animals—continued to migrate with relatively few problems, and none of them were major.

Bree spent some time on Tearmann, getting the animals all settled in and recruiting some of the younger deities to help monitor them. Then, she came back through to stay with me to ensure any straggler animals were taken care of.

Slowly at first, then with increasing frequency, portal attendants reported that their areas were clear and their portals could be closed. I continued to mark them off the master map, and by the tenth day, there were only a few hundred portals still open.

We were making extremely good time, and it seemed we'd only need one more day to complete the migration.

The next morning, I called the security team together and requested they go through the portal at The Hacienda. After the rest of the team went through, Randy refused.

"I can't leave you here unguarded."

Pointedly, I glanced around. "There are only a few thousand people left on the entire planet, Randy, and I doubt they'll try to come here to hurt me. You need to go. Please. We're down to the wire now, and I'll be very busy from here on out." I sighed. "I can't be distracted by people I care about hanging around."

He blinked at me. "You... care? About me?"

"Of course I do, you big goof." I lightly punched his massive bicep, and immediately regretted it. It'd been like hitting a rock, and my knuckles were sore. "Now go. I'm counting on you to help keep order on Tearmann. I'll be there as soon as I can."

Finally, I'd convinced him; he nodded and left.

As I'd previously arranged with Odin and the deities on other realms, I now severed the connection between each of those realms and Earth. They'd be safe, but on their own, until after impact.

But I also opened portals between those realms and Tearmann, so they could move freely between.

Throughout the day, portal attendants trickled in as they completed their assigned areas, and they wished me well before they went through the main portal.

Lugh was one of the last. Unexpectedly, he embraced me.

"It has been an honor to serve You, my Lady," he said, somewhat formally. "Be safe, and join us soon."

"Thank you." I blinked away sudden tears. "I will."

By dinnertime, it was done. The only humans left were the ones who'd refused to leave, and they numbered about three thousand, scattered all over the world. They seemed to believe either the asteroid would completely miss the planet, or their chosen god would save them.

So be it. Their fates were their own; I couldn't worry about them from here on out.

The portals were all closed except for the last, here at The Hacienda.

Dinner was quick leftovers, since I'd already sent Brianna through the portal earlier in the day. I spent the evening with my family, who'd insisted on staying until the end: Arddhu and Kevin, the Morrigan and Reshep, and Bree. None of us talked about the migration or the asteroid. We played card games, told jokes and stories, and hugged each other a lot.

Tomorrow, everyone would leave for Tearmann.

That night, I spent in my bed with Arddhu and Kevin, and it was glorious.

The following morning, I woke before anyone else. I pocketed the flask Maggie had given me, then sent my birthday gifts and a few other treasured items to my pocket universe. Then I went outside to install the shield around the planet. High above me, the shield appeared as a thin overcast that transformed the deep blue of a typical Arizona sky to a muted baby blue. It partially filtered the sun, giving it a hazy appearance, but was transparent enough so I'd be able to see the asteroid as it approached.

I'd connect it to Earth later, after everyone left.

Silently, my family and I ate breakfast, one of the meals prepared in advance by Brianna. It was as if no one knew what to say, so we didn't say anything.

After the meal and dishes were done, I cleared my throat. "It's time."

"Already?" Bree asked, her voice quiet and face pale.

Kevin didn't say a word, but he was obviously upset: his eyes, wide with fear, stared at nothing and his breath hitched.

Arddhu's face was stricken. "But there are many days left until the impact. I will stay with you."

I shook my head. "It could show up at any time. I need to know you're all safe."

Of all of them, only the Morrigan and Reshep stayed totally calm.

I held the panel in the window-wall open, and my family reluctantly went through. Just beyond the patio, near the portal, I took the leather cord from around my neck. It held the blue bead I'd found at Ard na Mara. I slipped it over Bree's head.

"Keep this safe for me."

She nodded with tears in her eyes, and I realized she was as tall as me now. When had she grown those last few inches?

"Who will help you with the shield?" Arddhu stubbornly asked.

"I don't need help. I've got this."

"I will not leave you here," Arddhu said.

"Yes, you will. I order you to. I can't be distracted when the asteroid hits. I'll need every bit of concentration."

He opened his mouth to continue arguing, but the Morrigan laid a hand on his arm. "She'll join us on Tearmann as soon as she is able."

Kevin added, "The humans on Tearmann will need to be calmed down. We can do that while we wait for Dee to battle the asteroid."

Ooh, I liked that. What a great way to put it: *battle the asteroid.*

"It'll be okay, Daddy Arddhu," Bree said. "I *know* it will."

He locked eyes with her, then finally nodded. "I do not like this, but I understand."

Bree stepped close and hugged me, hard. "You'd better not prove me wrong and die," she said, fiercely. "I'll be really pissed at you if you do."

"I will do everything in my power to live," I assured her, blinking away tears. "I love you so much, honey."

Just as I began to pull away from her, pain lanced through my body, centered on my left wrist. I grimaced and watched in disbelief as Anu detached herself from me and became a ball of blue light that rose to eye level.

"*Anu, what's happening?*"

"*Once, I foretold there would come a time when You would no longer need me. That time has come. However, there is one who does need me, and I will go with her now. Be at peace, Deirdre. Much love.*"

Already, my pain had faded.

Anu—the Sphere—floated toward Bree, who watched it in fascination. In a bright flash, Anu was gone. Bree gasped and lifted both hands to her neck, but by the time I'd taken only two steps toward her, she'd recovered.

"I'm okay," she insisted, dropping her hands to her sides. "I'm fine."

Around her slender neck, a shiny silver torque had appeared. On one end, a milky white stone softly glowed. The cobalt blue bead from Ard na Mara was affixed on the other end. Nothing remained of the leather cord I'd put it on.

Bree cocked her head and stared vacantly, as if listening to someone, and lightly brushed the torque with the fingers of one hand.

Anu was probably speaking to her now, and the pain of loss filled me for a moment. Again, I blinked through the tears. Gods, I'd miss Anu. But apparently, Bree needed her more than I did right now. I had to remember: everything wasn't always about me.

I hugged Bree once more, and my voice was hoarse when I spoke. "Anu will take good care of you until I can join you."

"I know." She paused, then added, "I love you, Mom. And I'll watch for you every day."

Next, I turned to Arddhu, and swallowed the lump in my throat.

Fuck. This was a lot harder than I'd thought it'd be.

"I love you." I kissed him and held his face in my hands. "Watch over Bree."

He nodded, seemingly unable to speak.

Then it was Kevin's turn. I gave him the flask. "This is Maggie's magick flask. Take care of it for me." I kissed him deeply, drawing him close.

"I love you so much," he murmured. "You'd better come back to us."

"I love you, too. I will. And you'd better stay out of trouble."

At least, he hadn't said he had a bad feeling about this.

I turned to Reshep and joked, "Don't start any wars over there."

"Never." His dark eyes glistened with unshed tears as he smiled wryly, then turned serious. "It has been an honor to serve on Your Council, Lady. I look forward to continuing my service to You."

I nodded, and lastly, hugged the Morrigan.

"Take care of them," I whispered in her ear. "And I love you."

"Always," she whispered back. "Love you, too."

Then, they stepped through the portal and were gone.

I didn't hold back the tears as I closed the portal and severed its connection to Earth.

Now, with no one around to hear—not even the coyotes—I threw my head back and released all the pain and frustration in a long, loud howl.

That's when the doubts came.

What if I never saw any of them ever again? What if I failed? What if I did, indeed, end up sacrificing myself for this godforsaken planet?

My legs gave out and I hit the dirt, chest heaving as I screamed and cried and wailed.

Eventually, of course, the tears stopped. By then my throat was raw.

But I felt better, somehow. Cleansed. Ready.

I took a deep breath, wiped my face with the hem of my tee shirt, and stood. One last thing to do to prepare for the asteroid.

I connected the shield to Earth, and as the power rose up into it, a soft hum filled the eerie silence. The shield flared briefly with the influx of power, then steadied.

Now, the waiting began.

For the next couple of days, I sat outside and kept my eyes on the sky, using my enhanced vision to spot Eris. Far above my head, the shield's hum somehow harmonized with the Earthsong that was finally loud enough for me to hear.

At night, the shield was almost completely transparent, allowing me to clearly see the stars and planets.

On the second night, I finally saw Eris.

A solitary flickering light in the dark sky. The sun illuminated it, just like it did the moon, but not as brightly. I tracked it for an hour, and realized I still had a few days yet.

It must've slowed down again.

The Fourth of July came and went, and the asteroid slowly grew larger as it came closer. I still couldn't see it during the day, not even with my enhanced vision. So I tracked it at night.

Somehow, the shield's hum seemed louder at night, but that also could've been because Earth was so quiet. No traffic, no humanity, no animals, no birds. Even the hum of electricity was loud in this unnatural silence.

Less than a week after the Fourth of July, the asteroid was now bigger than anything else in the sky except for the moon and the sun, and had a slight aura of dust surrounding it.

One night, while lying on the chaise by the pool and watching the asteroid approach, I must've nodded off. Something woke me with a start, and I blinked my eyes in confusion.

A tall woodland creature stood watching me with large brown eyes that were too round to be human-like. As clothing, it wore leaves of every shade of green, yellow, and orange, draped to its feet. Green vines with yellow and white blooms curled around appendages that were similar to arms, ending in twig-like fingers entwined with ivy leaves. It smelled like rich, fertile soil: dark and earthy.

I'd thought all the magickal creatures had been evacuated? But there was something about this one... my heart skipped a beat.

"Who are you?" I asked.

Something that sort of resembled a mouth stretched into something that sort of resembled a smile, with no teeth showing.

"Who do you think I am?"

The voice was all harmonics, with an underlying deep hum that seemed familiar.

Wait. It was familiar because it was Earthsong.

Oh gods. This could only be Gaia, Mother Earth herself.

I stumbled out of the chaise and knelt on the ground in front of her.

"My Lady, I am honored."

"Rise, Deirdre, my priestess."

Obediently, I stood, feeling small compared to her towering, tree-like presence. Then, her words registered: I was her *priestess*?

She hadn't stopped smiling, even as she glanced up at the approaching asteroid before returning her gaze to me.

"I have a gift for you." One vine-wrapped appendage extended, and when the twig-like fingers opened, a box lay in the center.

I recognized it immediately. It was the same box I'd sent deep within the Earth, in the hopes that no one would ever find it.

It held the Ring of Ur.

"But Kevin hid the key," I murmured. He'd specifically not told me where.

She laughed, and the beauty of a waterfall was in that sound. "You don't need a key. You have the power to open it yourself."

Still frowning, I took the box. "I don't understand."

She glanced at the asteroid again. "You will need it to survive this threat."

I could only stare at her in shock.

I wouldn't survive the impact without the Ring of Ur? I remembered Kevin telling me it granted incredible power to the wearer, but only at a cost.

Which was worse: dying, or going insane?

"But I don't want to lose my sanity, my Lady."

Her laughter bubbled again. "That only happens to mortals. You have nothing to fear, my priestess. Nothing of mine can ever harm you."

Nothing of hers? *The Ring of Ur belonged to her?*

Now I was even more confused.

She extended that vine-wrapped appendage again, and gently caressed my cheek with the ivy-tipped twigs. "Be well, Deirdre. I will be here when you need me. Always."

Then she was gone, as if swallowed up by the Earth.

I stared at the box in my hand.

I had to trust her. If she said it wouldn't hurt me, then it wouldn't. I glanced up at the asteroid and realized it'd grown even bigger, which meant it was much closer.

Just how much time had passed while I'd spoken with Gaia?

But now, at last, I could see the asteroid's trajectory: it was heading in at an angle to my right.

It wouldn't be much longer now.

I touched the lock on the box with my finger, and it sprang open, as if it hadn't been locked at all. The Ring whispered to me in its unfamiliar language, and I clenched my jaw with determination.

I'd do whatever it took to survive this. For my family. I'd promised, after all.

Dropping the empty box, I slipped the Ring onto my finger, and it fit as if it'd been made for me.

Power rose, filling me completely, and I lifted my arms to the sky. To the shield.

The shield glowed with energy, its hum growing loud enough to drown out the Earthsong.

Because I was connected to both the shield and Earth, I knew the exact moment the asteroid made contact with the shield. It wasn't pain, exactly. More like an earthquake that I felt throughout my body.

It had hit beyond the horizon, so I didn't see if the asteroid had exploded, and I didn't see if it'd plunged through the shield. I sent a probe out, and couldn't detect a breach.

As far as I could tell, the shield had held.

I'd just breathed a sigh of relief when the sky turned bright orange-red. A strong wind knocked me off my feet and sent me tumbling across the hard-packed earth.

The last thing I knew, I hit something solid—the house, maybe—and lost consciousness.

EPILOGUE

B REE, IT'S DINNER time," Kevin says as he walks up to his daughter. She's almost as tall as he is, now.

Every day at this hour, she stands where the portal to Earth was. She waits for it to open and for her mother to come through. She's never given up hope.

Kevin has tried like hell not to give up, but it's getting harder every day.

Dee should've been here by now. He'd expected her to stay and heal Earth for a few months, at most.

But it's been five years, and that can only mean something bad happened.

After the first year, he'd tried to open the portal himself. They all did, even Bree, with her new powers granted by the Sphere. But it remained stubbornly closed.

Earth was lost to them, and with it, Dee.

Arddhu was convinced she'd died. In his mind, Anu wouldn't have detached from Dee and attached to Bree unless Dee had been doomed to failure.

Kevin's not so sure about that. Bree has always insisted she *knows* her mother is alive.

But Arddhu's heart was so broken, he wouldn't listen. Listless and depressed for months, he'd wandered around their home in a daze, unable to appreciate the simple beauty that was Tearmann, Dee's magnificent creation.

He'd recently started to smile again, but only briefly, and only when he thinks no one else is watching.

The Morrigan spent a few months to herself but refused to call it grief. Then she threw herself into building a life with Reshep, while taking especially good care of Bree as a surrogate mother.

They'd all settled here, in a zone similar to the Flagstaff area, where the portal had brought them. Their house wasn't nearly as big as The Hacienda, but they'd made it work.

Kevin watched a large herd of Earth elk move peacefully through the woods nearby, and remembered how Bree had taken control as soon as they'd arrived. She'd recruited a large team of deities and humans— mostly younger ones—to help her care for the Earth animals, and they soon thrived.

The humans were surprised the animals left them alone, and soon became accustomed to sharing their world in peace.

The animals seemed devoted to Bree, as were the humans and deities, who affectionately called her the Mistress of Animals, an ancient title that once referred to the Neolithic Mediterranean Goddess who later became Artemis of Olympus.

After the first year, they'd decided to build a temple, dedicated to the Goddess of Earth. A stone carver well-known to the Túatha created a beautiful statue of Dee for the cella of the temple. It's such an excellent likeness, sometimes Kevin expects it to smile at him when he enters the cella.

Every morning, Arddhu lays a perfect flower on the altar. Reshep goes at lunchtime and lights a cone of incense. The Morrigan attends in the early afternoon, sitting and talking for an hour about everything and nothing. Kevin goes in the evening and leaves an offering of a bit of sand from the replica Ard na Mara beach.

Of all of them, Bree is the only one who doesn't go to the temple; she only comes here, to the portal site. Every day, just before dinner.

Many of the deities have kept Bree busy with her education. Although her actual Earth age is only six years, she's an adult in mind, body, and soul, and they treat her like one.

The Morrigan teaches her battle magick and how to play poker—and win. Kevin teaches her math and science; Arddhu teaches history, literature, and working with her natural talents. Reshep teaches battle strategy; the Dagda teaches spellcraft and herbal concoctions; and Athena teaches music and art. Kali and Brianna teach cooking.

Bree has received a well-rounded education, but she continues to learn every day.

Athena and Ares are quite content with their decision to come to Tearmann instead of their own realm. They're friends with Kali again, and even have regular movie nights together, taking turns making the popcorn.

The humans have also settled in well, and although there have been a few rumblings now and then from some malcontents, most everyone is grateful and pleased with this paradise that the Goddess of Earth created just for them. They, too, have built some temples to her, and although she is no longer available to answer their prayers, they've discovered the other deities are more than happy to help—as long as the deities get some devotion in return.

Thing is, there really aren't many reasons to pray any more. War and strife is nonexistent, as is poverty and sickness. Soon after the migration, everyone discovered that anyone who'd been sick was healed by the magick that powers Tearmann. That same magick continues to prevent any illness or disease.

Kevin doesn't know if Dee planned it that way or if it's just part of living in paradise.

The politicians, of course, got bored quickly. Most of the humans don't pay them much attention because the politicians don't do anything for them anymore. Especially when the Túatha showered the humans with attention.

The humans adore the Túatha. The politicians, not so much.

Now, Kevin steps closer to Bree. "C'mon, it's time for dinner."

She leans her head on his shoulder and speaks quietly. "Dad, I'm scared."

She stopped calling him Daddy Kevin some time ago. Now, he's just Dad, and so is Arddhu. But she has a knack for letting them know to which of them she's speaking, so somehow there's never any confusion.

"Why?"

"I'm starting to forget what she looks like," she says, quietly. "And the sound of her voice."

Fuck. What can he tell her? Any pictures or videos taken of Dee over the years were left behind on Earth. Their phones don't work here, something Dee either planned or somehow missed. The humans weren't too happy about that at first, but they learned how to create and use new technology with the magick reservoir, and adapted.

He swallows the lump in his throat and blinks away the tears. "That's totally normal, sweetheart. It happens to everyone."

She glances at him. "Are you forgetting, too?"

"Not yet. But I probably will, someday."

"But I don't want to," she insists. "I want to remember everything. The way she always wore her hair in a ponytail. Her smile. Her laugh. Even the way her eyes would sort of flash fire when she was angry."

Bree always wears her hair in a ponytail too, but he doesn't mention it.

"I want to remember everything, too," he says. "But for now, let's go eat dinner. Brianna made lasagna. After, maybe we'll play some poker with the Morrigan."

She snorts. "She lets me win too many times."

"She does *not.* You're just that good."

Bree sighs, and reluctantly turns away from the portal. She and Kevin walk toward the house.

They've only gone a few yards when a noise behind them makes Kevin glance over his shoulder. A rabbit, maybe. They've been prolific, getting into the garden and munching on the lettuces.

But it's not a rabbit.

Light is streaming from the portal.

At first, he can only stare, but he quickly returns to the portal and stands there, fidgeting.

Of course, Bree is beside him.

"Dad," she says, with urgency.

"I know." He's breathless.

And then, she's there, stepping through the portal.

His Dee.

She looks like shit. Her face is filthy with old blood and dirt. Her lips are bleeding. Her once-beautiful long auburn hair is burned to a bristly stubble. It's so patchy he can see her scalp, covered in dirt and scabs. Her clothes are torn, showing any exposed skin as bloody and blistered.

"Go get... everyone," he tells Bree, who ports away.

"Kevin." It comes out as a groan, and Dee stumbles toward him. The portal closes behind her with a snap.

He manages to catch her, but loses his balance. He falls to his knees, cradling her in his arms. He blinks rapidly, eyes blurry with tears, and lays one palm gently against her cheek.

"Oh, love, what have you done." His voice is hoarse.

"What I had to do."

She's clearly in severe pain, and he knows it's going to take a lot of work to heal her.

"But look at what it cost you."

Despite her suffering, she smiles. But it's only a weak smile, and it makes her cracked lips bleed even more. "Fucking. Worth. It."

Kevin tries to stay strong, to keep the tears from falling, but he can't. It hurts his heart so much to even look at her. And he doesn't even know where to start with the healing.

He reaches for her hand, and brings it to his lips. That's when he notices it, and his heart drops.

The Ring of Ur.

"What have you done?" he repeats, but doesn't think she heard him. She's fading in and out of consciousness.

Then, the others are there.

The Morrigan and Reshep kneel beside Kevin, wordless.

Arddhu makes an inhuman sound and he's on his knees at her side, Bree beside him.

"Mom," she says. "We can heal you. Just hang on. For us."

Dee opens her eyes, looks at her daughter, and nods. "Counting on it." Her eyes close again, and when she speaks again, it's a bit more forceful. "I need a fucking vacation."

Dee, Bree, Arddhu, Kevin, the Morrigan, and all the characters we love will return in the forthcoming Mistress of Animals trilogy.

ACKNOWLEDGEMENTS

Many writers aren't blessed with an awesome alpha reader for a spouse, but I am. From countless hours spent throwing strange shit against the wall to see what would stick, to the often heated discussions while playing our evening Egyptian Senet game, he has been incredibly patient. Love you so much, hon.

Deep gratitude to beta readers Heidi and Tabi. Their feedback was invaluable and helped me to make this a much better book. I truly hope they enjoy this finished version.

My favorite graphic artist, Farah Evers, has once again created an amazing cover. Her talent never ceases to amaze me, and I always look forward to what she'll come up with next.

My editor, Jen has again worked her magic. Thank goodness for her wit, wisdom, and patience. (And a side note to readers: any errors in this book are mine and mine alone.)

Much love and gratitude to my family for their unwavering support.

And finally, to each and every reader of my first and second books, I can't thank you enough for your feedback, support, and encouragement. I truly hope you enjoy this labor of love.

Please help support independent authors: leave a review on Amazon or Goodreads.

AUTHOR'S NOTE

Throughout this series, the spelling of "magick" is used instead of "magic" to distinguish between the use of power (magick) and illusion (magic).

I have tried my best to be respectful to the deities of numerous cultures, while still maintaining the story. If you feel something wasn't treated correctly, please drop me a note and let me know. I'll do my best to make it right.

I based the asteroid Eris on 'Oumuamua, the interstellar object discovered in 2017 and previously unknown to astronomers (deepest thanks to Chuck).

Regarding sources used for this book: Wikipedia was my most-used research tool for the deities and cultures referenced, followed by specific mythology and religion websites. If you'd like to know the exact sources I used, drop me a line and I'd be happy to share.

ABOUT THE AUTHOR

After a lifetime of reading just about anything she could get her hands on (especially science fiction, fantasy, and anything related to Ireland) and dreaming of becoming an author someday, D M Youngblood was inspired by someone who said, "write what you want to read," and a new chapter in her life began.

She lives in suburban Phoenix with her husband and adorable Pomeranian doggies who love to bark and disrupt the creative process (the dogs bark, not the husband). She also has an unhealthy obsession with the Marvel Cinematic Universe, especially Loki. (Don't judge.) Other interests include knitting and casual gaming.

Follow the author on:
Facebook: DMYoungblood
Twitter: dianey2
Website: dmyoungblood.com

www.ingramcontent.com/pod-product-compliance
Lightning Source LLC
Chambersburg PA
CBHW020606040726
47498CB00003B/655